Sign up for our newsletter to hear
about new and upcoming releases.

www.ylva-publishing.com

Other Books by A.L. Brooks

Write Your Own Script
One Way or Another
Up on the Roof
Miles Apart
Dark Horse
The Club

the Long Shot

A. L. Brooks

Acknowledgments

I want to start by thanking my wonderful partner, Tanja, for her incredible support through the writing of this one. This book was written while I was in the middle of the planning and subsequent realization of my move from the UK to Germany, and I honestly couldn't have done either of those rather big things without her. My love, you always boost me when I'm low, shout from the rooftops at my successes, and, best of all, buy me chocolate and/or wine when all else fails. Top girlfriend points awarded to you!

As always, thanks to Ylva Publishing for all that you do to bring my books to the world. Thanks to Miranda and Amanda for a lovely editing experience and to Sandra for teaching me things about grammar I never knew existed. I promise to keep my dangly participles hidden from view in the future…

To my wonderful beta readers Erin and Katja. I love how you two never let me get away with anything and really push me to delve deep into my characters' motivations and desires. And thank you to Kym for the sensitivity read and advice.

Finally, a massive shout-out to Judy Comella, stalwart member of the Golden Crown Literary Society, for the excellent feedback and assistance on the behind-the-scenes life of the women's golf tour. Any mistakes remaining in that regard are purely down to me. And thank you to the GCLS for offering a database of experts who can be called on for things such as this—what a fantastic resource.

Chapter 1

THE BEAD OF SWEAT TRACKED its way down Morgan's neck. She exhaled slowly and tried to relax her tight shoulders.

Ten feet. That's all this putt was. Ten feet between her and a playoff for a chance to win the first major of her career.

But you've been this close before, a nasty little voice whispered in her head. *Twice. And each time you blew it.*

Strange how that voice only ever made an appearance at the pressure moments. Never on the practice rounds or in the gym or out on a run. Only when it was the crunch shot on the final green of the final round.

A tickle of warm breeze lifted a few loose strands of hair underneath her ponytail. Somewhere behind her someone coughed, and to her right the creek in front of the green gurgled as it trundled over the bedrock.

She shouldn't be aware of any of this. She should be focused only on the small, white ball in front of her, the weight of the putter in her hand. *Come on, concentrate!*

If Harry could read her mind, he'd be tutting. Knowing her caddy stood behind her, probably with his hands in his pockets and probably wondering what the hell she was up to, Morgan slowly inhaled before stepping forward to the ball.

The putter settled in her hands, the rubberized grip warm against her palms and fingertips. She glanced to her left, even though she knew exactly where the hole was. Licking her lips, she settled her feet into place. She adjusted her position in minute increments until she hit that spot, that perfect blend of balance and poise and calm, her head over the ball.

"It'll swing left but not as much as you might think," Harry had said when they'd lined up the shot only a minute or so before. It seemed like a lifetime ago. "Don't overcompensate. You'll twitch 'cause you're nervous, and that will probably be enough to send it on its way."

She'd rolled her eyes at him but appreciated what he'd tried to do—relax her, make it seem like any other putt on any other day.

Ten feet, that's all.

Breathe in, take the putter back, then breathe out and swing it back in to make contact.

As soon as the ball moved, the crowd noise erupted. Shouts of *"Get in the hole!"* came from all angles, but Morgan didn't react, didn't move, simply kept her head turned toward the hole, watching the ball roll, bobble a little, start to swing left, and…

The groans and gasps that surrounded her were loud, a rolling wave that threatened to drown her.

The ball swung by the hole, its trajectory too far to the left.

She closed her eyes and gripped the putter so tightly she wondered if it would snap.

Harry's hand on the small of her back brought her back into the reality, the reality she really didn't want to face. But she was a professional, and courtesy dictated she walk forward, tap her ball in from where it had come to a stop a mere three inches from the hole, and then step out of the way after acknowledging the muted applause from the crowd.

Kim Lee, her Korean opponent, stepped up and calmly slotted in her two-foot putt to confirm the win. As the crowd went wild, she raised her arms aloft, a huge smile splitting her face.

Morgan gave her a moment. After handing the putter to Harry, she shook his hand, then strolled across the green to congratulate Lee, who had now won the Women's US Open. Kim Lee was all smiles but patted Morgan on the shoulder as they grasped hands.

"Bad luck." Lee's words seemed heartfelt.

Morgan mustered a smile. "You played well. You deserve the win."

Hundreds of camera flashes pinged off around them. The ESPN and Golf Channel TV cameramen circled around them. Keeping her smile fixed in place, Morgan shook Lee's hand.

"Thank you!" Lee gushed before letting go and facing the applauding crowd, whose cheers rose in volume. Sure, most of the crowd would have rather seen a home winner, but they were golf fans above all else, and the best player had won.

Morgan, her face aching from maintaining the smile, walked over to where Harry tucked her putter back into the bag, his towel rammed into one of his pockets. His face was expressionless; he was the consummate pro, and she loved him for it. The last thing she needed to see right now was any sort of disappointment on the face of the man who'd caddied for her the whole of her professional career.

"I'm thinking pulled-pork burger and fries," he said when she reached him.

"What?" Even for Harry, that comment was way out of left field.

"Tonight. For dinner. I'm buying." He gave her a slow smile. "Might even shout you a beer too. Light, of course."

Morgan sighed. "Harry, you know I can't."

"Oh, all right, a soda, then."

She bumped his shoulder with hers. It was a constant source of annoyance to him that she was an inch taller than his five ten, and the shoulder bump always emphasized it. Which was why she regularly performed it.

"You know what I mean," she said, her voice not much more than a whisper.

Harry sighed, pulled the towel from his pocket, and wiped his hands on it before stuffing it into the side pocket of the bag that held all of Morgan's clubs and equipment. When he stood to face her again, his eyes were full of kindness and understanding.

A lump formed in her throat.

"I'd never tell you what to do, you know that," he said.

She placed a gentle hand on his bicep to stop him. "I know. But it'd hurt Mom if I didn't go."

Harry exhaled noisily and ran a tanned hand over his even more tanned face. His brown eyes held hers. "Jack won, by the way. Just so you know."

Morgan closed her eyes. "Shit." She shook her head. "Good for him."

"Burger with me instead?"

She opened her eyes and gazed fondly at him. "Thanks, but no. I'm a big girl. I can take care of myself."

"I know you can. I've never doubted that." His eyes crinkled as he grinned. "I'll see you after the circus?"

"Yeah. Let's have one drink at the bar before you head off, okay?"

"You got yourself a deal, little lady."

Morgan groaned. She hated it when he called her that. Which was why he did it. She stuck her tongue out at him; Harry roared with laughter. They hugged, his strong arms encircling her completely and making her feel safe and protected for just a moment.

Morgan sucked in a deep breath, stepped out of his embrace, and turned back to the melee of people who now crowded the eighteenth green.

ESPN still interviewed Kim Lee, but Cindy Thomson from the Golf Channel hovered only a few yards away, her hawklike amber eyes on Morgan and Harry.

"Looks like I'm up," Morgan muttered.

"You got this."

Handing her cap to him, Morgan swept a hand over her hair. She plastered her fake smile back on, then stepped over to Cindy.

"Bad luck." Cindy shook her hand limply, her look of sympathy as fake as Morgan's smile.

Cindy was one of those never-quite-made-it players who'd rapidly realized they'd do better in front of the camera talking about golf rather than playing it. She was now the lead roving reporter for the Golf Channel's coverage of the women's game and, therefore, someone Morgan had to make nice with on a regular basis, even though she loathed her. Cindy was all fake blonde hair—and, rumor had it, fake breasts too—with layered-on makeup and expensive shoes. An airhead, Morgan's father had called her once, and Morgan unfortunately couldn't help but agree.

With a snap of her hand, Cindy directed the cameraman behind her to get into position, and Morgan saw the light illuminate on the camera that told her she was live.

"I've got the runner-up with me here, Morgan Spencer." Cindy's gaze bored into Morgan's. "Morgan, can you tell us how you're feeling right now? Third major in a row you've been right up there and couldn't quite get over the line. That's got to hurt, yes?"

Gee, thanks, Cindy.

"Well, it's not easy, no," Morgan said with a wry grin.

4

If there was one thing her manager had always told her, it was to never rise to the bait from these kinds of reporters. Her own self-discipline, honed from years of being in the limelight, meant Morgan could switch into her autopilot mode of interviewing at will. No one looking on would ever know how angry or upset she was. No one got to see that side of her, not ever. Even Harry was spared it. A punchbag in a gym was the only witness, and she knew come tomorrow morning she'd really need that kind of workout.

Cindy was right: three majors in a row, and Morgan had blown it on the final hole in each and every one. In last year's British Open, it had been a poor drive. In the ANA International two months ago, it had been the approach that had ended up in the bunker. And here today, a missed putt. She knew exactly what the headlines would say and wouldn't bother buying any of the papers or checking online later.

And God knew tonight she'd hear all about it anyway.

Maybe Harry was right—maybe she should skip it and go for a burger with him instead. But then her mom would have to deal with the other family stuff on her own, and that wasn't fair.

Mentally gritting her teeth, she braced herself for Cindy's additional questions.

"It seems the nerves might get to you on those big moments. What are you going to do to try to resolve that?"

The sickening gleam in Cindy's eyes turned Morgan's stomach. She really was enjoying this.

Morgan kept her smile fixed on her lips. "Well, I'm not sure it is nerves. We'll take a look at the tapes later and see if there's anything we need to work on."

Her jaw ached from keeping her tone even when all she wanted to do was yell at Cindy.

"You're thirty-one now, and you've been a pro for about six years, I believe. Do you think a major is still in your future?"

It was like death by a thousand cuts. Every question was designed to inflict yet more damage.

"I think every pro wants to win a major, and I really believe I've got that in me. I wasn't lucky enough today, but there's another one not too far away."

"Will you speak to your dad? See what advice he can give you?"

And there it was, the one question trotted out every time she appeared in front of the cameras. The one that twisted her stomach in knots and had her clenching her fists.

"I'll be seeing my folks later tonight, so I'm sure we'll talk about the match."

The lies came so easily, as they always had, and hurt just as badly. The irony wasn't lost on her of how proud her father would be of her for handling herself so well in front of the press.

Cindy pressed one finger to her earpiece. "Thanks for your time, Morgan, and good luck for the next one."

Before Morgan could respond, Cindy whirled around and marched off in Kim Lee's direction.

Morgan just had time to inhale one deep breath before the guy from ESPN stepped up. She forced her smile even wider and stared into the camera.

Later, after finally escaping the post-match press conference, Morgan found Harry in the club's bar, as expected. He had a cold beer, half drunk, in front of him at a table in the quietest corner of the room. What Morgan wouldn't give for a long beer, just as cold, right now. But the way she felt, if she started with one, she wouldn't want to stop, and a late supper with her parents was not something she could turn up drunk to.

After ordering a Perrier with a twist, she slumped into the chair opposite Harry.

He looked her up and down. "Sharks didn't totally rip you to shreds?"

She grinned wryly. "Not quite, but they got in some good hits, as usual."

"Bastards." Harry rarely swore, but when he did, his target was usually the press. Either that or the divorce lawyers each of his three ex-wives had hired.

Morgan waved a hand. "They're only doing their job. And, hey, some of those questions are perfectly valid."

Like, why do I keep screwing it up in majors?

Harry shrugged and took a long drink of his beer. "So you heading off straight away?"

6

Stifling a yawn, Morgan nodded. "I may as well. It'll be good to see Mom again." She rubbed her chin. "How long's it been now? Jeez, I can't even remember."

Harry chuckled. "I think it's maybe…two months? Before the ANA, I think."

"I think you're right. Wow. I had no idea."

"Say hi to Bree for me."

Morgan smiled. Harry had always had a soft spot for her mom. Maybe even a little crush. "I will."

"How is she?"

"Well, I haven't seen her in two months or spoken to her in two weeks, so I can't say. God, I'm a bad daughter." She smiled ruefully. "But last time I did speak to her, she was pretty tired. You know she does all that charity stuff, and it takes up a lot of her time."

He nodded. Morgan wasn't surprised he didn't ask after her father; the two men had never seen eye to eye.

Morgan sighed. She was usually better at speaking to her mom more regularly, but now that she was a top-ten—usually top-five—finisher in every tournament she played, free time to head home and see her folks was rarer. She didn't even like to guess when she'd last seen her brother, Jack. At that thought, her stomach twisted again, and she sighed. "How did you know Jack had won?"

Harry didn't look surprised at the question. "I set up an alert on the app on my phone. Just after your drive at the eighteenth, I snuck a look. I figured if you knew in advance…"

"Thanks." She tipped her glass in his direction.

"Any time."

Morgan downed the last of her drink and inhaled deeply. "Okay, time for me to get going."

Harry stood with her, then walked around the small table to give her a hug. "Take it easy."

"I'll try. Tuesday morning, eight?"

He nodded. "If you're late, I'll make you run up every fairway."

She laughed. "I'm never late, and you know it."

Harry opened his mouth to say something, then shut it again.

"What?" She tilted her head.

"Not necessarily Tuesday, but sometime before Thursday we need to talk about what happened out there today. We need to fix it."

"I know. We will. Definitely."

He squeezed her forearm, then sat back down to his beer.

Morgan left the now busy bar with only a handful of people stopping her to commiserate. She accepted their words with her practiced grace, ignoring the twinge in her heart each time those words made her think about missing that putt.

It didn't take long to retrieve her overnight bag and stow it in the trunk of the rental car. Normally, she'd stay on at the hotel for the night after a tournament before being whisked away in a sponsor's car straight to the airport the next morning and then either home or on to the next tournament, but not tonight. Although the room was still booked for the night, for once she was mistress of her own time. Even though where she headed filled her with a certain amount of hesitancy, the freedom to hit the road on her own was wonderful.

She turned up the volume on the radio as she hit the highway and sang along as loud as she could to one banal pop song after another. Belting out the lyrics to songs that spoke of simple things like first kisses and secret looks across a dance floor was one of her few guilty pleasures. She laughed as she imagined the looks on the faces of all those reporters if they saw her cutting so loose. Someone had given her a nickname ten years ago, when she'd really started to climb up the rankings, and it had stuck: Morgan "Ice" Spencer. They all called her that now. Equally cool on the course as off it, she had a reputation for never letting out a hint of what she felt inside. Only a few people knew she wasn't that cold—Harry, her mom, Jack to a certain extent, and... No, she wouldn't think about *her*. That was still way too painful.

Pushing those thoughts away, Morgan concentrated on the road. And on preparing herself for what she was bound to walk into in around twenty minutes' time.

"Darling!" Her mom rushed forward as the door swung open and pulled Morgan into a warm embrace.

"Hey, Mom." Morgan clung on, wishing she could spend the whole evening right here in her mom's caring arms and not have to deal with the rest of it.

"Bad luck, darling. You played well."

"You watched?"

Her mom stepped back, a wide smile on her face even though her eyes showed her concern. "Of course I did! I'm afraid I couldn't look at that last putt, though. The tension was too much."

Morgan chuckled. "Yeah, I had my eyes shut too."

"Oh, you!" Her mom nudged her with a beautifully manicured fingertip. "I'm sorry it didn't work out."

"That's the way it goes sometimes." Morgan shrugged. "Another day they go in."

"Very true. Well, come on in. I have food keeping warm in the oven."

"You've eaten already?"

Morgan stepped through with her small overnight bag and placed it on the marble floor of the foyer. Her parents' grand house could easily grace the cover of every home-and-garden magazine and be admired by many, but its clinical, almost cold finish did nothing for Morgan.

"No, I'll join you. Your father…ate earlier."

Her mom ran a hand through her hair, the soft waves of it lifting with her fingers but settling back perfectly into place once they'd passed.

Ignoring the comment about her father for now, Morgan followed her mom into the expansive kitchen that ran the width of the house. Split into two sections, the main area held the kitchen itself, and the slightly smaller area to the left was where casual meals were taken at a large oak table.

As her mom spooned their food onto plates, Morgan poured them each a small glass of wine from the open bottle she found in the refrigerator. She smiled as they moved around each other. Even though Morgan hadn't lived with her parents for nearly ten years now, she'd fallen right back into the same pattern of sharing an evening with her mom as she had way back then.

There was still no sign of her father as they sat down to their food, but for once she didn't have the energy to ask, and her mom didn't volunteer anything. It should have been awkward, but it wasn't, and so she accepted the clink of her mom's wineglass against her own before tucking into her food with gusto.

"I didn't realize how hungry I was," she said after a few rushed mouthfuls.

Her mom smiled. "Well, you have been rather busy today."

Morgan grinned and continued eating, the tuna casserole hot and filling.

"Up eight ranking places!" Her father's voice from behind her made her jump in her seat.

She met her mom's eyes, inhaled, and turned. "Hey, Dad."

Her father, his iPad clutched in his hand and raised somewhat triumphantly, also startled and stared at her. "Morgan. I didn't hear you come in."

"A little while ago. Just catching up with Mom and having some food." She waved her fork at her plate.

"Good. Good." He stepped forward and awkwardly leaned down to kiss her on the cheek. "Did you hear about Jack's win?" He straightened, his face lit up with pride.

Morgan's anger rose. *Wow, less than ten seconds to make it all about Jack. Must be a record.* "Uh, yeah, Dad, I did. That's great for him."

"Isn't it? And I just got the updated rankings. Up to 108. He keeps going like this, he's gonna break back into the top one hundred soon."

"That's marvelous." Her mom reached out and covered Morgan's hand briefly before she continued. "And obviously, Morgan did well today too, Gordy."

Her dad, to Morgan's surprise, did at least have the grace to look embarrassed but only for one fleeting moment.

"Oh, sure. Of course. Second place is a good result."

And there it was, hidden in the tone and the choice of words. Good but not good enough. Certainly not good enough for the daughter of Gordon "Gordy" Spencer, winner of six majors on the men's tour over the course of his career, including two US Opens and a Masters.

His eyes narrowed as he looked down at her. He was still imposing, even at the age of seventy-five. Although tall, he had a slight stoop, and her mom had mentioned on their last call that his right hip gave him some trouble.

"Jack's coming home tomorrow. Will you be here to congratulate him?"

Resisting the urge to roll her eyes or, worse, scream, Morgan shook her head. "Need to be on the road early. I've got a flight west tomorrow."

She could have elaborated, told him which tournament was up next, what her hopes were for it, what she thought she'd need to work on in her game, but she knew that tonight, after Jack's win, she'd be wasting her breath.

"Well, that's a shame. Boy's worked hard this year," he said. "That tennis tour is tough. Winning any tournament out there when you've got the likes of Nadal and Djokovic winning everything else is something to be celebrated."

"I know, Dad." Morgan tried not to sound exasperated, but her mom's fingers tightening against hers indicated she might not have succeeded.

Her dad bristled, but she held up a hand.

"I'm not trying to be difficult. I have places to be. I'm committed to playing the full year, I've got sponsorship requirements, and I *want* to play. I can't just drop that to stay home and pat Jack on the back."

It came out much sharper than she'd intended, and she knew she'd gone too far when her Dad stood as tall as he could, his chest expanding as he did so.

"This is important," he snapped. "Jack could break back into the top one hundred players in the world soon! He needs all of our support to do that."

"*I'm* world number four." Morgan's throat, damn it, tightened as she pushed back her chair and stood to face him. "Me." She jabbed a finger into her chest. "Me. I'm the world number four in women's golf."

"Don't start that again." Her father turned away.

"Gordy." Her mother half rose from her chair, but it was no use.

Without another word, Morgan's father strode out of the room.

Morgan closed her eyes, her hands clenched into tight fists at her sides. *Always the same. Why the hell did I expect anything different?*

"Thanks for supper, Mom." She finally opened her eyes and looked at her mom across the wide table. "It was good, but I think I'd better get back on the road tonight after all."

"I...I thought you were staying?" Her mom's eyes went wide and shimmered with wetness.

"I can't." Morgan's voice cracked, but she willed herself to keep it together. She wouldn't cry, not for him.

"I'll talk to him." Her mother wrung her hands together.

Morgan sighed. "No. Don't. It's not worth it." She walked out to the foyer, grabbed her lightweight jacket from the hook where she'd hung it up less than an hour before, and pulled it on.

"Please stay," her mom whispered, her hand tentative on Morgan's arm.

A sob choking her throat, Morgan shook her head and pulled her mom in for a long hug. "I can't. Not now. I'm too angry and… Well, you know."

"I know. I'm so sorry, Morgan. And I'm so proud of you, for what you're achieving."

"Thanks." Morgan swallowed. "And I'm proud of Jack too. You know that, right?"

Her mom stepped back slightly, staring at Morgan. "Of course I do, honey!"

"I'll call him later and congratulate him. If he's not too drunk by then." Morgan managed a smile, and her mom returned it.

"You do that. And you call me when you get to California, okay?"

Of course her mom knew where she headed next, and the thought that she had Morgan's schedule memorized like that allowed a small ball of warmth to push back at the coldness her father's words had caused her.

"I will. Take it easy, Mom."

"Of course, darling." Her mom hugged her one last time, then opened the door.

Morgan stepped out into the cool night, the air refreshing on her face, where anger and hurt burned just beneath the surface of her skin.

She opened the rental car, climbed in, and started the engine. The inbuilt GPS pinged to life, and she tapped the name of her hotel into the destination box and then hit a few more keys to choose the longer route back, avoiding the highways. She needed the drive and the solitude. And the cheesy pop music, of course. An old Madonna track came on, and she grinned. Yeah, that would do.

Chapter 2

"SHE BLEW IT! AGAIN!"

Adrienne looked up from her laptop as Jenny stomped into the office and flung herself down into the guest couch. The leather gave way beneath her with a soft sigh, and the huge vase of flowers on the side table wobbled but stayed upright.

"Who blew what?" Adrienne asked, although she had a pretty good idea what Jenny was ranting about.

Jenny threw her arms up. "Morgan Spencer! How could she?"

She groaned and sunk her head into her hands, nearly crashing her legs into the low oak coffee table that stood between the couch and Adrienne's desk as she slipped down further into her seat.

Adrienne chuckled. She was a big fan of women's golf, but Jenny was fanatical. And she was particularly fanatical about Morgan Spencer, whom she'd had a huge crush on for years. Every time Morgan failed to live up to the heights of the pedestal Jenny had placed her on, it was rather amusing to watch the resulting meltdown.

"Well, obviously she did it entirely to upset you," Adrienne said drily, and chuckled when Jenny thumped the leather seat.

"She's so frustrating! I totally get why the press go after her like they do. Although Cindy Thomson was particularly vicious, that bitch."

Adrienne snorted softly in agreement. Oh yes, Cindy Thomson was indeed a bitch—Adrienne had firsthand experience of that when they'd clashed during the filming of a doc about the history of the Solheim Cup. Cindy had wanted more screen time, keen to get exposure at the start of her TV career. After Adrienne had refused for genuine production reasons,

Cindy had gone over Adrienne's head to someone she knew on the board of directors at the TV company, undermining Adrienne's position with her peers.

It pained Adrienne deeply every time she saw Cindy's face on her TV screen, knowing how many people Cindy had stomped all over to get to where she was now, the golden girl of women's golf presenting.

"So did you just drop in here to get all that off your chest, or was there something else?" Adrienne inquired, needing to push thoughts of Cindy Thomson out of her mind.

Jenny grinned sheepishly, scratching at the back of her head. "No, just the rant. Sorry."

Adrienne smiled in understanding at her assistant. Jenny was in her mid-twenties, still learning all there was to know about making TV sports films, and full of the passion that went with her youth and enthusiasm. More than a few times, Adrienne had needed to rein her in when her fiery nature threatened to derail a project or upset an A-lister, but Jenny was rapidly becoming a fine producer's assistant and would make a fantastic producer one day, if that was the direction she wished to go.

"You okay?" Jenny asked as she stood. "Wanna coffee or something? I think I spotted some leftover Danish in the conference room a minute ago." She bounced on the toes of her orange sneakers, the shoes the only splash of color in her outfit. Her black long-sleeved T-shirt and black jeans fitted her lean body like a glove. It wasn't Jenny's usual look—there was normally much more color involved—but it worked, especially with her black spiky hair, which she'd gelled up particularly high today.

"Coffee, yes, Danish, no."

"On it."

Jenny bounded out of the room, and Adrienne chuckled.

Oh, to be that young again. But even as the thought crossed her mind, she shook her head. No, she didn't want to be that age again, actually. And that was in spite of all that had happened to her this past year, knocking her back in ways she would never have imagined. No, forty-nine-year-old Adrienne was a better person—mostly—than the Adrienne who'd once been in Jenny's shoes, and the experience she'd gained from life since then sat comfortably with her.

Well, not all of it, but she'd challenge anyone to feel comfortable about being left out of the blue by their partner of ten years for a woman twenty years younger…

She sighed. *Yeah, like I really need to be thinking about all that again.* The trouble was, no matter how hard she tried, and no matter how much she'd thrown herself into her work since then, the day when Paula had come home and told her, in a cold and distant tone, that she was leaving and moving in with her new young love would never leave Adrienne's mind. The pain still cut deep, as did the embarrassment once all their friends found out. Left for a younger model. What a fucking cliché.

Straightening at her desk, she rolled her shoulders a couple of times and focused back on her screen. When Jenny returned with her coffee and placed it on the *I love San Francisco* coaster on the corner of the desk, Adrienne was almost too engrossed to notice, mumbling a sound that could have meant "thanks" and scrolling slowly down the proposal that had landed in her in-box overnight.

Well, well, well. Interesting.

Adrienne reached for the coffee, blew on it for a moment, then sipped cautiously. Perfect. Her gaze drifted to the tall bookcase on her left, her awards proudly displayed in amongst photos of the wonderful people she'd worked with over the years. Was there a chance to add another one to her treasured collection? She read over the proposal again. It had been sent by one of the development execs upstairs, Daniel, and, as he said in his e-mail, was such an obvious addition to the project they were already working on it would be foolish not to pursue it. And when it came to her work, Adrienne wasn't a foolish woman.

She picked up the phone and called him.

"Thought I might be hearing from you." She could hear the smirk he wore as he spoke. He was an oily character, and personally she loathed him. She'd seen him act like a predator when it came to the younger female members of the staff, and it pained her that no one seemed willing to do anything about it. He did have more great ideas than not, she had to begrudgingly admit, so she'd spent the last three years swallowing down her feelings about him, and instead they'd worked together to put out a brilliant portfolio of work for TC Productions.

"I like the idea," she said, as usual getting straight to the point. She and Daniel were not the sort of people who wasted time on social niceties.

"And shouldn't take too much effort to tag on, no?"

"Not at all. Except for access."

"Yes. Do you know her manager?"

"Not personally, but I know how to reach out to him."

"Great. Keep me posted."

He hung up, and Adrienne rolled her eyes. He would take all the plaudits for this once she'd done all the running around to make it happen, but she'd still have her name on the credits, and, if she pulled this off the way her brain was already imagining, who knew what else it might lead to.

A glow warmed her body. This was what she needed to take her mind off everything else—a big, fat, juicy project that she could really sink her teeth into.

Perfect.

The apartment was cold. Adrienne threw her keys on the table near the front door and shivered. Stupid New York weather—forty-five degrees in early June was insane. After opening the narrow cupboard housing the heating controls, she turned them up, hearing the system kick in moments later.

God, how she missed her house. Their house, the one she and Paula had bought a year after they got together and had lived in until a year ago when Paula dropped her bomb on their relationship. The house had had to be sold—partly because she couldn't afford the upkeep for it on her own, but mostly because suddenly, overnight, it didn't feel like *home* anymore. Not after what Paula had done.

She stood in the bland hallway of the apartment she now rented instead and sighed. Beige walls, fake wooden floor, plain furniture. When she'd first looked at it, caught up in the throes of her grief, she chose it precisely because it was so bland. It made her feel nothing, and that was good back then because she'd ached and hurt in so many ways. She hadn't wanted to come home to anything that challenged her any further. But now it depressed her.

Maybe that was a good sign. Maybe that meant she was, as her friend Tricia had been trying to tell her for a while, ready to put some color back into her life. Of course, Tricia's version of color was for Adrienne to date again, or at least get laid, but Adrienne wasn't remotely ready for *that*.

After finally removing her coat when she thought she could cope with the lukewarm temperature of the place, she walked into the small kitchen and poured herself a glass of the red wine she'd opened the night before. She yawned widely after her first sip; it was already past ten, and she'd put yet another ridiculously long day in at the office. Still, it was worth it, as the project she'd been working on for the last three months was about to really get off the ground. Just one key phone call to make tomorrow…

The buzzing of her cell phone interrupted her thoughts. The caller display showed Tricia's name, and she smiled as she answered.

"Isn't it past your bedtime?"

Tricia laughed. "Ha ha. I have been known to stay up past ten on a school night, you know. Sometimes even eleven!"

Adrienne chuckled at the reference to school night. Tricia was an associate professor at NYU. "So how are you?"

"Good. This summer semester's already kicking my ass, but I'm still alive."

"Tough class?"

"Meh. More like disinterested. Which makes no sense when they've all paid so much to get here. Feels like I've been talking to a blank wall most days."

"Are they just overwhelmed? I mean, they're all from overseas, so…"

"Yeah, maybe that's all it is. Don't worry, I'll think of something to light them up."

"I don't doubt that."

Tricia's laugh was soft. "So how about you?"

One of the things Adrienne loved most about Tricia was her refusal to sugarcoat things. Everyone else who had asked Adrienne that question for the last twelve months had done so with that "oh, poor you" inflection in their tone. Like they were afraid to actually ask in case Adrienne told them the truth they didn't want to hear—that she was still angry and bitter and upset. Tricia just asked her normally, like she would with anyone else she knew, anyone who hadn't had their heart ripped to shreds last year.

"I'm pretty good." She glanced around the kitchen. "I'm sick of this apartment, I finally realized."

"Yay!"

"I know. You've never liked it."

"No, but I also get why you took it. Still, I'm thrilled you've finally realized the beige cave of doom is not for you. Thank God."

Adrienne laughed out loud. "Well, I'm not actually going to do anything about it yet, so don't be holding a party. I'm hopefully about to go on the road for a few weeks, so I may as well leave it here with all my belongings until I get back."

"But when you get back, you'll look for something else? Please? Promise?"

"I will. I promise."

"I'm fist pumping right now. And jigging."

"And you can jig with the best of them."

"I can." There was a pause, then Tricia's voice turned serious. "You sound good. Really good."

Adrienne's heart skipped a beat, then settled again. "I...am. Work is good. This project is finally getting going, hence me leaving town, and Daniel—"

"The snaky one?"

"Yes, the snaky one." Adrienne grinned. "Well, he actually came up with a brilliant addition to it that I hope I can pull off."

"Ooh, I'm intrigued. Tell me more. This is the women's golf documentary, yes?"

"Yes. So far I've just had a crew out gathering film of the first two majors of the year. You know we're doing a kind of life-in-a-year of the women's majors, yes?"

"Yeah, I remember. Not focusing on any player in particular but more the tournaments themselves, why they're so special to the players, et cetera."

"Wow, you really do listen to me sometimes."

"Oh, hardy har." Tricia snorted. "Go on, what's this extra part?"

"Well, did you hear Morgan Spencer failed again this past weekend? Missed a putt to go into a playoff for the Women's US Open, so that's three majors in a row she's blown it on the last hole."

18

"Hm, I might have caught a headline about that in today's sports pages. Wow, that's got to hurt."

"Well, that's the thing. I saw a tape of her press conference, and she didn't look bothered at all. I mean, I know they call her Ice, and she's got this reputation for being so cool out there, but I would have thought there would be *some* show of emotion after that loss. But no, nothing. It was almost like she was…bored by it all."

"Okay, but everyone reacts to disappointment and loss in different ways, right? Especially people in the public eye with her kind of background."

"True, but… Anyway, that's Daniel's idea, and I think it's worth doing."

"What idea?"

"Make Spencer the focus of the series. The woman who can't seem to win a major, talking about the majors, talking about her dad's six wins, yada yada yada. We'll couple that with recent winners of majors on the women's tour, get their take on what it meant for them to win one. And who knows, while we're tracking Spencer, maybe she'll actually win one at last, and we get to show it."

"And she's up for this?" Tricia sounded dubious, and for some reason it rankled with Adrienne.

"Well, she doesn't know yet. I'm reaching out to her manager tomorrow, but I can't see why she wouldn't be. It's a great story."

"I guess…"

"What?"

"Nothing, ignore me."

"No, tell me!"

"I don't know, Addy. There's just something about it not sitting right with me."

"Oh."

"You don't think it kind of invades her privacy a little? Like, maybe she wouldn't want this kind of exposure or attention?"

"She's a top sportswoman. They get this kind of attention all the time."

Tricia was silent for a while. Then she said, her voice quiet and concerned, "Just don't forget she's a person too. I know this is important to you and your career and portfolio. But she's a person with feelings, even if she is in the public eye."

Adrienne bristled, her stomach tight with tension. "I'm not completely heartless, you know!"

"I know, I know! That's not what I was saying. It's just…" Tricia sighed. "Since Paula stomped all over your heart, you've been kinda…cool. Aloof. I'm just saying, just because you're still feeling numb about everything, don't let that get in the way of other stuff."

The truth in Tricia's words was hard to deny, so she didn't bother trying. "Okay. Understood."

"I love you. You know that, right?"

"I do." Adrienne exhaled slowly. "Look, it's getting late. I'd better get some sleep. Say hi to David for me."

"I will. And hey, good luck with the project. I hope it all works out."

"Thanks. I'll call whenever I can, but you know how these things go."

Tricia's laugh was gentle. "I do. Don't worry. If I think it's been too long between calls, I'll bombard you with text messages until you have no choice but to contact me to shut me up."

Adrienne rolled her eyes. "Yes, that sounds exactly the sort of thing you'd do."

Tricia was still laughing as she said good-bye and hung up.

The alarm startled Adrienne awake at six. She'd been in a deeper sleep than she would have imagined, given how unsettled she was when she'd got into bed the night before. The call with Tricia had played on her mind as she'd gone through her going-to-bed routine, in particular Tricia's comment about her being aloof and cool.

As she moisturized after her shower, she did something rare: She actually looked at her own body. Since Paula had left her for someone so much younger, she'd avoided looking at herself too closely, afraid of what she'd see.

Objectively, it wasn't that bad, was it? Her face was reasonably smooth and soft, only a few wrinkles around her eyes and the corners of her mouth really giving her age away. Her naturally light-brown skin helped, of course, and for the thousandth time she thanked her mother for her French-Moroccan genes.

Her hair was…well, just her hair. It never grew the way she wanted it to and needed daily taming with a variety of products. There was a little grey, and it had been tempting—*very* tempting—to cover that up after Paula left. Adrienne became obsessed for a short time with the age of Paula's new partner and doing her utmost to make herself look as young as possible. Her mind had concluded—with twisted logic, she now realized—that if she made herself look younger, then Paula would want her again and come back.

Her glance swept downward, albeit briefly. Just long enough to take in a body that was…okay. Her breasts were still pretty firm and not yet pointing at her feet, which was a relief. Her overall shape wasn't, obviously, as trim and tight as it had been twenty years ago, but she could live with it.

Would anyone find this attractive enough to want to make love to it? Would she *want* anyone to make love to it?

The thought still didn't appeal, but she could also acknowledge that her hurt was dissipating over time. Just like everyone said it would. The only times it still really stuck like a knife in her belly was when someone in her social circle—the social circle she had shared with Paula until recently—let slip something about Paula and *that woman* being seen out and about. It might have been Adrienne's imagination—Tricia kept telling her it was, anyway—but she thought such little slips were intentional. That the comments always held an unspoken "Oh, and she's *gorgeous,* and hasn't Paula done well for herself, trading you in for something younger and brighter and perkier?"

Adrienne shook out the tightness that had enveloped her body and stepped into the bedroom to dress. Time to start the day. *The* day, when hopefully she'd be able to work her charm on Morgan Spencer's manager and give her already good project a boost up into a *great* project.

She walked into the office an hour later, feeling determined to make the most of her day.

Jenny said nothing as she walked past her desk but came trotting in two minutes later with Adrienne's morning coffee and a plate holding a croissant and a small cup of fruit salad.

"Thank you, Jenny."

"So what's the plan for this morning?" Jenny stood expectantly in front of Adrienne's desk, her hands clasped behind her back. Her spiky hair was today tipped with bright purple, and the shirt she wore matched the color.

"Nice hair." Adrienne smirked, and Jenny grinned. "Okay, this morning, we're aiming big." She scribbled on a Post-It note and handed it over to the puzzled-looking Jenny. "Get me the number for this guy."

Jenny took the piece of paper and glanced at it. "Who is he?"

Adrienne smiled, her skin buzzing with the anticipation of what the day might bring. "That's Morgan Spencer's manager."

"Morgan…" Jenny bit her lip. "You want Morgan Spencer for the doc, don't you?"

"Yep."

Jenny grinned widely. "Nice." She exited Adrienne's office at speed. Twenty minutes later, she returned. "I may have just sold my first child, but here it is. He's expecting your call this morning."

Adrienne took the proffered piece of paper. "I knew I could count on you."

Jenny tilted her head. "You could easily have done this yourself, couldn't you?"

"I could. But you need your name out there too, and as long as you weren't unbelievably cheeky or rude, you probably just made a new ally."

"I wasn't. And I did. Turns out his executive assistant went to the same college as me, although he graduated a couple years before me."

Adrienne nodded. "Remember, it's not—"

"What you know. It's who you know." Jenny beamed. "I get it. Thanks."

"Good. Now leave me in peace so I can set this up."

Jenny mock saluted and dashed out of the room, shutting the door behind her.

God, she'll wear me out before I've got her fully trained. But it'll be worth it.

Inhaling deeply, Adrienne sat up straighter in her chair and reached for the phone.

"Hi," she said. "This is Adrienne Wyatt calling for Hilton Stewart."

"One moment, please, Ms. Wyatt."

Silently thanking Jenny for her prep, Adrienne patiently waited for Hilton to join the call.

"Ms. Wyatt," he said, his voice a little nasally in a fashion that told her it was always that way and not due to him having a cold or the flu.

"Please, call me Adrienne," she said. "And thank you for taking my call, Mr. Stewart."

"That's no problem. And please, call me Hilton. So what can I do for you?"

"Well, I think it's more a case of what we can do for each other, Hilton," Adrienne began smoothly. "As you know, I work for TC Productions, and we're currently making a documentary, commissioned by ESPN, about the women's majors this year."

"Yes, I definitely heard something about that happening." There was a chuckle in his tone.

"Of course. So I have a proposal for you and your client Morgan Spencer, which I think will only increase her already high profile and probably improve her ability to maintain or even improve on her current sponsorship position." It was bold, but it was how she felt after pulling herself out of her introspection at the start of her day, and she knew she could sell it.

There was a slight pause. "Hm, okay, I'm listening."

And hooked, Adrienne thought with a triumphant smile.

Chapter 3

Jab, jab, upper cut.

Body punches—one, two, three, then right hook.

The punchbag swung crazily on its chain. Morgan blinked the sweat out of her eyes before delivering a final one-two to the center of the bag. She stepped back, her tired arms dropping to her sides.

A door slammed somewhere behind her, and she sighed. Her private time was over. She'd had no trouble waking early to get into the hotel's fitness suite before six so that she was its only occupant; she'd hardly slept all night. Anger and hurt had kept her brain wide awake—at one point, she'd even been tempted to drive back out to her parents' house and have it out with her father. Common sense had eventually prevailed and kept her tucked beneath the sheets even as her body tossed and turned.

She hadn't, after all that she'd said to her mom, called Jack yet. A quick text message to say "Congrats, Big Bro" had gone unanswered, but that was fine with Morgan. Good for him, going out to celebrate the win. She hoped he had an it-was-so-worth-it hangover this morning.

Grinning at the thought, she peeled off the gloves, stowed them on the equipment rack, and then picked up her water bottle and drained it. The shower she stepped into five minutes later was a welcome relief from her workout, which had perhaps been slightly more strenuous than usual. It was amazing what frustration could make a woman do.

She ate a light breakfast in her room before checking out and loading up the rental car. Having convinced her sponsors to give her twenty-four hours of freedom before she needed to be on a plane for the next tournament, she made the most of the drive back to the airport. Her flight wasn't until three, so she meandered more backroads, drifting through small towns with cute centers where everyone seemed to know each other as they passed on the street. She'd never had "real" life like that. Growing up in her dad's shadow had meant that nothing was normal or what she imagined normal to be.

Jeez, you're getting maudlin in your old age.

Smiling ruefully at herself, she swung the car onto the interstate, the one stretch of highway she had to drive in order to get to the airport. With reluctance, some twenty minutes later, she pulled the car into its allotted slot in the parking lot. A porter loaded up a trolley for her, and soon she was checked in, her bags trundling down the belt, her carry-on slung over her shoulder.

The flight out to the West Coast was much the same as any other flight she took most weeks: long and boring, even in business class. And then there she was, checking in to yet another hotel after the sponsor's car had collected her from LAX. At least this room had a view and a balcony that overlooked the hotel's extensive pool area.

She flopped down on the bed, pulled her phone from her pocket, and dialed her brother.

"Hey, Sis!"

He sounded hoarse, and she grinned. "Heavy night?"

Jack chuckled. "Yeah, something like that."

"Congrats. I haven't seen any of it yet, but I bet you were awesome."

"I was. Obviously." He cleared his throat. "Bummed for you."

"Meh. You win some, you lose some."

"Yeah, but..."

"I know."

"Did you still go to the folks' after?"

"Yeah."

"Regret it?"

"Hell yeah."

They both laughed, but it sounded hollow.

"Sorry. I wish he was—"

"Hey, nothing for you to apologize for. He is who he is. Nothing any of us can do to change that."

She didn't add what she wanted to add, which was that Jack *could* actually try harder on that score, in her humble opinion. Whenever they were together as a family, and her father talked nonstop about Jack and his success, her brother never thought to jump in and deflect some of that attention to Morgan. Usually, her mother pulled that heavy load alone. However, there was no point getting into that now and definitely not on the phone.

"How was Mom?" Jack asked after a moment.

"Good. Really good. Made me tuna casserole."

"Hah, of course she did! Man, I miss her tuna casserole."

"Then you should get home more. You know she'd love that."

"I know, but it's so hard to find time. This tour's a killer, especially if I want to push for the one hundred."

Especially for a guy who was thirty-three already and up against the much younger and fitter men, those new faces that joined the tour almost every week.

"I know, I know."

"So where are you now?"

"L.A. Got a smaller tournament in Anaheim starting Thursday."

She heard sounds of many people in the background and Jack's muffled, "*Yeah, just a sec!*" He came back on the line. "Well, look, good luck, okay? I gotta run."

"Yeah, okay. Speak soon," she said, but the line was already dead.

She threw the phone onto the bed and lay back, gazing up at the nondescript ceiling. As calls went with her brother, that was about as good as it got, so she couldn't complain. But the tense knot in her stomach told her otherwise, and she sighed.

Jack wasn't a bad guy, not really. But he'd allowed himself to get sucked into their father's view of the world, and whether he'd ever admit it or not, he also treated Morgan's sport and her achievements as somehow *less than*. Jack *was* a pretty good tennis player, she knew that. But *she* was an exceptional golfer whose gender negated everything she'd accomplished in the eyes of her father and, to a lesser extent, her brother.

The joke of it was, after naming his son, his firstborn, after one of, if not *the* best golfers of all time, Jack Nicklaus, her brother had shown zero interest in following in their father's footsteps. Morgan had, loving the game from the minute she could hold one of Jack's discarded small plastic clubs, but that had never been good enough for Gordy Spencer. Jack was aware, she knew that, but she wished he would try a little harder. She also knew there probably wasn't much point. Her father was old school, one of those misogynists who didn't even know he was doing it, it was so ingrained. And the fact that he did it to his daughter didn't register at all.

She forced herself up to a sitting position and glanced at the time on her phone: 6:30 p.m. Food, that was what she needed now. And then a very early night to make up for the one before.

Her phone buzzed in her hand.

Hey! You here yet? Need dinner? I'm in the Calypso bar (dumb name), and they have fried shrimp!!!

She smiled. Charlie McKinnon. Yeah, dinner with Charlie was just what she needed. Morgan jumped up and quickly pulled off the clothes she'd been in all day. A short shower freshened her up, then she tied back her hair, dressed in some casual attire, and left her room.

"Shit, you look *tired*!" were Charlie's first words when Morgan sidled up to her at the bar.

"Gee, thanks, honey."

Charlie laughed and pulled her into a tight hug. "You know I'll never lie to you."

"True." Morgan sat on the stool next to Charlie's and pointed at the plate of fried shrimp in front of her. "Any good?"

Charlie shrugged, her mouth quirking up at one corner. "It isn't *bad*, but I've definitely had better."

"Then I'll pass. Besides, I'm not sure I could handle fried food today."

Charlie wiped her hands on a napkin, took a quick sip of her soda, then looked at Morgan with a serious expression. "What's up?"

Charlie was the one person Morgan had confided some of her family secrets to—not all of them but enough hints that Charlie would know what Morgan meant when she said, "Spent the evening with the folks last night. It was the usual."

"Ah." Charlie frowned. "Sorry."

Morgan shrugged, then placed her order with the bartender for a Cobb salad and a Perrier before turning back to her friend. "I knew going in it was likely. Jack won yesterday."

"Yeah, I saw." Charlie patted Morgan's arm.

"Hey, what's this I hear about you getting snippy with some reporter yesterday?"

Charlie rolled her eyes. "Idiot. Asked me if I was aware that people were calling me the female Tiger Woods."

"Seriously? That again?"

"I know!" Charlie laughed. "I may have been a little sharp when I told him that actually, I am the golfing equivalent of Serena Williams, thank you very much."

Morgan laughed and gave her friend a mini fist bump. She knew Charlie, being one of the few black women playing golf, was sick of being compared to Tiger Woods, so she could well imagine how her response to the reporter would have been delivered.

Charlie finished her fried shrimp. "Want to talk about that putt?"

Morgan groaned and dropped her head into her hands. "You were watching."

"Of course I was! Just because I couldn't play didn't mean I wasn't there in spirit."

"How is the knee?"

"Don't deflect!" Charlie scowled at her. "And it's fine, actually. It was the right move to not play last week. But I'm itching to get out there this week, so watch your ass. I'm coming for you!"

Morgan laughed and squeezed Charlie's arm affectionately. "I'll be so far ahead of you, you won't see me."

Charlie huffed. "Probably true." She laughed. "Anyway, you're still deflecting. That putt?"

"Yeah, I know," Morgan said soberly. "It was there and then…and then it wasn't."

"Did you twitch? I bet Harry said you'd twitch."

"He did. But I don't think I did twitch. I think I just read it wrong. Or I didn't listen to his read on it." She shook her head. "I don't think I twitched."

Morgan's "twitch" was something the press had started talking about after she'd failed to win the previous two majors, and it bugged her. They all thought she couldn't take the pressure of winning the big ones, of finally getting a major on the board, so they thought she'd developed a nervous twitch that was the reason she'd missed those key shots.

"So who's our toughest competition this week, huh?"

Grateful for the slide away from the previous topic, Morgan dived wholeheartedly into a conversation about their rivals on the tour. When her food arrived, she stabbed eagerly at it with her fork, alternating mouthfuls of food with her thoughts on which women were there to be beaten this weekend. Before she knew it, she and Charlie had blown two hours at the bar, and with satisfaction, Morgan realized she'd shaken off everything she'd brought with her from the trip back east. Being with Charlie could usually do that for her, and once again, she was so grateful for their friendship.

"Okay, next subject," Charlie said with a wicked grin. She swirled her drink. "Any hot chickies out there for you at the moment?"

"'Hot chickies?'" Morgan asked incredulously. "What are you, fifteen?"

Charlie snorted into her drink. "Okay, so what do you prefer—hot babes? Hot mamas?"

"Women, Charlie, they're just women. Just like you and me."

"Hey, speak for yourself!" Charlie poked a finger into her own chest. "I, for one, am definitely a hot babe."

Morgan laughed and wrapped an arm around Charlie's shoulders. "Yes, Charlie, yes, you are." She rolled her eyes. "But no, there are no women out there for me at the moment." Her voice fell. "And you know I can't. Not yet. Not after…"

Charlie kissed Morgan on the cheek. "I know. I just…" She sighed. "Sorry, I just want you to meet that *one*, you know? That one who gets how wonderful you are and totally worships you as the goddess that you are."

"Goddess?" Morgan quirked an eyebrow. "Are you sure that's just soda you're drinking?"

Chuckling, Charlie pushed a fist into Morgan's bicep. "You know what I mean."

Morgan shook her head. "What about you? Any hot hunks on your horizon?"

Charlie's eyes went wide. "You did *not* just say 'hot hunks' to me."

Morgan laughed so hard her sides ached.

"You're late," Harry said, looking stern, his hands on his hips, Morgan's bag at his feet.

Morgan glanced at her watch. "It's 7:59 a.m. I'm early."

Harry rolled his eyes, then broke into laughter a moment later. "So how you doing? You seem pretty perky."

"I don't do perky," she replied with a growl, then grinned as he tutted. "I'm good. Ran into Charlie last night."

"Hey, how is Mac?"

"The same." Morgan smirked. "She said to tell you that you read that last putt wrong and I should fire you."

Harry glared at her. "She did *not!*"

Morgan shrugged. "What can I say? She's a smart cookie."

"Whatever," he muttered, turning away from her and picking up the bag. "Come on, we've got stuff to do."

She sighed. Yeah, he was right. The tournament this week wasn't as significant as the Open last week, but she knew all eyes would still be on her, wondering if she'd lost it, if she would crumple even further under the pressure everyone thought she was experiencing. It was funny—she'd chosen to play this one because she thought it would be a relaxing change straight off the back of a major. Now she wasn't so sure.

"Let's start on the green," Harry called over his shoulder, and she sighed again.

I knew he was gonna say that.

She followed him onto the area where various practice putting greens were set up. There were three other golfers already there, and she cast a quick glance around to see who. Laurie Schweitzer, of course. Currently world number two and still one of the most ambitious—*i.e., hard, callous,* Morgan thought with a wry smile—women on the tour, even after being near the top for twelve years. So Park, who was quiet, serious, and had the best drive on the women's tour right now. And Lotte Karlsson, one of the older players on the tour but still able to hit the top ten on a regular basis. Only Laurie failed to acknowledge Morgan's presence, but that was no real loss.

"Bitch," Harry muttered. He wiped the putter on a fresh towel before passing it to Morgan.

"Now, now, play nice, Harry." Morgan threw him a smile.

"I will if she will."

Morgan chuckled. On the outside, Harry looked like a gruff old bear—tall, solidly built, and with a manner of speaking that most people would take as rude. But Morgan knew better; no one had ever had her back more than him, and the insult he'd directed at Laurie was purely in support of Morgan.

Harry dropped a ball at her feet. "Are we going to talk about it?"

Morgan looked up at him. There was no judgement or disappointment in his face. Quietly, making sure that Laurie especially didn't hear, she said, "I didn't twitch. I swear. I think I just read it wrong. There was more of a slope than I anticipated."

He nodded, but before he could speak, she rushed on.

"But the problem wasn't the putt. It was the second shot."

His smile was slow but warm. "Good girl. Yes, it was. By hitting *that* into the rough, you never gave yourself a chance of getting close to the pin." He shrugged. "Sure, a ten-foot putt should be a piece of cake for someone as good as you, but you just added more pressure into an already high-pressure situation." He stepped back. "I just wanted to be sure about the twitch. Now I know what we need to focus on. And it ain't actually your putting."

She smiled in gratitude. Harry had been her caddy for years now, and she wouldn't trade him for anyone because he was way more than a caddy. She deliberately paid him the extra to accompany her on training sessions and practice rounds because he was more coach than mere bag carrier.

Exhaling slowly, she rolled her shoulders a few times, then pushed the ball around with the putter until it sat true on the cropped grass.

"Don't do that," Harry griped. "Play it from wherever it lands."

"Yes, boss." She grinned up at him, and he wagged a finger at her before stepping back.

She practiced putting—short, medium, and long—for about half an hour. Even though they'd both agreed that her putting wasn't really at fault for the loss of the Open, Harry knew it calmed her to start the day on the green rather than going straight into a round, and putting practice could never hurt.

They trotted down the rough pathway that led to the first tee; her first practice round tee-off time was nine, and she arrived in plenty of time to see So Park hit an immaculate drive straight down the middle of the fairway.

"Nice."

Morgan whistled, and Park flashed her a pleased grin before striding off down the fairway, her playing partner, another Korean whom Morgan didn't recognize, walking alongside her, chatting animatedly. Morgan, as usual, would play her practice round alone. She knew some of the press highlighted that as yet more evidence of her icy persona, but she couldn't care less about what the press thought. For her, practice was something she needed to concentrate on and always had, and she really didn't need the presence of another player alongside her disrupting that concentration.

Morgan retrieved first her cap, then her glove from the bag and pulled them both on. She watched the Koreans disappear down the fairway, but she wasn't really seeing them. Instead, she assessed the breeze on her face, judging its direction and strength, and took in the lack of cloud, the already warm sun on her upturned face.

When both the Koreans had played their second shots, Morgan finally turned back to face Harry.

"All right, Spencer." He handed her the driver. "Show 'em what you got."

She took the club and leaned on it to place her ball on the tee.

"Remember, it dog legs to the left, but the wind today is from the right, so aim farther right than you'd think to draw it back in."

"Sure." She swung the club a few times, loving how that always felt at the start of a day, and feeling, somewhere deep in her muscles and bones and sinews and tendons, that today was going to be a *good* day.

She stepped up, addressed the ball, then, moments later, sent it arcing into the sky into a perfect landing roughly 270 yards down the fairway.

"That'll do." Harry winked as he took back the driver. "That'll do."

"Fourteen and fifteen were the toughest, I think," Morgan said as she strolled up to where Harry finished packing the bag. She pulled off her cap and the tie around her ponytail and shook her hair out, running her fingers through it to ease out the tangles.

"Yeah, but you nearly made a mess of six too. That big bunker's right at your driving distance—you'll need to be way more accurate with the tee shot."

"True." She gulped from her water; the day was hot, the sun beating down relentlessly from the clear blue sky.

"Lunch?" Harry asked, hauling the bag up onto his shoulder.

"Love to."

She followed Harry down the path that led from the eighteenth green to the impressive clubhouse. The building had been recently redeveloped, the owners keen to get a top tournament on their books and willing to spend the money to make that happen. It was modern and airy and boasted four eating areas, one of which they headed toward once Harry had secured her bag in the trunk of his car.

They'd barely made it to the door when a voice called, "Morgan!"

Morgan spun around, and her mouth dropped open. "Hilton? What the—?"

Hilton Stewart, her manager, stood in the lobby between two of the eating areas, looking as sharp as ever in one of his Armani suits, a wide smile on his ridiculously handsome face. It was such a shame he was very happily married to his wife of twenty years, or Morgan could see herself engineering a meeting between him and Charlie.

"And it's lovely to see you too," he said as he walked over, his long legs making the distance in only three strides.

"Well, sorry, but you being here is such a shock. Did I miss an e-mail or something?" She grinned sheepishly as she leaned in to kiss him on the cheek.

"No," he said, drawing out the word, which made it sound even more comical with his naturally nasal tone. Anyone else hearing that sound would mistake it for him whining, but she knew better. "Can't I just drop in to see my favorite client? Perhaps treat her to lunch?" He waved a hand in the direction of the smartest restaurant area.

"Oh." Her eyes were wide as she turned toward Harry. "I was just about to—"

"No problem." Harry held up his hands. "You two talk business. I'll amuse myself until you're done."

"Sorry, Harry. And thank you." Hilton shook his hand. "It is rather important."

Harry saluted and ambled off to the counter where they dispensed burgers, which made Morgan chuckle. Of course that's where he would head. She was jealous—no doubt Hilton would now buy her a lunch that barely covered the plate it was presented on and she'd be craving something more substantial within two hours of eating it.

"Shall we?" Hilton motioned toward the restaurant with his head.

They took a quiet table near a large picture window that overlooked the ornamental gardens and both ordered water to drink.

"So what gives?" she asked after a few sips.

Hilton meshed his fingers together and leaned forward. "Well, I've had an interesting proposition that I want to run past you. And I'll be honest, I'll be really disappointed if you don't agree to it."

Wow, that wasn't like Hilton. Normally he was much more conciliatory and open. She tried hard not to bristle at the way he'd spoken, but her shoulders tensed. "Okay, what is it?"

"You might have heard about the documentary ESPN commissioned about the women's game?"

She nodded.

"I got a call yesterday from the producer. She wants to up the ante on how they're going to approach their story of the majors." He leaned in closer and lowered his voice. "She wants to make you the feature player. Follow you for the final three this season, have exclusive access to your training and practice, and a couple of sit-down interviews somewhere away from golf. Perhaps at your home."

Before he'd even finished speaking, Morgan's shoulders were so tight it was a wonder bones weren't popping out of their sockets.

"No. Absolutely no!"

He held up a hand. "Wait just a second, please. Think about it. This puts you front and center in the first major documentary about your sport in years. It'll be broadcast in every country where ESPN has a presence. It will put your name out there in a way that just isn't happening at the moment."

"Because I'm not winning majors," she snapped bitterly. "Is that it?"

He sighed and blinked a couple of times before responding. "I will admit, that is not helping my cause, no."

"And just what *is* your cause, huh?" Her fists clenched against her thighs.

Hilton gazed at her for a moment. "To get you the best exposure, the best publicity, and most of all, the best sponsorship deals." He sipped from his glass. "And by you doing this film, I'll be able to get the likes of S Pro interested at last."

S Pro was one of the largest manufacturers of sports goods in the world, right up there with Nike and Adidas. Having them as a sponsor would certainly be a coup.

"No, you won't." Morgan's voice was tight. "Only me winning a major will make that happen."

He blinked as he looked at her. "You know I met with S Pro two months ago, yes?"

"You said you were going to, but you never really said how it went. I assumed badly precisely because of that silence."

"Morgan, it is not your lack of major wins that worries S Pro." He leaned forward again. "I haven't bothered telling you this before because I've been trying to work out the best way to resolve it." His expression gentled. "The problem they have is how…cold you are."

Morgan flinched. "Cold?" She hated the catch in her voice.

"Their word, not mine. Your nickname has stuck. Ice. And, rightly or wrongly, no one wants to put money behind a woman who doesn't want to talk to anyone. Sunday was a case in point—that press conference you gave?" He shook his head. "You gave everyone in that room and watching on TV the impression that you didn't give a shit about what had just happened. You'd just lost the US Open, but there was no emotion. No fire." He held up a hand when she made to interrupt. "*I* know that isn't you. So does Harry. But that's the trouble, *no one else does.*" He pressed a hand into the pristine white tablecloth to emphasize the point.

Morgan slumped back in her chair, closing her eyes against the irritation that every one of his words stirred.

"The resolution to that," he continued, his tone so gentle it caused her to open her eyes and stare at him, "is to do something like this film. Open up. Let other people see what a wonderful person you are." He paused. "And finally step out of your father's shadow and be *you.*"

Chapter 4

"OKAY," HARRY SAID, HIS VOICE low, as he stepped up beside her. "This is a complete waste of both our time. Whatever Hilton said to you at lunch has clearly screwed you over for the rest of the day." He took hold of the sand wedge and tugged until Morgan gave it up. Ramming it into the bag, he shook his head. "Go back to your hotel, find your usual punchbag, and work it out."

She stared at him. "H-how did you know about the punchbag?"

He shuffled. "Stumbled across you doing that one morning last year. After the British Open. Realized that was your stress reliever."

Morgan nodded. "Okay." She sighed. "And yes, I'm sorry. Hilton's news *has* put my mind somewhere else." And to the point where she wasn't even ready to talk to Harry about it. She motioned to the bunker they'd been practicing in since lunch. "I know I'm screwing this up now. You're right."

He patted her on the shoulder. "You're not a robot. Stuff's allowed to affect you. But you have to be able to work past it to make this"—he gestured with a big sweep of his arm at the whole golf world around them—"still work. Go on. Go beat the crap out of something. I'll see if I can find a fishing spot somewhere nearby." He grinned. "I'll see you tomorrow. I'll even let you sleep in. We'll start at nine. Don't be late."

Her throat tightened. Moisture pricked at her eyes. "What did I do to deserve you?"

"Guess you were just born lucky," he said and winked. He hoisted her bag up and marched off. She knew she'd embarrassed him when he didn't look back.

After making an effort to say hello to the other women practicing their short game this afternoon, Morgan quickly departed the practice area and made her way to the front desk. A few minutes after she'd requested it, a car pulled up out front to drive her back to her hotel.

The meeting with Hilton really *had* thrown her for a loop. She realized part of the problem was entirely self-inflicted. Because she avoided the media reports of her tournaments like the plague, she hadn't known quite how bad her reputation was out there in the real world. She focused so hard on her game, on perfecting her play, she never remembered that there was more to being a professional than that.

Now she found herself wondering if that's why the autograph hunters always approached her with a certain apprehension. Did they think she would refuse, or worse, bite their heads off for asking? Not for the first time, she found herself wishing she could ask her father for advice—how had he managed it all, the fame and the media? Mind you, back when he was playing, the media wasn't the shark-infested frenzy it was these days, so would his advice actually hold water?

She was in a daze as she walked back into the hotel and up to her room, and when her phone rang the minute she'd pushed the door closed behind her, she was tempted to ignore it. Then she saw the name "Mom" in the caller display and hit the answer icon.

"Hey, Mom, everything okay?"

"Of course, darling. I didn't actually expect you to answer. I was just going to leave you a voice mail."

"Oh! Well, okay, you got me. How are things?"

"What are you doing answering in the middle of the day? Shouldn't you be out practicing?"

Her mother always had been the sharp one.

"Um, yeah. Kind of taking the afternoon off." A thought popped into her head—her father might not be approachable, but her mom had lived through all of it by his side, so maybe... "Hey, Mom, can I talk to you about something? Do you have time?"

"For you, darling, of course! Wait, let me get comfy out here on the veranda."

Morgan heard a chair being pulled into position and then a gentle sigh as her mom sat down.

"Okay, that's much better. What's on your mind?"

Haltingly, not quite sure of her words but managing to make mostly coherent sentences, Morgan told her all about the proposal from Hilton, the backdrop to it, the sponsor issues, the works. Her mom listened patiently, only occasionally interrupting with questions.

"Well, I can certainly see why this has you bothered," her mom said eventually. "And I'm sorry to hear you are upset. But which part disturbs you most—being the focus of the documentary or the fact that you didn't know that was how you were perceived?"

Morgan rubbed her thumb across her chin as she paced the room. "I guess both, but maybe that second one more than the first. I mean, it's not like I haven't been called cold before by someone else, but..."

"Ah, yes. The delightful"—the way she said the word made it sound anything but—"Naomi. Is she still around?"

Chuckling at her mom's obvious distaste for Morgan's ex, she said, "No. I mean, she's still playing, but a shoulder injury is keeping her away from the tour at the moment." *Thank God.*

"Good." Her mom huffed. "Morgan, what she said to you, those were the bitter words of someone who didn't want you leaving her, you do know that, yes?"

Morgan sighed. "I know, but I have to be honest. She was right in some ways. I *do* struggle with, you know, the whole warm and cuddly thing. I always have. But only because I've just been so driven to be the best golfer I can. I just thought she was different, that she'd get it, given she's on the tour too. I thought she'd be more patient with me."

"And then she betrayed all that. I know."

"Yeah."

"Do you want my honest opinion, darling?"

"Of course!"

"Do it. Do the film. It will challenge you, and you might struggle, but I think Hilton's right. I think other people need to see how wonderful you are. Your father and I, and Jack, we know, but the rest of the world needs to know."

Morgan almost snorted at the inclusion of her father in that endorsement but let it slide. "Did Dad ever have to do anything like this? How did he handle the media?"

"Well," her mom said, her tone turning a little flat. "Obviously the media back then wasn't the circus it is nowadays." She paused. "He tried to hit a balance between giving them something but not all of it. Perhaps that's what you need to think of. You've kept back more than you've given. Maybe it's time to even that up a little."

"Adrienne, I've got Hilton Stewart on line two." Jenny's voice always sounded like a ghost of herself on the intercom.

"Thanks, Jenny."

Adrienne's stomach flipped, and she sucked in a breath before picking up the call. "Adrienne Wyatt."

"Hi, Adrienne, it's Hilton Stewart."

"Hi, Hilton, how are you?" *Please have good news for me!* She crossed her fingers in front of her on the desk.

"I'm very well. And I call with good tidings."

Yes!

"She'll do it?"

Hilton chuckled. "She will. Only one condition—no interviews in her home. That really is her private space, and she'd like to keep it that way."

That was a small disappointment, but Adrienne wouldn't push it. Maybe once Morgan Spencer had gotten used to working with her that could be readdressed.

"I have no problem working with that."

"Excellent!"

"Hilton, thank you. I'll have someone get contracts over to you today, tomorrow at the latest."

"I look forward to receiving them. Thank you. I appreciate you reaching out on this."

They said their good-byes and hung up, and in the next moment, Adrienne leaped out of her chair and jigged a few steps on the worn rug beneath her feet.

"You okay, boss?"

Face burning, she stopped moving and grinned sheepishly at Jenny, who stood in the doorway, her eyes comically wide.

"I am. I am more than okay, actually." She beamed at Jenny, her heart racing. "We just got Morgan Spencer!"

"Oh. My. God." Jenny pressed a hand to her chest. "Seriously?"

Adrienne nodded and exhaled slowly, willing her pulse to settle. "So we've got a lot more work to do."

"Bring it." Jenny nodded slowly. "So worth it."

"Yes, I really think it will be."

Jenny trotted off, and Adrienne sat back in her chair. The only thing that ruined the moment was the condition that Spencer had put on the deal. Viewers loved an insight into a player's private life, and seeing Morgan in her home would have been a perfect scene to film.

I hope she's not a diva. I didn't peg as her one, but you never know.

In spite of that last thought, she couldn't help the smile that spread across her face. It finally felt like something good was coming Adrienne's way after the year from hell.

Sure, her work had kept her steady and helped her get out of bed every day when all she'd wanted to do was crawl in a hole and weep, but she hadn't worked on anything this tempting in a while. Being able to bring Morgan Spencer in at such short notice would need some quick thinking and handling, but she was up for the challenge. If nothing else, it might help dispel the remaining fragments of the aftermath with Paula and *that woman*. As long as Spencer played ball—she rolled her eyes at her own unintended pun—this project could be fantastic.

"Morgan!" James Morrison, the reporter for the National News Network she'd grown to loathe over the last couple of years, thrust his hand into the air and was so vigorous about it she had no choice but to take his question.

We're only ten minutes in, and already I want a pencil to stick in my eye. Anything but face their damn questions.

"James," she acknowledged coolly.

"Clearly you had no trouble winning today, so how can you explain that in comparison to last weekend?"

Well, that had to be a record. Normally, he took at least three questions before he aimed for her jugular. Channeling Hilton, knowing that if he were here, he'd be counselling her to tread lightly, she bit back her gut retort and instead smiled as sweetly as she could manage. Cameras flashed.

"Well, James, every tournament is different, as you know." As if he did—the guy had never lifted a club in his life, she'd bet. "Every one of them presents different challenges to overcome." She grinned. "Guess I got that right today."

The win had been sweet. Three ahead going into today's final round in Anaheim, and everything had run as smooth as silk. Even Harry had been happy with her. She'd hit every fairway and nearly every green—only fourteen and fifteen, as she'd anticipated earlier in the week, proving tricky.

Charlie had given her a good run for her money but had had to settle for second, five shots behind in the end. Still, that was Charlie's best result of the year, so Morgan would be sure to share a beer with her later to celebrate. And tonight she *could* have beer, as she had the next week off. Her mouth watered at the prospect.

"Well, yeah, I guess. But how do you explain *not* being able to get it right last week when you were in pole position?"

He was like a dog with a bone, and even a couple of other reporters winced at his snide tone. She wasn't even sure what it was about her he didn't like, but it was obvious it was something.

"Like I said," she replied through gritted teeth, "every time we go out there it's different. Yes, you hope you can get everything right on every day, that your swing won't let you down, that your putting will be true." She shrugged. "But sometimes the universe has other ideas."

Praying for someone else to raise their hand, she nearly groaned aloud when James pounced again.

"Wait, so you're now blaming some higher being, is that it?" His tone was beyond sarcastic, plunging well into the zone of scathing.

There was a shocked silence in the room for a moment, but in Morgan's head there was no such quiet. White noise filled her ears. Who the hell did he think he was, coming after her like that? She opened her mouth before reason could set in, but as she made to speak the words that had leaped to the forefront of her brain—one of which was *asshole*—a disturbance to her right had her swiveling in her seat.

"Hi, everyone! Sorry I'm late. What did I miss?"

Charlie lightly ran up the three steps that led to the small stage and dropped quickly into the chair alongside Morgan. She didn't look at Morgan, but her hand quickly found Morgan's leg under the table and gave it a light squeeze, which told Morgan she had heard every part of that exchange with James. Had she run in to rescue Morgan? If so, that was a whole new level to their friendship, and Morgan swallowed rapidly against the emotion that engendered.

The assembled mass of reporters chuckled, breaking the tension in the room, and Patty from CBS shouted her first question at Charlie, effectively cutting James Morrison out.

"Your best result this year, Charlie. How does that feel?"

Charlie whooped, loud and long, and the laughter in the room was genuinely warm. "Does that answer your question?" she asked with a grin.

Later, when they'd escaped the room, and each had given their prearranged, one-on-one interviews with ESPN, they found each other again in the hotel's bar. Not the Calypso this time but the quieter, more formal Browns, where they threw themselves into a burgundy leather sofa and ordered ice-cold beers from the frowning waiter.

"Do you think we've just broken a rule?" Charlie asked, one eyebrow quirked. "Are women allowed to drink beer in a bar like this?"

Morgan laughed. "He didn't kick us out, so I think we're good."

"Ugh, I can't believe we have to go to this dinner thing this evening. I just want to hang out with you and drink beer."

"I hear you." Morgan raised her glass and waited for Charlie to follow suit. "My friend, congratulations on your highest finish this year. You played really well, and I'm so proud of you."

Charlie dipped her head. "Hey, you're the one who won. We should be toasting you!"

"Come on, don't be so modest. This was an awesome result for you. I'll tell you, when you got within two shots at the ninth, I got a little worried."

"Yeah?" Charlie beamed. "Cool."

They clinked glasses and drank.

"Oh, yeah, *that's* what I needed." Charlie's eyes closed in rapture.

"Hell yeah." Morgan took another long drink, then set her glass down. "And there's one other thing I want to thank you for."

Charlie looked at her, eyes twinkling.

"Your timing at that press conference was *immaculate*. And I don't think I'm wrong in assuming it was deliberate?"

Charlie's laugh was bubbly and infectious. "Oh my God, no, you're not wrong! Your face when he started in on you? I expected him to turn into a frozen popsicle right there on the spot." She narrowed her eyes. "You were about to really let him have it, weren't you?"

Morgan sighed. "I was. I can't deny it. I'd been channeling Hilton through the whole thing, remembering what he told me about being more approachable and, you know, *nice*. And then Morrison gets in my face, and I was ready to rip him a new one."

Her response to Morrison had shocked her. Normally, she was an expert at keeping her emotions in check, but somehow, this past week or so, lots of things she'd normally repress were bubbling way too close to the surface to be comfortable.

"He's such a jerk. And it's not just us players who think so. I overheard Patty moaning about him to that woman from *Golfing Today*."

"Well, that actually makes me feel better."

"Good." Charlie slowly drank some more of her beer, then said quietly, "So Hilton's been saying stuff, has he?"

"Uh, yeah." Morgan rubbed her chin. "There's been a development this week. Because you and I have been in our zones, I haven't had a chance to tell you."

"Tell me what?"

Morgan sketched out for her what had transpired from her meeting with Hilton. It was hard to report back what S Pro thought of her, but Charlie merely patted her hand and sipped at her beer, letting Morgan finish.

"Okay," Charlie said, when Morgan stopped and took a drink. "You know I'm someone who gets you and loves you and all that, yeah?"

Morgan smiled and nodded.

"So don't be offended when I say that I totally get what S Pro and Hilton are saying. And your mom too. It really is time to let the world in a little. Now, I know it isn't going to be easy for you. So just remember, wherever we are, whatever tournaments we're playing, whether that's together or not, you know I'm always at the end of a phone, right?"

Morgan smiled wider and squeezed Charlie's forearm. "You have been, and continue to be, a great friend, Charlie. Thank you."

"Aw, stop, you're going to make me blush." She swigged the last of her beer. "When do you meet the TV woman?"

Morgan stretched back in her seat and rubbed at her neck to ease out the kink that had built up during the day. "Thankfully not until Phoenix. I've got a week at home first, and I can't wait for that."

"Yeah, me too! Haven't seen my mama in so long. But wait, how come you're meeting this woman in Phoenix? I thought the TV thing was about the majors, but the next one isn't until the PGA in July."

Morgan rolled her eyes. "Yeah, this is the dumbest part of the whole deal—she wants to do two sit-down interviews away from the majors. We're meeting on the Monday after the tournament finishes for her to grill me. I can just imagine the kind of ammo she's going to fire at me when she gets me in front of a camera."

"You sound *so* enthusiastic about this opportunity, it's wonderful," Charlie said wryly, and Morgan couldn't help but laugh.

"I know, I know. I need to just get on with it, but honestly, I hate this crap."

"I know. But I go back to what Hilton said—this is the right thing to do, especially with where the extra sponsorship could take you. You *will* be number one, Morgan. And probably soon. And number one deserves the best this crazy sporting world offers, so that means S Pro or someone like them."

"I guess." She shook her head. "All I ever wanted to do, though, is just play golf, you know? I never asked for any of this other stuff."

Charlie shrugged. "Yeah, me too. But you're the daughter of Gordy Spencer, and as soon as you started playing golf properly, you were never going to get away from all this other stuff because of that. All you can do is try to make it work for you and fuck the rest of 'em."

Morgan snorted and laughed and pulled Charlie into a one-arm hug. "You should put that on a greeting card. It'd sell millions."

Charlie's eyes lit up. "Hey, I might just do that!"

The driver helped Morgan with the bags, but only as far as the front door, at her request. She let very few people into her house, and the drivers who escorted her to and from airports were not on that elite list. After waiting for him to back down the short driveway, she turned the key in the lock and let out a contented sigh when her foyer came into view.

The house had been her biggest treat to herself since starting to win serious money on the tour about five years ago. Everything else she'd invested for the future, but this house was her pride and joy, not least because she'd earned it herself. Her parents had paid for her entire college tuition and most of the first two years she was on tour, and while they'd not allowed her to repay that, they had respected her need to be independent as soon as she could. The house was relatively small by Sea Cliff's standards, but it was plenty big enough for her. It even afforded her space for a workout room that she'd be taking advantage of most days this week.

After dragging her bags into the house, she locked the door behind her and finally relaxed, properly, for the first time in four weeks. The fresh scent everywhere told her that Renata had been in earlier that day. Morgan was sure the outside areas were immaculate too, with Alejandro, Renata's husband, in charge of the garden and grounds. They had been keeping house for her ever since she first bought the property. Both hardworking and conscientious, they also made Morgan smile with their constant gentle bickering, which, she was sure, disguised a deeply held love for each other.

"Unpacking can wait until tomorrow," she said into the empty space of the foyer.

It was already past five in the afternoon, and she had only two things on her mind: a run to ease out the stiffness from yesterday and the—albeit short—travelling today, and then a night of indulgence in front of her TV. She had a catch up of *CSI: NY* to get sunk into.

The run did exactly what she needed. San Francisco had, for once, had a pleasant day of June weather, an even sixty-five all day with bright sunshine. She'd run through the Presidio, along with many other people all with the same idea, and returned home hot, sweaty, and feeling infinitely better.

She settled in front of her awesomely large TV screen, a bowl of her favorite coffee ice cream on her lap. After a few mouthfuls, she let her mind return to the conversations with Charlie, Hilton, and her mom. She knew they were all right, deep down, and that this TV thing *was* something she should really embrace. But she hated talking about herself, and she'd never been good at letting people in. It was why Naomi had turned her back on her in the end, making it easy for Morgan to end things when Naomi had decided she would apparently get more forthcoming "conversation" from the receptionist at their hotel in Miami. Catching them in the act had been one of the most devastating moments of Morgan's life to date. And mainly because she had, for her, really begun to open up to Naomi. Just not enough, it seemed, for Naomi to be happy.

Which reminded her—she'd heard through the grapevine that Naomi was slated to make her comeback in Chicago the week before the Women's PGA.

Ugh.

She shoveled more ice cream into her mouth and let the intense flavor distract her.

Come on, CSI *is what you need.*

She had three whole days with no commitments whatsoever and wondered how many episodes she could get through in that amount of time.

"Come on, Morgan! Harder! Faster!"

Damon's voice, although smooth and melodious, made Morgan's teeth grind. He was, without a doubt, the best personal trainer she'd worked with yet, but sometimes she hated how hard he made her work. Especially after three days of binging on *CSI* and coffee ice cream.

Yes, she'd run daily and made use of the weights in her workout room, but Damon always took things to another level. Right now, he had her doing run-squat combinations down the pathway she kept clear on the left side of the garden for such fitness purposes. She'd agreed with Damon months ago that whenever she was home, he'd work with her every other day to make sure her overall fitness, not just her muscle tone, was at a high level. She was one of the few female golfers who took their fitness this seriously—most definitely did something, but she and a few others worked it as hard as the top male players like Rory McIlroy. Damon saw her as a unique challenge and loved their time together.

Of course he would. He gets to inflict all this pain on me. Sadist.

"Four more!" he shouted from his comfy position leaning against the wall of the house at the end of the path.

Grunting with the effort, she went into a squat position at the far end of the garden, then straightened and turned in as fluid a motion as she could manage before sprinting back toward him.

"Oh, my poor Miss Morgan!" Renata called from across the terrace. "What is he doing to you?"

"Working off that damn ice cream you left her in the freezer," Damon said with a wicked grin.

Renata threw up her hands in mock surrender. "I am only the paid help," she said in a mournful tone. "I do as I am told."

"Hah!" Morgan puffed out scornfully as she reached Damon. She went into the squat, then turned and sprinted away from him again. Renata's laugh followed her all the way down the path.

"What is this, some sort of conspiracy between the pair of you?" she panted, once she'd finished the other three reps and bent over, hands on her knees, next to them.

Renata chuckled, and Morgan grinned, loving how it felt to be so relaxed. Around people like Renata and Damon, in the comfort of her home—her sanctuary—she could completely be herself. Out on tour, she always felt the need to remain on her best behavior, if only to always present to the world as worthy of being Gordy Spencer's daughter.

The phone ringing on the outdoor table where she'd left it at the start of her workout brought her out of her reverie.

"Hi, Mom."

"Hello, darling. How are you?"

"I'm well. A little out of breath after Damon ran me into the ground, but yeah, okay."

Her mom's laughter was soft and understanding. "I don't know how you do it. Your father never did anything like this. I'm not sure he even stretched when he got out of bed in the morning."

Morgan snorted. "Yeah, it's a different world now."

"Indeed. Anyway, talking of your world and your father."

"Yes?" Something unpleasant churned in Morgan's stomach—she had a feeling she wasn't going to enjoy whatever was coming next.

"Well, it's all rather exciting. Your father has been approached by ESPN to be one of those expert commentators!"

"Oh! Wow, that's actually pretty cool." Okay, maybe this wasn't so bad after—

"Yes, and the first championship he'll be working on is your PGA next month!"

And there it was, the sucker punch.

Ouch.

The idea of her father, who'd never given her game or the women's game in general the time of day, being a so-called expert in front of the ESPN cameras had Morgan's stomach not only churning but clenching and twisting, like she was on the most hideous rollercoaster ride ever.

The good mood her workout and the banter with Renata and Damon had engendered flew out the metaphorical window.

"Morgan, are you still there? Did you hear what I said?"

She worked hard to pull herself together when anger threatened to spill over. "Uh, yeah, Mom, I heard. That's really great."

God, she hoped she sounded sincere. Her mom didn't need to be in the middle of Morgan's issues with her father. Well, no more than she had been for the last ten years anyway.

"I know. I'm *so* excited."

And what about how he feels, huh? Is he *that excited? I bet he isn't. Come to think of it, why the hell did he agree to do it, given how little he values the women's game?*

"So, um, Dad must be really pleased. First time he's been approached since that documentary a couple of years back."

Her mom cleared her throat. "Yes, well, obviously he's thrilled." She sighed. "Morgan, I have to be honest. This wasn't exactly his first choice of events to cover, but it appears they already have a full panel for the men's events right through to the end of the year, and, well, he thought this would at least—"

"Get him in the door, so to speak?"

Her mom paused. "Yes. He sees it as a stepping stone."

"And nothing else, I bet." She couldn't help the bitter words, despite her vow of only moments earlier to keep her mom out of this. Her mother stayed silent, and Morgan sighed audibly. "It's okay, Mom. I get it."

"It's...it's not okay," her mom whispered. "Not at all. I'm so—"

"Don't. Those aren't your words to say. I appreciate it, I really do, but just...don't."

"Okay, darling. I...I understand."

Morgan didn't know what else to say then. Both Renata and Damon had wandered away during her call, perhaps picking up enough of her side of the conversation to know this was a contentious one. Suddenly, she wanted nothing more than to be alone.

"Okay, gotta go, Mom. I'll call soon."

"Have a good flight to Phoenix tomorrow."

"Thanks."

She hung up before her throat could fully close and swallowed the lump that caused the discomfort. When she looked up, Damon was saying good-bye to Renata as they walked back to the house.

"Morgan, I'll catch you after Phoenix, okay?" he called.

Thankful for his intuition, she nodded and waved. Renata cast her a sympathetic look before heading back into the house with a downcast face.

Alone in the garden, Morgan stood with her hands on her hips and tried to breathe away the hurt and anger. She turned her face up to the sun, hoping its weak warmth would somehow overcome the coldness that had settled into her chest.

Chapter 5

"BOSS, YOU NEED TO GO. Now. Or you'll miss your flight." Jenny hovered in the doorway, her eyes wide with worry.

"I know, I know. Give me just…one…second." Adrienne clicked send on the e-mail, then shut down her laptop. She grabbed her jacket from the back of her chair while the laptop did its thing and crammed that into her bag once it had gone dark. "Okay, I'm ready."

She hurried toward the doorway, where Jenny now leaned against the frame, her face transformed from panicked assistant to kicked puppy. Adrienne chuckled.

"Get over it. You'll meet her on Monday, and then you can make those goofy eyes at your big crush."

Jenny snorted and tried to look affronted but crumpled under the pressure, instead collapsing into laughter. "Sorry, it's pathetic, isn't it?"

Adrienne patted her arm and walked past her. "Yes, it is, but I won't hold it against you."

"Gee, thanks, boss!" Jenny called after her.

There was a spring in Adrienne's step as she exited their offices and walked over to the waiting cab. She needed this, this time out of New York. Everything here had stagnated for her in the last twelve months, and time away, even if it was somewhere like Phoenix, which had never been on her list of must-see places, would do her a world of good.

She'd made a deal with herself, admittedly at Trish's demanding prompting, that she would try to do as little work as possible on the flight, and so two hours in opened the March issue of *National Geographic*. She ignored the fact that she was three months behind and instead lost herself in features about cultures and places she'd never heard of and would probably never experience firsthand. That didn't detract from her enjoyment, however, and she allowed herself a small smile at the thought that she'd been an avid reader for over thirty years and through that had been all over the world from the comfort of a chair.

One day, she'd have a house big enough again to have her entire collection on display. She'd managed it in the house she'd bought with Paula, but now everything was boxed up again and in storage. Her mood threatened to dive at the thought, and she pushed it away while summoning the flight attendant and ordering herself a second glass of champagne. Because why the hell not?

After checking in to her hotel an hour or so after she'd landed in Phoenix, Adrienne spent some time on her laptop, figuring out where she was headed the next day. The first meeting between her and Morgan Spencer was slated for eleven on Monday morning, after the tournament finished, but Adrienne had deliberately arrived in the city in time for the first round on Thursday, which started in a little over twelve hours. She was determined to watch Morgan over the few days of the event without her knowing who Adrienne was so that she could get a feel for what kind of person Morgan was when she was out there competing. And to see if she could garner any clues as to why Morgan could regularly win on the tour except at the majors.

Adrienne considered herself a pretty good reader of people—it was partly what had made her the success she was. Something told her she'd need to be at her best to get Morgan's story, her *real* story, over the coming months.

The applause was muted as Morgan's tee shot sailed down the center of the fairway, but Morgan wasn't surprised. The first two days of the women's tournaments rarely attracted large crowds, and in some ways, Morgan preferred that. It was nice to have that quiet hum of people in the background without the over-exuberant cheering and shouting that tended to come to the fore on the last day.

As she handed Harry the driver for stowing away in the bag, her gaze caught on a striking woman standing at the edge of the press area behind the first tee. The woman stood maybe a couple of inches shorter than Morgan, with short reddish-brown hair, light-brown skin, an oval face, and a full mouth. She wore press credentials on a lanyard, but Morgan was convinced she'd never seen her at any of the press calls before—surely she'd remember someone so beautiful.

She blinked as that thought filtered through her brain. *Okay, way to lose your focus on the game, Morgan.* She shook her head, then turned away from the woman's intense brown eyes only to be caught by Harry's inquiring gaze.

"Something wrong?" he asked impatiently.

With a start Morgan realized her playing partner, Lotte Karlsson, and her caddy were already some fifty yards ahead of them on the walk down the fairway.

Shit.

"No, all good," she bluffed, striding after the Swedes.

Harry's tut was loud.

The round went well, both she and Lotte hitting all the sweet spots and coming in at the end with both of them in a three-way tie for the lead with So Park on three under for the day.

"Good start," Harry said as they headed into the referee's office to hand in Morgan's card. "You just need a little more spin on all your irons, but otherwise, don't change anything."

"Got it." She smiled as she handed over her card and had it validated.

They left the office and found the path that led around to the area set aside for the press.

"You meeting Charlie tonight?" Harry asked.

"No, I'm having a quiet one. I'll eat in my room and see you in the morning, okay?"

He tilted his head. "You okay?"

"I am. A little tired. And I need to just get this done so I can relax."

Morgan gestured toward the waiting press, and her attention was snagged once again by the beautiful woman she'd seen at the start of the day. She stood at the back of the group of reporters, her gaze scanning the approaching players.

"Harry, who's that?" Morgan nodded in the woman's direction.

Harry narrowed his eyes. "No idea. Why?"

She tried not to blush. "No reason. Just never seen her before and was curious."

"Right." His tone let her know he'd seen right through her.

Clearing her throat, she patted him on the arm. "I'll see you tomorrow."

He smirked and wandered away.

Lotte appeared alongside Morgan as she strolled up to the waiting press. "Hey, Morgan, it was good playing with you today. We haven't been paired in a while, and I'd forgotten how much you make me work to keep pace with you."

Morgan chuckled, but the praise gave her a warm glow. "That's sweet of you. It's an honor to play alongside you—you're a legend of our game."

"Are you calling me old?" Lotte's grin told Morgan she was teasing.

"No, never." Morgan placed a hand on her heart and smiled sweetly.

Lotte laughed and patted her shoulder. "Looking forward to tomorrow."

"Me too!"

They reached the press area and separated, Lotte to talk to Cindy Thomson, Morgan to face the print news reporters with their handheld recording devices. Out of the corner of her eye, as she answered the banal and repetitive questions pushed her way, she saw the beautiful woman watching her again. For some reason, even though she wore press credentials, she never stepped forward to ask any of the players questions. *Who is she? What is she doing here?*

And why can't I stop looking at her?

Embarrassed that her gaze *did* keep drifting, Morgan made a concerted effort to focus on the reporters. She also tried to smile a little more and inject more warmth into her answers. A few raised eyebrows told her the effort wasn't going unnoticed, and the thanks she received from them seemed genuine, for once. It felt strangely nice.

The next two days passed in pretty much the same way. She played well, kept to herself in the evenings, and woke up on Sunday feeling good about her prospects. She was one shot ahead of So Park, two ahead of Laurie Schweitzer. Lotte had fallen behind during the third round, so for the final round, she'd be playing with Schweitzer, while Morgan and So were the last pair to tee off.

Not only was the win up for grabs, but Morgan, if she won, would move up to number three in the world, behind Kim Lee in first and Laurie in second. It would be Morgan's highest ever ranking, and she wanted it. Badly.

"Well," Harry said, as he met her in the staging area. "I don't need to give you any kind of pep talk this morning, do I? I could see the fire in your eyes from twenty yards away." He grinned. "Good."

She smiled back at him. "Yeah, it's feeling good this morning. Let's do it."

They fist-bumped, and she went through her exercises to loosen up while Harry double-checked the bag. When it came time to tee off, Morgan was as focused as she could be. Her drive off the first was perfect, and the whoops of the crowd only lifted her mood.

Game on.

So that's what she looks like when she finally gets in her zone.

Adrienne saw it from a mile off. Morgan Spencer appeared two inches taller, her shoulders looked as if they were made of iron, and she practically glowed with confidence and the hunger to do well. It was rather stirring to see.

Following Morgan these past few days had been an interesting experience. While Morgan was clearly focused on her game and hardly spent any time interacting with anyone, either other golfers, the press, or the crowd, there was something about her that didn't quite add up. Sometimes she looked sad; perhaps haunted would be the better word. It was fleeting, and Adrienne was never sure she'd totally read it correctly, but it had stayed with her each time she'd caught the briefest glances of it.

She'd hadn't seen Morgan in any of the club's restaurants or bars in the evening, and a couple of quiet inquiries had told her this was fairly normal. Morgan Spencer liked to keep to herself. For someone with her background, her looks—which, Adrienne could admit now she'd seen her close up, were very attractive—and her success, she came across as either shy, socially inept, or reluctant.

Adrienne had scribbled copious notes in her production notebook, starting to formulate how their first sit-down interview might go on Monday. Something told her Morgan would be a hard nut to crack, and she'd have to be careful what questions she asked this first time around and how.

Zipping up her light jacket in the face of the cooler than expected breeze that blew across the course this afternoon, she walked with the crowd that followed Morgan and So Park on their final round.

Morgan's caddy, Harry Carr, seemed to be the only person Morgan relaxed around. Adrienne often saw them chuckling with each other as they discussed which club to use, and each of those interactions transformed Morgan. The lightness in her face as she looked at Harry was remarkable. There was clearly a level of affection between them that no one else, as far as Adrienne could determine, got to experience from Morgan.

Are they involved?

She snorted at the thought. No, it wasn't that kind of affection. Harry seemed more like a father figure to Morgan. Interesting. Besides, she'd heard on the grapevine that Morgan Spencer was into women—there were rumors of something between her and Naomi Chase, who was currently missing from the tour as she recovered from a shoulder injury.

Adrienne smiled as she walked the course, watching Morgan extend her lead to three shots by the fifteenth. She mentally rubbed her hands together at the thought of interviewing Morgan in the morning. It would be a challenge, but she couldn't wait.

"Toby, I think here will be best for you. I like that portrait as a backdrop." Adrienne pointed to the wall ahead of her, and the cameraman murmured his assent.

"Yeah, the lighting's cool here. Not too much glare from that window but enough natural light for me not to need the full spot."

He stepped away, looking at angles, and she left him to it. She'd worked with Toby many times before for this type of piece and trusted him to get it right without her interfering.

Diane, the sound woman, was busy setting up her equipment. They were using a boom rather than lapel mikes. Adrienne always hated how those little things drew the eye when attached to someone, and she wanted her audience only focused on Morgan's face and words.

Jenny buzzed into the room long enough to say that the local makeup assistant they'd hired was waiting in the lobby and she was off to retrieve her. She hopped from foot to foot, her eyes wide, a huge grin on her face.

Adrienne rolled her eyes and made a mental note to have a quick word with her overexcited assistant. Sure, it was cute how pumped Jenny was to be finally meeting her biggest sporting crush, but she still needed to maintain her professionalism.

"Is she always so…wired?" Diane asked, her southern drawl stretching out the last word.

Toby guffawed. "Hell yeah. She's like the Energizer bunny. You kinda get used to it, though."

"You do." Adrienne smiled at Diane, who shook her head and turned back to her equipment. "Right, I'm going off to meet Ms. Spencer for a coffee." Adrienne pulled her papers together and pushed them into her bag. "Should be back in about half an hour ready to start, okay?"

"Sure," Toby and Diane said in tandem. Neither bothered to raise their heads from their tasks, and Adrienne smiled. She did like working with pros she could trust.

She stopped at a bathroom en route to her first meeting with Morgan, taking a few minutes to make sure she looked professional but not too formal. Morgan had been told to wear whatever she felt most comfortable in, and Adrienne didn't want her subject feeling underdressed if she chose to come in super casual, so she herself had opted for a long denim skirt over knee-length brown boots and a simple cream cotton sweater that hung loosely on her shoulders.

Once satisfied she looked as good as she was going to get, Adrienne exited the bathroom and made her way to the club's small private dining room. A man dressed in a sharply-cut suit waited inside when she pushed open the door. There was no sign of Morgan, but a quick glance at her watch told Adrienne it was still ten minutes before their agreed meeting time.

"Adrienne?" The man stood, holding out his hand. "I'm Hilton Stewart."

She shook it firmly and smiled. "It's great to meet you in person, Hilton. Thanks for helping to set this up."

"My pleasure." He motioned to the club chair beside his, and Adrienne dropped gracefully into it. "Coffee?"

"Yes, please."

Hilton reached for the pot sitting on the table beside his chair and poured her a cup, adding a little cream when she nodded at his raised eyebrow. He was a handsome man, with a strong jaw, an easy smile, and a shaved head, his brown scalp shining in the light of the chandelier that dominated the ceiling above them. His suit was obviously expensive, and a glance at his shoes told her the man knew how to dress to impress. Given how much he must be earning off representing the likes of Morgan Spencer, she wasn't surprised.

"Morgan will be here shortly," he said as he passed her the cup of coffee.

There was something in the way he said it that gave Adrienne pause. "Everything okay?"

Morgan had easily won yesterday's tournament and was up to number three in the world as a result, so Hilton should have been looking much happier than he was right now.

He sighed. "Morgan is… She's a quiet, private person. Doing something like this is not high on her wish list."

"Ah." *Damn.* Did that mean she was going to be more difficult than Adrienne had imagined? "Is there anything in particular I can do to make this easier for her?"

"Other than not doing it?" Hilton smiled ruefully. "Probably not. Simply understand that about her and carry it with you over the next few weeks."

Adrienne nodded. "I can do that. I would have thought, though, that she was used to all this, given who her father is?"

Hilton made a so-so motion with his hand. "Yes, she's been in the public eye for most of her life, especially since she started to show such an interest in playing golf. But…well, let's just say it's sometimes not easy for a child to follow in their famous father's footsteps."

There was something more to that, she could tell, but before she could press him, the door swung open and Morgan Spencer walked in. Adrienne caught the startled look Morgan gave her before the younger woman swiftly covered it with a lukewarm smile.

"Morgan!" Hilton stood and walked over to usher his client into the room. "Come and meet Adrienne Wyatt."

Adrienne also stood and took two steps forward as Morgan approached. She held out her hand and smiled widely, wondering why her heart raced as the tall, beautiful woman neared. When Morgan's hand gripped hers, she noted the coolness, the strength, and had the distinct impression that Morgan held back just how firm her grip could be.

"It's a pleasure to meet you," Adrienne said. "Well done for yesterday's win and the step up in the rankings."

"Thank you." Morgan's voice was soft, and again Adrienne had the impression something was being held back. "It's a pleasure to meet you too."

She lies well. Adrienne tried hard not to stare at the young woman, even though the flecks of gold in Morgan's light-brown eyes surprised her with the way they shimmered in the room's lights. Her eyelashes were most distracting; long and lush, they framed the beautiful eyes that now beheld Adrienne with something akin to puzzlement.

Adrienne realized she still had a hold of Morgan's hand and quickly let go. She motioned to the chairs behind her. "Shall we sit?" she asked, thankful her voice didn't croak.

Morgan nodded, then stepped past her and sat in the chair that Hilton had previously occupied.

While Hilton fussed with pouring Morgan a coffee, Adrienne surreptitiously observed her. She sat rigidly in her chair, her shoulders straight, her hands clasped together in her lap. With one leg crossed over the other, an expanse of tanned calf was revealed by the knee-length black pants she wore. Somewhere in Adrienne's brain it registered that Morgan was *very* fit—the muscle tone on display was impressive, to say the least. Morgan had chosen a plain, thin purple hoodie to wear over the pants, and Converse sneakers with matching purple laces. While her clothes looked comfortable, her posture screamed anything but.

Hilton sat in another chair, and Adrienne snapped out of her perusal of Morgan.

"Thanks for agreeing to do this today, Morgan," she said. "I know you have a plane to catch later, so this interview won't be a long one."

Morgan nodded again but said nothing.

"Do you have a set list of questions?" Hilton asked.

"I have some, yes," Adrienne said, not taking her eyes off Morgan, "but I always leave room for the conversation to take its own course."

Morgan frowned. "What if I don't want to answer a question, set or otherwise?" Her tone was almost prickly, and Adrienne held back the urge to roll her eyes.

"Then just say so, and we'll edit that part out."

"What if I don't want to answer *any* of your questions?"

"Morgan," Hilton said quietly.

Morgan sighed before facing him. "I know." She turned back to Adrienne. Her fingers twisted together in her lap. "I'm sorry, Ms. Wyatt. I don't mean to appear rude. I'm just really not a fan of opening up like this, and not knowing what you're going to ask me is…unsettling."

"It's Adrienne." She smiled, hoping to elicit even a small one in return from Morgan, but nothing was forthcoming. Okay, this was not the best start. *Tread lightly.* "I was obviously going to show you the set questions first for us to have a read through and think about how you'd like to answer them. Do you want to do that now?" She kept her tone light and gentle; it was as if she were talking to a spooked horse.

"Okay."

Morgan was the epitome of tension; her posture had not relaxed at all since she'd first entered the room.

Adrienne risked a quick glance at Hilton as she reached down to her bag to retrieve her notebook. His frown was deep as he tried to catch Morgan's eye.

Adrienne pulled the notebook from her bag and flicked through to the page where she'd written down her initial questions. Normally, she'd take the subject through the questions, and together they'd work out any kinks in her approach, but something told her that wouldn't work today. She hesitated only a moment before she ripped the page out and passed it to Morgan.

"Why don't you both take a look through this? I'll be back in a few minutes."

Morgan took the paper, her wide eyes staring at Adrienne as she did so. There was surprise in her gaze and something that looked very much like gratitude.

Adrienne gave her a subtle nod, then left the room.

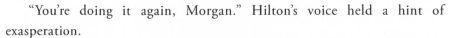

"You're doing it again, Morgan." Hilton's voice held a hint of exasperation.

Her petulant side wanted to say something childish, but she bit it back and instead let out an extended sigh. "I know. I'm sorry."

She stood and walked over to the window that looked out over the eighteenth green. It looked so plain now that it was empty of crowds, players, and officials. Less than twenty-four hours ago, she'd stood out there, surrounded by people, and accepted the small trophy and the large check. She'd felt just as alone then as she did now.

"I thought you were fine to go ahead with this."

"I was. Am."

She shook her head. It had to be *her*, didn't it? The gorgeous woman who'd caught Morgan's eye on day one of the tournament was, of course, the woman she would now spend weeks with by her side for this in-depth profile. Up close, Adrienne Wyatt was stunning, although older than Morgan had realized. Not that age mattered, of course. But Adrienne's beauty and poise flustered Morgan; it wasn't just the questions she would ask that had her all hot under the collar.

Jesus, get a grip. So she's a beautiful woman. So what? She's here to do a job, so why not let her get on with it, and the sooner she does, the sooner it will be over.

Grateful to Adrienne for giving her this time alone with Hilton, Morgan squared her shoulders and turned back to her manager. "Okay, sorry. I'm here now. Let's look at those questions."

He tilted his head. "Anything we need to talk about?"

She strode back across the room to her chair. "Nope. We're good." She picked up the sheet of paper, pulled her chair closer to his, and they bent their heads over the questions.

The first few were fine, relatively innocuous and standard questions about how Morgan felt the year was going so far, her highlights, and what a regular week looked like for her when she wasn't on the road. Unfortunately, that one segued into asking about how much time she had with her family now that she was so ensconced in the LPGA tour.

She could only imagine where that might lead with follow-up questions.

"How much of this project is supposed to be about me the person versus me the golfer?" she asked quietly.

Hilton stared at her. "I would assume mostly the latter, but I'm not sure you can explore that fully without some of the former."

"Yeah."

"What are you not telling me?"

She bit her lip but stayed silent.

"Morgan, if you're worried about the whole gay thing, don't be."

Morgan laughed. "No, it's not that. It's not exactly a secret, is it?"

"True, although you've never actually come out in an interview. That might change by the end of this project."

"I guess." She shrugged. "But I'm okay with that."

"So what is it?"

She'd never told Hilton much about her father. He, like everyone else in the golfing world, automatically assumed that her father must be over the moon to have such a successful golfer in the family. Any time her father had been asked an opinion by the press, he'd said all the right things, and everyone had taken it as gospel.

"There are...some family things that I'd prefer not to talk about. I'm concerned they'll come up in Adrienne's questioning. Either today or over the next few weeks."

Hilton frowned. "Do I need to know what these family things are? Maybe I could help steer her away?"

Morgan huffed out a breath. "No. I guess I can just handle that myself."

If he was hurt by her exclusion, he didn't show it. "Well, all right then. But if you need my help with anything, you just let me know."

"I will." She reached out and quickly clasped his forearm. "Thanks. I promise I'll try to do this right. I know I've been pretty immature about it so far, but I'll shape up."

"I know you will." He smiled. "You've never let anything best you yet, so I can't see a little thing like an interview getting in your way."

She hoped like hell his confidence wasn't misplaced.

Chapter 6

"AND HOME IS SAN FRANCISCO, correct?" Adrienne asked, smiling encouragingly.

Morgan had done well so far. When Adrienne had returned to the dining room, she'd been pleasantly surprised—and relieved—by the transformation in Morgan's demeanor. She still came across as shy, although Adrienne wasn't sure that was the word she was looking for. But she also seemed to have crossed a mental hurdle and was quick to apologize for her earlier shortness.

They'd got started soon after that. Hilton had left, then Jenny had been introduced to Morgan. To Adrienne's delight, Jenny had greeted the golfing superstar with the utmost decorum and civility. Although Jenny had met some celebrities before, she'd never met someone she so openly admired—and crushed on. Adrienne hadn't known what to expect, and her relief was coupled with the realization that she had done her assistant a disservice by assuming the worst.

Morgan was patient with the makeup artist and Toby and Diane as they set her up in the perfect position for both light and sound. And she had answered Adrienne's first few questions with more ease than she'd dared hope for.

"Yes, it is. I visited the city when I was a kid and fell in love with the cable cars and hills and, of course, the Golden Gate Bridge. It was always a dream of mine to live there one day, and I'm lucky enough to do that now."

"So how much time do you get to spend there?"

"Not as much as I'd like!" Morgan smiled ruefully for the camera, and it was endearing. "The tour is long. We don't have to play every tournament, so we can pick which weeks to take a break, but obviously the more you play, the more ranking points you can hopefully earn, so..." She shrugged and grinned.

"And what do you do on your breaks?"

Morgan laughed, and it was the most natural Adrienne had seen her yet. It was amazing the difference it made to her usual serious face. "I spend time with my personal trainer, who helps me work off the ice cream I eat too much of when I'm home."

Adrienne chuckled. "Ice cream?"

"Yeah, it's my Kryptonite!"

"What flavor? Or will anything do?"

Morgan gave a look of mock horror. "Oh no, it *has* to be coffee."

Adrienne glanced down at her notes. "Presumably you also like to catch up with your family when you've got free time." There was the briefest of drops in Morgan's expression that almost threw Adrienne off her spiel. *What just happened?* "As most viewers will know, your dad is Gordy Spencer, six-time major win on the men's tour, and your brother, Jack, is a pro tennis player, ranked 108 as we speak. That's a pretty successful family!"

Morgan nodded slowly, but her eyes had lost some of their sparkle. "It certainly is."

Okay, so that was not the answer she'd expected. She almost floundered. "Must make for some interesting conversations over the dinner table, comparing wins and achievements?"

Morgan shifted in her chair, glanced away from Adrienne to look directly at the camera, then back again. "I'm sorry, I'm... What was the question?"

"Do you need a short break?"

Morgan shook her head. "No, it's not that. It's... You can edit this, right?"

Adrienne nodded.

"Okay, then ask me again, and we'll carry on."

Wondering just what the hell she'd stumbled into, Adrienne asked her question again.

"Yeah, obviously all three of us have been very successful in our careers," Morgan said, but it sounded flat. "My mom always jokes about how she

63

feels left out, but she does some incredible charity work that deserves just as much publicity, in my opinion."

Hm, interesting deflection. Deciding to run with it for now but determined to revisit this clearly touchy subject, Adrienne asked Morgan to give the viewers a little more detail about what her mom did. She'd probably cut this section later, but it seemed important to get Morgan back on track.

"So, as we speak, you've just had back-to-back wins and climbed up to third in the world, your highest ever rank."

Morgan grinned.

"Is that going to give you more confidence heading into the Women's PGA in Williamsburg? Perhaps help you finally notch that first major?"

"I hope so. Winning always boosts your confidence, whether you're number three in the world or number thirty. But yeah, back-to-back wins does make me feel I'm doing everything right to put myself in the strongest position for a good run at the PGA."

"Can you win it?"

"Yes, I can."

"Will you?"

Morgan chuckled. "I'll certainly do my best."

"Okay, let's leave it there," Adrienne said after a quick pause to give the editors a gap to work with. She knew they hated it when interviewers or commentators talked over natural cut-off points. Later their narrator would record a voiceover that provided a link between that segment and the next, and it would all appear seamless.

"Was it okay?" Morgan asked nervously.

"You were amazing!" Jenny stepped forward from the corner where she'd watched the interview. "Really good."

"It was fine, Morgan," Adrienne said. "Don't worry."

Morgan nodded and stood. "Well, okay. I'll see you in Chicago."

She walked quickly across the room, but Adrienne, instinct kicking in, called after her. "Hey, Morgan, I was wondering. Do you have time for lunch before you leave?"

Morgan's eyes were wide as she turned back. "Lunch?"

"Oh, yeah, lunch is a great idea! I'm starving," Jenny said, and Adrienne wanted to groan. She should have known Jenny would invite herself along.

Morgan looked between them. "Sure," she said, although she sounded as if she'd rather do anything else on earth.

Morgan was having a surprisingly good time. Jenny was fun company, and Adrienne, although quieter, had a dry humor that delighted Morgan. Discovering earlier that Adrienne was the attractive woman she'd spotted hanging around in the press area all week of the tournament had clicked all the pieces into place—why she followed Morgan on the course, and why she hung back at the press conferences afterward, not asking any questions but simply observing. Strangely, it didn't make Morgan feel uncomfortable; she understood why Adrienne would have kept her distance and respected her for not attempting to talk to her earlier than the planned interview.

They ate at a Mexican restaurant in the city just a couple of blocks from Morgan's hotel. Adrienne's thoughtfulness on that arrangement had also touched Morgan and only added to the positive impression she was gaining of this woman. She never thought she'd feel so comfortable so quickly around someone who was essentially here to poke into her life. So far, Adrienne had been courteous, respectful, and careful. *Long may that continue.*

Although she'd feared their conversation would be awkward and stumbling, after the first few minutes, they'd all relaxed around each other. Morgan realized with a shock that this was the first social time she'd spent with anyone not directly related to her golfing life in quite some time and was pleased she could remember how to act in such situations.

"So," she said, as she scooped up the last of her chicken fajita and used it to mop up the remaining sauce on her plate. "Do either of you play golf? You both seem to know a lot about it."

She popped the morsel into her mouth and chewed while she waited for their responses. They both did seem very knowledgeable about her sport, and it had been yet another surprise.

Jenny snorted. "I'd love to be able to tell you that I'm a keen player with a handicap of whatever, but I'd be lying."

Adrienne smiled. "You have to tell her the whole story."

Jenny rolled her eyes and laughed.

"Oh, you do now." Morgan grinned at Jenny.

Jenny flushed, then cleared her throat. "Well, my dad is a big golf fan, and he plays a pretty good game. I grew up with golf on the TV and in conversation all through the weekends. I begged my dad to let me try it. He waited until I was old enough, in his eyes, to properly hold a club, and he finally took me out to his local course when I was thirteen." She took a sip of her water and carried on, her words warmed by her smile. "So we head out to the driving range. He hands me a four iron and gets me in position and talks through the swing, et cetera. He steps back a little and tells me to take a practice swing, nice and slow. Well," she said, chuckling, "I'm feeling all full of myself at this point and determined to show him I can handle this."

"Uh-oh," Morgan said, engrossed in the story and in the amusement dancing in Jenny's eyes. Next to her, Adrienne laughed softly, and she caught her gaze, amazed once again at what an incredible color Adrienne's eyes were, a deep brown that was almost the color of scorched earth. They smiled at each other.

"Yeah, exactly! I try to give it a full swing but somehow lose my grip completely. The club shoots *backwards* out of my hands and slams into my dad's shins!"

"Oh. My. God." Morgan laughed, shaking her head. "How bad was he hurt?"

Jenny looked shamefaced. "He's still got a scar on his left leg from the stitches he needed. Only three," she said, when Morgan raised her eyebrows, "but needless to say, I was never allowed to play golf with him again."

"Oh, dear."

Jenny sipped the last of her water. "I did try again later in college—my boyfriend at the time thought it would be a fun day out. We argued the whole way around the course because I wouldn't take it seriously enough for him. I think I realized then I'm definitely an armchair fan."

"Nothing wrong with that." Morgan turned to Adrienne. "And you, do you play?"

"No. Never lifted a club. I'm not so fanatical about it as Jenny is, but I like to watch it on TV sometimes. I really enjoy the Solheim, actually. I like the team camaraderie."

Morgan nodded. She'd not made the team last year, but she had high hopes for next time around, especially on her current form.

As if reading her thoughts, Adrienne asked, "Would you want to play in it?"

Smiling, Morgan nodded vigorously, and the two women watching her laughed. "Yeah, that's definitely a dream."

"God, imagine how proud your dad would be after he played in four Ryder Cups and won it twice!" Jenny said, her eyes wide.

Morgan's stomach sank. "Oh, yeah, sure."

Adrienne caught her eye. There was a question in her expression, and Morgan braced herself, but it never came. Instead, to her surprise, Adrienne looked quickly at her watch.

"Jenny, we need to let Morgan go. She's got some things to do before she heads out to the airport."

"Oh, God, sorry!" Jenny pushed back her chair. "I've just rambled on. It's just been so cool to talk to you." She blushed. "You're one of my favorite players, so this has been a real honor."

"You're welcome." Morgan smiled, then looked at Adrienne. That question was still there in her eyes. Why hadn't she asked? *And why did she offer me an escape?*

"So we will catch up with you in Chicago, okay?" Adrienne said, her voice smooth and giving nothing away.

"Yes, of course. Hilton said you wanted to film some of my practice time?"

"That would be ideal, yes. Let us know which day works best for you. Here, this is my number." Adrienne pulled a card from her purse and pushed it across the table.

"Great, I'll do that."

They parted company outside the restaurant. Jenny shook her hand with enthusiasm and repeated what a pleasure it had been to meet her. There was something else there too, in her eyes and her smile, something that took a few moments to register because it had been so long since Morgan had looked for it. Well, perhaps that was something she could think more about—Jenny was cute, fun, and so very different from Naomi.

Adrienne's hand in hers was warm, her handshake firm but not as vigorous as Jenny's. She smiled at Morgan. *God, she really is beautiful.* The thought hit Morgan out of the blue. Yes, she'd registered Adrienne's beauty earlier that day and even before that, but up close with their hands still clasped together, there was a presence about Adrienne that only added to her physical beauty. It left Morgan feeling a little shy and breathless.

"Looking forward to working more with you," Adrienne said, and her voice was like velvet, sending a shiver through Morgan's chest.

Jesus, what is wrong with you? Calm down.

"Likewise. And again, I'm sorry about not being that friendly earlier. I'm—"

Adrienne held up her hand. "No need to apologize or explain. It can't be easy letting a complete stranger into your life like this. I very much appreciate that you are."

Morgan couldn't think of a response to such heartfelt words, so she merely nodded and smiled and finally let go of Adrienne's hand. She missed the feel of it immediately. Flustered, she stepped back, lifted a hand in a goofy wave, and turned away before her blush revealed itself.

"She's amazing!" Jenny said in the cab back to their hotel. "Wow."

Adrienne smiled but wondered why her stomach sank a little at Jenny's words. She hadn't missed that moment between Jenny and Morgan—Jenny's attraction for the golfer was plainly written on her face, and it seemed Morgan had responded ever so slightly. Why did that disappoint her?

She moved on from that uncomfortable thought to the other one that had lurked in the back of her mind since Jenny had made the comment about Morgan's father. It had been slight, but Adrienne hadn't missed it: Morgan had flinched. That was the second time today a comment or question about her family had caused Morgan discomfort. *What am I missing?* Every time the Spencer family had featured on the news or in the papers, they gave the impression of being a regular, albeit very public and successful, all-American family. *Is there something behind all that which means it isn't that rosy? Interesting.*

"So the hotel in San Antonio finally confirmed our reservations." Jenny switched subjects so quickly Adrienne blinked a couple of times to register. "I don't know what their problem was, but it's done. The only thing left to finalize is Laurie Schweitzer's interview. Her manager is, quite frankly, a bitch, and I may need you to step in on that one."

"What's her problem?"

Jenny sighed. "'I'm not sure I understand why Ms. Wyatt can't talk to me herself,'" she mimicked in a whiny tone. "I think she thinks I'm too far down the food chain, even though all she has to do is say yes or no to a short one-on-one interview for Schweitzer on Wednesday morning before the Pro-Am gets started."

Adrienne patted Jenny's arm. "Some battles just aren't worth fighting. I'll take this one when we get back to the hotel."

"Okay." Jenny's voice sounded small.

The cab pulled up in front of their hotel, and Adrienne paid him before joining Jenny in the lobby. She glanced at her watch and then at her despondent assistant. "Hey, tell you what. Let me deal with Schweitzer's manager now while you go and find us two comfy chairs in there." She pointed to the hotel's cozy-looking bar just beyond the lobby. "Order me a dry white wine, preferably something Californian, and whatever you want for yourself." Jenny's face lit up. "We're taking the afternoon off, okay?"

"Aw, you're the best, boss." Jenny grinned. "Thanks."

The call with Schweitzer's manager took all of two minutes. When Adrienne hung up, she scowled. *Egos, good God.*

Yes, Laurie Schweitzer was currently world number two, and yes, she'd been on the tour for twelve years, but really, the way her manager had acted, you'd have thought Adrienne was asking for an audience with the Pope. She could only hope the golfer wasn't as full of herself as her manager was.

Jenny had ordered Adrienne a deliciously crisp white wine, and she sipped from it enthusiastically after falling into her leather chair. Jenny grinned as she raised her glass.

"To the afternoon off!"

"Hear, hear."

They drank in silence for a few moments.

"So." Jenny put down her glass and sighed. "Schweitzer all lined up?"

Adrienne nodded. "Patience," she said when Jenny's brow creased into a frown. "Trust me, I will get your name out there, and it won't be long before that sort of thing won't happen to you. But for now, just remember, pick your battles. Don't waste your energy on people like that; you'll never change their minds."

"If you can't go through something, go around it."

69

"Exactly." Adrienne tipped her glass in Jenny's direction and laughed. "You *do* listen to me."

"Sometimes." Jenny smirked and reached for her drink, a lurid pink concoction with fruit chunks lining the edge of her glass.

"Dare I ask what's in there?"

Jenny laughed. "I don't think you really want to know."

"As long as I don't have to carry you up to your room."

Jenny waggled her eyebrows.

Adrienne rolled her eyes. Jenny, she had come to realize, flirted mildly with pretty much anyone, but it was always in this gentle, teasing manner. Except when she was seriously attracted to someone. Then, inexplicably, she'd become tongue-tied and blush with alarming regularity. *Hm, rather like her behavior with Morgan at lunch.*

"I bet Morgan could carry me up to my room," Jenny said, her tone wistful. She stirred idly at her drink with its ridiculously bright cocktail umbrella.

Adrienne's memory served her up an image of Morgan's arms, that muscle definition that she'd tried so hard not to look at these past few days. Yes, Jenny was probably correct. Those arms would feel wonderful wrapped around her, holding her tight as she carried Adrienne up to her room, kicking down the door and laying her gently on the bed...

In a flush of heat, she chided herself—*the woman is seventeen, no, wait, nearly eighteen years younger than you.* Thinking about her like that was... wrong. But was it? Paula's new young paramour was twenty years younger, and everyone seemed to be applauding her for landing such a youthful catch. Adrienne seemed to be the only one in their circle who found it distasteful. Of course, everyone else just assumed she was jealous. Which she was, but it wasn't only that. What was that word for women who had much younger lovers? Tiger? No, *cougar*, that was it. She shuddered. Ugh, imagine walking around with that label hanging over your head.

No, her admiration of Morgan's physical attributes was just that— admiration. Anything else was too ridiculous to dwell on.

She sipped her wine and tried very hard to push thoughts of Morgan's arms out of her mind.

Chapter 7

LAURIE SCHWEITZER WAS NOT A nice person. Adrienne used patience she didn't know she possessed to keep herself from rolling her eyes every few minutes at the words spouting from the golfer's mouth. She'd worked with some egos in her time, both in front of and behind the camera, but Laurie was one of the worst. Sure, Adrienne could acknowledge she was an incredible player who'd been at the top of the women's game for years, but that didn't mean she had to be an asshole about it. Laurie was very good at making snide little remarks about former and current players behind statements that seemed innocuous on the surface, but Adrienne had seen through each and every one of them. *I'm going to have to cut a lot of this.*

Adrienne sucked in a deep breath. "Sorry, I'm going to have to interrupt you there, as we're running low on time." She sweetened her words with a big smile.

Laurie shifted in her chair, and a nerve above her left eye twitched. "What would you like to finish up with?" she asked in a tight voice.

"Well, as you know," Adrienne said, ignoring the faint scowl on Laurie's face, "the main focus of the film is the majors. You've won two yourself, and I'm wondering what you would say to all the up-and-coming golfers who've yet to win one. What do they need to have to reach that pinnacle?"

Laurie's smile was almost feral. "Well, a major certainly isn't going to be handed to you on a silver platter."

Adrienne's stomach flopped—that comment could only be a dig at Morgan Spencer or at least at the public's obsession with Morgan not yet achieving what her father had, thinking it should be a given. She'd heard a rumor that some top players were fed up with that angle being beaten to death in the press. Clearly, Laurie was one of them.

"Focus," Laurie said. "Your focus needs to be 100 percent at a major. You're up against the very best, and any slip in concentration will cost you, as some have already learned." Her smile widened but if anything became colder. "Only the best of the best win the majors on our tour. Some great golfers never have and never will. Great isn't good enough. You have to be exceptional."

Adrienne motioned to Toby to cut.

"Thank you for your time, Laurie," Adrienne said.

"My pleasure." Laurie stood and stretched. She was about Adrienne's height but with a slightly stockier build. "Are you staying around for the whole tournament?"

Toby and Diane packed up their equipment, and a member of the hotel staff appeared to clear away their coffee cups.

"No, we leave tomorrow afternoon."

"Want to maybe get a drink later tonight, grab a bite to eat? I have a suite."

Adrienne looked up quickly, trying to keep her shock from reflecting in her expression. "Um, that's kind of you, but I have plans."

Laurie didn't even look perturbed. She leaned in and whispered, "Well, if you change your mind, just have the lobby staff call up to my room."

With one last lingering look at Adrienne, she turned and left the room.

Adrienne glanced around, but neither Toby nor Diane gave any sign of having heard that last exchange. Relief flooded through her. It was bad enough that...*snake* of a woman had propositioned her. *Ugh.* She felt unclean after forty minutes in Laurie Schweitzer's presence.

"Toby, you okay to finish packing this up? I'm going to head back to my room."

"Sure thing, Adrienne."

"Great, thanks. I'll see you later for that taco I promised you."

He grinned. "You bet."

When she reached her room, she dumped her bag and notes on the bed and ran the shower. Ten minutes under its heat and she felt somewhat restored. She was still reeling from Laurie's approach. *Did I give her any hint I was interested? I've been out of the game for so long, I probably wouldn't know it if I did.* She counted it back. A year single and not looking since Paula left, plus ten years with Paula and a couple of years before that of happily doing the single thing. *So, yes, thirteen years since I was last out there looking. God, I feel even older now.*

Her phone rang just as she finished dressing. "Hey, Jenny. What's up?"

"San Antonio is kicking my ass."

"You probably deserved it."

"Ha ha. Seriously, Adrienne, this heat! I'm wilting by the second."

"Oh, my poor sweet child. Did you get the shots I wanted?"

"Jeez, your sympathy sounds *so* sincere." Jenny snorted. "Yes, boss, I got your shots. Can I come home now? I really need a shower and a beer."

Adrienne smiled. "Sure, come on back. I just wrapped up with Schweitzer."

"Ooooh, how'd it go?"

"It was…interesting. Buy me a glass of wine, and I'll spill everything."

"You are *on*! See you soon."

"She did not!" Jenny's mouth dropped open.

Adrienne smiled ruefully. "I'm afraid she did." She shuddered. "And I'm only telling you this so that you're aware this kind of thing happens. It's not the first time an interview has ended that way for me."

"Really?" Jenny leaned in. "Have you ever accepted an offer like that?"

"I don't kiss and tell." Adrienne smirked when Jenny huffed. "But seriously, be aware. It's one reason why you should always make sure you are never alone in the room with the subject. Unfortunately, these days, far too many people think these situations are easy pickings."

"What if…?" Jenny picked at the label on her beer bottle.

"What if what?"

It was obvious what she wanted to ask, but Adrienne wanted her to say it out loud.

Jenny sighed. "What if you want to do the asking? Or what if it's someone who you'd happily go out with?"

"One, never, ever do the asking. No matter how much you like them. If it got back to the company, you'd be fired. It's unprofessional. Two, if they ask you, make an arrangement with them for once the project is complete.

If they don't want to do that, then you know they're only really into you for that night and nothing else. Absolutely not worth it."

Jenny tilted her head. "Voice of experience?"

Adrienne sighed. "My first and only such mistake many years ago. Luckily for me it was the last day of the project, so when a whisper got back to my boss, she gave me a warning but let me keep my job."

Jenny chugged the remainder of her beer. "Okay, advice noted."

She looked a little shaken, but Adrienne was pleased. It was a harsh world they operated in, and Jenny was still too green to know all the pitfalls that could await her.

Jenny sat up straighter. "So Chicago next!"

"Yes. I'm looking forward to it. We've got the pre-tournament filming with Spencer and with So Park, and it'll be interesting to see how each of them takes to that."

"Yeah. And, of course, Naomi Chase returns."

"Indeed."

"You heard the buzz? That she and Morgan were dating but not anymore?"

"I did hear that, yes. I don't think it's a secret that either of them is gay, but they did seem to want to keep that one quiet."

"*I* heard it all crashed and burned after the Miami Open last year. That Morgan found Naomi cheating on her with someone at the hotel they were staying in."

God, no wonder she wants to keep to herself. I know what that kind of betrayal can feel like.

Adrienne hadn't realized she could have something so fundamental in common with Morgan, and it frustrated her. As a producer-cum-journalist, she'd like nothing more than to get to the bottom of both that story and whatever it was that went on behind the scenes in the Spencer family. But now, armed with the knowledge that Morgan had also been cheated on, she was swamped with sympathy for the younger woman, and her desire to hunt down a good story was less than sharp.

"So what time is Toby meeting us?"

Jenny's question saved Adrienne from her thoughts, and she was thankful. Morgan Spencer was merely the subject of the film Adrienne was making. There was no room for personal feelings about anything that Spencer might or might not be going through.

Adrienne could almost hear Tricia tutting in her ear.

"You did good." Harry smiled and heaved the bag onto his shoulder.

"Thanks. It *felt* good." Morgan rolled her shoulders and gazed up at the bright blue Chicago sky.

He cocked his head at her when she looked back and met his eye. "You seem...different. Something's changed since Phoenix." In the next moment, his eyes went wide. "You got *laid*!"

"I did not!" She glared at him. "And even if I had, I wouldn't tell you."

"Oh, you so would. You wouldn't be able to keep it to yourself." He laughed as Morgan stomped past him. "So if you didn't get laid, what *did* happen?"

She couldn't tell him. It would sound...dumb. Maybe Charlie, but even she would probably roll her eyes and laugh.

"Nothing. Nothing happened. We had a good day's practice. That's all."

"No, it's not just that."

Jesus, he was like a dog with a bone.

"Harry, nothing happened. Now, is there anything you think we should work on tomorrow?"

"Isn't tomorrow when the camera crew arrives? And that woman from the production company?"

She couldn't help the little flutter that ran through her. *God, now I want to roll my eyes at myself.* "Yes, but they don't want to meet with me until the afternoon. You and I could get a serious practice session in earlier if you think we should?"

"Do you think so?"

She hated when he did that, answering her question with a question, but she also knew why he did it, so she took the time to think it through.

"No, actually, I don't. This was good. Everything seems to be working as I want. I'd like to lose that slight drift to the right I seem to be getting on my drives, but that's all."

"Yep, that drift started to happen back in Phoenix. I'll take a look at some tapes from there and see if I can nail it down because it isn't obvious."

"Cool, thanks. Want a drink with me and Charlie later?"

"Hell yeah."

Back in her hotel room, she changed into her running gear before heading out to the Lakefront Trail. She was thankful their hotel was in the city and not out near the golf course they'd be playing for real in a couple days' time. She ran for forty minutes, enjoying the strong breeze that whipped across from the water as it cooled her heated skin. Harry's observation pinged back into her mind, and she smiled ruefully. She hadn't realized her mood had lifted so much after Phoenix, but it made sense. *Adrienne just made me feel so at ease. That's all. There's nothing more to it than that. There can't be, for crying out loud.*

That last thought sobered her and brought her back to reality. There was no room for anything complicated in her life right now. She had just climbed to her highest world ranking, and she'd be pretty stupid to let anything compromise that. If there was one thing she'd learned from observing her father when she was a child, it was to remain focused on the goal. And her goal was twofold—to win her first major and to get to number one—so she needed to be even more vigilant. No matter how attractive the alternative.

"So you ready?" Charlie asked, after wiping her mouth.

They'd eaten healthily for once, both of them aware they had a tough stretch coming up, with key tournaments back-to-back. The superfood salad had been surprisingly filling, and Morgan felt virtuous as she washed it down with a diet soda. She would allow herself one small light beer tonight, then no more alcohol until the tournament was over.

"Yeah, I am. It's all feeling pretty good. How about you?"

"Ditto. The knee's doing really well, which is a big relief, I can tell you."

"You didn't say you were worried about it."

Charlie sighed. "Yeah, I was worried I'd jinx it if I said it out loud. I know the doctor said it would be fine, but until you put it through a couple of tournaments, you never know."

"True. Well, I'm pleased for you."

"Thanks." Charlie looked at her watch. "What time did Harry say he'd get here?"

"About now. Want to move to that comfy couch?"

"You read my mind."

They settled into the couch; the big stuffed chair opposite would be fine for Harry.

"So before Harry gets here, some gossip." Charlie leaned in, her eyes shining. "Want to hear it?"

"Always." Morgan didn't know how Charlie did it, but she always had the scoop on everybody after each tournament she played and even some she didn't.

"Laurie hit on one of those TV women, in San Antonio, and got shot down in smokin' flames."

Morgan clenched her fists. "What?"

Charlie blinked. "You okay?"

"Um, sure. Which one?"

"Which one what?"

"Which one did she hit on?"

Even saying the words made her feel sick. The thought of Laurie trying anything with either Jenny or Adrienne was revolting. Morgan had heard plenty of rumors, of course, about Laurie Schweitzer but had never seen her in action herself. *Probably because you never go to any of the social events or hang out with the other players long enough.*

Charlie looked at her quizzically. "The older one, the one who's running the show. Alison?"

"Adrienne." Morgan's stomach jumped, and heat spread across her chest. "Laurie didn't, um, touch her or anything, did she?"

"Ew, no! No, just asked her out and got turned down. Apparently this Adrienne looked horrified. Well, who wouldn't?" Charlie shuddered.

Morgan chuckled and willed her heart to resume its normal pace. "Well, yeah."

"You sure you're okay?"

For a split second, she was tempted to tell Charlie, to try to explain why the thought of Adrienne made her pulse pound and her hands shake and had been doing so since they parted in Phoenix, but she couldn't even explain it to herself, so there was no point.

At that moment, Harry strolled over to their cozy corner and threw himself into the big chair.

"Hey," he said by way of greeting, and Morgan didn't know whether to be thankful or annoyed that he'd interrupted their conversation.

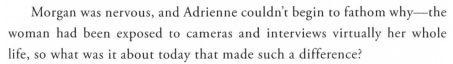

Morgan was nervous, and Adrienne couldn't begin to fathom why—the woman had been exposed to cameras and interviews virtually her whole life, so what was it about today that made such a difference?

Harry, whom Adrienne had taken an instant liking to when being introduced half an hour ago, frowned, his tanned, weather-beaten face a landscape of crevices and creases. Morgan had just missed two short putts while Toby filmed her, and Adrienne knew they'd have to try again. It wouldn't do to show Morgan Spencer missing every shot on a documentary about the best women's golfers.

"Let's take a break," Harry said gruffly before Adrienne could offer.

Morgan said nothing but handed Harry the putter and followed him as he walked briskly off the practice green. Adrienne had requested use of one of the course greens, but the club had refused, reluctant to have it risk being damaged so close to the tournament itself. It was less than ideal. There were other players coming and going, with all the attendant background noise that generated, and the filming so far had been a complete waste of time.

Jenny appeared beside her. "What's going on? She doesn't look so good." She motioned with her head toward Morgan, who conferred with Harry and looked agitated at whatever he said.

"I'm not sure," Adrienne said, watching Morgan and Harry.

Should I step in?

She glanced down at her schedule. They really only had this chance with Morgan today, unless she could perhaps push Kim Lee to tomorrow. That would seem particularly rude, though, asking the world number one to bump because the world number three had a bad day. *Screw it. Morgan's just going to have to make this work.* It was the same attitude she'd have for anyone she filmed.

So why did it not sit right when applied to Morgan?

She drew in a long breath and strode over to Morgan and Harry.

"Hi, sorry to interrupt, but we've only got so much time this morning, and we need to press on."

Harry glared at her, his contempt plain to see. Ouch. But she'd been subjected to worse; Harry was a teddy bear in comparison to some of the people she'd butted heads with. He opened his mouth to speak, but Morgan's hand on his arm stopped him.

"No, she's right." Morgan smiled at Adrienne, but it was half-hearted at best. "I'm sorry. It's me. For some reason, being filmed today is making me over aware of everything I do in making a shot." She shrugged. "I feel like I'm under a microscope."

"And it's putting stress on her she doesn't need two days before a tournament starts." Harry's eyes narrowed.

Adrienne held up a placating hand. "I understand. All of it." She turned to look Morgan in the eye and found herself distracted once again by the remarkable color of those eyes. The gold flecks were almost mesmerizing in the way they shifted and shimmered in the sunlight.

Morgan stared at her, and the faintest of blushes stole across her cheeks.

Oh great, now she thinks I'm going to tell her off.

"Morgan, the last thing I want to do is put any pressure on you."

Harry snorted.

"I thought this would be an interesting segment for people to watch," Adrienne continued, keeping her gaze on Morgan. "To see how you and Harry work together. Is it just today that it's giving you an issue, or do you think it would be the same no matter which day we chose?"

Morgan's chuckle sounded strained. She shook her head. "No, it's…" She glanced away and sighed. "You must think I'm some kind of diva."

"Not at all." Adrienne chuckled. "Trust me, I know what a diva acts like, and you are not it."

Morgan looked back at her, and this time her smile seemed real. "Thanks. Look, can I just have five minutes to grab a coffee?"

"Sure. Want Jenny to go get it for you?"

"Oh, no, I'd rather go myself. Does anyone else want one?" She threw the question out in the direction of Jenny and the crew, who all shook their heads.

Not really in need of a second cup but recognizing an opportunity when it stepped in front of her, Adrienne said, "I'll come with you if that's okay."

Morgan's eyes widened ever so slightly. "Sure." She turned on her heel.

Harry shot Adrienne one last glare before she followed Morgan.

The clubhouse buzzed with activity, but the coffee bar was thankfully quiet. Morgan ordered her coffee—black, no sugar—and turned to Adrienne.

"And for you?" Her voice held a hint of huskiness that sent a shiver down Adrienne's spine, a shiver that had no right to come into being.

"Oh, uh, with cream, no sugar. Please."

As they waited for the coffees, the silence between them was awkward, and Adrienne searched for a way to break it.

"It's not really my thing," Morgan said, her voice low.

Adrienne blinked, not understanding.

"Being the center of attention." Morgan gave her a wry smile. "When I'm out on the course, I'm one of many, and I can lose myself in that." She sighed. "But put me up front on my own, and I...struggle."

"I guess I owe you an apology, then," Adrienne said quietly.

What did they say about the word *assumption*? Oh boy, did she feel like an ass now. Just because Morgan grew up with fame didn't automatically mean she was comfortable with it. *Idiot.*

"Why?"

"Because I made an assumption, based on who you are. Or rather, based on your name and your background, not on who *you* really are."

"Ah. You thought I'd be used to all this?"

Adrienne nodded.

Morgan sighed again. "Yeah, not so much."

Their coffees were ready, and they each took a proffered cup. Once again, Morgan led the way, and Adrienne hurried to keep up with her long-legged strides. So much started to make sense after Morgan's admission. Why she always appeared so aloof and cold in press conferences, why she kept herself apart from the crowds. *And yet I've still got a project to deliver. Shit.*

"How about if Toby films most of the practice stuff from farther away?" It was a big compromise and one she really didn't want to offer. But understanding so much more about Morgan now, it seemed the right thing to do. "We can always do a separate interview after with you talking about practice, and we'll use it as a voiceover?"

Morgan slowed her pace and faced Adrienne. "Will that give you the best result?"

Okay, just how honest should I be? Adrienne took in Morgan's expression, her head tilted slightly to one side, her eyes narrowed.

Tell her.

"No, it won't. What I want is a more intimate scene, with the audience really seeing how you work and how you and Harry communicate. I won't get that with a long shot."

Morgan pursed her lips.

Adrienne waited her out, sensing that somehow this was the make-or-break moment of the entire project. If Morgan wouldn't go for it, Adrienne would have to put her foot down, and then their working relationship would be a shadow of what it could be, of what it had already become. And Morgan would think less of her as a result, and that thought stung.

"I've never done anything half-assed. Everything I put my energy into, I give it 100 percent." Morgan smiled, but Adrienne could see the hint of nerves in the tightness of her mouth. "And as much as I was pushed into this by Hilton, I *did* agree to it, so I need to do it right. Or at least try my best to." She shrugged, then sipped her coffee. "So let's do it right, okay?"

Adrienne smiled, nodded, and raised her cup in salute.

Morgan laughed, and it changed everything about her in an instant. Suddenly, she was carefree, open, and...God, *beautiful.* Adrienne fought hard against the overwhelming urge to say the word out loud.

No. You are not going there. She's way too young, and this is just, quite frankly, embarrassing. Get a grip.

"What did she say to you in there?" Harry looked puzzled.

"Not much." Morgan reached for her putter and grinned when Harry growled. "Come on, we need to get this done. And I'm fine, okay?"

"I hope so." He handed her the putter. "I'm still not sure this TV thing is a good idea."

Morgan made to speak, but he held up a hand.

"Look, I get what Hilton said about getting you more exposure. But these people, they're...parasites. I've seen them pull other players down by never leaving them alone. I don't want that to happen to you." He paused. "Do you really want to carry on with this?"

Morgan pondered his words for a moment. She knew they held some truth, but they were countered by Adrienne's thoughtfulness and her attention to Morgan's needs in the process. Somehow, she knew Adrienne wasn't like the other press and TV journalists Harry warned her about.

"I do. I really trust her to do this right. But I appreciate your concern." He sighed, then nodded.

Morgan smiled at him, bumped his shoulder, then turned back to the TV crew.

"Okay!" Morgan called, thrilled at the big smile that painted Adrienne's full lips in response. *I want to make her smile like that all the time.* She nearly groaned aloud. *Oh God, this crush has to stop!*

Because that's all it was: a silly crush. She'd been aware of it since they met, since she'd held on to Adrienne's hand a little too long as they parted after their lunch in Phoenix, as she'd stared into those incredible brown eyes. It was the main reason she'd struggled earlier that morning with the filming session. Knowing that Adrienne was close by and watching her every move had turned her into a pile of jelly. It was ridiculous. Adrienne was so out of her league, all sophistication and poise, and yet Morgan couldn't stop thinking about her.

Toby approached, his camera settled firmly on his shoulder.

"All right, Harry," Morgan said with a grin. "Time to make you into a TV star." It helped, teasing Harry like this, taking her mind off Adrienne's presence.

"Whatever," Harry grumbled, but his wink told her he was game.

They resumed the putting practice, and this time, Morgan could put the camera out of her mind. Talking with Adrienne had been a curious dichotomy. On the one hand, explaining to Adrienne about her nerves in front of the camera had helped relax her into accepting the filming session. On the other, spending time alone with Adrienne had made her nerves tingle to the point where she thought she'd never string a coherent sentence together in her presence again.

She and Harry worked a practice session for the camera for fifteen minutes before Adrienne started throwing occasional questions in.

"How hard does he work you usually?"

"Too hard!" Morgan said quickly, grinning for the camera when Harry scowled at her.

"She needs it!" he said.

Adrienne's soft laughter reached them across the green. Off camera, Jenny beamed as she watched the whole thing with a rapt expression.

"Aw, he's the best." Morgan threw an arm around Harry's shoulder. "I couldn't have done any of this without him."

They broke apart to set up for a long putt. Harry read it for her, she checked it and confirmed, and all the while Toby tracked quietly around them.

"Is she a good student?" Adrienne asked as Morgan walked around the putt.

"Don't tell her I said so, but she's the best I ever had," Harry said.

Morgan whipped her head up, genuinely astonished, and a flush of pride swamped her as Harry looked at her from fifteen feet away.

"We're not talking to you," he said gruffly. "You just get on with what you're doing."

This time, even Toby and Diane chuckled.

"And cut!" Adrienne called. She walked quickly over to Morgan. "That was *perfect*! Thank you!"

Morgan's face burned. "You're welcome. I'm pleased it worked out."

They stared at each other, the air between them charged with something Morgan had never experienced. Every hair on the back of her neck stood up, and for a moment, she thought her heart would burst out of her chest. Adrienne looked at her with such…admiration. It was almost too much to take. Morgan lifted a hand, then dropped it just as quickly. *God, what are you doing?*

The slight hint of disappointment that flashed across Adrienne's face did nothing but confuse her even more.

Chapter 8

ADRIENNE PACED HER HOTEL ROOM, phone in hand. *Come on, she's your best friend. If you can't talk to her about this, who can you talk to?*

Before she could out think herself, she pressed down on the keypad.

Tricia answered quickly. "Hey, well done! I didn't even have to nag you to get a call."

Despite the circumstances, Adrienne grinned. "You have me well trained."

"And it only took me twenty years. So how are you?"

"I'm…okay."

"All right, there's a story here, and I need wine. Hold on a sec."

Adrienne smiled. Tricia was, as usual, all in, even before she knew what was coming. And yes, wine wasn't a bad idea, actually. Adrienne propped the phone under her chin while she opened the mini bar and poured herself a glass of the white wine the hotel provided. It wasn't too bad, but at this point, she really didn't care about its provenance, only the calming effect it could have on her taut nerves.

"Okay, shoot," Tricia said, as Adrienne eased into one of the chairs at the small table.

"Well, the project itself is going well. As usual, Toby and Diane are handling it all without any protest. I think Toby's enjoying this one, lots of nice scenery making a change from boring conference rooms and football stadiums. And Jenny's having fun and learning a lot too."

"You're stalling, Wyatt. Cut to the chase." There was a smile in Tricia's tone that softened her words.

Adrienne sighed. "All right, all right. Well, um…" *How do I even say it?* "The thing is, I seem to have found myself in a situation that's rather embarrassing, and even though I know it's ridiculous, I can't shake it off." And that was the most frustrating element—she couldn't damn well stop whatever it was she felt for Morgan. She took a long sip of her wine to fortify herself.

"I'm going to take a guess that this involves a woman, yes?"

Adrienne slumped back in her chair. "Yes, it does. A woman I have no right having an attraction for. It's completely inappropriate, never mind unprofessional." *God, and I was only lecturing Jenny on this the other day. Ugh.*

"Let's set aside the unprofessional part for a moment. Why is it inappropriate? Is she with someone? Straight? Both?"

"No, actually, it's neither. She's…she's much younger than me. I mean, I'm old enough to be her damn mother. It's…" Adrienne shuddered. "It's very wrong, and I'm deeply ashamed of it."

"Okay, that sounds a tad dramatic. And I don't like hearing you say you're ashamed of yourself. It can't possibly be that bad. Unless you've done something that—"

"No! God, no. I just feel that a woman my age has no business being interested in someone that young."

"How big an age gap are we talking?"

"I'm eighteen years older than her," Adrienne whispered, mortification heating her cheeks.

"Oh." There was so much weight in that one simple word.

"I know."

"Look, hon, I get it. You've been hurt, and you've been alone a while now. It's obvious if someone shows a hint of interest in you, especially someone so young, then—"

"But that's the problem. It's not her. It's me!" Adrienne groaned and dropped her head into her free hand. "I'm the one acting like the lovestruck teenager. She's just being as friendly as our situation calls for."

Tricia said nothing for a moment, then sighed. "Can I be frank?"

"Of course."

"I'm worried there's an element of wanting to, shall we say, compete with Paula here. She got herself a hot young thing, so subconsciously you think that's a way to perhaps get back at her?"

Is that where my brain is going?

"I honestly don't know. I just know I'm in danger of making a fool of myself."

"Well, at least you're recognizing the problem. And I mean, just for the record, I don't necessarily think an age gap is a problem. You're forty-nine, but you don't look it, and I know damn well you don't feel it. But…how would you feel if people said the same things about you that you've been saying about Paula all this time? I mean, Paula and Zoe do look very happy together, despite what you might think, but even so…"

"You've seen them?" Adrienne was shocked. Paula and Tricia had never moved in the same circles, so why—?

"We bumped into them at the Met, at that new exhibition of Frida Kahlo's work. It seemed rude to ignore them, so we said hello, chatted for a few minutes." She sighed. "They genuinely seemed very happy, very comfortable with each other. Yes, they look different in age, but they didn't act it, not at all."

The tears welled up, but Adrienne wasn't even sure why. Many reasons—pain for the loss of what she had with Paula, and strangely, a tinge of happiness that Paula was okay. That what she'd done to Adrienne hadn't all been for nothing.

"However," Tricia continued, before Adrienne could speak, "that's them, and this is you. I suspect you would be worried about everyone pointing fingers at you and being all 'Oh, look, Adrienne was all jealous of Paula, so she's gone and gotten herself her own toy girl'."

"Is that how *you* would feel?" Adrienne wasn't sure she wanted to hear the answer.

"If that was why you were pursuing this woman, then yes."

"I'm not *pursuing* her! And even if I did, that's the last reason I'd do it," Adrienne snapped, words spilling from her with no thought. "Morgan is much more than that. She's smart, dedicated, thoughtful, passionate about what she does, and—"

"Morgan?" Tricia interrupted. "Morgan *Spencer*, the subject of your film?"

"Argh, yes." Adrienne groaned. "You see, it's totally unprofessional of me."

"Hm."

"Hm?"

Tricia sighed. "Addy, you've said yourself you're not ready for a new relationship. I hardly think getting involved with the subject of your film, someone who's in the public eye, is the best way to dip your toe back in to the dating pool, do you? Never mind the extensive age gap."

Adrienne groaned again. "No, God no. You're absolutely right." She exhaled slowly. "This is why I needed to talk to you, so that *you* could talk some sense into me."

"You're welcome. And, hey, look, there's no need to be silly about this. You are working with her, and getting to know her in order to make the best film you can would still be a wise move. So don't clam up completely, okay? Just remember those boundaries."

"I will."

Morgan had a spring in her step and almost laughed out loud at herself. It was the day before the tournament got underway, and this morning's practice had been fantastic. When it all worked like that, she felt on top of the world. All she'd ever wanted to do from the time she could lift a proper club was play the best she could and win as much as she could. Not to the point of becoming obsessed, but because she knew she had it in her, and she wanted to see how far her talent could take her. And because, just once, she'd like to hear her father say, "Well done, Morgan," and know he meant it. It hadn't happened yet, and it was another reason she was mad at herself for blowing the last three majors she'd had a chance to win. Surely winning one of those would elicit that response at last.

Refusing to let that last thought sour her mood, she strode through the hotel lobby. She'd just pushed the button to call the elevator when her phone buzzed in her pocket. Adrienne's name was on the caller display, and Morgan's stomach fluttered.

"Hi, Adrienne."

"Morgan." Adrienne cleared her throat. "How was the rest of your day?"

"Good, thanks. Really good. Harry pushed me hard, but it was worth it."

"Great! So, um, I was wondering. Do you have any plans for dinner this evening? I'd like to go over the ideas I have for the PGA, and I don't think there'll be time on Monday before we all travel to Virginia."

Morgan's stomach completed a full roll. Dinner with Adrienne, even a working dinner, was equal parts exciting and terrifying. *What if I get all tongue-tied in front of her and make a fool of myself?* Her reaction to Adrienne mystified her. Morgan hadn't done a lot of dating in college or since, but she'd done enough to consider herself reasonably confident in the presence of a woman. But not with Adrienne.

"Morgan? It's okay if you have plans."

"Oh! No, sorry, was just thinking about timings." *Liar.* "Um, sure, dinner sounds good. But could we meet around six? I know that's a bit early, but—"

"No, that's fine. I totally understand. How about in your hotel's brasserie, then you don't have to travel either?"

So thoughtful. Again. "Oh, that's perfect, thanks. I'll see you then."

Morgan killed an hour in the hotel's fitness suite, doing mostly stretches and some light weights before a soak in the small steam room and a cool shower to finish off. She was relaxed and refreshed on the outside but a jumble of nerves on the inside. *Come on, it's a quick working dinner!*

Yeah, but with a woman who makes my heart pound and my insides melt.

She changed into her softest jeans and a green, long-sleeved T-shirt, throwing a thin scarf around her neck in case the air-conditioning in the brasserie was too fierce. The last thing she needed was a cramped neck on the eve of a tournament—it had happened once before years ago, but she'd learned her lesson. She brushed out her hair, leaving it to tumble around her shoulders. Any chance to literally let her hair down was a welcome one, given she spent most days with it tied tight in a ponytail.

Adrienne waited for her at a table by the window that looked out over the terrace. Some hardy patrons were seated outside despite the cool evening, and Morgan was grateful Adrienne had chosen a table inside. As Morgan approached, Adrienne's eyes went wide before she dipped her head to look back at the menu she held in her hands.

"Hi," Morgan said as she slipped into the seat opposite Adrienne. "How are you?"

Adrienne took a moment to meet her gaze, which was puzzling. "I'm good. Achieved a lot today, so…"

"Good."

They stared at each other for a moment. Morgan forgot all the promises to herself not to look so deeply into Adrienne's eyes or to drink in the beauty of her skin, those lips, the way her hair perfectly framed her oval face—the hair that Morgan ached to touch, to run her fingers through.

"So," Adrienne said roughly, then cleared her throat. "Should we order, and then we can talk?"

Morgan shook herself out of her daze and hoped her cheeks weren't flushing too red as she pulled her gaze away from Adrienne. "Sure. I'll be having some kind of salad, but don't let that stop you ordering something less boring."

Adrienne chuckled. "I actually prefer a salad."

"Really?"

Now Adrienne laughed, and her eyes sparkled as she did so, drawing Morgan back into that place where nothing else mattered except being in the same space as this beautiful woman.

"Yes, really. Don't get me wrong, I'm not averse to something richer, but I spend so much time in hotels and on the road, it's too easy to fall into the habit of eating heavy food every day."

"Yeah, I know what you mean. Okay, then let's check out the salad options together."

Once they'd placed their orders, Adrienne pulled a notebook from her purse and opened it.

Okay, so she really does mean business. The disappointment cut deep.

They talked through the ideas Adrienne had for the short time that was available before the PGA. That mainly involved another short sit-down segment, which Morgan was okay with until Adrienne elaborated on the subject she wanted to cover.

"So this time I want the main focus to be on following in your father's footsteps." She held up a hand when Morgan stiffened in her seat. "Yes, I know you must be fed up of being asked about it. But I can't do this film and *not* mention it in some way." She softened her tone. "You must realize that, yes?"

Morgan sighed. "Yes. Of course."

Adrienne fiddled with her water glass. "Morgan, is there...? Are you close to your family?"

The anger hit her without warning. "Is that on or off the record?"

Adrienne made an unintelligible sound and leaned forward. "Morgan, I have to be honest with you. It's a bit of both." She stared intently at Morgan.

All Morgan wanted to do was change the subject and move them back into that nice zone where they were at ease with each other.

"Morgan, the professional in me knows there's something not quite right in the Spencer house. You've flinched each time the subject of your family has come up during this project. I'd be slacking on my job if I didn't ask you. But I'll be honest, the human in me is asking because I...care." Adrienne visibly swallowed. "Because I don't like to see anyone hurting about something. Now we've spent some time together, I can see that's what's happening to you." She shook her head. "God, now I'm rambling. Maybe we—"

"He doesn't support me. Or have any belief in the women's game in general."

The words fell into the space between them, and Morgan saw their impact. Saw how, in a split second, Adrienne processed what that meant for both Morgan herself and for Adrienne's perception of the big American golf hero, Gordy Spencer.

"Shit," Adrienne said.

Morgan burst out laughing. Adrienne's response was so far from what she'd anticipated, she couldn't do anything *but* laugh out loud.

Adrienne smiled ruefully, shaking her head. "Sorry, that wasn't exactly the most professional response, was it?"

"No," Morgan said, still chuckling, "but it was the most human response." And it meant the world to her that Adrienne's first reaction had come from within herself, not her TV-producer self.

"So, um, how—?"

"Morgan, I thought that was you."

Adrienne watched in astonishment as Morgan folded in on herself. The woman she'd just shared an important moment with and then laughed with about it was instantly a shadow of herself at the sound of that voice. Adrienne turned toward it a moment after Morgan, so she had a split second to see the pain, hurt, and anger that zipped across Morgan's face before she shut down.

What the—?

"Naomi." Morgan said the word with little energy, and Adrienne saw, out of the corner of her eye, her fold her arms defensively across her chest.

"I'm sorry, am I interrupting?" Naomi asked, but her tone was so far from sincere Adrienne nearly snorted.

Of course you are, but you really don't care, do you?

Adrienne looked at Naomi Chase, and what she saw in her eyes and on her face caused bile to rise in her throat. This woman had hurt Morgan and hurt her badly as far as Adrienne could tell, and she stood here looking between Morgan and Adrienne with a smirk on her face that could only be described as vicious.

This wasn't Adrienne's battle. Hell, it wasn't even her business, but something flooded through her and straightened her spine and lifted her head.

"Yes, actually, you are. Adrienne Wyatt, TC Productions." She held out her hand and stared Naomi Chase down.

To Adrienne's intense satisfaction, Chase looked startled and quickly shook Adrienne's hand even as her mouth twisted into a scowl.

"If you'll excuse us," Adrienne continued as Chase opened her mouth, "we're in the middle of a meeting and have lots to discuss."

It was delivered in Adrienne's best cutting tone, the one she rarely used but when she did always had the desired effect. She watched as it worked now.

Chase took a breath, stood up straight, and turned to Morgan.

"Another time," she murmured and walked away without waiting for a response.

There was a silence in her wake, and regret poured through Adrienne. *Well, way to go, Wyatt. Why not act like the macho man protecting his damsel in distress?* She almost didn't want to look at Morgan, but then a gentle snort followed by a throaty chuckle brought her head around to face the woman opposite her.

Morgan's laughter gently rocked her entire body.

Adrienne's discomfort waned slightly. "Are you…? God, I'm sorry, that was—"

"Completely wonderful," Morgan finished, meeting Adrienne's eyes at last. "But how did you know?"

Adrienne paused. "Jenny. She heard a rumor. I don't know how."

Morgan nodded slowly. "Yeah, we weren't that public about it, but we were seen out a few times. Not that we had anything to hide, but I didn't want the press making it into a mountain, given who I am, yada yada yada."

Adrienne sighed. "I *am* sorry, though. It wasn't my place to say anything."

"Adrienne, honestly, I'm grateful. I knew she was here this week, but I'd hoped to avoid her. I never expected she'd just walk right up to me." She shook her head and looked dazed.

"Is it true, what she did?" Adrienne asked quietly, wondering if that was a step too far.

Morgan seemed unfazed by the question. "Cheated on me? With the woman who worked at the reception desk of our hotel?" She huffed out a breath. "Yep. It's true."

"God, I'm so sorry." She hesitated only a moment before continuing. "I know how that feels. I…I can empathize."

"Yeah?" Morgan raised one eyebrow.

She nodded. Her heart thudded as she prepared the words, words that still hurt no matter who she said them to. "My partner of ten years cheated on me, then left me. Last year."

"Ouch." Morgan winced. "Ten years. That's tough. I'm sorry." She yawned, rapidly covering her mouth. "God, sorry. I'm… Suddenly I'm really tired."

"Hey, it's okay. I understand. A lot just happened there." *And I didn't help, asking about your family.* In all the drama of Naomi's appearance, Adrienne had completely forgotten Morgan's admission about her father.

"Yeah, it did." Morgan stretched. "Look, our food's on its way. Do you mind if we just eat and run? Can we talk another time this week about that interview you want to do?"

"Of course."

The last thing Adrienne wanted to do was press Morgan now. At the same time, she really did want that interview—not to get Morgan to publicly criticize her father, of course. That would be crass. But to perhaps get her to open up about what it was like to grow up in such a famous family and any pressures that might have bestowed on her.

"Thanks, Adrienne. For everything."

The smile Morgan sent her way made her breath catch in her throat, and she had to cover her emotions by reaching for her water glass. "You're welcome."

This getting-to-know-Morgan-but-stay-within-the-boundaries plan was an emotional minefield. One she wasn't sure she would survive.

"You did good, kid." Harry patted her shoulder and grinned when she scowled at him.

"You know I hate it when you call me that," Morgan whined.

He shrugged, laughed at her as she tutted, then held open the door for her.

They stepped into the lobby of the hotel and wove their way through the throngs of guests. Morgan kept her head down, not wanting to be rude but in need of some time to decompress. The round had been tough but had seen her end the second day three shots clear of everyone else.

They headed toward the restaurant, less people blocking their route the farther they travelled. As they passed the bar, noisy with revelers, Morgan glanced down one of the many hallways that led off the extended lobby. She stopped short when she spotted the unlikely pairing of Adrienne and Naomi in conversation.

"What's up?" Harry asked, peering over her shoulder. "Oh. Her." His tone was scathing.

Morgan threw him a glance, a wry smirk on her face. "Which one?"

Harry snorted. "That stupid ex-girlfriend of yours."

Morgan sighed and turned back to observe the interaction between the two women. Naomi looked smug; Adrienne looked awkward.

What is that about?

"Come on," Harry urged, with a little nudge in her back. "Whatever that is, it's nothing to do with us."

He was probably right, but whatever was going on between the two women nagged at her.

"Look, give me a minute, okay? You go ahead and get us a table. I'll be there soon."

Harry frowned and folded his arms. "Morgan."

She held up a hand. "I promise. I'll be there soon."

I just need to check she's okay. God knows what crap Naomi is pulling, but I know it can't be good.

Harry glared at her, then dropped his arms, shook his head, and walked on.

Morgan watched as Naomi placed her hands on her hips and spoke sternly to Adrienne. Adrienne squared her shoulders and responded in what looked like a calming manner, and then Naomi nodded sharply and strode off down the hallway, away from where Morgan spied on them.

Adrienne dropped her head back and huffed out a long breath before rolling her shoulders.

Morgan took a couple steps forward. "Adrienne?"

Adrienne whipped around to face her, and even with the distance still between them, Morgan could see the fire in her eyes.

Whoa.

"Sorry," Morgan said, holding up her hands. "I just wanted to check you were okay."

Adrienne closed her eyes, then smiled as she opened them. "I'm fine," she replied, slowly walking toward Morgan.

Adrienne was all grace and yet utterly powerful as she approached. The charcoal-grey pants she wore clung to her hips in ways that made Morgan fight for breath. The teal, off-the-shoulder silk shirt teased at Morgan's mind with the way it alternately emphasized the shape of Adrienne's breasts and then hid them from view.

Is it me or did the temperature in here just go up ten degrees?

"Are *you* okay?" Adrienne said softly as she stopped a few feet away.

"Uh, yeah. Yeah, I'm good."

Morgan inhaled deeply and fought hard to bring herself back to a place where she *wasn't* thinking about how incredible it would be to wrap her arms around Adrienne and pull her in close.

"What did Naomi want?" *Yep, perfect—think about your ex. If ever there was a mood killer...*

Adrienne sighed. "An apology."

"For what?"

"For my rudeness the other day. She made a complaint about me. I had to suck it up."

"That... She's..." Morgan's anger ravaged her insides.

Adrienne held up a hand. "It's okay. She was right. I *was* out of line. However satisfying it was at the time." She smirked.

Morgan shook her head. This woman. "Well, I'm still sorry you had to do that. She's... She can be very manipulative."

"So I gather," Adrienne said drily. She shrugged. "It's not the first time someone's nose got put out of joint by me, and I'm sure it won't be the last. The joys of dealing with egos in my line of work."

"I guess."

"Oh, hey, great play today! You must be pleased."

Morgan's face heated at the praise, something that never normally happened whenever anyone else complimented her game. "I am. It was a good day."

Her words brought Harry to mind, and she knew she had to get to the restaurant, however tempted she was to stay and talk with Adrienne.

"I, um, I have to go. I'm meeting Harry for dinner and a debrief."

Adrienne looked disappointed. Or was that wishful thinking? "Of course. Don't let me keep you." Adrienne smiled then and looked relaxed for the first time since Morgan had stumbled across her. "And thank you for checking up on me. I really appreciate it."

"You're welcome. Anytime. Although obviously I hope you're *not* going to have to deal with Naomi again."

Adrienne chuckled. "No such luck. Part of the deal with the apology was giving her a slot in the film. I have to interview her on Sunday after the last round."

"Oh, no..."

"Hey, I'm a big girl. I can handle her," Adrienne said with a wicked grin, and Morgan's libido shifted into fifth gear.

Oh, holy hell. I really am in deep trouble here.

Chapter 9

MORGAN STEPPED OUT OF THE press room, smiled and waved at various people she either knew or thought she should at least be polite to, and then exited the building, breathing in a deep lungful of crisp air as she did so.

Her nerves jangled but in a good way. She'd played an awesome third round today and had extended her lead out to five shots going into tomorrow's final round. As long as nothing crazy happened out there the next day, she'd win her third tournament on the run, something she hadn't achieved thus far in her career. The thought gave her a thrill, which she quickly tamped down.

Don't jinx it. Don't think that far ahead.

"So are you *ever* going to talk to me again?"

Morgan stumbled at the harsh words and looked around quickly to find the person who had spoken them.

Naomi leaned against the wall of the building, arms folded, legs crossed at the ankles. She was beautiful—Morgan could still acknowledge that—but her features now were scrunched into an angry frown that negated that beauty.

She supposed she should have known this would happen at some point. Morgan had done her utmost to avoid Naomi all week, while at the same time not obsessing over it to the point where it would interrupt her focus on the tournament. But now there'd be no getting away from it. From her.

"Naomi, I really don't think we have anything to say to each other."

Morgan made to move on, but Naomi caught up with her, and a firm hand on her bicep pulled her to a stop.

"Naomi, don't. Please."

She didn't want a scene, didn't want anything more to do with the one woman she'd let close since college. The woman who'd stomped all over her heart.

"Morgan, this is ridiculous! We're both on the tour. Avoiding each other is pretty much impossible. I think you ought to be a grown-up and just deal with this so that—"

"'Deal with this'?" Morgan stepped in closer to Naomi, ignoring the beautiful blue eyes and the tightly curled blonde hair that had always felt incredible clenched in her hands when they'd made love. "You broke my heart, so forgive me if my need to stay away from you comes across as immature. Believe me, it's not. It's by far the most sensible thing I can do in the circumstances."

"You know it didn't have to be the end of us. We could have worked out that little...misunderstanding."

She reached out to brush Morgan's cheek, but Morgan flinched away.

Naomi frowned. "Am I really that repulsive to you now?" she asked, her tone full of wonder.

How could she not get this? It was as if they spoke a different language.

"Naomi, you *cheated* on me. It wasn't a misunderstanding. I walked in on the two of you in your hotel room, the room where we had slept together the night before." Naomi tutted, but Morgan rushed on before she could interrupt. "I trusted you. I gave you more of myself than I've ever given anyone, and you threw it right back in my face with that...that *groupie*. So, no, we couldn't have worked it out. Not at all."

Naomi snorted, and her expression turned hard again. "And just how much of yourself *did* you give me, huh? Jesus, talking to you about how you felt was like trying to get blood out of a frigging stone. Every time I thought I was getting close you pushed me away! Some days I felt like I didn't know you at all. You were just some other golfer I knew on the tour, not the woman I was supposed to be in a relationship with. A relationship that no one else knew about, I might add."

"Now hold on, we both wanted to keep it on the down low. Don't you dare try to pin that on me and say it had anything to do with our breakup. And while we're at it, don't you dare blame me for you cheating on me! Talk about immature. Face up to your own responsibility. If you weren't happy

97

with our relationship, you could have talked to me. Then we might have worked it out. But you took that choice away when you slept with that woman."

"And just when the hell was I supposed to talk to you? You were never present. Even when we were together, alone, you were off somewhere else up here." She gestured with a twirling finger at her head. "Morgan world, where no one else gets in. And don't even start with the whole 'you don't understand what it was like for me' crap about your daddy and growing up famous and all that other shit." Naomi glared at her. "You fell back on that way too often. Such a great excuse to avoid actual feelings."

Morgan's throat tightened but damned if she was going to cry in front of Naomi. She forced her voice to be calm and rational when all she wanted to do was scream. "This is pointless. We didn't agree about it when I caught you, and we're not going to agree about it now. We didn't fit. I realize that now." She sighed. "I suppose you want us to be friends now, is that it?"

Naomi grimaced and exhaled slowly. "I'm not sure what I want," she said quietly, and it was probably the most honest thing she'd offered to Morgan since that infamous day back in Miami.

"Well, take it from me, friendship seems unlikely. I mean it, Naomi, whether you can accept it or not—you broke my heart that day." She shook her head. "I thought you knew how I felt about you. I thought you understood what I meant when I talked about my feelings. The fact that you could crap all over them, that hurt. Still hurts." She blinked away the tears. "But yes, trying to avoid you completely on the tour is ridiculous. So maybe we can at least say hi whenever we pass by and be professional if we ever get drawn against each other for a round. But that's all I can give you. Nothing else."

Naomi huffed out a breath and looked skyward for a moment. The sun was setting, and the golden light that spilled across her face softened her features.

"Then I guess that will have to do." She brought her gaze back down to Morgan's. "But it would also help if you could tell your girlfriend to treat me with a bit more respect in the future."

Girlfriend?

"What the hell are you talking about?"

Naomi scoffed. "Oh, come on, I'm not blind. That TV producer you're seeing. Adrienne Wyatt. Treating me like I was a piece of dirt she'd spotted on her shoe." Naomi jabbed a finger at her. "I've accepted her apology this time, but if she tries anything like that again, I'll do more than put in an unofficial complaint to her boss, you hear me?"

Morgan clenched her hands at her side. "You have no idea what you're talking about. Adrienne is not my girlfriend. We're just working together on that documentary they're making. And if she thinks you're rude and wants to call you out on it, that's her choice."

Naomi smirked. "Yeah, whatever. *Working together*—that's a nice way of putting it. A tad old for you, though, isn't she? Still, maybe that would suit you—I doubt at her age she has much of a sex drive, so all those issues you had with sex won't need addressing at all, will they?"

She threw Morgan one last glare and strode off into the descending darkness.

Williamsburg was surprisingly cold for July. Cold *and* wet. Morgan sighed as she gazed out the window of the car taking her to her hotel. *I hate playing in the rain.* The rain matched her mood. She should have been feeling way more positive going into the week ahead after the great win in Chicago, but after the run-in with Naomi on Saturday night, she'd slipped into a bit of a funk. Unfortunately, the forecast said the rain would linger all through Thursday and Friday, so she'd have to deal with it for the first two rounds at least. *At least I can try to improve my mood in the meantime, given the weather is out of my control.*

The hotel lobby was busy with other arriving players and their entourages. She spotted Charlie and waved. Hell yes, time with Charlie would definitely help her mood.

"Hey!" Charlie bounded over and wrapped her in a crushing hug. "Dinner tonight?"

"Yes, please." Morgan sounded desperate even to her own ears.

Charlie threw her a concerned look. "You okay?"

"Yes. No." She rolled her eyes and chuckled. "Later, okay?"

Charlie patted her on the arm. "Cool. I have to run, but let's say seven, somewhere not here?"

Morgan glanced around. Yeah, the hotel's restaurants would be full of everyone from the tour tonight. "Good thinking. Work your magic. Find us something quiet?"

Charlie saluted, grinned, and charged off.

Chuckling, Morgan stepped up to the desk and checked in. As she turned away from the desk to point the bellboy in the direction of her bags, she came face-to-face with her mom.

"Darling!" her mother exclaimed and pulled her into a warm embrace.

"Mom?"

"Surprise! Dad and I just arrived. We hoped you were in the same hotel. Gordy, look, it's Morgan. Isn't this perfect?"

Her father, who had been talking to someone Morgan couldn't see, turned around. He smiled, and even though it didn't reach his eyes, it was an improvement on their last meeting, so Morgan decided she'd better run with it.

"Hey, Dad."

He stepped forward and wrapped an arm around her shoulders. "Here's my girl!"

Cameras flashed, and Morgan's heart sank. *Oh, so that's why we're doing the loving father routine. I should have known.* She plastered the Spencer public smile on her face and posed for a few shots for the fans who'd pressed closer, her dad's arm tight around her shoulders.

"Congratulations on the Chicago win!" someone said, and Morgan's smile this time was genuine.

"Thanks!"

"Yes, great result," her father said before he let go of her shoulders and stepped back one pace.

The three Spencers turned into a private circle, and her mom grabbed Morgan's arm. "And you're only a few points off number two! We're so proud of you."

"Thanks, Mom." She dared a look at her dad.

He smiled, and the sight startled her. "Well, we'd best get checked in, Bree," he said, and the moment was gone. "I've got to be at the course in an hour."

"Oh?" Morgan asked.

"Preparation for Thursday. We're walking the course. Well, I'm riding it in a cart because of this damn hip."

"Ah, yes, you're part of the commentary team." Morgan smiled with as much encouragement as she could manage. "I hope that goes well."

"Oh, I'll be fine. I know what I'm talking about," he said gruffly, then stepped past her to the front desk.

Her mom looked embarrassed by her husband. "I think he's more nervous than he's letting on," she whispered, leaning in. "Don't mind him."

If only it were that easy.

"So," her mom continued. "Do you have time for a coffee? Just you and me. Let's catch up."

Morgan had planned on going for a run, but she hadn't seen her mom in weeks, and the happy coincidence of them sharing a hotel was too good to go to waste.

"Sure, that's a great idea. Meet you back down here in about half an hour?"

"Perfect!"

They decided to walk out of the hotel, in spite of the rain, and find somewhere downtown. A cute place on a corner a few blocks from the hotel caught their eye. They soon lounged in comfy chairs by an old, blackened, currently empty fireplace.

"So, darling, how are you?" Her mom clasped Morgan's hand. "You've been doing so well, but we've barely spoken the past few weeks."

"I know. I'm sorry about that. I've just been working really hard on keeping that momentum going."

"Oh, I understand. Don't worry!"

"How are things with you?"

"I'm fine. I've been busy, of course. Your father's hip is really getting him down. I think working on this tournament will really give him a lift."

And in that Morgan read that her dad had been a grouch and her mom couldn't wait for them to have a few days apart to give her a break.

After taking a sip of her coffee, her mom asked, "And how is Harry? And Charlie?"

Morgan smiled. "Both good. Harry's working me hard, but that's a good thing."

Her mom nodded. "And how about that TV film?"

101

She wasn't sure why she nearly choked on her mouthful of coffee. Although mention of the TV film always conjured up an instant image of Adrienne, so she shouldn't have been surprised.

"Oh, darling, are you okay? Do you need some water?"

Morgan waved her mom off. "No," she said in a strangled voice once she was nearly recovered. "I'm good."

Her mom frowned at her over her mug. "Is something wrong? Is the TV film proving difficult?"

Morgan's mother could never be called stupid.

"Uh, not wrong, not exactly, no."

Was it worth getting into? So far, Morgan's perception of her own behavior was that she was in danger of making a fool of herself with a woman who wasn't remotely interested in her. But if that should change, there was one thing about the situation she'd appreciate some advice on, and who better to give it than her mom?

"There is something. It's nothing much, not yet, but I guess it might be if I'm lucky."

Her mom waited, eyes narrowed.

"Well, I've met someone."

Her mom's smile split her face.

Morgan rushed on. "She, um, she's part of the TV team. And I really like her, and although I'm not sure if she likes me, maybe she might. But the thing is, she's a lot older than me, and I wondered, did the age gap between you and dad ever factor in to anything? Like, did it hold either of you back from, you know, pursuing each other?"

Her face heated, and it intensified as her mother chuckled.

"Pursuing each other? Morgan, honey, sometimes you're so sweet."

"Whatever."

Her mom laughed again. "You know, I don't think either of us really thought about it. I mean, it's not like I met him when I was eighteen. I was thirty, and he was only in his early forties. It just wasn't that big of a deal." She pinned Morgan with a penetrating look. "How old is this woman?"

"You know, I'm not really sure. But I'm guessing at least ten years older than me, maybe a little more."

"Okay." She nodded slowly, then sighed. "I'm the last person on earth who should try to talk you out of being involved with someone older, but I think you should think very carefully about it. You have to make compromises when the age gap is that big. If she's that much older than you, she may be looking for very different things in a relationship than you are. You don't want her holding you back."

Morgan pondered her mom's words. Adrienne didn't seem that much older, even though Morgan knew she must be. She still seemed pretty young at heart, and you'd never know there was any gap from the way they talked to each other. But she had to acknowledge that she really didn't know Adrienne or what she wanted from life. At the same time, she herself wasn't exactly the young woman about town who hopped from club to club, staying out late and partying until all hours. Maybe she and Adrienne would have more in common than anyone realized.

"Okay, I get what you're saying." She sipped her coffee. "And I note your concerns," she added with a grin.

Her mom smiled. "I want you to be happy. Please don't mistake my warning as me trying to stop that from happening."

"I know. And I won't."

Her mother smiled again, but her eyes told Morgan she was worried.

Adrienne finished taking her notes on the dailies she'd just watched and sat back in her chair. Toby and Diane had done a good job of gathering the fill-in shots she'd need to slip from one player interview to another in the segment featuring this week's major, the Women's PGA. Toby's reliability was a boon, no doubt.

"How is it looking?" Jenny asked, lifting her head up from her laptop. She blinked a couple of times as she focused on Adrienne. Today's hair color was the black base but with pink tips on the spikes and one bright pink streak on one side of her head. It was odd yet strangely beautiful.

"Not bad at all. There's nothing that looks like it needs redoing, which is good news for the budget."

"Yeah, about that. We're a little behind again after having to do that extra thing with Naomi Chase on Sunday."

Adrienne shrugged. "I assumed we would be. Don't worry, we'll find somewhere else we can claw it back. I'm seriously considering not going to Miami next week so we can save on travel costs there." At Jenny's gasp, she smiled and continued. "I'm happy for you and Toby to get what we need there, given we have no sit-down interviews planned."

Jenny's eyes were wide. "Seriously? You'd let me run those two days?"

"I would." Adrienne smiled. "You've been paying attention. You know what I need."

It didn't matter, other than the money it would waste, if what Jenny brought back wasn't that good, because by now Adrienne probably had more than enough footage of all the players prepping for tournaments. But she really wanted to give Jenny a small part of the project to call her own and see how she ran with it, and this was as good an opportunity as any.

Jenny chair-danced, her smile wide. "This is awesome!"

Adrienne laughed then reached for the remnants of her coffee. She grimaced at how cold it was. "Ugh." She put the cup back down. "I need a fresh one of these. How about you?"

"No, I'm good, thanks."

"All right. I'll head down to the coffee bar. Back soon."

Jenny waved distractedly, her attention already back on her spreadsheets and schedules.

The coffee bar in the hotel was next to the main bar. At four on a Tuesday afternoon, there was only a smattering of people sitting at the bar itself or at one of its small tables. As she passed by, she noticed the TV screens above the bar were running ESPN, and she paused when she realized it was Gordy Spencer on screen. His ruggedly handsome face, tanned from years of being outside on a golf course, filled the screen. For a man in his seventies, he still looked good, with steely grey hair that was thick and combed back in a smooth wave and brown eyes the same shade as Morgan's, although his were missing those amazing gold flecks.

Curious as to what he was talking about, she sidled closer to the bar to listen.

"And winning a major, for any golfer, is a big step forward." He smiled at his interviewer; it looked like a live shot as part of their extended daily news segment. "I remember when I first won the US Open. Took days for it to really sink in. I kept seeing all the newspaper headlines—we didn't have the internet back then." He laughed. "And they were all calling me the US Open champion, and it didn't seem real."

"Was that hard to deal with?" the interviewer asked.

"At first, yes. But actually, once that first one sank in, the others got easier and easier." He held up his hands. "I'm not saying I took them for granted, but I knew I was a good golfer, and winning majors was what I was meant to do."

"So here we are, two days before the Women's PGA championship at the beautiful, Jack Nicklaus-designed, Sweet Springs course in Williamsburg, Virginia. Your daughter, Morgan, is, of course, one of the hot tips to take the win, coming off a three-tournament winning streak…"

Adrienne's curiosity rose as a small twitch flickered in the corner of Gordy's eye. He nodded and smiled for the camera, but there was something…off.

"And we at ESPN are thrilled that you are going to be a part of our team this week. Tell me, how is it going to feel watching Morgan battle it out for the title?"

"Well," Gordy replied gruffly, "obviously I will need to remain neutral. I'm there to commentate on all the girls."

Women, Adrienne mentally corrected, and she bit back the urge to tut.

"Oh, of course," the interviewer chipped in, chuckling. "But surely it's going to be a tense time for you, waiting to see if Morgan can pull it off?"

"Oh, yes, of course." It sounded flat.

"And do you think she can?"

The hesitation was so slight, Adrienne wasn't sure many other people would notice, people who didn't spend a lot of their time interviewing others, but it caused her to suck in a surprised breath.

"Oh, yes, of course. She's a great player. I don't doubt her first major isn't too far away." That sounded as rehearsed as hell, and Adrienne's shoulders tightened with tension and…disappointment for Morgan for having this man as her father, a man who clearly, as Morgan had already hinted at, didn't rate her at all. *Jesus.*

The segment finished, and the anchor segued into a piece about baseball. Adrienne swallowed hard and let out a slow breath. Gordy Spencer was an asshole as far as she could tell.

Poor Morgan.

She turned away from the TV, waving away the attentions of the approaching bartender, and stopped dead in her tracks.

Morgan hunched down in a chair at one of the tables a few feet away. A half-drunk glass of ice water dripped condensation onto the table. Her eyes were unfocused as she looked off into the distance.

Don't tell me she heard all that. Oh, God.

She could just leave Morgan alone, leave her to whatever thoughts consumed her, but the pull was too strong. *Don't do it*, she thought, even as her feet moved. A few paces later, she stood next to Morgan's table.

"Quite the performance, wasn't it?" Morgan said softly.

Adrienne hadn't realized Morgan even knew she was there. Carefully, she pulled out the chair next to Morgan's and slipped into it. Only when she'd relaxed back did Morgan raise her head and meet her concerned gaze. What she saw in Morgan's eyes clutched at her heart, and before she could stop herself, she reached out and gently placed her hand over one of Morgan's.

Morgan blinked but didn't retract her hand.

"I'm sorry," Adrienne said. It was the most useless of responses, but she didn't know what else to offer.

Morgan huffed out a breath and smiled wanly. "Why do I keep caring?" she asked, but Adrienne knew she wasn't looking for an answer, at least not from her. "I know what he's like. I know how he thinks. Yet every time he cuts me down like that, it's like he's kicked me in the gut. I've tried. So hard." She fell silent.

"Tried what?"

Morgan snorted. "Tried to put up a wall to protect myself from it. All that got me was a girlfriend who cheated on me, and I *still* give a shit what good old Daddy thinks of me." She pulled her hand away and stood, her face pink. "God, I'm sorry, you don't need to hear this."

Adrienne attempted to re-take her hand, to keep her there for just a few moments longer, but Morgan stepped back.

"Sorry." She strode off.

Adrienne watched her go, observed the tight set of her shoulders, the stiff swing of her arms, and sighed.

I know I'm going to regret this, but I honestly can't do anything else.

She stood and walked quickly after Morgan.

106

"Morgan, wait!"

Adrienne's velvet voice came from behind Morgan as she neared the bank of elevators, and she groaned. God, no, this was embarrassing enough. Couldn't Adrienne leave her alone?

She rapidly hit the call button a few times. "Come on, come on," she whispered, but the elevator gods conspired against her today.

Adrienne arrived alongside her. "Morgan, are you okay?"

"No," she snapped, then instantly regretted her tone. "Sorry."

She finally plucked up courage to look at Adrienne. Yes, there was the expected sympathy in her gaze, which twisted in Morgan's gut—the last person she wanted to appear pathetic in front of was Adrienne—but there was also anger there, which surprised her.

"You're allowed to be angry," Adrienne said firmly. "And you're allowed to let your emotions out."

The elevator finally arrived, sparing Morgan from answering. Without looking back at Adrienne, she hurriedly stepped into the car and punched the button for the third floor.

She jumped when Adrienne said, "I'm here if you need someone to talk to," and turned to see that she too had entered the car. Before Morgan could ask her to leave, the doors slid shut.

Great. Just great.

"I don't need to talk to anyone. I appreciate you trying to help, but I don't need it, okay?"

Why couldn't people get this? She was better off alone, just getting on with what she liked doing best: playing golf and winning tournaments. *That* life was perfect.

Okay, *not* perfect but definitely enough.

"You're lying, Morgan, to me and yourself."

Morgan faced her at last, her anger sparking. "Who the hell do you think you are? You barely know me! Yes, I know, I said some things down there"—she gestured vaguely in the direction of the lobby below them—"but that doesn't mean you have the right to push me on this."

The elevator came to a halt, but as the doors began to open, Adrienne stepped in front of Morgan and pressed the 'Close doors' button. She held her finger there, glaring at Morgan.

"What the hell are you doing?" Morgan asked, staring at Adrienne and trying to ignore the parts of her body that appreciated how attractive this infuriating woman was up close.

"I have no earthly idea." Adrienne shook her head. "But for some reason, I care about you, about what is happening to you. Your father"—she almost spat the word—"is treating you appallingly. This upsets me. Perhaps more than it should, but it's so unfair to you, especially when you are *this* good and this close to winning that first major. I refuse to let you deny how that makes you feel when you could be fighting back against it."

"Oh, wait, I get it. This is all about that interview, isn't it? You want me to go on national TV and bad-mouth my own father!" Morgan's tone was snide. "This isn't about me at all. This is all about you getting this year's TV hit!" She was practically shouting now but couldn't seem to stop.

Adrienne's eyes went wide, then narrowed. She pulled away from the elevator controls; the doors stayed closed, keeping them cocooned in the small interior. She took one step forward, her face slightly flushed. The movement brought her, and her delicious scent, within inches of Morgan. Her deep-brown eyes were almost luminous, her breathing fast but shallow.

Morgan could feel the heat emanating from her, and something stirred in her, something deep down low.

"How dare you?" Adrienne's voice was as taut as piano wire. "You say I don't know you, but you *really* don't know me if you think that's what this is about. Right now I couldn't care less about my TV documentary. This is all about *you*, Morgan." She moved another step forward and exhaled in a huff. "I think all this shit from your father is affecting you more than you know, and I hate to see it happening to you. You deserve so much better," she finished, her tone passionate and her voice half an octave lower.

She was so close now; her gaze bored into Morgan. Her heat and her perfume overwhelmed Morgan and any sense she might have possessed only moments before.

Morgan's hands moved a millisecond before the rest of her, but it all came together in one heated rush. She clutched at Adrienne's lush hips as she pulled her in and kissed her hungrily.

One agonizing split second later, Adrienne responded. A low groan leaked from her throat as her arms wrapped around Morgan's shoulders and pulled her even closer. Adrienne flicked her tongue over Morgan's bottom lip, and she opened willingly to let Adrienne in.

The heat that flashed through her at the first touch of Adrienne's tongue on her own seared her inside and out. For one fleeting, exulting moment she thought she would immolate from it. Instead, she sunk deeper into the kiss, consumed by the need to take as much as she could from the gorgeous woman in her arms.

Adrienne gave back as good as she got and more. They crashed against the wall of the elevator car, Adrienne pressed between it and Morgan. As their mouths devoured each other, Morgan tried to connect to every inch of Adrienne.

And then it was over.

Adrienne wrenched away, a hand on her mouth as she stared at Morgan from two paces away.

"Adrienne…" Morgan's voice cracked.

"No…no, we…can't." Adrienne spun around and pressed the 'Open doors' button.

The doors slid slowly open, and Adrienne squeezed through them before they'd finished parting.

"Adrienne," Morgan pleaded, as she took a step forward. Her body hummed, but her mind was an utter blank.

Adrienne fled the car without even a backward glance.

Chapter 10

MORGAN STARED AT HER BREAKFAST tray, the congealing apple-and-cinnamon oatmeal—usually her favorite—looking decidedly unappetizing. She threw her spoon down and leaned back in her chair. At least eating breakfast in her room had been the right move; God knew she wasn't in the mood for company. Morgan knew Charlie was getting suspicious, having blown her off for dinner the night before and now breakfast this morning, but after the elevator incident, she just needed to be alone.

Kissing Adrienne had been a particularly dumb move. Her face heated with embarrassment thinking about it. Her rational mind knew that, for a few moments at least, Adrienne had kissed her back, and so the mistake wasn't only Morgan's, but that was little comfort. The look of horror on Adrienne's face as she'd pulled away made it abundantly clear there'd be no repeat.

Which really was a shame, given how completely mind-blowing that kiss had been.

Naomi's spiteful words about Adrienne had played in Morgan's mind on a regular repeat ever since she'd stepped out of the elevator and stumbled to her room. Which had then led to a whole flood of unwelcome memories of her time with Naomi, from both last year and Saturday night in Chicago. Sleep had been a rare commodity as a result.

She sighed. Emotions swamped her, but in a little over two hours, she'd be out on the course for her second practice round. Harry would rip her a new one if she turned up in this frame of mind. So she did what she'd become exceptionally good at since she was a kid: locked all these confusing feelings up tight somewhere in the back of her mind. And yes, that made

Naomi's words come back to her, but it had worked for years, and there was no point doing anything else now.

After pushing the breakfast away, she stood up and walked to the wardrobe. Her fitness gear sat in a neat pile on one of the shelves, and a couple minutes later, she was ready. She grabbed a bottle of water from the minibar and headed out.

Half an hour later, she slowed the treadmill and settled into a walking pace to cool down. Sweat tickled her forehead, and she brushed it away with a towel. She wasn't alone in the suite, but she'd kept her eyes focused only on her machine and plugged in her iPod to make sure the other guests got the message. She was, therefore, surprised when someone tapped on her arm. She only just held back a glare as she faced her unwelcome visitor.

Charlie stood by the machine, her hands on her hips, a scowl on her face.

Uh-oh.

Morgan stopped the treadmill, wiped down her face once more, and tried a smile.

"No, that smile isn't going to cut it." Charlie kept her voice low, but her words were sharp. "Why are you avoiding me?"

"I'm not." Morgan flinched as Charlie's eyes went wide. "Well, okay, I am, but—"

Charlie raised a finger. "Why don't we take this up to your room?"

Knowing there was nothing she could do to escape her doom, Morgan nodded and stepped off the treadmill.

They rode the elevator in silence, Morgan all the while trying to figure out what she could tell Charlie that would pacify her without revealing the entire embarrassing story. Her mind refused to cooperate, however, and no plausible story had formed in her brain by the time she unlocked her room and ushered Charlie in.

"Are you sick?" Charlie asked, as soon as the door was closed. "In trouble with the law? Pregnant?"

Morgan, who had been on the verge of a strong denial to the first two options, instead burst out laughing at the third and rolled her eyes when Charlie said quietly, "Gotcha."

"Sit down." Morgan gestured to the armchair by the table, wincing when she realized the remnants of her abandoned breakfast sat there, looking definitely worse than they had when she left them.

Charlie merely shoved the tray out of the way, then looked up at her expectantly.

"I kissed Adrienne."

Okay, that hadn't been the plan *at all*.

Charlie's mouth fell open. "Adrienne? The hot TV lady?"

"You think she's hot?"

"Morgan, I'm straight, not blind."

Morgan chuckled despite the mortification heating her face. Then she slumped down on the edge of the bed and sighed.

"Yeah, her."

"Okay, this should be a happy Morgan, but I'm not seeing that. Is she a bad kisser?"

Morgan shook her head. "Hell no."

"Then what?"

She took a deep breath then told Charlie everything—from the TV thing with her dad through to the scorching kiss in the elevator to Adrienne running from her so fast she'd left a sonic boom in her wake.

"Huh," was all Charlie offered at the end of the tale.

"That's it?" Morgan threw up her arms in disgust. "That's all I get?"

"I'm thinking." Charlie glared at her. "Shush."

Morgan glowered but leaned back on her hands on the bed. She swung her legs in her impatience to hear Charlie's wisdom on the events. As she waited, it slowly dawned on her that she'd never really had this, a female friend to share this kind of stuff with. It was kind of scary but nice.

"Stop with the feet." Charlie pointed at Morgan's swinging legs, her eyes narrowed.

"Jesus," Morgan muttered, but she stilled her legs and did some light stretches of her back and shoulders before she tightened up too much after her run.

"Okay, here's what I think," Charlie announced.

Morgan sat up straight, her heart pounding.

"I think she's into you but doesn't want to be." Charlie sat up straighter too. "Could be the whole age thing. Could just be because you're working together. Not sure." She rubbed one finger over her chin. "You could push it, but that would probably make her run more. So I think you're just going to have to give her some space. You're going to be seeing more of her anyway over the next few weeks, so you can take your time."

"Take my time with what?"

"Wooing her."

Morgan snorted, then guffawed and clutched at her sides. "Woo... wooing her?" she eventually managed to squeak out.

Charlie looked affronted. "Yes. You want this woman, don't you? You really like her. I can tell. And trust me, if she kissed you back that hard, she's got some feelings for you too, whether she wants to admit it or not. So, yeah, you woo her. Slow and easy."

"Charlie, I love you, but really, I'm not the...wooing kind."

"Have you ever tried?" Charlie's stare was piercing.

"Well...no, but—"

"So there you go. Nothing to lose, everything to gain."

"I wouldn't have the faintest idea where to start!"

"Hell, just be *you*. You're a sweetheart, something that bitch Naomi couldn't have figured out if she had a century to do so." Charlie stood and walked over to Morgan. "Now, go get a shower because, trust me, you need one, and I will see you later on the course."

She patted Morgan's shoulder, then turned toward the door.

Morgan, a warmth deep in her chest from Charlie's words, stood. "Charlie, wait." Her friend turned, a small smile on her face. "Thanks. For...for being here and for giving me your own special brand of advice."

Charlie laughed, then wagged a finger. "It's worth a fortune, trust me. You don't know just how good I am."

Morgan laughed. "Uh-huh, I think I have a pretty good idea." She grinned as Charlie rolled her eyes.

Powerful arms enfolded her, pushing her back against the elevator wall. The cool marble at her back did nothing to tamp down the heat that engulfed her body as a hot mouth plundered hers. Her heartbeat pounded in her ears; she clutched at the woman who kissed her so passionately, and in the next moment, she would sweep round to cup Morgan's breast and—

Adrienne's eyes popped open, and she sat bolt upright in the tub. Water cascaded over the rim and faucets. She'd been in that half state between asleep and awake, and the memories of that kiss had dared to invade her brain without her permission. Again.

Dammit, why couldn't she wipe those images from her mind? Because she should, she really should. She had no business revisiting them as often as she had done in the last twenty-four hours. If only the memories weren't so pleasant...

Tutting, she hauled herself out of the tub and toweled down. The soak was supposed to have been a way to shake off the irritation she'd felt ever since the elevator incident, but that clearly hadn't worked. Morgan kissing her had stunned her but only momentarily, and then she'd wholeheartedly given herself over to it. It was only when she'd had the thought of touching Morgan, of caressing her, and then suggesting they go to one of their rooms that reality had walked up and slapped her in the face and she'd shoved Morgan away. Morgan's confused expression had only made the whole situation worse, and Adrienne cringed at the thought.

She couldn't meet her own eyes in the mirror above the basin; she didn't want to look at the face of a forty-nine-year-old woman who should have known *way* better than to kiss Morgan.

She kissed you first, said a small voice in her head.

Like that was any kind of excuse.

After she'd pulled on some soft yoga pants and a sweater—the air conditioner in her room was set to fierce, and she couldn't find a way to turn it down—she sat at the desk, hoping that immersing herself in her work would stop this ridiculous mental treadmill she'd found herself on. It was a long shot; the next thing she had to work on was the sequence of shots she wanted to get of Morgan on the PGA course, the first major they'd be filming her playing.

Her phone rang, and she snatched it up, grateful to whichever human was on the other end of the line for offering her a chance to be distracted for a little while.

Tricia's chirpy voice said a breezy "Hello!" in her ear.

That's what they have caller display for, you idiot.

"Hey, you," Adrienne replied, then cleared her throat when her voice croaked. "How are you? What have you been up to?"

Good plan, get her talking about herself so she doesn't have time to ask any pointed questions.

"I'm good and nothing much. But enough about me, how are you?"

Adrienne groaned. She knew there was no escape other than hanging up, and her good manners prevented that drastic action.

"Addy? What's wrong?"

"Nothing's wrong. I'm fine."

"That groan didn't sound like you were fine."

Adrienne pushed her fingers into her hair and held back the curses that wanted to leap from her mouth. "She kissed me."

Silence greeted her announcement.

"Tricia, you still there?"

"Uh-huh. Just processing."

"Oh."

"Addy…" Tricia's voice sounded dangerously close to patronizing.

Adrienne's hackles rose. "What?"

Tricia exhaled loudly. "Did anyone see you?"

"No! We…were stuck in an elevator." Well, it was half the truth.

"Well, that's something at least. Right, this is rescuable. You'll probably have to take a step back from the project. Perhaps send that chirpy assistant of yours out to do the face-to-face interviews from now on and—"

"Stop! Please, just…stop."

There was a brief silence, then Tricia asked, "What the hell is going on?"

"I can't shake it off. I like her."

"Addy…" Tricia's tone was loaded with warning.

"I know! All right? I know."

"Okay," Tricia said, clearly trying to keep her voice even and calm. "Let's set aside the work thing for now. What about that age gap? I mean, have you thought about that at all? That all your cultural references are different, the music you grew up with, everything?" She sighed. "At the risk of sounding cruel, you do realize you were just starting college when she was a newborn baby, yes?"

Adrienne closed her eyes as the truth of Tricia's words sunk in. Her friend was right—even without the work project between them, the age gap was…ridiculous.

Oh God, and I kissed her back.

"You're right." Adrienne sighed. "You're right. Sorry."

Tricia also sighed. "No, *I'm* sorry. I didn't mean to come down on you so hard, but you know you love your job. I'd hate for something this silly to take that away from you." She laughed half-heartedly. "Although at least you are attracted to someone new—she's the first woman who's caught your eye since Paula left. That's progress, right?"

Adrienne chuckled. "Yes, I suppose it is. I'm not dead yet, it seems." Far from it, if the heat from that kiss was anything to go by.

"And hey, I really would like to see you with someone again, you know?"

Adrienne snorted. "Despite what's been going on with Morgan, I really don't think I have it in me, actually. I think I'm still too broken."

"Well," Tricia said quietly, "I respectfully disagree, but I accept that you need to find your own time for when you think you will be ready. Don't be scared off by this. I'm worried you'll go scurrying back into your lonely cave to hide away, and if you leave it too long, you'll miss the boat."

"People still fall in love in their sixties, you know."

Tricia gasped. "You're not seriously telling me you're going to hibernate for over ten years?"

Laughing, Adrienne shook her head. "No, no, but just because I'm not ready yet at forty-nine does not mean it's all over."

"Okay, point taken." Tricia huffed out a breath. "You okay?"

"Mostly. I will be. Promise."

"All right, I'll leave you in peace then. Call me in a few days, okay?"

Adrienne said good-bye and set the phone back down on the table. She leaned over the smooth wood and laid her head on her arms. A twinge of guilt tugged at her: She hadn't been entirely truthful with her best friend.

Yes, there was a part of her that didn't think she was ready to be out there again. But a bigger part, a more worrying part, couldn't handle how much she'd craved more of Morgan during that kiss. How she'd wanted to lose herself in it, to give herself over, completely and utterly, to the extraordinary level of emotion kissing that incredible woman had generated within her. To drop into that wonderful rush that came from being with someone new, where you lost all sense of yourself and allowed yourself to be swept away, not caring where you ended up because the ride was the only thing you were focused on.

That scared the shit out of her.

"Didn't you want to watch Morgan's practice round?" Jenny asked as Adrienne walked into the small conference room they were using as their base for the tournament.

It was just after five in the afternoon, and her assistant looked mystified at Adrienne's appearance.

"No need. I'll watch the first round tomorrow."

"Oh, okay." Jenny paused. "Sorry, I'm confused, you said yesterday that—"

"I know what I said yesterday. Today I changed my mind." She *knew* her tone was harsh. She knew it, yet she couldn't seem to stop it.

Jenny's eyes widened, then she turned away and tapped furiously at her keyboard.

Adrienne inhaled slowly. "I'm sorry. I... Bad day."

Jenny threw her a quick glance coupled with a brief smile. "Apology accepted."

Adrienne pulled out her chair and flopped into it. The sound of Jenny's fingers flying over her keyboard was strangely soothing, and for a few moments, Adrienne sat still and let her gaze drift.

"So, um, if you don't want to go watch, can I?"

Jenny sounded nervous, and Adrienne didn't blame her. *Probably thinks I'll take her head off. Come on, Wyatt, you're a better person than this.*

"You know what, why don't you? Let me know how she's looking." She paused. "I mean, you know, her play, her demeanor."

"Yeah, I got it."

Jenny seemed oblivious to Adrienne's verbal stumbling, and she breathed a sigh of relief.

"I'll only catch the last four or five holes, but it'll be worth it." Jenny pulled on her zipped hoodie. "Anything to get another look at those arms. Have you *seen* the muscles?" She grinned and held up a hand before Adrienne could respond. "And no, I won't do or say anything inappropriate. I've taken very seriously what you told me the other day. But I figure there's no harm in looking, right?" She waggled her eyebrows. "Still, imagine all that *power* wrapped around you…"

Adrienne wanted the ground to open up and swallow her before her blush gave her away.

Jenny laughed. "Oh, boy, I need to find me someone with arms like those, clearly." She flushed slightly. "Sorry, boss, none of that was remotely appropriate, was it?"

Despite her inner turmoil, Adrienne smiled. "Within these four walls," she said, gesturing to their small room, "you're good. Don't worry."

Jenny grinned and practically jogged out of the room.

"Oh God." Adrienne moaned and dropped her head onto the table.

Harry was pissed, if the set of his shoulders was anything to go by. He marched ahead of Morgan down the narrow pathway to the first tee, and she sighed as she trotted after him. She'd been late to their allotted time for practice—only by ten minutes, but it was eleven minutes later than she'd normally be. Harry had raised one eyebrow, she'd shaken her head, and then he'd made a kind of growling sound as he hefted her bag of clubs. Now she stared morosely at his back, knowing that Harry, a stickler for punctuality, was disappointed in her unusual tardiness.

Luckily, she had, as usual, opted for a solo practice round, and only Lotte was slated to play behind her. She'd gracefully accepted Morgan's apology for the delay and shooed her off with a smile on her face.

"Harry," Morgan said as she finally managed to catch him where the path made a sharp turn toward the tee. "I'm sorry."

He grunted, stepped onto the tee, and placed the bag on the ground. Only then did he turn to face her, casting a quick glance around before stepping closer.

"What's going on?" His voice was gruff, but his eyes were soft.

She suddenly knew it wasn't only annoyance he'd been feeling; he was concerned too.

She wouldn't tell him. He knew her pretty well, but he didn't need to know *that*.

"I just didn't sleep too good. Then I went for a run to wake myself up, and time got away from me." Not entirely a lie, but even so, it didn't sit right in her gut.

He sighed. "Morgan, I..." He shook his head. "Nope, forget it. I really don't need to tell you, do I?"

"No."

And he didn't. She knew what key words would come out of his mouth if he did. Professionalism. Focus. Work ethic. All the things he'd helped instill in her during his time as her coach and caddy.

All the things she was forgetting for the sake of a woman. And okay, that woman was pretty amazing, but even so...

"But you're okay?"

"I am. Honest." She straightened her shoulders and inhaled deeply. "I'm here. Let's play."

He nodded once, then turned back to the bag and reached for the driver.

"Hey, Morgan?"

Morgan froze. *No, not now of all times.*

Naomi stepped onto the first tee, a course official only two steps behind.

"What does she want?" Harry muttered, not exactly quietly.

Naomi shot him a withering glare, then turned back to Morgan all smiles.

"Hey, sorry about this. There was a mix-up with times this morning, and I missed my slot. I know you've booked a solo round, but would you mind very much if I played along with you?" She held up her hands as Morgan opened her mouth. "We don't have to speak. We can just do our own thing, but I'd really appreciate it."

Everything in Morgan screamed "No!" but with the official looking on, her smile friendly and unaware, Morgan was loath to appear rude or unhelpful. Her mind worked a mile a minute.

"Um, well..." In desperation, she turned to the official, a plump woman who looked to be in her sixties, iron-grey hair cut short with bangs that rode high on her long forehead. "I really do prefer to play solo. I don't mean to be awkward, but can't Naomi just play a solo round at the end of the day behind Lotte?"

The official smiled warmly. "You know, she could, but she did specifically ask for a round with another player. Although, come to think of it, I did see Mrs. Karlsson back there, and I know she's playing solo. We could always ask her. Not sure why I didn't think of that before." She turned to Naomi, who looked like she'd just eaten something very sour. "If you'll just give me a second, I'll go check with her."

Naomi gave her half a smile, then glared at Morgan. "Really? You can't even do this?"

Morgan moved closer, not wanting this argument to carry to any other ears. "You know I like solo practice rounds. Believe it or not, this isn't about you." Well, not totally. "I'd be asking the same if it was any other player."

Naomi snorted. "Oh, yeah. Sure." She folded her arms.

Morgan shook her head and stepped back, refusing to engage with her anymore.

They stood like that for a couple of minutes, Harry quietly going about his business to Morgan's left, whistling tunelessly as he did so.

Naomi's caddy had clearly deemed it wise to stay the hell out of whatever was going on and leaned on her bag some fifteen feet away back down on the path.

Eventually, the pleasant-faced official returned, puffing slightly but beaming.

"Mrs. Karlsson said she'd be happy to have you join her," she said to Naomi. "Miss Spencer, we're sorry to have held you up even further."

Morgan grinned victoriously. "Oh, no problem. Have a nice day."

"And you." The woman turned to Naomi. "Okay, Miss Chase, let's head on back."

Naomi threw Morgan a spiteful look, then stomped off the first tee.

"Wished I'd had popcorn for that," Harry said in Morgan's ear.

She laughed softly.

"Something going on there?" he asked, thumbing in the direction of Naomi's retreating back.

Morgan sighed. "No, not really. She ambushed me in Chicago last weekend. We had…words."

"She always was a dumb one," he said dismissively. "Now, are we playing or what?"

"Yes, sir, we are playing!" Morgan snapped a salute. Relief washed over her at a bullet dodged.

Harry shook his head, handed her the driver, and stepped out of the way.

Chapter 11

COME ON, YOU'RE AN ADULT. *Act like one!*

Adrienne glared at her reflection in the hotel bathroom mirror and sighed. She'd been doing a lot of sighing since getting up this morning. The knowledge of what she needed to do in the next few hours made her stomach clench.

It had been easy to avoid Morgan the last two days, but today was the first round, and it would look very odd to the people Adrienne worked with if she didn't put in an appearance. But that would also mean being near Morgan, and every time she thought of her, a cold sweat formed at the base of her spine.

She was afraid. Afraid to appear unprofessional by not being able to set that kiss aside and just get on with her job. Afraid that she had upset Morgan by steering clear of her, by not talking to her, by continuing to send Jenny down to talk with her about the shots they'd be taking today.

Adrienne shook her head. Jenny, of course, loved it. One-on-one time with Morgan put a spring in her young assistant's step that would be sweet in any other circumstance if it wasn't so damn annoying.

Jealous, are we?

Yes, she was, and *that* made her squirm even more. Jenny was full of the stories of how well she and Morgan were getting on, the fun they were having talking about the tournament, the other players, and the less-than-stellar food in the press area. Jenny was, however, always careful to make sure Adrienne knew she wasn't crossing any boundaries.

Every time she made a point of saying it Adrienne wanted to crawl into a cave and hide.

She reached for her toothbrush and vigorously cleaned her teeth. After rinsing her mouth, applying a thin sheen of lip-gloss and a spritz of perfume, she drew herself up to her full height and stared at herself in the mirror.

Get a damn grip and get on with your damn job.

Pep talk over, she strode back into the bedroom and pulled on her jacket. The pantsuit was overkill for a day of watching golf, but it was almost her armor, reminding her just what her role was here today. Her one concession to the reality of the day was a pair of white Reeboks rather than her pumps. She tied the laces quickly before pulling her large bag over her shoulder and heading out of the room.

Jenny, Toby, and Diane were already down in the lobby, their equipment bags at their feet.

"Good morning," Adrienne said breezily as she reached them, and she gave them all her widest smile.

"Hey, boss. Here, coffee." Jenny thrust the large cup forward, and Adrienne took it gratefully.

"You, young lady, will go far in this business," she said, nodding sagely before taking her first sip.

"Suck-up," Toby said, then laughed when Jenny stuck her tongue out at him.

Diane, always the quiet one, rolled her eyes, but she smiled too.

"Okay, ready to go?" Toby asked, as he bounced on his toes.

Adrienne smiled and nodded, ignoring the lurch in her stomach.

The drive to the course took less than fifteen minutes, and no more than ten minutes after they'd arrived, they were walking toward the press area. It was a cool morning, but the sun tried vainly to break through the low, hazy cloud. Around them, small crowds of people flowed like water, excited chatter emanating from them like static on an old-fashioned radio.

Adrienne waved at everyone she knew, and with each step she took, her assuredness increased and her posture strengthened. All that poise almost deserted her, however, when she caught sight of Morgan coming out of the clubhouse with Harry, but she forced herself to keep her focus on remaining as professional as possible.

If only Morgan didn't look so delectable in the mint-green, short-sleeved polo shirt and white three-quarter-length pants, a white sweater draped over her shoulders, her tanned biceps on prominent display.

"Morgan!" Jenny called, furiously waving one arm. "Over here!"

Okay, here we go.

Adrienne pulled herself up to her full height and plastered a bright-but-not-overly-so smile on her face as she waited for Morgan to join them.

"Good morning," Morgan said quietly as she drew up alongside Jenny, who beamed in response.

Harry nodded at them all, clearly eager to get this part of the day over with as soon as possible, if his scowl was anything to go by.

Adrienne could empathize.

"Good morning," she replied. She made sure her eyes didn't linger on Morgan's for too long.

Morgan's gaze darted left and right; she looked as uncomfortable as Adrienne felt.

"So, ready to get out there and kick their butts?" Jenny asked, a chuckle in her voice.

Morgan visibly relaxed. She turned away from Adrienne and focused on Jenny. "You bet."

"Cool." Jenny flipped open her notebook. "We're going to be tracking your first round today, but I promise you won't even know we're there, okay? Right, boss?" She turned back to Adrienne, her look expectant.

"Absolutely," Adrienne said coolly. Her mantra of *stay professional, stay goddamn professional* cycled through her mind. "Please do tell us if we encroach on your boundaries at any point."

"You bet I will," Harry growled.

They all chuckled, but their laughter died quickly at the fierce look in his eyes.

Morgan appraised Adrienne, her eyes slightly narrowed.

Adrienne looked away, not daring to get caught in that gaze. "Okay, team, let's get set up and leave Morgan to do her own prep."

Toby and Diane smiled, and Toby tapped his head in a small salute before they both strode off toward the first tee.

"Good luck." Jenny smiled at Morgan, and a faint blush formed on her cheeks when Morgan smiled warmly back.

"Thank you."

Morgan flicked one last glance at Adrienne. It was brief, but the pain it illuminated cut Adrienne to the bone. Then Morgan turned and walked away, Harry smoothly falling into stride beside her.

Adrienne's stomach finally relaxed, but that did nothing to alleviate the ache in her heart.

"Goddammit," Morgan muttered as her tee shot on the fifteenth veered left, *way* too left.

"*Left!*" she shouted next, waving her arm to warn the crowd.

People ducked, threw their arms up over their heads, or gazed aimlessly at the sky, as they searched in vain for a small white ball dropping out of the cloud. From the sudden parting of a section of spectators near the path that paralleled the fairway, she had a pretty good idea where her ball had touched down and could now only hope it had a decent lie.

She reined in her temptation to hurl her driver into the shrubs that fenced in the tee and took two deep breaths before she turned and handed the club back to Harry, whose expression was impossible to read.

This was, without a shadow of a doubt, the worst round of golf she'd played in a *long* time. She was one over par, which didn't sound terrible unless you glanced up at one of the big scoreboards dotted around the course and saw that the leader was five under. Six shots behind and she still had this hole and three more to play.

Okay, so think positive. That's four chances to get some of those shots back. Although perhaps not on this hole, now that she'd gone so far left on her drive. But maybe the last three, each of which certainly offered the chance of a birdie—if only she could get her head back in the game.

I should never have agreed to this damn documentary.

She set off down the fairway, her strides purposeful.

I certainly shouldn't have kissed the damn documentary maker.

She tried hard to compose herself before she spoke to Harry.

"So," he said quietly and stepped in close. "If we're lucky, you're on some of that grass that's already been trampled by the spectators. Of course, you could be stuck behind one of those big-ass trees, in which case, we're fucked. Could be looking at playing some little squirt of a shot just to get back on the fairway."

125

"I'm sorry," she whispered, mortified as tears pricked at her eyes. Why the hell couldn't she get all her emotions back in the box she'd crammed them into the night before?

"Is there something going on? Are you sick?"

"No, I'm not sick. I'm..." God, this was hardly the time or place, was it? "Look, my head's just not here today, and I'm really sorry. I'll try hard to get out of the mess of this hole and focus on the next three. Maybe if I can grab birdies on two of them, that'll put me in a better position."

"It will, but I'll be honest, I don't really care about your score right now."

She risked a glance at him, and the worry on his face touched her even as it threatened to make her tears spill over.

Her gaze caught on movement parallel to Harry's shoulder. Adrienne. She and the team were walking the course as planned, and Morgan wished to hell they weren't. She'd tried so hard to ignore them, to ignore Adrienne. When they'd met first thing that morning, it was obvious Adrienne wanted to put the kiss behind them, doing everything she could not to look at Morgan or engage with her any more than she had to. So Morgan had tried to do the same, to be professional, cool, and collected. The trouble was she'd focused so hard on shutting Adrienne out of her mind, she'd lost her concentration on her actual game.

She pulled her gaze away from the stirring sight of Adrienne marching along in her navy-blue pantsuit, her bag slung across her shoulder, her leather notebook in one hand and a pen in the other. When she did finally manage to pull her gaze back, she found Harry staring at her, his expression knowing.

Morgan opened her mouth to speak, then shut it again. He wasn't stupid; he'd clearly figured it out. Nothing she said now would make any difference.

They marched on, veering to the left when they saw the section in the crowd that had been parted and pushed back by the course officials around where her ball had presumably come to rest. She summoned polite smiles for the crowd when they applauded and called encouragingly. Then she saw how her ball had landed and only just smothered a groan. It was, as Harry had feared, backed up behind one of the big-ass trees. *Shit.*

"Come on, Morgan!" someone yelled. "You can do it!"

You know what, my friend, I really don't think I can. Not this time.
She exhaled and turned to confer with Harry.

"I don't think she's ever played so badly."

Jenny looked visibly upset, and Adrienne bit back her irritation. They were here to do a job, not get so invested in the subject of their project.

Uh-huh. You should try remembering that yourself.

It had been painful to watch this round disintegrate for Morgan, she had to admit. She knew golfers had days like this, days where nothing quite worked and they could never quite pull it together. But seeing it happen to someone she knew and liked from up close was hard to witness. Especially when she felt responsible for it. The hurt in Morgan's eyes earlier made it crystal clear how she felt, so now Adrienne was racked with guilt over her role in putting Morgan off her game.

"Unfortunately, she's just having one of those days."

Adrienne knew it sounded trite, but the white lie was all she could muster. God knew she wasn't going to tell Jenny the truth. She fought so hard against an urge to walk over to Morgan and pull her close. To hug that frown off her face, smooth down her hair, and whisper soft words of encouragement and hope. *Why am I so drawn to her? Is it some latent maternal instinct I never knew I had?* It wasn't, though. She knew that for sure. There was nothing maternal at all about what she felt for Morgan Spencer.

She stayed where she was and settled for grinding her teeth in frustration. She watched Morgan size up the shot she needed to play. Adrienne knew Morgan would likely lose another shot on this hole and then only had three more to play to repair some of the damage. *And the way she's playing, that seems a remote possibility.*

Harry finally stepped back, the officials called for quiet, and Morgan approached the ball.

Adrienne leaned in next to Toby, who had zoomed his camera in to highlight Morgan, tall and steady, braced in position behind an ancient gnarly tree. Her face was the epitome of concentration as she took a few practice swings with her club. Toby had captured the scene perfectly, with the late morning sun shining directly on Morgan's face.

She's so beautiful.

Adrienne fought down a sudden surge of desire, her face heating at her own thoughts.

Supposed to be getting past that, remember?

Morgan settled, swung the club, and pitched the ball out from behind the tree. It landed on the fairway about twenty yards ahead. Polite applause surrounded them, and Morgan vaguely acknowledged it with a wave before turning back to Harry to hand him the club. As she did so, her gaze met Adrienne's. Morgan's eyes narrowed, and she shook her head, almost imperceptibly, then strode off the path and back onto the fairway.

Harry turned to see what she'd looked at, and he caught Adrienne's eye. His gaze was stern, yet there was something else there, something understanding.

Adrienne sighed and turned away.

"Everything okay?" Toby asked, shifting the camera on his shoulder.

"Yes," Adrienne replied, hoping she sounded more confident than she felt. "Fine."

The path at the back of the seventeenth green was as empty as Morgan had hoped. She scuffed the soft wood chips that covered the path and shoved her hands into the pockets of her windbreaker. The sun dipped down behind the trees that hid her from the rest of the course, and the temperature dropped along with it, although it was still warm enough to be pleasant.

What a disaster of a day. She'd finally carded a seventy-three, pulling one shot back with a sweet nine-foot putt on the seventeenth. Pars at the holes on either side meant she'd staunched the flow of awfulness that had dominated much of her round.

She'd skipped the press call afterward; she knew Hilton would not be happy about that, but really, what was the point? She knew what sort of questions she'd face, and she had no answers for them. Well, she had one but there was no way she was sharing that with anyone.

"Why did I play so badly? Oh, well, see, there's this woman I can't seem to get out of my head, and everywhere I looked today, there she was, tormenting me."

She chuckled. Yeah, that would go down *really* well.

Her phone buzzed in her pocket, and she pulled it out. Her mom. Again. She'd tried calling twice and now was messaging her.

I know today was hard, but you'll turn this around. I know you will. Stay strong, darling. Love you. Mom xx

Morgan ought to at least call her. She didn't need her mom's comfort—nothing would make this feel any better—but she had been brought up with good manners. Leaving her mom waiting too long for any sort of acknowledgement of her attempts to reach out was not something that would sit right with Morgan.

Harry had gone surprisingly easy on her, although he had suggested they meet a couple hours before her second round tee time to "go over a few things."

But Morgan knew the only thing that would fix what had gone wrong today was for her to get her head back to where it needed to be, and right now, wallowing in a tank of self-pity, she couldn't make that happen.

"Hey," a quiet voice said.

Morgan whipped round, heart pounding.

Adrienne stood on the path behind her, a long but light coat over her pantsuit, her hair a little mussed from the evening breeze.

"I...I saw you walk over this way, and I...I thought we should talk." Adrienne hadn't stepped any closer, her expression one of sad resignation.

Morgan didn't know whether to run or stay. Running would be easy, but staying and hearing what Adrienne had to say, although difficult, might at least help.

"Okay."

"I know I've been avoiding you." Adrienne shrugged. "But I pride myself on being a tad more mature than that, so here I am."

"I'm sorry," Morgan said quickly. "For what I did in the elevator the other day."

Adrienne shook her head. "There were two of us there that day. I could have stopped you much earlier than I did."

Morgan swallowed. She had to know. "Wh-why did you stop?"

Adrienne looked away for a moment. "Many reasons." She looked back up at Morgan. "We're working together. The age gap." She paused. "Fear."

Morgan's stomach lurched. "Fear?"

129

Adrienne's eyes widened, and she took a step closer. "Not physical fear!" Morgan's insides relaxed.

"No, simply fear of what it could mean to be involved with someone again, with…you." Adrienne sighed. "I'm sorry. For running away, for not explaining. But to be fair, I don't think I could have explained it that day. I needed some time to think it through." She shrugged again. "I am attracted to you. I won't lie to you about that. But I can't… This can't happen."

Morgan closed the distance between them, her spirits lifted to a level she hadn't felt in two days. Adrienne's confession of attraction laid to rest the doubts Morgan had been swamped with ever since the kiss. At least Adrienne hadn't run away because Morgan kissing her was the last thing she wanted.

"But if we're both attracted to each other, why can't this happen?" she asked softly. She stared intently into Adrienne's eyes, trying to read what she saw there.

Adrienne sighed. "Morgan, I just told you. I can't. Never mind the working relationship and the disparity in our ages. *I'm* not available. I don't have it in me yet to let someone else in."

"And if you did have it in you, could that someone be me?" She had to know, and she held her breath, waiting for Adrienne to respond.

"Morgan…" Adrienne looked away again. She jammed her hands in the pockets of her coat. When she finally looked back, her expression was one of deep regret, and Morgan's stomach plummeted to the floor. "No, it couldn't. I'm sorry. I… You're too young, and we're in different places in our lives." Before Morgan could interrupt her, challenge her, she plunged on. "I really want us to be able to work well together. I think this project is a great opportunity for you and for women's golf in general. I really just wanted to talk to you today so that we could set aside the…other things and find a way to get past them to get back to working together without this hanging over us."

Morgan bit back her disappointment. She wanted to fight Adrienne, tell her the age gap didn't matter, but if Adrienne felt it did, Morgan had no right to argue with her. She was crushed by the rejection but, at the same time, grudgingly impressed with Adrienne's honesty. So maybe now that she knew where Adrienne stood, and she didn't have to lie awake wondering, maybe she *could* push her attraction away. After all, she really didn't have time to be in a relationship, did she? And look what the distraction of a gorgeous woman had done to her game. That alone was reason enough to nod, murmur her agreement, and force a smile onto her face.

"You're right. Absolutely." She stood a little taller, working hard to believe her own words as she delivered them with a firmness that she hoped would convince Adrienne they were on the same page. "We're working on the same project, and that's all we'll need to focus on. Are you guys filming me again tomorrow?"

Adrienne blinked, as if startled at how quickly Morgan had turned herself around. *Isn't that what she wanted?*

"Um, yes. Well, not me. The team will be there, but they'll also be filming other players from the top ten to give us a balance. I'll be working on something else back at the hotel."

"Oh. Okay."

It was for the best, Morgan knew that. Maybe tomorrow, knowing Adrienne wasn't going to be there watching her every move, *maybe* she could relax and play some actual golf instead of the charade she'd managed today.

"I'll see you on Sunday, I expect," Adrienne said, and she smiled weakly. "I have every confidence you'll turn things around tomorrow and make the cut."

In spite of the disappointment coursing through her, Morgan snorted out a laugh. "Well, I'm glad someone does."

Adrienne looked quizzical. "You don't?"

Morgan sighed. "Actually, yes, I do. I just lost my focus today. I'll get it back by morning."

Adrienne's flush told Morgan she knew *why* that focus had deserted her, but neither of them said anything.

"Okay, well, I'll say goodnight, then." Adrienne offered her a small smile, warm yet sad.

"Want me to walk you back?"

"No, I'm good."

Morgan nodded, and Adrienne turned and walked back the way she'd come. Morgan watched her until the darkness of the trees swallowed her up.

Chapter 12

"AND YOU JUST LET HER walk away?"

Morgan withered under Charlie's scathing glare. "Uh…yeah."

When Charlie snorted, Morgan threw up her hands. "She's…she's bad for me! Look what happened to my game today. And she doesn't want me. She made that very clear."

"I call BS." Charlie drained the last of her soda and sat back, arms folded.

They were in Morgan's room, keeping away from prying eyes. After Adrienne had left Morgan alone in the gathering gloom, Morgan had wandered for a few minutes more, locking down her feelings, turning her thoughts to the golf, to the steps she'd have to take tomorrow to fix the mess she'd created by letting Adrienne unravel her.

Then she'd called Charlie. It was a big step, reaching out to a friend for help and advice at a critical point like this. Up until now, Morgan would have relied only on herself, battling through whatever troubled her, refusing to let anyone come to her aid. She'd had to be self-sufficient growing up; sure, her mom was a sweetheart, but she'd also been pretty good at brushing off emotions as something to be worried about another day. Although not so much lately, Morgan realized. She'd arranged to grab a quick breakfast with her mom in the morning—she had sounded very worried about Morgan when they'd spoken just before Morgan arranged to catch up with Charlie.

"Look, I know you're kind of romantic and you want me to have some big happy ending after what Naomi did. But I'm not sure that's really me."

"Again," Charlie said, rolling her eyes, "I call BS."

Morgan was close to throwing an actual tantrum—the urge to stomp her feet was strong. "Will you stop saying that? I know my own feelings."

Charlie sighed, unfolded her arms, and leaned forward. She placed a gentle hand over Morgan's on the small table between them. "I'm not saying you don't. But I do think you're scared." She held up her other hand. "And yes, I totally get why. Naomi broke your heart, and who wants to get out there again when their heart's all broken in pieces?" She smiled, understanding written in her hazel eyes. "I guess I just thought, from everything you said, that Adrienne was different. Worth it. Worth fighting for, even just a little. Because despite what she said this evening, I think she *does* want you. She's just scared too."

Morgan pursed her lips. "That might be true, but...I just can't. It's screwing with my head, and I can't have another day like today. I want to win a major," she said fiercely. She turned their hands so that she could grasp Charlie's. "And for that I need to be 100 percent focused on my game. No other distractions."

Charlie squeezed Morgan's hand, then let it go. "For now, I'll let you have that."

Morgan chuckled. "Why, how kind of you."

Charlie stuck out her tongue. "But I think you and I both know Adrienne is much more than a distraction. Or at least has the potential to be. So will you promise me one thing?"

With trepidation, Morgan slowly nodded.

"Don't shut her out completely. While you're working on this documentary together, you'll still need to spend time with her. Don't be an ass when you do."

Morgan snorted and laughed. "I'm never an ass."

Charlie smiled. "Yeah, actually, that's true. You're not." She stood up and pulled Morgan with her. As she hugged her close, Charlie whispered, "I just want you to be happy, you know? And I get that golf does that for you, but there *is* more than golf in that outside world. That's all I'm saying."

Morgan hugged her back. "Thank you for listening."

"Sleep well," Charlie said, then she pulled away and headed for the door. "See you on the course."

Morgan shut the door behind her and walked back into the room. She kicked off her sneakers and flopped onto her back on the bed.

Jeez, being a grown-up sucked sometimes. She remembered being a teenager, willing every school day to pass quickly so she could get home and practice shots on the small green-and-bunker combo her dad had built in the corner of their extensive backyard. He'd built it for himself, of course, but when he was on tour, Morgan would make the most of his absence and play out there for hours. It was an easy life, a life that had suited her perfectly. Her mom had worried about her lack of friends, yet at the same time was happy her daughter was home every night straight after school and not getting into any kind of trouble.

College was pretty much the same pattern: studying hard and golfing at any opportunity she got until she'd finally plucked up the courage to enter some amateur tournaments. Her father had scoffed at the idea, but she'd grown up enough by then to finally ignore what he thought. Well, mostly. Besides, once he realized how good she was, he'd come around, wouldn't he?

She blinked away tears. Yeah, so that hadn't happened yet. She vaguely wondered how he'd got on with his first day of calling the tournament. The remote was by the bed, and ESPN was bound to be showing a highlights reel on one of their channels. *Should I? Ugh, maybe not.* If he was an ass about the women's game, *her* game, that was the last thing she needed to hear today. A quick glance at the digital clock built into the TV told her it was 9:30 p.m.

Okay, rock star, let's call it quits for the day.

As she brushed her teeth, she worked some more on pushing images of Adrienne back into a box marked "secret" in the back of her mind.

Her mother stood as Morgan entered the hotel's breakfast room the next morning, and Morgan sighed as her warm arms embraced her.

"Hey, Mom."

"Hi, darling." Her mom held her at arm's length as she examined her. "Hm, you look a little tired. Did you sleep okay?"

Morgan shrugged. "As well as I could expect after a day like that."

She knew her mom would think she meant only the golf, and she was happy to keep it that way, not feeling the need to share the Adrienne situation with her. If nothing else, it would keep Adrienne out of her own mind.

Her mom sat back down, and Morgan slid into the seat opposite her.

"What happened?" her mom asked quietly. "I can't remember the last time you played a round over par."

Which was a polite way of putting it, Morgan thought with a wry smile. "Actually, I've had a few over-par rounds this year, but I know what you mean. I've been on a pretty good roll the last couple of months, so, yeah, a round like that hurts a little."

Her mom patted her hand. "You'll figure it out today, I'm sure."

"Yeah, I think I will."

And she actually believed it. Mostly she'd slept well, but more than anything she'd woken up with a new determination to be who she was meant to be: the world's number-one golfer. And to do that, she needed to go out there today and shoot her best round of the year. Of course, she did know it helped that Adrienne wouldn't be following her today or even be at the golf club. Did Adrienne really have other work back here in the hotel, or was she just using that as an excuse to stay away?

Okay, stop. You're doing it again—not supposed to be thinking about her, remember?

"And therefore I think I'll find myself a good spot on the eighteenth and watch you all finish."

Guiltily, Morgan realized she hadn't been listening to her mom. "Oh, okay, that sounds good."

The waitress appeared, and they placed their orders.

"Your father's already at the course, having breakfast with the team. He's enjoyed catching up with Lou again."

"Lou?"

"Oh, you remember, honey—Lou Thomson. Won a few tournaments when your father was at his peak. Cindy Thomson's father. You know, the girl on TV."

"Oh, right. Is Lou on the ESPN team too, then?"

"Well, yes." Her mom leaned in. "I heard Cindy got him a spot. Lou's had a little money trouble, you see, and Cindy, of course, being such a sweet girl, put in a good word for him."

I'll just bet she did. I can just imagine the demands or threats she made.

"You okay, sweetheart? You're frowning."

"Oh, sorry, Mom. Just thinking ahead to the day." *Why do I seem to be lying so much these days to the people who know me?*

"Are you worried?" Her mom's expression scrunched into concern.

Morgan sighed. At least with this question she could be totally honest. "A little. I know what I need to do to make it better, but you never know what's going to happen out on the course."

"I understand. But you know, you've always been so strong, ever since you were a little girl. I know you can do this. Please believe it yourself."

The words touched Morgan, and she smiled at her mom. "Thank you. Your support is very important to me."

Their food arrived, and they ate in companionable silence. When they'd finished and their plates had been cleared, her mom leaned in once more, her hands clasped together on the table. She looked nervous.

"So I was wondering, darling. How about having dinner with your father and me tonight? We haven't seen you in quite some time, so it would be nice if the three of us could sit down for a meal."

She wanted to say no because the last thing she needed in the middle of a tournament was any kind of tension with her dad. But if she said no, wouldn't that in itself create tension?

Ugh.

"Sure, Mom, that would be great."

For one brief moment, her mom looked surprised but covered it with a quick clap of her hands. "Lovely! I'll find out what time he's finishing up with the TV people, and I'll let you know."

"Sounds good." Morgan glanced at her watch. "Okay, gotta run."

As Morgan rose, her mom pushed back her chair and stood too. She held out her arms and enveloped Morgan in another warm hug.

"You go out there and show them, darling," she said in Morgan's ear. "I'll be waiting for you on the eighteenth."

"See you there," Morgan said through a tight throat.

Watching her on TV didn't count, right?

Adrienne rolled her eyes but still reached for the remote and found the ESPN coverage.

Lotte Karlsson lined up a monster putt at the tenth hole. Off to one side stood her playing partner for the day, Naomi Chase. Adrienne scowled out of pure reflex, then laughed at herself. Yeah, so this whole forgetting about Morgan except in a purely professional sense seemed to be going great.

She sat at the table she used as a desk and leaned her chin in her hands, elbows propped on the table.

When she'd followed Morgan out to the secluded pathway near the seventeenth the night before, it had seemed so clear in her head what she had to do. And even as she'd walked away, she was convinced she'd done the right thing for both of them. Then, alone in her room, mellowed from a glass of rather good Pinot Noir ordered from the hotel's bar, the doubts had started to creep in and then kept her awake half the night.

So here she was. Holed up in a small conference room in the back of the hotel, hiding from the world and trying to hide from her feelings. The main one of which was regret. But she had done the right thing, hadn't she? Like Tricia had said, Adrienne would be risking an awful lot to get involved with Morgan. Besides, she was too young, and they were both at very different points in their lives to be reckless and attempt to make something of this attraction they had. Except that every time they talked, they didn't actually seem to be so different…

Come on, focus! Get on with your work. You made your decision last night, and you can't back down now.

She stared at the notebook in front of her. What the hell was she actually supposed to be doing today?

"And here's Spencer at the fifth. Already two under today and in with a great chance of birdie here."

She swung round to stare at the TV. Two under after four holes?

Yes! Go, Morgan!

Knowing it was ridiculous, she held her breath as Morgan pulled the putter back, then made a good connection with the ball to send it on its way toward the hole. A couple moments later, it dropped in, dead center, and Adrienne let out a whoop as the sounds of the crowd's applause filtered out of the TV's speakers.

Her phone pinged next to her.

She's killing it today! This is awesome to watch!

Jenny, who had a ringside seat for what was so far a stellar round for Morgan.

And here I am, hiding away.

It was for the best. It really was.

Wasn't it?

Work had helped. After over two hours with only coffee to keep her company, Adrienne had finally detailed an outline for the next project she'd be working on: a pre-season look at next year's WNBA championship.

While one part of her grumbled at always being given the women's sports to work on, another part of her reveled in it because it gave her the opportunity to show those sports in the best light possible. At least her company made such shows and continued to promote women in sports, even if they were a tad sexist in always putting a female producer in charge.

She was using it to her sex's advantage, as much as she could, by hiring as many women to work for her as possible. She would have kept Toby on camera for the WBNA film, though, if it wasn't for the fact that he'd been offered a project that featured his favorite sport: Formula Three car racing. He had, however, recommended a female camera operator in his place, so Adrienne forgave him for his desertion. Diane would reprise her role on sound, and Jenny would be given more responsibility on this project. Adrienne hadn't worked as hard as she had to get to where she was without making sure she used her position to help those coming up behind her.

She'd left the TV on but muted the volume once she'd realized she did have to get serious about the plan she was working on, so now she swiveled in her chair and reached for the remote.

Kim Lee was on screen about to drive off at the last. The score box at the bottom left showed she was co-leader, on seven under for the tournament. A good score after only two rounds. Her drive, as always, was perfect.

The picture snapped to Morgan, taking her second shot at the sixteenth, and Adrienne's eyes widened when she saw Morgan's score box on screen: five under for the tournament, which meant she was six under for this round. And only two shots off the lead.

A broad smile painted Adrienne's lips, and pride for Morgan's abilities swelled her chest.

Maybe I'll find her later and congratulate her. A colleague would do that, wouldn't they? Or a friend?

"So Morgan's really pulled it around, hasn't she?" It was Lou Thomson's voice on the microphone, as the camera tracked Morgan's shot to where it landed just on the edge of the green. "I know we need to be neutral, but that's got to make you proud, Gordy."

"She's done well," came Gordon Spencer's voice. "But I don't think she'll make birdie there. She's landed too far from the hole. Could have done with half a club more. Besides, you know, there's a lot of golf left to play over the weekend."

You couldn't just say it outright, could you?

Adrienne tutted. What was it with that man? All he'd had to say was, "Yes, very proud," and then he could still have gone on with his cautious "there's a lot of golf left to play" comment. Why was it so difficult for him to openly praise his very successful daughter?

She angrily hit the mute button again, then pushed her chair back and intently watched the screen. Unfortunately, Gordy Spencer was right— Morgan didn't make a birdie on sixteen. She did make one on seventeen and parred the last, almost a mirror image of how she'd finished her first round. She'd shot a sixty-six, one of the best rounds over the first two days, and finished just two shots behind Kim Lee and So Park, the joint leaders, and one shot behind Laurie Schweitzer in second place.

The cameras caught Morgan walking off the eighteenth, laughing with Harry, who looked pleased. Well, as pleased as that gruff old face could manage. Morgan's smile was relaxed, and it pulled at Adrienne's heart. Bree Spencer, looking as immaculate as always, her blonde hair shining in the afternoon sun, appeared from the crowd and hugged her daughter. *At least someone in that family cares.*

Jenny called a minute or two later. "Did you see any of it?" she asked breathlessly. "She was incredible!"

"I caught the last couple of holes, yes. Good score."

"*Amazing* score! I overheard Schweitzer whining as she left the eighteenth. I think she's worried Morgan's gonna stomp all over her ass tomorrow."

Adrienne chuckled at the image that conjured up. It would be worth seeing.

"So how did the filming go today?"

"Really good. We got all the shots you requested and some good close-ups of all the current top ten. Toby'll get the first cut of them to you soon."

"Sounds good." Adrienne glanced at the clock on the wall. "Okay, in that case I'm going to grab something light to eat right now. Want me to get you guys something?"

"Thanks, but no. I think we're all going for beer and pizza later once we've wrapped up with you."

"Okay, then I'll see you back in the conference room when you return from the course."

"Cool. We'll see you there."

Adrienne leaned back in her chair and stretched her arms above her head.

"Toby, this is all really good. Thank you."

He grinned and closed the lid on his laptop. "Thanks, boss."

"You know, I think I'd be happy with you camping out at the eighteenth tomorrow and just getting some shots of the top ten finishing their rounds. I don't think we need to go in-depth again until the final round."

Everyone around the table nodded.

"Which means," Adrienne continued, "you all get the morning off."

"Yay!" Jenny fist-pumped.

Wide smiles from Toby and Diane indicated they shared Jenny's sentiment, and who could blame them? It was only a little after six, so they'd have a whole evening and morning to have some downtime.

Adrienne laughed and motioned them all out of the room. "Have a good evening."

"We're grabbing some beers. Want to join us?" Jenny asked, her eyes hopeful.

"No, I'm going to get out for some fresh air, then have an early night. But thank you anyway."

Jenny shrugged. "Okay, see you tomorrow."

When the others had left, Adrienne gathered up her stuff and sorted it neatly into her large shoulder bag. Her room was icy cold again when she returned to it, her complaint to the front desk clearly having made no difference. *I'll deal with that when I get back.* First, she needed to get out of this building and see some of the world outside.

She changed clothes, pulling on a pair of dark-blue jeans, a light-green sweater, a brown leather jacket, and brown ankle boots. Not sparing her makeup a second glance—however it had looked during the day would be fine now—she stuck some money in her pocket along with her room key and left, almost skipping down the hallway in her joy to be heading out.

The hotel was a few blocks from the old colonial center of Williamsburg, but Adrienne didn't care; a good long walk to literally stretch her legs was just what she needed. Besides, it was a mild night, so it wasn't like she'd freeze. She chuckled softly. It was actually warmer outside than it was in her room.

She walked at a good pace, taking in the sights around her but never slowing to linger. She finally stopped at the Governor's Palace, staring up at the impressive structure, allowing herself to focus only on the architecture and not the somewhat checkered history of its former inhabitants.

"Looks like someone else had the same idea," a voice said from a few feet away.

Adrienne turned. Her gaze took in the speaker, Charlotte McKinnon, but lingered on who stood next to her.

Morgan.

"Hi, I don't think we've been properly introduced," Charlotte said, and she stepped forward with her hand outstretched. "Charlotte McKinnon, but you can call me Charlie."

Adrienne smiled and hoped her voice wouldn't let her down in the middle of the bout of nerves that had just clutched at her stomach. She shook Charlie's hand. "Adrienne Wyatt. It's lovely to meet you."

"Hi," Morgan said. She shuffled from foot to foot a few paces away.

"Hi." Adrienne inhaled slowly, but before she could say more, Charlie raised a hand to her face.

"Oh, crap. I just remembered I'm supposed to be somewhere. I don't mean to be rude, but I've got to go."

She faced Morgan, who scowled.

"Where are you supposed to be?" Morgan asked Charlie, her eyes narrowed, her voice overly sweet.

"It's private." Charlie smirked. "I'll catch you later. Bye."

She waved at Adrienne and, before either Morgan or Adrienne could respond, strode off in the direction of the hotel.

Adrienne stared at Morgan, who stared back. Then they both smiled wryly.

"Sorry, she can be a little…" Morgan waved a hand in the air. "You know."

Nodding, Adrienne said, "Well done today. That was a fantastic round you played."

Morgan dipped her head at the compliment. "Thank you. It felt good. Everything just worked."

"I'm really pleased for you. I know you were struggling with…things yesterday, but I always had faith you could turn it around."

"Thanks. That…that means a lot." Morgan looked away for a moment. When her gaze returned to Adrienne's, there was a hopeful look on her face. "Want to take a walk with me?"

"I…"

"It could be a working walk," Morgan said quickly, with a small grin. "Just two people who are working on the same project taking a walk to discuss that very project."

God, she looked adorable. And irresistible.

"Okay, a working walk. I can do that." Adrienne's stomach tumbled.

Morgan's smile made Adrienne's nervousness completely worth it. It was the same kind of smile she'd worn when she'd stepped off the eighteenth green earlier that day. The smile that said Morgan was truly happy.

"So," Morgan said, as she stepped alongside Adrienne. She pointed south toward the Palace Green. "How about we head that way?"

Chapter 13

ADRIENNE, MORGAN HAD DECIDED, LOOKED good enough to eat. Except thinking *that* made her brain short-circuit and other parts of her body threaten to burst into flames. What she'd said about Morgan's round today had reached other less physical parts of Morgan too; being on the receiving end of a compliment from Adrienne made her heart skip a beat. And while Morgan wasn't too thrilled with Charlie's blatant attempt to push her and Adrienne together, right here and now, with Adrienne walking along beside her and looking as good as she did, she couldn't really complain.

"So I suppose one thing we need to think about is when to do the next sit-down interview," Adrienne said, bringing Morgan back to the moment.

Morgan sidestepped a small group of laughing teenagers before answering. "Okay. I thought you were going to leave that until much later? Perhaps once we're all in Europe for the British Open and the Evian?"

"Yes, that was my original plan, but now I'm concerned that will all get a bit hectic for you." Adrienne smiled sheepishly. "I mean, I need to get my film made, but you've got quite a few tournaments to play back-to-back."

"True, but I said at the start that if I was going to do this film, I'd do it properly. So if that means squeezing that interview in somewhere in Europe, then I will."

Adrienne slowed as they reached a crossing and looked tentatively up at Morgan. The glow from the streetlights that had just begun to come to life for the night made Adrienne's auburn hair look like molten lava. It was mesmerizing.

"There could be a solution that didn't involve you squeezing it in," Adrienne said quietly.

"What?"

"Let us come to your home before you fly out to Europe."

Morgan sighed. Adrienne really was treating this walk and their whole situation since they'd spoken yesterday as purely business. Bringing up doing an interview in Morgan's home only emphasized that. But keeping it business shouldn't make her feel so disappointed. *This was what you wanted, after all: no distractions from gorgeous TV producers.*

When Morgan didn't immediately answer, Adrienne rushed on. "Look, I know you said that your home is your private space, and I do respect that. But even a small glimpse, perhaps of you hanging out in your backyard, would really pique people's interest in you. And, you know, sponsor interest too."

"Can I think about it?" Morgan stared intently at Adrienne to try to convey how big a deal this was for her. She got what Adrienne said, but even so… "I promise I'm not just saying this to brush you off, okay?"

Adrienne nodded. "Okay. Let me know after the PGA?"

"I will."

They crossed the street and came upon the Fountain Garden.

"Oh, that's lovely," Adrienne said.

They leaned against the railing, standing close but not touching. Even so, Morgan was aware of Adrienne, every one of her senses on high alert.

"So what did you do today?" Morgan asked. "How does a TV producer fill her day when she's not watching her subjects?"

Adrienne chuckled and faced her. "It's all rather boring, actually. I was planning the timeline for my next project." She paused and blinked a couple of times. "And, you know, I did have ESPN on in the background. To see how all my subjects were doing."

"Oh." Did Adrienne just blush? "How was their coverage?"

Adrienne looked away. "It was fine."

"Well," Morgan said drily, "that's a ringing endorsement."

Adrienne snorted and turned back. "It was just that…" She stopped and stared up at Morgan.

Morgan was drawn inexorably to those stunning brown eyes. Suddenly, they seemed really close to each other, closer than they had been when they'd first stopped to admire the garden.

How did we end up right back here again?

"Morgan." Adrienne's voice was barely above a whisper.

"Yes?" Morgan swayed forward.

"I… This is wrong," Adrienne whispered, but she didn't move back or step away.

"So you keep saying," Morgan said with a hint of frustration. She knew she *could* step back, could stick to her own pledge to not get distracted by this woman, but knew in the next moment that was simply impossible.

Adrienne leaned in.

Morgan's gaze flicked to Adrienne's lips. "You drive me crazy," Morgan said softly. Her heart hammered.

"I don't mean to." Adrienne blinked. "I just can't…seem…to…"

Whatever she was going to say next was lost as she kissed Morgan. It was feather soft, but it sent a bolt of heat flashing through Morgan's limbs.

Morgan groaned, low in her throat.

Adrienne stepped back.

"Don't tease. Please," Morgan begged.

"It's not my intention to." Adrienne stroked Morgan's cheek, her fingers cool against Morgan's skin. "I don't know what to do about…this. About us. I tell myself it can't happen, but as soon as I'm alone with you, I…" She shook her head. "I'm too old for you," she murmured.

"I don't even know how old you are," Morgan said, and Adrienne's soft snort of laughter made her smile. "So how about you tell me, and then I can decide if that's 'too old.' Although I have to warn you, my parents have a pretty big age gap in their relationship, and they seem to have done okay."

Adrienne sighed. "I'm forty-nine. I'm eighteen years older than you. That's a *big* gap."

"Well, I would have taken at least five or six years off your age, so really it's only thirteen, and that's less than the gap between my parents, so…"

Adrienne shook her head, but she laughed. "We're from a different generation. You're still yet to peak in your career, and, hopefully, you've many years ahead of you at the top of this game. You've got parties to go to and sponsor events, and I'm really more of a stay-at-home woman, with—"

"Adrienne," Morgan said, and she cupped Adrienne's face in her hands. God, her skin was so soft. "Do you know what my favorite Saturday night involves?"

Sighing, Adrienne shook her head.

"It is *not* going to some hotshot's party or the latest club or whatever it is you think all women my age do." Morgan grinned. "It's sitting under a nice, warm throw on my couch with one of my favorite movies on TV and a pint of ice cream or maybe a beer or two." She rubbed small circles with her thumbs on Adrienne's cheeks. "Yesterday I convinced myself to let you walk away from the possibility of this, but now I don't think I will."

Adrienne quirked up an eyebrow. "Don't I get a say in that?"

Morgan smiled. "Of course. But that means we have to talk about it together. Yesterday you made all the decisions, and I let you. But not anymore."

"Hm, bossy much?" Adrienne's eyebrow rose even higher, but a smile danced around her lips.

"I like to think of it as assertive," Morgan said. She laughed when Adrienne rolled her eyes.

The loss cut deep when Adrienne gently stepped back, but she let her go.

"Can I think about it?" Adrienne repeated Morgan's question from a few minutes ago. "And just like you said, I'm not doing that just to get rid of you."

"Okay, I guess that's fair." Morgan stepped closer and dared to dip her head and brush another soft kiss over Adrienne's warm lips. The small moan she received in response made her stomach clutch in the most delicious way. "Please think quickly, though."

Adrienne shook her head as if coming out of a daze. "There is another element at play here." She pointed at each of them. "We work together. It is not a good move on my part especially to be seen...fraternizing with the subject of my film."

"Oh." Shit, she hadn't realized that. "How bad would it be for you?"

"Worst-case scenario? I could get fired."

"Ouch."

"So," Adrienne said, her tone rueful, "even if I did think we should see what this could be, we couldn't do anything about it until after the filming wraps." She shrugged. "I'm sorry, but I'm not risking my career for anyone. If that sounds harsh, well, that's too bad."

"No, it's okay. I'd much rather you were that honest with me." *God knows I could do with some of that in my next relationship.*

"Well, okay then." Adrienne stepped back again and pulled her jacket close around her body. "Maybe I should get back."

Morgan looked at her watch and swore softly. She was already late for dinner. "Me too. I'm having an early dinner with my folks. I can walk you back as far as the restaurant where I'm meeting them." She saw Adrienne's hesitation and smiled. "No ulterior motive. Just as working colleagues," she added with a grin.

"Just as colleagues," Adrienne agreed slowly, but she also grinned.

They walked briskly. Morgan worked hard not to look at Adrienne every minute or so. She also tried not to hope too hard, but Adrienne had opened a small window into the idea that they could take a chance on what was obviously between them, and it made Morgan's steps lighter and her mood lift considerably. Being with Adrienne was easy. Well, not easy in that they both, so far, had kept trying to fight this. But when they *were* together, the conversation flowed, and there seemed to be no pretense or dissembling of truth between them. With Naomi, every conversation had felt like a battleground, and it had worn Morgan out.

A couple minutes later, Morgan spotted the restaurant across the street and slowed her steps.

"This is my stop." She thumbed in the direction of the cozy-looking French brasserie.

Adrienne glanced across at it and nodded. "Looks lovely." She looked up at Morgan and smiled warmly. "Thanks for walking me."

"My pleasure. Will you be on the course tomorrow?"

Adrienne shook her head. "No, and the team will only be on the eighteenth. So you'll have a whole day of being left alone." She grinned. "I'm sure that's a pleasing thing to hear."

Morgan chuckled, then shrugged. "Harry will be thrilled."

Adrienne laughed.

"Actually, I think I'll kind of miss it," Morgan said. "Well, I'll miss seeing you."

If she'd thought about it in advance, she probably wouldn't have said anything quite so…sappy, but the effect the words had on Adrienne totally made it worthwhile. She softened, and—Morgan was pretty sure, even though the lowering dusk made it difficult to really know—she blushed, and a smile crept across her face.

Adrienne cleared her throat. "You're more of a charmer than you realize, I think."

"Well." Morgan shuffled from foot to foot, nervous excitement making her toes tap the sidewalk. "Charlie did say I should woo you."

Adrienne laughed. "Oh, she did, did she? So she knows about…?" She pointed between them.

"Oh, is it okay that I spoke about you to her? I totally trust her and—"

"It's fine." Adrienne smiled. "I spoke to a good friend of mine about you, so fair's fair."

"Uh-huh. And what did *your* friend say?"

Adrienne sighed. "Actually, she tried to warn me off."

"Oh?" Morgan's stomach plummeted to her feet.

"She's concerned about my career, amongst other things."

Morgan could tell Adrienne didn't want to elaborate on what those other things were, so she bit back her curiosity—and fear—and shrugged, trying to act as nonchalant as possible even though her insides churned.

"Well, I guess it's good to have a friend looking out for you."

"It is." Adrienne nodded. "But please don't take it personally. It's not really about you."

"It's okay. I understand." *Well, maybe.* "And, again, thank you for your honesty."

They stood in silence for a couple moments and simply gazed at each other.

"Okay, I'm going," Adrienne said eventually. "It was… This was nice. I'm glad we talked."

"Me too."

They stared at each other for a little longer before Adrienne smiled again, then continued walking up the street back toward the hotel.

Morgan watched her go. She chuckled as she realized how wide a grin she wore, then inhaled a deep breath before heading across the street to the brasserie.

The warmth of the place hit her the minute she opened the door. She quickly shucked out of her jacket and handed it to the coat check. The hostess approached and smiled when Morgan told her who she was meeting.

"Oh yes, of course, they're at the table. Let me take you through."

Her parents sat at a table near one of the windows, a small glass of wine before each of them and closed menus beside them. They'd clearly been here a while, and Morgan braced herself. Tardiness was not an admired trait in her family.

"Hi, I'm sorry I'm late," Morgan said as she quickly slid into her seat.

"Who was that woman?" her father asked instantly, his tone hinting at barely repressed annoyance.

Morgan blinked, then glanced out the window. *Oh shit, prime view.* She inhaled slowly and willed herself not to blush. "That was Adrienne Wyatt, the producer and director of the TV documentary."

"Oh?" Her mother's eyebrows rose majestically.

"What did she want at this time of night?" her father asked before Morgan could react to her mother.

Shit. "Um, we were just, you know, discussing the next moves. Shots, I mean."

Her father looked pointedly at his watch. "And you couldn't get away sooner, considering you were meeting us?"

"I really am sorry, Dad. I didn't realize how late it had gotten."

How did he do this practically every time? Make her feel like she was about eight years old and being scolded for some childish misdemeanor?

"Oh, Gordy, she's not *that* late," her mom offered, peacekeeping as usual. "We've barely looked at the menu."

"I know what I'm having," he said, still staring at Morgan as if he could drill into her mind for her secrets.

"Well, let me quickly choose, and then we can catch up." Morgan opened the menu, grateful for a moment's respite from her father's glare. She spotted a Niçoise salad and shut the menu. "I'm ready."

Her mom caught her eye and gave her a gentle, understanding smile.

Morgan swallowed, blinked, then reached for her water glass so she'd have something to do other than blurt out everything to her mom. She'd barely had time to process everything she and Adrienne had talked about, but she couldn't shake off the hopeful excitement that warmed her blood and body. Adrienne hadn't outright said no, and those brief kisses they'd shared by the garden were cause enough to give Morgan joy at what might become of them.

Woo her, Charlie had said. Well, she hadn't exactly made any progress in that respect, but she had apparently charmed her, so there was that.

"Morgan! Didn't you hear what I said?"

It was her father, and his frown made it abundantly clear he was pissed.

"Sorry, Dad." Her face burned. *Come on, focus!* "Could you repeat it?"

He tutted. "I asked what time you were teeing off tomorrow. I haven't seen the start list yet."

The waiter arrived at that point, which gave Morgan another couple minutes to get her head in this game. It was one she didn't actually want to play but it always transpired whenever she and her father had to spend more than five minutes with each other.

After the waiter left with their orders, Morgan sat up a little straighter in her chair and answered her father. "I'm at 1:30 p.m., as I'm in the penultimate group. I'll be playing with Laurie."

Her father grunted and took a sip of his wine.

"What's it like playing with her?" her mom asked.

Morgan grinned. "She's tough. She doesn't like to chat on course, and she can be a little, you know"—she leaned in and lowered her voice—"stuck up. She's pretty conceited."

"Morgan," her dad snapped. "There's no need for that."

Morgan stared at him, her irritation rising. "For what?"

"Gossiping about other players," he responded. He clasped his hands in front of him on the table.

And here comes the lecture.

"In my day, professionalism was everything. We all respected each other. We all worked well together. Yes, we all wanted to win but not at the cost of our dignity."

"Dad," she said carefully, "I wasn't gossiping. Mom asked for an opinion. I gave it. I have the greatest respect for Laurie—she's done a huge amount for the women's game, not just here in the US but around the world."

"I'm going to the restroom," he said and stood.

As he walked away, Morgan caught her mom's eye.

"How are you, Mom?" There was no way she was going to reference what had just occurred.

"Oh, I'm fine, darling." Her mom leaned in, also seeming happy to ignore what her husband had said before he left the table. "You seem... happy. Well, not that you were unhappy, but you know..."

Morgan smiled. "I had a good day today."

"Are we only talking about golf?" Her mom's eyes twinkled.

Waggling her hand back and forth, Morgan chuckled.

"She's beautiful," her mother said, and Morgan knew she had easily put two and two together. *She always could read me so well.* "I mean, I only saw her from across the street but even so."

Morgan nodded. "She is. And it's not just on the outside. She's a lovely person and wonderful to spend time with."

"And what sort of time *are* you spending with her, hm?" Her mom grinned conspiratorially.

"We're...negotiating that." Morgan smiled. "There may have been some progress on that this evening."

"Well." Her mom sat back and lifted her wine glass. "Here's to more progress if it makes you this happy."

Morgan touched her mom's glass with her own, and they sipped.

Morgan's father returned and retook his seat, wincing slightly as he did so.

"You okay, Dad?"

He grunted and made a chopping motion with his hand in the direction of his hip. "Just this acting up. It's rather cold in the studio, and sitting around all day didn't help."

"Are you enjoying the work?"

He shrugged. "It's okay. I'd rather be doing a proper tournament, but it's a start."

Morgan bristled at his words. "'*Proper*'?"

He waved off her protest. "You know what I mean." He lifted his wine glass and took a healthy mouthful.

"Actually," Morgan said icily, despite her mother's warning glance, "I don't. Please enlighten me."

Her father glared at her. "We are not doing this now. We're here to eat."

"Oh, no, you started it, so you can finish—"

"Don't be so childish," he snapped.

Morgan made to retort, but the waiter appeared to deposit their meals on the table. Under the table, she felt her mom's hand come to rest on her knee and squeeze gently.

With every ounce of mental strength she possessed, Morgan swallowed back—again—all the words she wanted to say and picked up her fork. She shot her mom a quick glance, a look that said, "Okay, I'll keep quiet," and concentrated on her food, even though her stomach was in knots and her pulse thudded painfully in her veins. She really didn't know how much longer she could keep on keeping quiet.

Chapter 14

HARRY RAISED HIS BEER. "YOU didn't win, but I'm proud of the way you turned it around."

Morgan smiled and tapped her glass to his. "Thanks. I really don't feel so bad about this one. Me and Laurie didn't stand a chance once Kim and So raced ahead."

She and Laurie had tried, pushing each other to try to catch the Koreans during the last round, but having both started the day three shots behind Lee in second place, it was a big ask. Although Laurie had shot a sixty-eight and Morgan a sixty-seven, the Koreans had each shot a sixty-seven, with So Park taking the Women's PGA title by one shot from her compatriot Kim Lee. Morgan was delighted with her third place, all things considered.

"Yeah, I heard they were sinking thirty-footers like they were nothing. We were all outclassed this week." He paused, tilting his head to one side. "But what else was going on this week? Is there something I need to know?"

Morgan blinked, unsure how to answer. She knew Harry would be asking for two reasons. One, would whatever it was affect her play, and two, because he cared about her as a person. They didn't do emotional stuff, though. Not really. So telling him everything, even though she suspected he'd guessed the basics already, would feel a little awkward.

"Is it Adrienne?" Harry asked, eyes narrowed.

Her face burned.

Harry chuckled.

"I ain't blind," he said, shaking his head. He picked at the edges of the paper coaster his beer glass rested on. "And, you know, we don't have to talk about these things." His voice was gruff. "But a happy Morgan makes a better golfer, so…" He shrugged.

Morgan's heart swelled with affection for this man who'd stood by her for so long.

"Yes, it's Adrienne," she said. She kept her voice low; there were plenty of people from the tour in the bar, the official end-of-tournament dinner having finished around half an hour earlier.

"But it's good, right?"

Morgan smiled. "Let's just say, I'm hopeful. We talked, and, well…"

Harry held up a hand. "It's okay. You don't need to tell me anything else. As long as you're okay."

"I am. Promise."

Harry opened his mouth to speak, then his gaze flicked away and narrowed.

"What?" Morgan itched to turn around and see what had caught his eye.

"Cindy Thomson and Naomi have their heads together in a corner," he murmured before bringing his gaze back to Morgan. "And that can't be good."

Harry had never liked Naomi for Morgan, she'd always known that, but she was surprised at the venom in his tone when he spoke Cindy's name.

Morgan took a quick peek over her shoulder. Yep, there they were, sitting close together, their conversation animated but certainly looking friendly enough. She hadn't realized they knew each other that well. But then, there were a lot of things Naomi had kept from her.

"Hm," she murmured, and turned back to look at Harry.

He grimaced and picked up his beer. "That Thomson woman is in the class of journalists I warned you about. In fact, from what I hear, she's one of the worst. Watch yourself with her."

"I will."

Morgan was about to ask him how he knew all this stuff when he nodded at something behind her.

"Incoming."

Before Morgan could respond, a chirpy voice called, "Hey, Morgan!" and she turned to see Jenny bounding the last few steps up to their table.

"Oh, hi, Jenny."

154

"Sorry, am I interrupting?" Jenny's eyes went wide as her gaze moved from Morgan and Harry.

"No, not really. We're just having a last beer and shooting the breeze after the day." Morgan mustered up a bright smile, trying to forget about Cindy and Naomi and whatever they were up to.

"Oh, okay. Well, I just wanted to say well done." Jenny blushed slightly. "I think you did really well, especially after, well, you know, that first round." Her blush deepened. It was kinda cute.

Harry rolled his eyes at Morgan over the top of his glass and drained his beer. "You know what, I'm done. Morgan, I'll see you for breakfast, yeah?"

"All right. About eight, okay?"

He saluted her and wandered off with a murmured "Good night" in Jenny's direction.

Jenny looked like a rabbit caught in the headlights. "Sorry, did I...? I mean, is he leaving because of me?"

"No, he's just tired." *I bet he isn't. He's made it pretty clear he doesn't have much time for TV people, as he calls them.* Morgan smiled and motioned to Harry's vacated seat. "Want to sit down?"

Morgan wasn't quite ready to call it a night, but neither did she want to sit here alone in case either Cindy or Naomi got any dumb ideas about approaching her. Besides, Jenny was fun company, and it might be nice to hang out with her for a while. Of course, she'd rather hang out with Adrienne, but apart from exchanging a few casual text messages the last couple days, Adrienne had left Morgan to play golf, and Morgan had left Adrienne to that thinking time she wanted.

It had been the right move. Morgan *had* been able to focus completely on her game, and from the tone of Adrienne's messages, Morgan knew she was appreciative of the space Morgan gave her. They were meeting for coffee after breakfast. Ostensibly to talk about the next steps for the project, but Morgan was hopeful they'd talk about "them" too.

"That would be great," Jenny said as she eased into the chair. Her hair, which changed color on a weekly basis as far as Morgan could tell, was currently black on one side, bright red on the other—even her bangs were half and half.

"Your hair looks good," Morgan said with a grin. "I'd never be brave enough."

Jenny laughed and visibly relaxed. "Thanks. I never really think about it being brave. I just love bright colors and figure that doesn't have to stop at my clothes."

"Do you want a drink?" Morgan asked, spying the waitress walking in their direction.

"Oh, sure." Jenny faced the young woman. "Can I get a rum and Coke?"

"No problem," the waitress said with a smile.

Morgan took a sip from her light beer. "I can't wait for November, when I can have a real drink again."

"You really don't drink during season?"

"I try not to. Some of the early starts and all the travel really don't fit well with hangovers. And I am a bit of a lightweight when it comes to alcohol anyway. Always have been. So the occasional light beer during season, but I indulge a little over Thanksgiving and Christmas."

"And where do you spend the holidays?"

"Oh, with my family. And you?" Morgan asked it quickly, hoping to head off any family-related questions.

Jenny's smile was small, and she didn't answer straight away, pausing as the waitress placed her drink on the table. Once she'd walked away again, Jenny took a sip, then responded.

"I usually spend it with my chosen family. Some really good friends from college." She hesitated. "My family disowned me when I came out. I don't have any contact with them."

"God, I'm sorry to hear that." Morgan shook her head. "I will never understand families like that."

Jenny shrugged. "They're very religious. I was brought up in the faith but just couldn't reconcile it to who I really was. I thought they'd feel differently if it was their own daughter, but I got that wrong, it turns out." Her chuckle was humorless. "I was out the door, with my bags at my feet, before I could even blink." She took another pull on her drink. "Still, I had this great group of friends who all rallied round, and within hours I was living in someone's guest room."

"Well, I'm glad you had them."

"Me too."

"So how did you end up working for Adrienne?"

Jenny's entire demeanor lifted, and her smile was wide. "Oh, that was part luck, part me being pushy."

Morgan laughed. "Okay, now you have to tell me more."

Smiling, Jenny leaned forward and launched into a tale involving a presentation Adrienne had delivered to Jenny's media class at college, Jenny trailing her afterward to a coffee shop downtown, and then informing Adrienne why she'd be the perfect assistant Adrienne never knew she needed.

"I still can't believe she didn't just get up and walk out of the coffee shop," Jenny said with a grin. "She told me after it was because her feet were hurting so much from the heels she'd worn that day, she literally couldn't face getting up again. She figured she'd be able to tune me out, just make noises like she was really listening until I went away." She sat up like a strutting peacock. "But I totally wowed her, and she was mesmerized by my pitch."

"Well, she must have been because here you are."

"Yep. Best job *ever*. I love it."

"What's she like to work for?" *Hm, fishing much?*

"Oh, she's amazing. She's so cool about sharing stuff that I know other managers keep to themselves. She's not all about protecting her own job to the detriment of anyone else. I kinda suspect that might be her age. I figure she doesn't want to still be doing this when she's, like, eighty, so she's happy to pass things on to give me a chance at establishing myself. I guess, too, she knows I won't crap all over that. She's been too nice for me to turn around and kick her in the ass."

"Yeah, she seems like she always encourages all of you to think for yourselves and take some chances from what I've seen of you all working together."

It was wonderful to hear that Adrienne was that good a manager. It fit with everything Morgan had already learned about her and made her even more admiring of the woman she was becoming so attached to.

Jenny nodded. "Oh, yeah. I know Toby loves working with her because she gives him so much freedom with shooting angles, et cetera. She doesn't seem to have any of the control freak tendencies I hear other PAs moan about." She smiled and blushed. "I could talk about her for hours. She's kinda my hero."

"I get it. I sort of feel that way about Harry, believe it or not."

"Harry? The grumpy one?" Jenny grinned.

"Yeah, he's a grumpy old grizzly on the outside, but trust me, that guy's been there for me for a long time. I can't imagine working with anyone else."

"Yeah, I can see that with you two. It's sweet."

Morgan snorted. "Don't let him hear you say that."

Jenny laughed, and they easily fell into a discussion of the tournament's highs and lows and what they thought might play out in Miami. Jenny was very knowledgeable about the women's game, and although sometimes Morgan felt her questions were bordering on pure gossip collection, Jenny did seem to have the utmost respect for all the players.

"So how come you're skipping Miami this year?" Jenny's next question seemed innocent enough, but there was something in her eyes that told Morgan she knew all about Naomi.

"Well, when we worked out the schedule for this year, we took into account what happened last year." Jenny's eyebrows shot up, but Morgan plunged on before her obvious question. "Playing Miami, then flying straight out to the UK to play both the Scottish and British Opens was all a bit much. I arrived at Sunningdale feeling pretty tired, and we're sure that played a part in me not winning there."

If Jenny was disappointed in the work-related answer and not the lowdown on the Naomi incident, she hid it well, to her credit.

"Oh, yeah, that totally makes sense. It's a pretty heavy season for you all."

"It is. It's always a juggling act, working out who to disappoint each year."

"Well, *I'm* disappointed I won't get to hang out with you more in Miami," Jenny said with a smile that suddenly went a step beyond friendly. "But maybe we could do this again in the UK?"

"Sure," Morgan said but alarm bells clamored in her mind. She ostentatiously looked at her watch. "Damn, sorry, I think I'd better go. I've got a couple of calls to make before I go to bed."

Jenny looked crestfallen for a moment, then rallied and smiled perkily. "Oh, of course!" She stood as Morgan did. "It was great talking with you."

"It was." Morgan smiled in a way she hoped was warm without being *too* warm. "I'll see you in a couple weeks."

"Yes, you will." Jenny's smile promised an awful lot if Morgan wanted to go there.

Doing her best not to be too obvious about it, she walked away as fast as she could.

"Okay," Adrienne said as she reached for her purse. "I'm off to have a quick meeting with Morgan. I suspect you might be gone by the time I get back, so have a good trip."

Jenny smiled from across the room where she was busy stuffing her carry-on with notebooks, pens, and her laptop. "Thanks, boss. And say hi to Morgan for me, will you?"

There was a gleam in Jenny's eyes that created a small knot of unpleasantness in Adrienne's belly.

"Oh, um, sure." Adrienne watched as Jenny grinned and continued packing her bag. "Jenny," she began, then stopped. How could she phrase this without sounding like she was accusing Jenny of something she'd already said she wouldn't do? She had to trust Jenny, didn't she, or what kind of message would that send?

"Hm?" Jenny didn't look up, distracted by the fact that her large bag of peanut butter M&Ms wouldn't quite fit in the side pocket of her bag.

Adrienne exhaled slowly. "Nothing. Call me tomorrow."

"Sure thing."

She gave her assistant one long last look and did her best to quash her discomfort. God knew she had enough to be uncomfortable about without adding Jenny and any possible inappropriateness into the mix.

The two days of not seeing Morgan had been good, just what she needed to sort through the maelstrom of emotions, fears, and worries their heart-to-heart had created. That Morgan had respected her need for some distance only made her admire her more, and she'd had to accept that Morgan's age meant nothing as far as her maturity went. In fact, in thinking things over, she'd come to realize that immediately judging Morgan for her relatively young age was probably just as bad as someone else judging *her* for her older age. Adrienne hated it when she was on the receiving end of it, so why had she thought it was okay to do the same to Morgan?

Because it was an easy excuse to use. *Yes, albeit with some merit—we are, after all, from an entirely different generation.* But using Morgan's age to immediately discount her, despite how strongly Adrienne was attracted to her—and vice versa—was a coward's way out.

And Adrienne Wyatt had never been a coward.

As she exited the elevator in the hotel lobby, she inhaled a couple of deep breaths. Now composed, she walked around the corner to the bar. Morgan wasn't yet there, so Adrienne took a table and ordered a pot of coffee from the waitress.

"Hi, Adrienne."

She looked up, expecting to see Morgan even as her brain registered the voice wasn't quite right.

"Cindy," Adrienne managed to reply, her entire being automatically going into a high state of alert. What the hell did Cindy Thomson want?

"Waiting for someone?" Cindy motioned to the chair on the opposite side of the table.

"Um, yes, actually."

"Oh, well, I won't keep you. I just want to hear how the filming's going."

Cindy looked and sounded pleasant enough, but there was an overly bright glint in her eyes that said something different and a hint of... triumph in her tone?

"It's going well, thank you."

"Excellent. I'm still available for all the voiceover slots, you know."

Over my dead body.

"Thanks, but we already have Annika lined up for that." *You know, a real golfer.* "But surely you must be busy enough with the Golf Channel?"

That seemed to take some of the glimmer out of her gaze. "Oh, of course. I just thought you might need a favor, given how difficult things had been."

"Difficult?"

Now Cindy's smile turned feral. "Oh, yes, with Morgan Spencer. Such a diva," she whispered conspiratorially. "I'm surprised you haven't walked away already."

Flummoxed, Adrienne used all her experience of working in the industry to affect a casual air. "Oh, I think you're misinformed. Morgan's a joy to work with."

"Oh, really?"

Cindy leaned forward and patted Adrienne's shoulder, and it took all her strength not to flinch. She noticed Cindy's way-too-perfect hair didn't move one strand as she chuckled nastily, her shoulders jiggling. Was it spray-painted on?

"Well," Cindy continued, "actually, yes, I imagine you two would work well together, all things considered."

What the—?

"Cindy, I—" Adrienne attempted to rise from her seat.

"Oh, gosh, is that the time? I need to get going. Ciao."

She threw Adrienne a vicious grin, and then she was gone before Adrienne could wrestle her to the ground and beat the answer out of her. Just what the hell had she meant by all that?

"What did *she* want?" Morgan asked a few moments later as she approached the table, deep suspicion in her tone.

"I have no idea," Adrienne said tightly. The exchange had rattled her, and *that* annoyed her.

Morgan sat down and smiled at her, which helped. A lot.

"Sorry." Adrienne exhaled loudly. "She just… God, I don't even know how to explain it. I think she was accusing me of something, but if it's what I think it is, how could she know?"

"Huh?"

Morgan looked so confused, her forehead scrunched into a deep frown, that Adrienne couldn't help but burst out laughing.

"God, sorry, ignore me! I'm probably imagining it."

"Okayyy."

Adrienne sighed and leaned forward. They'd said they'd be honest, so… "I think she was obliquely accusing me of having some involvement with you that isn't entirely work related."

Morgan's eyes widened, and she sucked in a breath. "Seriously?"

Adrienne nodded and reached across the table for the coffee pot, then poured them each a cup, relieved her hands didn't shake.

"But how could she know?"

Adrienne smiled wanly. "I don't know. And it's not like there's a lot *to* know."

Morgan grinned. "Oh, I don't know. There *was* one rather heated moment in an elevator, I seem to recall," she said quietly.

Adrienne's face warmed, and she shook her head. "Stop that."

Morgan laughed as she picked up her coffee. "Can't. Won't," she said, before taking a sip.

There was a new confidence in her that was deeply attractive and had Adrienne in need of a fan.

"You seem…different," she said eventually.

Now it was Morgan's turn to blush. "Maybe I am. A little."

Adrienne bit at her bottom lip. She needed to steer this back to easier ground. "You had a good last couple of rounds. Are you happy with how it went? I know it's another major gone by, but…"

"No, I'm good. I screwed up in the first round, and I probably wasn't ever going to get back from that. But I am pleased with what I did this weekend. And now, with a week off, I think I'm going to go to Britain in much better shape than I did last year."

"I'm pleased for you, then. That's good."

"Thank you." Morgan sipped a couple of times from her coffee, then set the cup down. "So, um, how are you?"

"I'm…good."

Adrienne's gaze wandered over Morgan's features. She hadn't realized until now just how much she'd missed seeing her and being able to soak up her beauty. Especially since the tender moments they'd shared the last time they'd been together. And remembering that jogged her into action. "Listen, I have been doing that thinking I promised."

"You have?" Morgan sounded nervous.

Adrienne nodded and smiled, trying to infuse it with as much warmth as possible. "I have. And I… Well, I have decided that perhaps you, and Charlie, are possibly correct."

Morgan's mouth quirked up at one side, and her eyes crinkled. "'Possibly correct'?" she mimicked.

Rolling her eyes, Adrienne leaned forward. "Yes." She nodded slowly. "There might be something here," she said. She gestured between them and chuckled when Morgan snorted. "And it possibly is something we should pursue." As Morgan's face lit up, Adrienne held up a hand. "But not until after we've finished the project."

Morgan slumped back in her chair, but she smiled. "I guess that's as good as I could have hoped if I'm honest. And I completely understand."

"You sure? I don't want you to think I'm leading you on, or—"

"Adrienne, no, I don't think that at all."

God, the way she says my name...

"Okay," Adrienne croaked.

Morgan leaned forward again, her gaze intent. "But please don't tell me I can't spend time with you. I want to get to know you, to hear about your life, your dreams, your world." She fiddled with her coffee cup. "I'm not very good at talking about feelings and all that, and I don't want to sound like some sappy movie, but when I'm around you, I like how I feel. And I want to keep that feeling."

Oh God, she's going to break my heart, isn't she? Adrienne shook off the thought. *Come on, don't be a pessimist.*

"Actually, I think you're very good at talking about your feelings if that's anything to go by." Her voice was husky. "And no, I won't tell you not to spend time with me because then I'd be depriving myself of something I want too. Very much."

Morgan's smile lifted her worried features in an instant, and there it was, that shining beauty, dazzling Adrienne with its luster.

"Well, then that's good," Morgan said softly. "So I was doing some thinking too. How would you like to do that interview in my home this week? I'm feeling pretty relaxed, and I have a few days, so..."

"I would like that very much. And not just because it fits my documentary." Adrienne smiled shyly. "I'd be honored to see your home and learn some more about you in a place where you feel so comfortable."

Morgan nodded slowly. "Okay, then let's set it up." She grinned. "Is tomorrow too soon?"

Adrienne's laugh was rich and long.

Chapter 15

RENATA GLARED AT MORGAN FROM across the kitchen. "Miss Morgan, stop watching me. You are making me nervous. You are like a hawk."

Morgan startled and focused on Renata's worried face. "God, sorry! I didn't even realize I was doing it."

Renata chuckled and shook her head. "You don't usually get nervous about my cleaning. What is going on?"

Renata's familiarity wasn't overstepping. Morgan had been very clear from the start of their arrangement that Renata was not a servant. Over the last couple of years, she'd come to think of Renata as a kindly aunt, always looking out for Morgan. And clearly her aunt-like instincts were in full flow.

Morgan groaned and swept her hands through her hair. "Someone special is coming to visit."

"Special?" Renata's eyebrows rose, and her eyes widened. "A special lady, perhaps?"

Face hot, Morgan nodded.

Renata grinned and shook her finger at Morgan. "Why did you keep this a secret?"

Morgan shrugged. "Didn't want to jinx it?"

"Hah!" Renata chuckled. "*I* am the superstitious one, remember?"

Morgan laughed. Oh yes, Renata had a multitude of superstitions, every one of which, as far as Morgan could recall, she'd managed to break, much to Renata's horror.

"Maybe you're finally rubbing off on me." Morgan smiled.

Renata laughed out loud and, to Morgan's relief, returned to wiping down the polished breakfast bar. "Don't worry, Miss Morgan, I will have the house sparkling from top to bottom."

"Thank you, Renata." Morgan walked round the breakfast bar and gave Renata a quick hug. "You're the best."

"Oh, shush," Renata said, but her blush and her bright eyes told Morgan she appreciated the gesture and words more than she would let on.

Deciding she really should leave Renata to do her job, Morgan left the kitchen and strode down the hallway to the workout room. Since she was a bag of nerves, she knew a run on the treadmill would help. Within minutes, she had changed and paced easily on the machine, the Black Eyed Peas pounding from the room's inbuilt music system.

Despite her best efforts, her mind insisted on drifting to the next day, when Adrienne would be here in the house. She would bring a local crew, with Jenny, Toby, and Diane off in Miami, but had promised to keep their time in Morgan's private space to a minimum. Morgan wanted more time with Adrienne, not less, and wondered how she could convince the beautiful TV producer to stay for dinner in the evening.

Well, I guess I just need to ask her, she thought wryly.

Charlie's words came back to her, and she wondered just how hard she'd have to try to woo Adrienne into spending that time together. She also needed to make a final decision on what to cook if Adrienne did decide to stay. Morgan didn't get much time at home to cook, but she enjoyed it when she did, and she'd been complimented on her skills over the years. It would be nice to do that for Adrienne, given what she'd said about eating out on the road all the time.

Okay, so in that case, something light... Her mind started whirring. A big smile plastered itself across her face as she pounded the treadmill and worked her way through the many options in her culinary repertoire to present the tastiest yet healthiest menu to her guest. *Here's hoping she says yes; otherwise, I'll be eating all that lovely food alone.*

Adrienne didn't know whether to be grateful or annoyed that she had two other people with her as the cab dropped them off outside Morgan's home at a little after 3:00 p.m. on Wednesday. Late last night, when she hadn't been able to sleep for thinking about Morgan, she'd seriously considered calling the whole thing off. Only the realization that she'd have to explain the cost of the crew with no film to back it up had stopped her from picking up the phone; cancelling that late in the day, she would have had to pay for everything regardless.

So we'll just get in and get out. Quick and easy. Two hours tops.

And all the while two chaperones making sure Adrienne didn't give in to her increasingly swoon-worthy fantasies of throwing herself into Morgan's arms and letting their mutual desire run away with itself.

This is ridiculous.

She'd never been so…giddy. *You're going to be fifty next birthday. Get a hold of yourself.*

But she couldn't. Thoughts of Morgan filled her mind constantly. Had she ever been so enamored of Paula? Surely she had in the early days. Hadn't she? She racked her brain for the memories, but they wouldn't come, overshadowed by everything that had happened since. Unwittingly, an image of Paula and her much younger lover crept into Adrienne's mind, and she swallowed hard. *You'll be just like Paula if you follow through with this. People will point and laugh and ridicule you.*

Yes, but Tricia said Paula's doing okay with it, so why can't you?

Only just stifling a groan, she climbed out of the cab and shut the door behind her. As the crew—Tina on camera and Cheri on sound—lifted their gear from the trunk, Adrienne gazed up at the house before them. It wasn't huge, not by the standards of the area they'd just driven through, but it seemed exactly the sort of house Morgan would choose to live in. Not too fussy, no grand entrance, yet full of character.

"Wow, nice place!" Tina whistled.

Adrienne smiled, then led her two charges to the front door. It swung open as they approached.

"Hey," Morgan said cheerily from just inside the door, but Adrienne could already tell she was nervous, as her voice was a little too high pitched.

It'll be okay, sweetheart, she wanted to say, and the mental term of endearment nearly made her blush.

Remembering at the very last moment to keep her professionalism, Adrienne held back from a hug in greeting and instead held out her hand.

Morgan's quirked eyebrow hinted at her amusement, but she played along, and shook Adrienne's hand firmly.

"Nice to see you again," she said, and Adrienne had to bite her lip to keep from laughing.

Turning to the two women behind her—both chosen because she thought Morgan would feel much more comfortable with women invading her space rather than men—she made the introductions. Morgan motioned them into the house.

Inside the house spoke even more of Morgan's personality, and Adrienne smiled at all the cute touches displayed. The furniture was clearly chosen for comfort rather than because it was the latest statement. Pictures on the walls attested to Morgan's love of coastlines; she'd mentioned once that her dream getaway was a deserted beach anywhere in the world. The whole interior felt relaxed and casual, and Adrienne could understand even more why it was Morgan's sanctuary. And why her and the crew being here was such a big deal.

With that thought, she stepped into full business mode.

"Morgan, thank you so much for inviting us into your home. TC Productions really appreciates it."

Morgan, who had walked over to a smoothly polished stone breakfast bar in the small but beautifully appointed kitchen, turned and dazzled Adrienne with a wide smile.

"You're welcome," she responded quietly. She gestured to the display on the counter. "I have freshly brewed coffee and some fresh fruit and pastries if you'd like?"

Tina made appreciative noises, and Morgan chuckled.

"I'll take a cup of coffee for sure," Adrienne said and smiled as Tina and Cheri moved forward to help themselves to the gooey pastries arranged on a yellow ceramic platter. "But I'll pass on the pastries."

"Some fruit?" Morgan asked.

"You know, I'm fine with just coffee."

"Okay." Morgan flashed her that smile again, and Adrienne feared she'd melt into the floor.

Once they each had a cup of coffee in their hands, Adrienne pushed on with the reason for being there.

"When we spoke about this before, I suggested that to keep your privacy, we do this interview in the yard. As it's such a nice day, I don't see any reason to change that idea."

Morgan nodded. "Sounds perfect. Thank you."

Adrienne gave her a brief nod of acknowledgement before turning to her crew. "Why don't we step outside and see what we've got to work with?"

She's being so considerate, and the more she is, the more I want to tell the other two to disappear so I can have her all to myself.

While she knew Adrienne's actions were professional, especially with an audience looking on, she also knew they came from genuine care for Morgan's well-being. That knowledge gave her the sort of warm, fuzzy feeling she had never imagined experiencing.

Morgan shook her head. The effect Adrienne had on her bordered on ridiculous. Even if she wanted to protect herself from any potential hurt Adrienne could send her way, she wasn't sure she was capable. Zero defense. It thrilled her, while at the same time her heart rate increased with the pinch of fear running through her veins.

She walked over to the doorway and leaned against the frame, coffee cup in one hand, watching Adrienne and Tina discuss the best place to set things up.

Adrienne turned and met Morgan's gaze, and even though it was brief, the look they shared spoke volumes: Adrienne was struggling too.

After swallowing the last of her coffee, Morgan sucked in a breath and stepped out onto the terrace.

"So will it work?" she asked as she walked up alongside the three women.

"Yes, definitely. We'll pull the table over there." Adrienne pointed to the big patch of empty terrace that currently basked in the most sunlight. "And have you facing the house so all that lovely greenery is the backdrop." She faced Morgan. "And who does your landscaping? It's gorgeous!"

Morgan smiled. "That would be Alejandro, and I'll be sure to pass on your compliments."

Adrienne grinned, then spoke to Tina. "Okay, let's get started."

They were all set up about twenty minutes later, long enough for Morgan's nerves to build. She and Adrienne had agreed on the broad outline of the questions that would form this interview, but as usual Adrienne wanted some leeway to steer them in a different direction if the situation arose. She had, however, promised not to push Morgan on her relationship with her father, which was just as well, as a part of Morgan still seethed after the disastrous dinner in Williamsburg. Who knew what she'd say if asked something directly?

Morgan settled into the chair, a glass of water on the table beside her.

"You okay?" Adrienne asked. She stood just to the left of Tina, peering intently at Morgan.

"A little nervous," she admitted and was rewarded with a warm, comforting smile.

"Okay, let's start."

Adrienne waited a couple of beats before speaking. "So, Morgan, thank you for showing us your lovely home. Tell me, how long have you lived here?"

Morgan relaxed as Adrienne led her through some fairly standard questions about her home, her life on the road, her workout regime, and her nutrition.

"And now you've got a week off before flying to Europe to play a couple of big tournaments over there."

Morgan smiled deprecatingly. "Uh, yeah. Just the small matter of the British Open and the Evian to deal with."

Adrienne chuckled. "How are you feeling about those?"

"You know, I'm feeling pretty relaxed. It's been a good last few weeks for me, that first round at the PGA aside. I'm proud of the way I pulled that around, and I'm even more proud of my place in the rankings. So I'm taking a lot of confidence into the trip to Europe."

"Will you have a chance to catch up with your folks while you're there?"

To anyone watching it was an obvious question, and Morgan had to answer it, but she feared where it might go. Was Adrienne about to push her into talking about the issues with her father?

"I hope so." Almost the truth. "My dad's going to be working for ESPN over there, and I know my mom would love to see Britain again, so I'm hopeful we can find some time to spend together around my schedule."

"Is it tough trying to fit family and friends around the life of a pro golfer?"

Okay, that didn't go where I thought it would. "Yeah, it is. But my parents support me and my brother in our careers, and they understand the demands."

It was difficult to brace herself and keep calm on the outside; she hoped it wasn't noticeable on film. *All right, if she's going to go for it, I just gave her an in.* Morgan fervently wished Adrienne *wouldn't* go for it—Morgan wasn't sure what mood she'd be in afterward if she did, and that could ruin her plans for the rest of the day.

"Do you do anything different to prepare for a major?"

For a moment, Morgan wanted to laugh. At the relatively innocuous question and also because this week *was* very different preparation. Normally she'd be out on a practice range every day, not deliberately setting aside time to be interviewed and, hopefully, having dinner with Adrienne later.

"You know, it depends on my schedule. Last year I went straight from the PGA to Miami to Europe. I'll be honest, that turned out not to be the best plan." She held back a wince at the thought of why in particular Miami had not been such a good idea after all. "I was pretty tired by the time I got to Britain. That's the main reason I decided to take this week off this year. So I'll use this time to get some more practice in and hopefully rest a little. Maybe have dinner with a friend," she couldn't resist adding with a small smile.

Adrienne's eyes widened, but her professional poise didn't falter for one moment. "Sounds great," she said, and Morgan wondered if there was a hidden message for her in there somewhere. "And do you think about your opponents at all in the build-up? Come up with strategies on how to play if, say, Kim Lee's right up there with you in the final round?"

Morgan shook her head. "No, not at all. They're all great players, some of them legends in our game. I treat everyone with the same high level of respect and just go out there and play my game. At the end of the day, I'm the only one who can control my own round, and that's all I need to focus on."

A few seconds of silence. "And cut."

Morgan blinked. That was it? They were done? All that time, waiting Adrienne out, wondering if something a bit more hard-hitting would be asked, but no. Adrienne had stuck entirely to their script. Morgan wanted to hug her. Or kiss her. Preferably both.

Cheri lowered the sound boom, and Tina stepped back from the camera. Adrienne beamed. "Very nice job," she said. "Tina, any issues?"

"None. Walk in the park."

"Excellent." Adrienne dropped her notebook on the table and walked round to Morgan.

"You did really well," she said quietly.

Morgan smiled and gratitude raced through her. "Yeah, but thank you—you let me off easy. I know you said you wouldn't ask about my father, but I'll be honest, I'm still surprised you didn't."

Adrienne shrugged. "You know, when I said you should talk about it back in, um, the elevator, I didn't necessarily mean publicly."

"I know. But I still appreciate your effort. I know as a journalist you must be itching to get the full story."

"Yes and no. I'm not just a journalist with you now, am I? And that means I have different priorities." The words were a whisper, but their effect was electric.

They stared at each other for a moment before Adrienne broke the exquisite tension.

"So, um, what's the rest of your afternoon look like?" she asked.

Morgan inhaled. *Now or never.* "Well, I was hoping to invite you for dinner. Here. I'm cooking."

Adrienne's mouth quirked up at one corner. "'Dinner with a friend?'"

Laughing, Morgan nodded. She glanced over at the crew to make sure they still couldn't be overheard. "I'd love to spend some time with you, and at least here it would be nice and private."

Adrienne bit her bottom lip, and a slow heat spread through Morgan's body.

"It, um, sounds lovely." Adrienne flushed a little. "I just need to come up with a reason why they should leave without me." She looked back at the crew. "Give me a moment."

"Would you like a glass of wine or something?" Morgan asked from across the kitchen.

"Are you having any?" Adrienne replied and willed her pulse to slow just a tad.

They were alone now. Tina and Cheri had long departed in a cab back to the city; they'd easily bought Adrienne's explanation that she and Morgan were going to work on ideas for a final interview. They didn't need to know that one wasn't actually scheduled.

Morgan shook her head. "No, not this week. Probably not drinking any alcohol again until after the Evian, to be honest."

"Then I won't either, thank you. I'll have whatever you're having."

"Okay." Morgan smiled. "It's just plain seltzer. Is that all right?"

Adrienne laughed. "It's fine. With a slice of lemon if you have it."

"Of course." Morgan pulled a lemon from the refrigerator with a flourish, and they smiled at each other.

"You seem so at ease here," Adrienne mused. "I completely understand now what you meant about this place."

Morgan deftly sliced the lemon. "It really is my retreat. I worked hard to get this place, and I was determined to make it all my own. I had a few changes made before I moved in and chose all the paint colors and furniture myself. I couldn't be happier with it."

"Have you always lived alone?" Adrienne asked as her drink was handed to her in a tall glass.

"Since turning pro, yes." Morgan walked around the breakfast bar and settled into the stool next to Adrienne. "Back in college I roomed with a couple of other women but no dramas there. I just prefer to live alone."

"You and Naomi never lived together?" She tilted her head. "You don't have to answer if that's too personal or painful."

Morgan waved off her concerns. "Hey, no, it's fine. I…want to talk about our lives. Share our stories. I mean, that's all part of getting to know someone, isn't it?"

Adrienne nodded, sipped at her drink, then jumped and nearly spilled the contents when Morgan pushed her fingertips against Adrienne's free hand where it rested on the countertop. It was the softest, merest of touches, but she might as well have waved a flaming brand in front of Adrienne's body.

"Sorry." Morgan retracted her hand, her eyes wide. "Was that too—?"

Adrienne quickly put her glass down and reached out her hand. "No, it was… You just surprised me. That's all." She inched her hand closer to Morgan's, desperate for that warmth again, and sighed with relief when

Morgan entwined their fingers. "Thank you. That's better," Adrienne said with a smile.

Morgan grinned. "You make me feel so goofy." She shook her head. "Not with anything *you* do, but I mean, just when I'm around you. I've never been like this." She sounded puzzled.

"Well, if it's any comfort, neither have I. And at my age, I really should know better."

"Tsk, tsk," Morgan said, then chuckled. "Age is not an issue, remember?"

"I'm still undecided on that," Adrienne whispered. "Sorry, but that will take some getting used to."

"Okay." Morgan held her hand a little tighter. "I can respect that." She smiled. "So back to your question. No, Naomi and I didn't live together, although she wanted to. Within a couple months of us seeing each other, she was dropping not-so-subtle hints about bringing her stuff here."

"You didn't want to?"

"I guess deep down maybe I knew she wasn't to be trusted." Morgan let out a soft snort. "Wish I'd listened to that instinct a little harder."

Adrienne couldn't help the louder snort that escaped her throat. "God, I wish I'd had *any* kind of instinct about Paula."

"Your ex?"

"Yes."

She sighed. Telling Morgan wasn't essential, she knew that, but if they were going to really get to know each other, then sharing this kind of story was part of that process. She wondered how it would feel telling someone she was very much attracted to about the pain her last relationship had caused her.

"I told you she cheated on me?"

Morgan nodded and rubbed a thumb over the palm of Adrienne's hand, sending delicious tingles up her arm, sensations that definitely helped to distract her from the memories of Paula's betrayal.

"I had no idea," Adrienne continued. "Literally none. When it all blew up, she accused me of being so focused on my work that I'd never seen what was in front of my face. As if it was my fault she started an affair with a woman from her office who was twenty years younger."

Adrienne was surprised. Her words, the ones she'd delivered to few people since the fateful day Paula had ended their relationship, stung but not with the depth of pain she'd anticipated. *Huh, having someone beautiful holding your hand while you say them clearly does make a difference.*

"Well, that sounds a little manipulative. Kinda like Naomi. Maybe she and Paula are related."

Morgan's grin was wry, and Adrienne's laughter bubbled up without warning. Soon they both rocked in their seats, their laughter filling the room.

"You're good for me," Adrienne said, the admission taking her by surprise with its openness.

"I'm glad to hear it," Morgan replied quietly. Her gaze softened, and she returned to making those tantalizing, lazy circles on Adrienne's palm with her thumb. "I'm sorry for what Paula did to you. She took the coward's way out, and that's never good in my book."

"She did. Since it happened, I've wondered more than once if that's what upsets me most. Not that she left but the way she left." Adrienne sucked in a breath. "I don't miss her. And I haven't missed her for months. I think the baggage I've been carrying around is all about how and who."

"The younger woman?"

Face heating, knowing it had parallels with their situation, Adrienne sighed. "Yes. It hurt, being replaced by someone so much younger. I know you say age doesn't matter, but with all due respect, that's easy for someone so young to say."

"Point taken," Morgan said, thankfully not looking the least bit offended. "Is that part of why you've had so much trouble with our age difference?"

Adrienne nodded. "I was worried what people would think. My friend Tricia, for example, who's concerned I'm just chasing after you so I can have what Paula has."

"Ouch. I hope you're about to tell me that's not the case?" Morgan's calm composure slipped, and tension crept into her expression.

"I know it isn't," Adrienne said forcefully. She locked her gaze on Morgan's and squeezed her fingers. "Yes, I worried when I first realized how attracted to you I am, thinking I was having some clichéd midlife crisis. But...the more time I spend with you, the more I know you, the more I know that this, what I feel, is rather real."

Her voice had turned husky with emotion and a slow-burning desire that gradually made its presence known. They were alone, holding hands, and she was telling this remarkable young woman she really did have feelings for her. It was more than a tad scary, but she wouldn't change a thing, not right now.

"Adrienne," Morgan breathed, a pulse beating in her neck.

"Yes?"

"Can I kiss you?"

"God, *yes*."

It was the heat that she remembered. That and the exquisite softness of Morgan's lips as they moved slowly against her own. To hell with worrying about her job and her grand—now laughable—plan to keep things between them purely platonic until the project was finished. This, a kiss that burned its way through every defensive layer she'd built up over the last twelve months, couldn't be resisted or delayed.

Morgan nibbled gently at Adrienne's bottom lip, and a groan, deep and long, wrenched from her throat as she opened her mouth and let Morgan in. In the next moment, they eased off the stools and stepped closer. Morgan's strong arms wrapped around her, and Adrienne lost herself in every sensation that overtook her body at Morgan's touch.

The doorbell rang, breaking the spell. Morgan lifted her head, her eyes unfocused, although she kept Adrienne pressed close against her.

"Ah, shit!" Morgan muttered. "I completely forgot about that."

"What?" Adrienne murmured, and she leaned in to kiss along the line of Morgan's jaw, delighting in the shudder that rippled through the body in her arms.

Morgan chuckled as the doorbell rang a second time. "That's the grocery delivery. I'd better answer, or we'll go pretty hungry this evening."

Adrienne smiled up at her. "Well, yes. You promised me dinner after all, and you'd better deliver."

With a smirk, Morgan pulled way. "All right, smart-ass."

"But be quick," Adrienne said, her voice even huskier than before, her body already missing Morgan's touch.

"Jesus," Morgan murmured, before she stumbled backward out of the kitchen.

Chapter 16

AFTER TIPPING THE DELIVERY GUY, Morgan closed the front door and leaned against it. She needed a moment to…breathe. The kiss in the kitchen had been every bit as electrifying as the one in the elevator, albeit gentler and more tender. She was almost afraid of what might happen next, given how intense her desire was after that far-too-brief moment. The feel of Adrienne in her arms made her forget her own name, and the loss of control bordered on overwhelming. She'd never fully let go with Naomi, scared to fall too deep, but with Adrienne, holding back really didn't seem like an option. Her heart fluttered at the thought.

She took a couple more deep breaths, then straightened her shoulders. *Come on, you're a grown-up. Get back in that kitchen and focus on spending the evening with Adrienne. Whatever happens will happen.*

The two bags were reasonably heavy—possibly she'd gone overboard in her eagerness to prepare them a special meal—and she chuckled as she picked them up and carried them down the hallway.

When she entered the kitchen, Adrienne sat at the table, talking on her phone, and rolled her eyes at Morgan as she listened to whoever was on the other end.

Morgan smiled and set about unloading the bags.

"Yes, Daniel, I know. But I've literally just completed that last segment with Morgan Spencer, and we're well on track." Adrienne sounded tense, and Morgan occasionally glanced at her as she arranged the groceries on the countertop. "Yes, the budget will be *fine*, I promise." Another pause as whoever this Daniel person was said more. "No, absolutely not! I've already got Annika ready to go the minute the film's wrapped. With all due respect to Ms. Thomson, she's not in Annika's league. I don't care who she knows or what she's threatening." Adrienne rubbed her forehead with her free hand. "Daniel, do you want this film done properly or not? Right, in that case, you have to trust me, okay? Right, fine. Yes, I'll catch up with you then."

After ending the call, Adrienne mimicked smashing the phone on the table, then dropped it carefully into her purse instead.

"Trouble?" Morgan asked, leaning against the counter. She wanted to walk around it and wrap Adrienne back up in her arms, but there was a tension in Adrienne's shoulders that gave her pause.

Adrienne rolled her neck a few times before answering. "I'm not sure." She sighed. "That was my boss, Daniel McGovern. It seems Cindy Thomson might be trying to muscle her way into this film. Remember she was talking to me the other day?"

"When she dropped some hint that she thought there was something between us?"

"Yes. Well prior to that, she offered to do the voiceover for the film. It seems she didn't take my 'no, thanks' well and has been putting some pressure on a couple of the directors of the company. Apparently made some veiled threat about making things difficult for us if she doesn't get her way."

Morgan stared at Adrienne. "Are you worried?"

"A little," Adrienne admitted. A frown marred her features. "I'm not sure what she knows and whether she'd find a willing ear to listen to it. So far, it seems the directors think she's playing a silly game and are happy to ignore her, but she has a history of doing this to me, so I'm concerned, yes."

Now Morgan did walk around the breakfast bar to the table, where she placed a comforting hand on Adrienne's back and rubbed soothing circles.

"Sorry," Adrienne said, a rueful smile on her face. "It seems the, um, lovely mood we'd created has been shattered."

"Hey, it's okay. Not your fault." Morgan gave what she hoped was an encouraging smile. "We've got all evening. I'm sure we can find our way back there again if we want."

Adrienne smiled too and hooked an arm around Morgan's waist. "Maybe we can. I mean, it seems as if my big plan to not pursue this"—she pointed between them—"until after we've finished filming has gone up in flames anyway."

Morgan laughed, leaned down, and kissed the top of Adrienne's head. "How about you let me make you that dinner now, then? And we'll just see how things…develop?"

Adrienne blinked. "Sounds good."

"Morgan, is there anything you *can't* do?" Adrienne asked in mock exasperation after she swallowed her second bite of the incredible dish before her. "This is delicious!"

Morgan blushed sweetly. "Thanks, I'm really glad you like it."

Adrienne loaded her fork with fish, wild mushrooms, and a swipe of the delicate truffle sauce and chewed contentedly. "Who taught you to cook?"

"Well," Morgan said after taking a sip of her water. "I learned quite a bit from my mom when I was growing up. But we also ate out a lot, and each time a dish wowed me, I'd experiment with trying to recreate it at home. This one," she said, pointing her fork at her plate, "I had in London at a Michelin-starred restaurant in Kensington. I'm sure mine is only half as good as theirs, but I love the flavor combination, and I've cooked this a few times since."

"To impress the women?" Adrienne asked, and she smirked, even though her question made her stomach churn with a mild jealousy that was definitely unbecoming.

Morgan snorted. "Hardly." She sighed and shook her head. "Adrienne, I think you have this idea that I've played the field. Is it because I'm younger? I mean, at the risk of sounding rude, I'd imagine you've had more partners than I have."

She sounded mildly irritated, and Adrienne was immediately contrite. "I'm sorry. You're right. That was a cheap shot." She sat back in her chair and met Morgan's gaze. "I know I need to get away from this issue with our age disparity, and I promise to do better."

Morgan nodded and relaxed visibly. "For the record, you're only the third woman I've…dated. Are we dating?"

She looked so unsure of herself, Adrienne had to physically resist the urge to throw herself across the table and hug her. "I think that's a word we could use," she said with a smile. Then she grinned wryly. "And yes, you're right. I *have* had more partners than you. Though not by much—you're number six."

"Well, okay. That doesn't actually make me feel so bad."

"Why would you feel bad?" Adrienne was mystified.

Morgan fiddled with her fork. "Um, well, because you're... Well, I just assumed you would have more, um, experience than me, and I was a little worried I, you know, wouldn't measure up."

"Oh my God, you are... I don't even know what to say." She reached across the table, her heart pounding, and ran her hand over Morgan's. "Trust me, that is *not* something you need to worry about. Whenever we...take things further, there's not going to be any scorecards involved." She smiled as Morgan chuckled. "It seems we both have some issues with confidence. I mean, I still can't believe someone as wonderful as you is interested in someone like me. So please don't sell yourself short."

Morgan's smile was slow but lit up her face. "Well, then I'd say the same to you. You're incredible and beautiful, and I'm honored you're here with me now."

Adrienne swallowed the lump in her throat. "Well, okay then," she said. She pointed at her plate. "Now that we've got that settled, I'm going to finish this amazing meal, okay?"

Morgan nodded and smiled, then released Adrienne's hand. "Yes, let's eat."

After eating, they cleared the dishes together, chatting about anything that popped into their heads. The more they talked, the more Adrienne realized that Morgan's age was immaterial. She was sharp, knowledgeable about many subjects, and a good listener. The only thing that kept niggling at Adrienne's mind was the thought of getting more physical with Morgan. Not that she didn't want to—far from it. But that was the one area where their age difference still bothered her.

Morgan was fit—super fit—and lithe and, well, owned a body only thirty-one years old. Adrienne, while not exactly out of shape, hadn't been to a gym in about two years, couldn't touch her toes anymore, and had knees that creaked alarmingly whenever she sat down too quickly. And there were wrinkles in many places other than her face. In fact, the more she thought about it, the more her panic rose and the idea of ever being able to get naked with Morgan seemed ridiculous.

They finished loading the dishwasher, then Morgan stepped away to wipe the table. Adrienne watched her, mesmerized by the play of her muscles under the short sleeves of her checkered shirt. *Such an incredible physique, and, oh God, I so do not compare with that.* Adrienne's gaze drifted, her eyes unfocused as her thoughts enveloped her.

The heat from Morgan's body behind her startled her. Morgan wrapped her arms around her and nuzzled her neck. Shivers careered down Adrienne's spine, setting off a chain reaction somewhere south of her belly.

"You okay?" Morgan murmured. "You've disappeared on me." Then she tensed. "Sorry, is this okay?"

"Mm, yes," Adrienne said softly. "I'm sorry, I just…drifted."

She couldn't tell her, not yet. Besides, it wasn't like it was going to happen tonight anyway. Adrienne was not a sex-on-the-first-date kind of woman.

"Want to get comfy on the couch?" Morgan asked. Her lips, less than an inch from Adrienne's ear, sent pulses of heat throbbing along Adrienne's shoulders and collarbone.

It's been so long since I felt like this. And it had been. When the dust had settled from Paula's departure, Adrienne had come to the realization that they hadn't been intimate for at least the last year of their relationship—and Adrienne hadn't noticed. Of course, Adrienne realized much later, Paula hadn't mentioned it because she was already finding intimacy elsewhere. Adrienne pushed back her irritation at that thought and concentrated on the sensation of Morgan's arms encircling her.

Over two years since someone had touched her so intimately, and while it felt wonderful, it was also unnerving. Sensations she'd forgotten she could experience were sending her synapses crazy.

"Couch…would be…good," she managed to stammer out as Morgan's lips moved to the back of her neck and kissed a sweet trail across her skin.

Morgan chuckled and gradually let her go. "How about I make some coffee?"

Snapping herself back into the moment, Adrienne took a step back and remembered to breathe. "Decaf?"

"Sure, I can do that." Morgan gazed at Adrienne intently. "You okay?"

"Yes. No." *God, I can't even form proper sentences when I'm around her!* "I mean, I am, but I do have some things on my mind."

Morgan opened her mouth to speak, then paused. "Okay, I'll make coffee and join you on the couch. We can talk or just watch a movie. Whatever you're more comfortable with."

"Thank you."

Adrienne slowly walked out of the kitchen to the living area, her mind whirling. Why was she letting Morgan carry all the weight in this burgeoning relationship? So much for being the older, more mature woman.

She settled into the comforting softness of the big couch and laid her head back against the cushions. She would have loved to reach out to Tricia for some advice, but she feared Tricia would try to talk her out of this. If there was one thing she *was* sure of, she didn't want to be talked out of whatever this might be. Being with Morgan was scary, yes, but it was also fun and exciting and easy. They could talk about anything, it seemed, and do so with a calm honesty that Adrienne found a joy to experience.

Can I do this? Can I really embark on a relationship with this woman?

The answer that came back to her from deep in her gut was a resounding *yes*, because having had a glimpse of who they could be together, there really was no other option. Morgan's obvious respect and care for her was enough on its own, never mind the sizzling chemistry between them. Adrienne had known, somewhere in her mind, that at forty-nine, she wasn't dead yet, but she never would have imagined it would be a thirty-one-year-old who would make that crystal clear.

"So, I thought while coffee was a good idea, an even better idea was some dessert with that," Morgan said as she walked into the room.

She rounded the couch with a tray containing a coffee pot, two cups, a jug of what was presumably cream—and a pint tub of Ben & Jerry's *Coffee Coffee BuzzBuzzBuzz!* ice cream with two spoons resting beside it.

Adrienne laughed as Morgan placed the tray on the low coffee table in front of the couch.

"What?" Morgan asked innocently.

"You just happened to have that tub in the freezer?"

Morgan leaned in. "I always have at least three in there."

"I didn't realize your love of ice cream ran to addiction levels."

"Uh-huh." Morgan sat beside Adrienne but not so close as to leave her feeling breathless. "Can't help it. I've always loved the stuff."

"You're adorable," Adrienne said. She shook her head at the beam on Morgan's face.

Then she did what she knew she'd really wanted to do again ever since they were interrupted two hours previously. She leaned in and kissed Morgan, soft and slow, trailing one hand up into the incredible silkiness of Morgan's hair to wind her fingers deep in its luxurious strands.

Morgan whimpered, and the sound sparked a deep throb between Adrienne's legs. The power of it startled her and pitched her forward to hold Morgan even tighter.

They surfaced minutes later, both gasping for air.

"Adrienne," Morgan murmured. She held Adrienne's hips, her grip strong even through the rough denim of Adrienne's jeans.

"Hm?" Adrienne couldn't manage words in the haze of warmth and desire that swamped her body.

"You're making me feel…things." Morgan pressed her forehead to Adrienne's, her breath soft over Adrienne's nose. "I'm falling, and it's a little scary."

Adrienne exhaled slowly. "I know. Me too."

Morgan pulled her close, then leaned her head back to look Adrienne in the eye, her expression one of disbelief. "Yeah?"

Adrienne nodded and kissed her chin. "Yes."

Morgan groaned and claimed Adrienne's mouth once more, her arms encircling Adrienne's back as she swept her tongue into Adrienne's mouth.

Adrienne clung on, drowning in sensation, one hand frantic in Morgan's hair, the other snaking under the back of Morgan's shirt to feel, for the first time, the warm firmness of her body. Muscles tensed, then trembled beneath her fingertips.

Morgan moaned, the sound of it reverberating in Adrienne's chest where they were pressed so close together.

When Morgan pushed her back, easing her down onto the couch, she went willingly. With Morgan's weight fully on her, she ran both hands under her shirt, reveling in the heated skin. Morgan shifted her hips slightly, bringing their thighs together, and Adrienne's head arched back. When she slipped her fingertips beneath the waistband of Morgan's cotton shorts, Morgan surged against her. Her mouth deepened their kiss, and her hands moved under the fabric of Adrienne's silk shirt, up over her ribs to—

Adrienne jerked away. "Not...not yet," she said, breathless. Heart pounding, she eased away from Morgan and sat up. "Sorry, I—"

"Oh God, no, I'm sorry!" Morgan's eyes were wide. She sat upright and wriggled back on the couch a little. "I just got carried away, and..." She chuckled. "You're so sexy. I couldn't help myself. Sorry."

Adrienne brushed her fingertips over Morgan's soft, rosy lips. "No, no need to apologize. Believe me, there's a big part of me that wants to but..."

"But?"

Adrienne sighed then dropped a soft kiss on Morgan's mouth before sitting back again. She mentally sorted through the words she wanted to say, to explain what it meant to be on the cusp of being physical with Morgan. "I'm just not ready. And I'll be honest, mostly that's because, well, my body is a lot older than yours. I know you say my age isn't an issue, but in this one respect, for me this is, perhaps, the biggest hill to climb. I'll need some time to feel confident letting you...see me and...touch me."

"Adrienne." Morgan's tone ached with tenderness. "You are beautiful. Please don't ever doubt that. I totally respect what you are saying, of course, but please believe me, you have nothing to fear. I've...I've never had such a strong physical reaction to someone." She blushed and looked away. "I'm not known for my, um, sexual appetite. This is...quite new for me. And that's all because of you," she said, finally looking back. "That's what you do to me."

"Oh." She didn't think it was possible to feel even more emotion today, but there it was. "Thank you for sharing that with me."

"That's the other thing you do to me," Morgan said with a wry smile. "Make me want to tell you everything I'm feeling. That's new too."

Adrienne gazed at her in wonder, knowing that they'd just stepped up onto another level in this new relationship. And she was more than happy to use that word now—this *was* a relationship, not just some dalliance with little meaning.

"So, um, how about that ice cream?" Morgan shuffled to the edge of the couch and pointed at the tray. "Hm?"

Smiling, thankful that Morgan was comfortable in giving them this space, Adrienne nodded.

"I think ice cream is a wonderful idea."

Morgan fist-pumped and reached for the tub.

Two days later, Morgan was still on a high. She ran through the Presidio early on Friday morning, not bothered by the light summer rain that fell in a gentle curtain across the city and coated her hair and body. She'd replayed that evening in her mind so many times, and every time she did so, she smiled as a warm glow settled over her. *At this rate, I could save the city on heating costs.*

She eased down from her run a few blocks from home and walked the rest of the way. As much fun as it was to keep thinking about Adrienne and all they'd shared on Wednesday, today she really needed to get her head back to the forthcoming trip to Europe. The practice yesterday had been great; her swing felt as good as it ever had, and her hands had been light and deft on all the bunker shots. Today was putting and approach shots, and early tomorrow morning she'd play a full round with a club caddy before flying out to London overnight.

It would be easy to say that her game had only improved once she and Adrienne had realized they couldn't fight what was happening between them, but that wasn't the whole story. Yes, her emotional happiness played a part, of course it did, but working through what they were had made Morgan focus on what else was important. Somehow, she knew that even if she and Adrienne didn't work out, she'd be able to keep her focus on her game. That first round at the PGA had scared the crap out of her, knowing she could drop her concentration that badly because of whatever else was going on in her life. But not anymore. She'd learned a few things about herself the past few weeks, and it was satisfying to have done so.

She stepped into the house and smiled at Renata, who stood at the breakfast bar wiping down its surface. Morgan opened the refrigerator and liberated a carton of orange juice. After pouring herself a large glass, she also retrieved the one pastry left over from Wednesday and crammed half the delicacy in her mouth.

The phone rang just as she swallowed.

"Hey, Mom."

"Hi, darling, how are you?"

She sounded…nervous, and Morgan realized with a guilty start that she hadn't contacted her mother since that awful dinner back in Williamsburg.

"I'm good, Mom. Sorry I haven't been in touch."

"Oh, it's all right. I understand. That evening was…difficult."

Morgan blinked. It was very unlike her mom to admit something like that. "Um, yeah, it was."

Her mother cleared her throat. "Morgan, are you home any time today?"

Today? "Where are you?"

"I'm at the Fairmont." She sighed. "Here in San Francisco."

"What?" Morgan blurted, then stumbled on before her mom could respond. "Why are you guys in San Francisco?"

"Just me. I… There's some things we need to talk about. Can I come see you?"

"Of course! I'm free all morning. I have a sponsor thing this afternoon but that would be difficult to swap if—"

"Oh, no, this morning will be fine."

"Do you want to come to the house?"

"That would be lovely."

"Well, you jump in a cab as soon as you're ready. I just need to shower, but if you get here before I'm done, Renata will let you in, okay?"

"All right, darling. See you soon."

Morgan put the phone down on the counter and stared at it for a few seconds. What the hell was going on?

"Everything okay, Miss Morgan?" Renata asked.

Morgan lifted her head to find Renata looking at her with concern etched on her face.

"Um, yeah. My mom's coming to visit. I didn't even know she was in the city."

"I'll put some coffee on." Renata patted Morgan's hand and walked across the kitchen.

"Yeah," Morgan replied distractedly, "that would be great. I'm just going to…" She turned and walked out of the kitchen toward the bathroom.

She heard her mom arrive around twenty minutes later, just as she was pulling on her soft yoga pants. In the kitchen, she found her mom sitting at the table with Renata fussing over her, pouring coffee and asking if she'd like anything to eat.

185

"Oh, no, thank you, Renata. I'm fine with just coffee."

"Okay." Renata caught Morgan's eye. "I will go now."

Morgan smiled. "Thanks, Renata. I'll see you in a few weeks."

"Be well, Miss Morgan."

Renata left quietly, and Morgan turned to stare at her mom. "Hi."

Her mother stood to give her a hug before easing back into her chair and motioning Morgan to sit alongside her.

"Mom?"

Morgan was getting seriously worried now. Was her mom ill? Or her dad?

"This is difficult for me," her mom began. Her hands twisted together on the table. "I've never been one to talk much about emotions. I know that's where you get it from."

Morgan smiled wryly.

Her mother sighed heavily. "I kept excusing him because of the problem with his hip. I know he's been in considerable pain, and pain can make a person say or do things they would think twice about in better circumstances. But…"

Morgan waited, breath held. Okay, so no one was dying, which was a relief, but clearly something had happened between her parents. She braced herself for what would come next.

"He's always been so stubborn." Her mom shook her head slowly. "When he was playing, I assumed it was necessary, for him to focus, to keep going even when the odds might be stacked against him. But now, well, now it just makes him a pain in the ass."

The words, so unexpected from the rather refined tongue of her mother, made Morgan snort with laughter.

Her mom chuckled too, but it sounded hollow.

"I've told him I want a temporary separation." She said the words quickly, as if actually speaking them out loud would somehow bring the world crashing down.

Morgan grasped her hand, a thousand questions spinning in her mind.

Wetness shimmered in her mom's eyes. "I'm okay." Her voice shook a little. "Really. I just…had enough. Finally." She blinked a couple of times and wiped her eyes with her free hand. "And it was that dinner that was the final straw. I couldn't bear to see him treat you that way anymore. I'm sorry, darling, for not speaking up before, but I had become…blind to what he was like. Seeing you so upset that evening, especially after you seemed so upbeat about what was happening between you and Adrienne…" She sighed. "I don't know what came over me, but I confronted him about it when we got back to our hotel. He got a message from Jack talking about his latest win and couldn't stop talking about how proud he was of Jack. I just saw red, darling. All I could think about was how he'd insulted your game at dinner, and, well, I said a lot of things. Told him his sexism belonged in the past, told him how he was in danger of losing the love of his daughter." Her voice broke, and she waved her hand listlessly. "And lots more. It wasn't pleasant."

"Oh, Mom." Morgan got up from her chair and dropped to her knees in front of her mother, pulling her into a tender hug. She hated the idea that her mom had battled with her father, but at the same time, she burst with gratitude that her mom had finally called him on his misogyny.

Her mom sniffed delicately, her face pressed against Morgan's hair. "It's okay. It will be okay."

"How did he take it?"

At this, her mom snorted, a sound Morgan wasn't sure she'd ever heard her make. "Well, he looked like he'd been shot, to be honest. He didn't say much of anything for a couple of minutes, then told me I had no idea what I was talking about and switched on the TV!" She pulled back from Morgan's embrace and smiled down at her. "Well, that only fired me up again, and I gave him more of the same."

Morgan laughed. "Mom, I…I can't believe this. Is it okay to say I'm really proud of you?"

"Morgan, I love that man and always have, but what I said to him was long overdue. I'm not proud, not for letting it go on as long as I did."

"Mom, don't. You did it. That's the main thing. I'll be honest, I've been finding it really tough this year, hearing you make excuses for him all the time."

"I know, darling." She stroked Morgan's hair. "I wouldn't have blamed you if you'd stopped coming home or calling."

"It was getting difficult, I must admit."

Her mom hugged her close again. "I know."

"So what now? You told him you want to separate. Are you sure?"

"I am. He refused to engage in any serious conversation about all the points I raised that night or when we got back home. I…I nearly backed down, but then I kept seeing your face in my mind's eye, your hurt at the way he speaks to you, and I decided drastic action was the only way to get him to really listen." She rolled her eyes. "Of course, that may backfire on me if he thinks he's better off without me shouting at him all the time."

Morgan shook her head. "No, it won't. If there's one thing I've always been sure of, it's that he loves you. I'll be surprised if this separation lasts long."

"Well, like I said, darling, he's stubborn. He won't like the idea of asking me to come back, especially as I made it abundantly clear I won't do so until he's prepared to face up to his behavior and attitudes. But I have to hope you're right, that his love for me will be strong enough."

She looked haunted, and Morgan's heart lurched. "It will. I'm sure of it."

There was a part of Morgan's brain that found it a tad bizarre she was now actively fighting for her parents to stay together after all that her father had done—and not done—for Morgan over the years, but she recognized that his treatment of her and the love between her parents were two distinct things.

"I hope so, darling." She squeezed Morgan tightly. "But believe me, your love is just as important to me, and I won't risk that." She choked up, her quiet sobs tearing at Morgan. "I couldn't bear to lose you, Morgan."

"Oh, Mom." Morgan's throat tightened and tears welled up. "You won't. Never. Whatever happens, you'll always have me, okay?"

Her mom's only answer was to hold Morgan even tighter.

Chapter 17

"AND HOW IS SHE HOLDING up?" Adrienne asked. She sank back into her couch and noticed it was distinctly less comfortable than Morgan's had been.

Morgan sighed down the phone line. "She's quiet. My dad called her last night, wondering when she was 'going to stop this ridiculous charade and come home.' She asked him if he was ready to change, he made some noise about her making a mountain out of a molehill, and she hung up on him."

"Oh, dear."

"You know, actually, I think it was okay. She was steaming mad after, but she didn't regret cutting him off like that. It'll be interesting to see what happens in the next couple of days, given they're booked on the same flight out to London together on Monday night."

"You think she'll still go?"

"Oh yeah. Says she wouldn't miss watching me for anything, but I'm curious as to how they'll be with each other when they meet up at JFK." Morgan chuckled. "She's already messaged him and told him she'll meet him there. She's not going home first."

"Do you think your dad is going to come around?" Adrienne was almost afraid to ask, because as much as she admired Bree Spencer for finally standing up to her sexist husband, she knew what it was like to suddenly lose a relationship you'd relied on for so many years.

"I honestly don't know. I mean, I feel like I barely know him after the last few years. We've hardly talked. But I do know he loves my mom, and if she keeps pushing him, I think the fear of losing her will be too strong for him *not* to try to come to terms with her."

"Is she going to stay at your place even after you've left tonight?"

"Yeah, I insisted. I think being here has helped her, knowing she can truly relax here. I mean, the Fairmont's nice, but it's still a hotel."

"Of course. But don't sell yourself short—being around you, not just in your lovely home, will also help her relax, you know."

Morgan's chuckle was light. "Okay, okay. You might be a little biased, though."

Adrienne laughed. "I might."

"I...miss you," Morgan said softly. "And I know we can't really see each other while I'm playing at Wentworth or in France, but I wish we could."

"I know." Adrienne smiled. She really did feel like a lovesick teenager. "But just think, three more weeks and we can stop hiding from the world."

"That sounds wonderful. Are you...are you sure you'll be okay with not hiding?"

"Well, to be perfectly honest, I'm not. But that doesn't mean it isn't the right thing to do." Adrienne's stomach *did* lurch at the thought of her colleagues and peers knowing she was dating a much younger woman, and a woman she'd met while working on a project. But she also knew she would feel worse if she tried to keep Morgan her dirty little secret.

"We can wait. And we can make sure news filters out slowly."

"I know, and I appreciate what you are saying, but at the end of the day, my fear about it still comes down to how I think I will be perceived by others. And I really should be too old to be concerned about that anymore."

"Have you spoken to Tricia?"

"Ugh, no. That will be my next call." Adrienne glanced down at her watch. "Hey, what time are you leaving for the airport?"

Morgan sighed. "In about thirty minutes."

"And yet you're still talking to me."

"Hey, I'm all packed. I can see my bags from here. All I have to do is throw on some shoes and a jacket and I'm done. So forgive me if I want to spend as much time talking to you as possible. Trust me, I set up the day precisely so I could do this."

"You're doing it again," Adrienne said with a smile, her heart full.

"What?"

"Being adorable."

"Would you rather I was an asshole? Because I could try if it would help."

Laughing, Adrienne grabbed the nearest cushion and hugged it close, wishing it was Morgan she held against her. "No, you stay just the way you are, thank you."

They filled the rest of their call with talk about Morgan's practice, her schedule for the week leading up to the British Open at Wentworth, and when they might squeeze in at least a genuine working meeting if nothing else. Coffee on Wednesday morning seemed the only option, but they added it to their calendars anyway, not wishing to pass up even that small opportunity to properly lay eyes on each other.

"Okay, well, I guess I'd better get going," Morgan said eventually. "But you should know, I look like a kicked puppy right about now."

"*It's true!*" a voice called from somewhere.

Morgan snorted. "That's my mom. She just walked into the room to say good-bye to me."

Adrienne smiled. "Well, I'll leave you two to it, then. Safe travels. Message me when you get there, okay?"

"I will. And I know we won't speak before you leave tomorrow, so I hope your journey goes well too."

"Thank you." *Okay, you really have to say good-bye now, come on.* "Right, go, and I'll see you on Wednesday."

Morgan whimpered, then laughed. "Okay, I'm really going now. Bye."

Adrienne hung up and looked around her sterile living room. Nothing about this apartment appealed in the slightest, not like the warmth and welcome of Morgan's house. *As soon as this project is done, I'm moving.* She'd thought about it before, just as the project started, but now she absolutely knew she had to. And thinking that brought Tricia to mind, and she knew she needed to make that call now before she chickened out.

The call went straight to voice mail, so she hung up and messaged instead.

Hi, hon. Are you around for a call tonight or perhaps breakfast tomorrow before I head off to London?

Two hours later, just as she was readying herself for an early night, the response came.

Breakfast! Meet at Vinny's around 10?

Even though she was nervous at the thought of telling Tricia what had developed with Morgan, Adrienne replied in the affirmative and lay down to sleep, willing her brain to shut down long enough for her to actually get some shut-eye.

"Wow, you look amazing!" Tricia exclaimed as she approached the table Adrienne had secured for them beside the window at Vinny's.

They hugged, and the embrace plus Tricia's reaction settled Adrienne's nerves a little.

Tricia pulled back and held her at arm's length, scrutinizing her face. "You just look so…relaxed. How is this possible when you've been flying all over the country, working on that film?"

Adrienne motioned Tricia into the chair opposite hers. "Life is…good," she offered as a starter.

"It must be. Let's order, then you can tell me all about it."

Their waitress, a perky twenty-something who was new, took three attempts to get their order right but was so sweet with it neither Adrienne nor, it seemed, Tricia could complain. Once their coffee cups were full, Tricia leaned forward on the table and grinned at Adrienne.

"Okay, tell me everything."

Here goes. "The project is going well. All of the golfers are keen to have this film show off their world in the best way, so they've all been extremely helpful." She chuckled. "One wanted to take that a tad too far." She told Tricia about Laurie's proposition.

"Ew!" Tricia mimed sticking her fingers down her throat. "Who *does* that?"

Adrienne shook her head. "She has a reputation for it, apparently. At least she *did* take no for an answer. I was dreading she'd appear at the door to my room later that night."

Tricia laughed. "And there was me thinking only men could be that sleazy."

"Oh, no, unfortunately not." Adrienne sipped her coffee, then exhaled, preparing herself. "And, well, there is something else that's got me feeling good about life again."

"Oh?" Tricia's eyebrows rose. "Do tell."

Adrienne fiddled with her napkin. How to say it? "Well, Morgan and I are...seeing each other. Quietly, privately for now, while the project is ongoing, but it's...it's really good. It's...it could be something very special."

Tricia's eyes narrowed, and she took a moment to respond. "I thought you weren't going to risk it? I mean, okay, if you tell me it's good, whatever this thing is that you have going on with her, I'll believe you, but what about your job if anyone finds out?"

She'd expected it, of course, but it still stung. "I thought you'd be happy for me. You said yourself you didn't want me alone forever. Now I'm sitting here telling you I've found someone who makes me feel incredibly positive about the future, and you can't see beyond any risk there might be from it to my job?"

Tricia blinked a few times, her lips pursed, then sighed. "I'm..." She shook her head. "You're right. Being happy for you should have been my first thought." She paused and rolled her bottom lip between her teeth. "I just... Sorry, I guess I'm still a little cynical about your motivations for getting involved with someone so young." She threw up her hands as Adrienne leaned forward to protest. "I know, I know, it's grossly unfair. It seems I might be carrying around some prejudices of my own." She slumped back in her chair. "Give me a minute here. Please."

Adrienne bit back her words and let her friend ruminate while they drank their coffee. The waitress appeared with their food—an omelet each and a stack of pancakes to share—and set their plates down, casting a nervous glance between the two silent women as she did so.

"Is that everything?" she asked, her voice cracking.

"Yes, thank you." Adrienne offered her an encouraging smile, which seemed to relax the young woman before she bounded off to deal with her next table.

"Morgan really makes you happy? Genuinely happy?" Tricia said suddenly, her gaze intense.

"She does." Adrienne smiled, a wonderful mix of images of Morgan conjured up by just thinking about her. "Morgan is...amazing. Thoughtful, caring, fun, intelligent. She respects me and my feelings 100 percent." Adrienne's voice was full of the passion she felt for Morgan. "She's not putting any pressure on me to rush into...things and is also concerned about how what we have fits with my job. She's willing to keep us well under the radar until the project is over. At the same time, she's making it very clear that she's in this for real, not just for some quick fling or to tick 'older woman' off some imaginary list. I honestly don't think I could have found a better person to trust my heart to again."

"Your…heart?" Tricia's eyes went wide.

"Yes! Haven't you been listening to me? I'm in. All in. Morgan is… She's someone I'm going to fall in love with, if I'm not already there, and the more I allow myself to think about that, the more I want it. Want her."

Adrienne shuddered at her own words. This thing with Morgan had somehow crept up on her, but the power of it was undeniable.

"Wow." Tricia stared at her, then shook her head once and smiled ruefully before reaching for Adrienne's hand. "My friend, please forgive me. I didn't mean to be an asshole. I was just…"

"Looking out for me?" Adrienne had suspected, deep down, that was Tricia's motivation, so despite how lukewarm her reaction to Adrienne's news had originally been, she could quite comfortably forgive her now.

"Yes." Tricia squeezed Adrienne's hand. "But in an even more overbearing way than usual, it would seem."

Adrienne snorted, and Tricia laughed, and they clutched each other's hands to anchor themselves against the mirth.

"She sounds wonderful," Tricia said, her voice catching. "And you really do seem very happy, so I am truly happy for you. The way you talk about her says it all, and I can't wait to meet this woman who's brought my friend back to life."

"Then we'll have to arrange that very soon."

Tricia smiled. "I'd love that. Now, let's eat this plate of cholesterol before it goes cold, huh?"

The long first hole on the Wentworth West Course was a daunting yet magnificent sight, and Morgan's pulse sped up just gazing down its tree-lined length. This, and many of the other famous courses around the world, was the kind of course she'd dreamed of playing as a young girl. A wide grin split her face as she turned back from the view to walk over to Harry.

"You good?" he asked.

"Beyond good," she replied and grinned even more inanely at him.

He placed a hand on her forehead. "Hm, no fever, so that ain't it."

She batted his hand away and laughed. "Harry, look at this place!" She swung her arms wide. "This is *so* cool."

He rolled his eyes, then pulled the driver out of the bag. "You here to play golf or act like a fifteen-year-old?"

"Both." She impishly stuck out her tongue.

He cocked his head and stared at her, a faint smile on his lips. "All right, Spencer, what gives?"

"Nothing." She tried to pull away from his gaze but couldn't quite do it. "Just, you know, happy."

"Happy. Uh-huh. Wouldn't have anything to do with a certain TV producer would it?"

She studied him for any signs of disapproval but found none. "Okay, yes, that too. We're...we're in a good place."

"She cares for you?" he asked, his voice a little rough.

"She does," Morgan whispered, her heart full.

"Good." He thrust the driver at her. "Now, let's practice."

Morgan smiled. His abruptness was his way of masking his emotions, and it added yet another layer to her happiness to know that Harry was pleased for her.

Impulsively, she stepped over to him and gave him a one-armed hug, which he returned in kind, his whiskery cheek pressed against hers.

"What's that for?" he asked gruffly.

"I love you, Harry." She'd never told him and hadn't imagined she would ever say it out loud, but there would never be a better moment.

Harry said nothing, just pulled away to stare at her. He rubbed the back of his neck, then patted her on the back. "That's... Thank you," he said. "Now, we gonna play some damn golf or what?"

Morgan stepped back. "Sir!" She saluted with her free hand, then grinned when he tutted and walked away.

Placing her ball on the tee, Morgan composed herself. Much as she wanted to think about Adrienne, she cleared her from her mind. She also shunted away any thoughts of her parents and the troubled stalemate their relationship found itself in. She'd catch up with her mom for a late lunch after this practice round. All thoughts of anything but golf were quickly and efficiently locked into their appropriate boxes in her mind, and she inhaled deeply once, twice, three times before stepping up to the ball.

It was time to play, and Morgan was more than ready.

"Hey, Mom." Morgan leaned into her mom's proffered hug and held her tight. "How are you?"

"Well, jet lagged like you wouldn't believe, but I'll survive," her mom answered with a light chuckle.

Morgan sat at the table in the hotel's casual brasserie-style restaurant and dropped her bag at her feet. "Well, you look pretty good to me," she said, and it was true—her mom looked surprisingly unworried and relaxed.

"Thank you, darling. That's sweet of you to say. How was your practice? And how is that lovely girlfriend of yours?"

Morgan startled. It was the first time Adrienne had been referenced as such, and the word brought a satisfaction to Morgan that was hard to describe. "Adrienne is good. She arrived last night, but we won't be able to meet up until tomorrow morning. I have sponsor commitments this evening, and she has work to do to set up their filming this week."

"Well, like you said, once this project's finished, you'll be able to see much more of each other, and that will make your time even more special."

"You're taking this new relationship very well, Mom. I mean, when I first spoke to you about Adrienne, you seemed to be worried about the age gap and—"

"That was before I heard so much about her and how well you two seem to fit. I can't wait to meet her this week."

"Oh, well, I don't know when we can make that happen, but we can certainly try."

Her mother's eyes sparkled. "I might just take matters into my own hands, you know, and introduce myself to her out on the course. I assume she'll be following your rounds?"

Morgan blinked. This new version of her mom, the confident, playful one, was a joy to know. "Um, yeah, she will, so, hey, why not? I'd love to make the introductions myself, but if that doesn't happen, I'd... Well, it would mean a lot to me that you'd go out of your way to find her and talk to her."

"Of course I would. She's important to you, more important than anyone who's come before, I think. So I want to meet this woman and get to know her too."

"I think you're gonna make me cry if you don't stop being so nice."

Her mom laughed and patted Morgan's hand. "I'm sorry, darling. But I can't seem to stop—giving your father a large piece of my mind seems to have done wonders for my emotional health. Who would have thought?" She threw Morgan a wry smile. "Come on, let's order. I'm ravenous."

They placed their orders, and after the waiter had poured them each a glass of water, they chatted about Morgan's practice round. She'd shot a seventy, which was a solid start on a tough course.

"And everything's feeling good out there?"

"It really is. Harry's pleased, which is always a good sign."

"Good."

Morgan couldn't wait any longer. "Can I ask, how was the trip over with Dad?"

Her mom smiled in a way that Morgan could only describe as wicked.

"Well," she replied as she twirled the water glass in her hand, "I think your father has finally realized this is serious and he'd better do something about it."

"Oh, really?"

Her mom snorted. "He was the most chivalrous and attentive I've seen him since we were dating. He also went to great lengths to make it obvious he was studying his player notes ready for Thursday. And *your* profile was top of his pile."

Morgan opened her mouth, but no sound appeared. Her mom nodded and smiled smugly. "Yes. And when we got to the hotel, I made it perfectly clear we were now in separate rooms, and for the first time since I met him, he was literally speechless. In fact," she said, chuckling, "he looked rather like you do right now."

Morgan still couldn't make any sound, nor could she close her mouth.

Her mother shrugged. "Let's see if this is all just for show or whether he really is going to come around."

"Well," Morgan said, finally remembering how words were formed, "I hope for your sakes it's the latter."

"I only hope he realizes what damage he would do to us, to all of us, if he tries to fake this."

Morgan nodded in agreement. While it still concerned her that her parents' marriage was going through this rough patch—she didn't want to think about it as anything more serious than that right now—somehow her emotional balance was still good.

Probably because Mom seems to be turning into a badass. If she can handle it, so can I.

When their food arrived, they turned their conversation to lighter and easier topics, and the meal passed pleasantly.

Morgan charged the lunch to her room over her mother's protests, and they said their good-byes.

"I'll hopefully see you sometime tomorrow, perhaps after my final practice round," Morgan said as they hugged.

"Whenever you can find time, darling. But don't put any pressure on yourself. I'm going to enjoy myself this week and enjoy watching you play, and I know we can always catch up again after the final round."

"Well, I like your confidence that I'll make the cut." Morgan grinned.

Her mom stepped back, her hands wrapped firmly around Morgan's biceps, and she stared deeply into Morgan's eyes. "You will. I know it. You are in a better place than you've ever been, and that will count for a lot this week. You'll see."

Morgan smiled. "Thanks. Love you."

"I love you too, darling."

Morgan watched her mom walk away toward the doors that led to the hotel grounds, then bent to gather her bag. When she stood again, her heart boomed.

Her father watched her from across the restaurant, framed by the doorway that led to the lobby.

She hesitated for just a moment, then sucked in a breath and headed his way.

He held her gaze the whole way but made no move to come to her.

"Dad," she said as she reached him.

"Morgan." His tone was clipped.

"How are you?"

"Why are you doing this to me?" he asked and looked genuinely confused.

"I... What?"

"Encouraging your mother in this...this *crazy* scheme of hers."

"Dad," Morgan said, careful to keep her tone calm and neutral. He seemed rattled, and she'd never seen him this way. "I honestly don't know what you mean. I'm not encouraging her in anything. She's done this of her own free will."

"Yes? Then why is she living with you when she should be at home?"

"Would you rather she was in a hotel, surrounded by strangers?"

He blinked. "Well, no, of course not." He ran a hand over his hair. "I don't understand," he muttered. "I've given you everything. You never wanted for anything, did you? And this is how I'm repaid."

Her temperature rose, and Morgan counted to three before she replied. "I'm not 'repaying' you for anything. This is between you and Mom. Maybe you should just listen to what she's been saying and—"

"Don't you tell me what to do!" His cheeks reddened. "Just like your mother, trying to make me do things and be a certain way and feel things I don't feel."

"Dad." This time she couldn't hide her impatience. "Seriously, are you even listening to yourself? Mom's asked you to change some specific behaviors, namely the ones where you treat her and me and all women as somehow *less* simply because we're women. Why is that so difficult for you to grasp? And why is that so difficult for you to want to change? Do you *want* to treat us all as second-class humans?"

"And now you're just being ridiculous," he scoffed, but his eyes were shadowed, as if he didn't really believe his own words. "I might have known I'd get nowhere with you."

He turned and limped away.

Morgan watched him go and breathed slowly until her heart rate normalized.

Well, at this rate, Mom may be moving in with me permanently.

She sighed. She'd always known her father was difficult, she, and sometimes even Jack, staying well clear of him when he was in one of his moods. But this...this was a whole different level, and it saddened her more than she would have thought to see her father so...lost to them all.

Chapter 18

It took every ounce of self-control Adrienne possessed not to leap out of her chair and run into Morgan's arms when Morgan walked purposefully across the coffee shop—*tea shop*, she corrected herself—toward her at around ten on Wednesday morning. Instead, Adrienne settled for smiling widely at her and gripping the table to keep her hands from doing anything inappropriate.

"Hey," Morgan said quietly as she stopped about two feet away.

"Hi."

Morgan snorted then sat down with a thump. "Oh my God, this is hard. All I want to do right now is kiss you!"

She kept her voice low, but that really didn't help Adrienne's libido to stay in check; the huskiness of Morgan's tone only added fuel to the simmering fire.

Adrienne cleared her throat. "I know. And me too."

Nodding, Morgan stared at her, a big smile plastered on her face. "You look good."

It still took some getting used to, receiving compliments from this gorgeous woman, but Adrienne did her best to gracefully accept with a dip of her head and a murmured, "Thank you."

"How are you feeling?"

"Is that code for, 'you look tired, honey'?" Adrienne asked with a smirk.

Morgan laughed, then shook her head. "No! Trust me, if you looked like crap, I'd tell you."

Adrienne doubted that was true. "I'm fine. Less tired than I would imagine, actually. Flying business class did make a difference."

"Oh yeah! I still remember flying coach to Europe when I was a student. I felt like I'd never stand up straight again after I finally peeled myself out of my seat at Heathrow."

Chuckling, Adrienne made to reach across the table, then stopped herself. *Damn!*

"I know," Morgan said sympathetically when Adrienne tutted at herself and sat back.

Adrienne looked around. The tea shop wasn't part of the hotel complex they were all staying in, but even so, it was only a few hundred yards away from the hotel's main entrance on the edge of the small village nearby. Close enough that any form of intimate interaction between them was too risky if Adrienne wanted to ensure her job was safe until the project was over. Maybe she was worrying for nothing. Maybe she was just paranoid after Tricia had expressed so much concern for her position, but there really wasn't any reason to be stupid about this. Three more weeks and she could be as open with Morgan as she wished.

"So would you like a coffee? Something to eat? It's not table service here," Adrienne clarified, as Morgan lifted the quaintly printed menu from its equally quaint holder.

Morgan smiled. "Welsh Rarebit." She shook her head. "Still confuses me. But no, I've already eaten, so just coffee would be fine."

Adrienne stood and walked over to the counter, where the thin-faced, sallow young woman behind the display of cakes and buns looked up with barely a smile to take her order for two coffees, one with cream. When she returned to the table, Morgan watched her every move, and once again Adrienne's libido stirred in a delicious way.

"You need to stop looking at me like that," she said as she eased back into her seat.

"Why?" Morgan attempted an innocent look, but the quirk of her lips gave her away.

Adrienne rolled her eyes. "What have I got myself in for?"

Morgan laughed. "Okay, so in all seriousness, and I hate to say it, but I don't have long. I've got a press call at 11:00 a.m., then practice at 1:00 p.m. Then we've got the opening reception at 6:00 p.m. Ugh. So we ought to get on with this and talk about how much you want from me this week."

Her eyes widened, and Adrienne laughed.

"Well, that conjures up a very tempting list of possibilities." Adrienne kept her voice low, and she delighted in the blush that stole across Morgan's cheek at her flirty comment. *Wow, I haven't totally forgotten how to do this. How lovely.* "But let's focus on the film." She pulled her notebook out of her purse and opened it at the relevant page. "Here's what I was thinking."

Over the mediocre coffee, they agreed on the amount of time Morgan would be tracked by Jenny, Toby, and Diane. Adrienne was meeting them that afternoon to talk through her ideas and ensure they would deliver what she needed. She also penciled in a possible additional sit-down interview with Morgan on Monday, reluctant to say it out loud, but hopeful they'd be talking about Morgan's first major win at that point.

"Okay, I guess we can do another interview. If nothing else, we could talk about the weather," Morgan said with a wry grin.

"How's your confidence level?"

"Actually, pretty good. More than good. But let's not jinx anything, all right?"

Adrienne smiled warmly at her. "Deal."

Morgan glanced at her watch. "Crap. I have to go."

"I'll leave with you." Adrienne stood then gathered her things. "I want to pop into that little grocery store for a few items."

Adrienne paid for their coffee and followed Morgan out into the warm August air. The main street that ran through the village was busy with traffic, presumably most of it related to the upcoming tournament. A few heads turned in recognition as Morgan strolled along, but no one stopped her.

"Do you get used to that?" Adrienne asked.

"Um, yes and no. It's kind of odd, being looked at so much, but thankfully everyone's pretty respectful of my space, so it's easy to deal with. I wouldn't mind interacting with them, especially the young girls, because I know how valuable it is to get some encouragement from your sporting heroes, but at the same time, I've got to stay focused. And get to that press call."

They reached the grocery store and stopped in front of the large window displaying a selection of its offerings.

"I guess I'll leave you here," Morgan said softly, glancing around. "It's been really good to see you, and I can't wait until we can spend some more time together."

"Yes," Adrienne murmured, astonished at how the thought of not seeing Morgan properly for the next few days affected her. "But you go do what you do best and know that I'll be supporting you every step of the way as you do so. You're going to be brilliant, I know."

"Thank you." Morgan looked as if she wanted to say more, but with a slight shake of her head, she stepped past Adrienne, brushing her fingers against Adrienne's as she did so. "Miss you," she whispered, then was gone, striding purposefully up the street, her ponytail bouncing in sync with her steps.

Adrienne was annoyed, and it was not an experience she was that familiar with. She prided herself on being level-headed, professional, and able to handle any situation her job threw at her, but right here and now, she was pissed.

Although both Toby and Diane were jet lagged, having only arrived the day before due to budget constraints, they'd both assured her they'd be firing on all cylinders when needed. So, no, it wasn't their lack of energy causing her annoyance or the fact that Cindy Thomson had, to Adrienne's bafflement, thrown her a vicious look when they'd passed each other in the clubhouse lobby an hour or so ago.

Much to Adrienne's surprise and concern, it was Jenny's behavior that was the cause of her irritation, and she paced up and down the small room they were using for their meeting while she waited for her missing assistant to return from who knew where.

Jenny had responded to Adrienne's messages asking her whereabouts—and reminding her she'd missed the initial meeting with the crew—with short, some would say terse, responses and a vague comment that she'd be back soon. Adrienne had no choice but to dismiss Toby and Diane for a while, suggesting they might want to check out the course, vantage points, et cetera, while Adrienne awaited Jenny's return so the four of them could finalize the shooting schedule.

When the door opened and Jenny walked in, a scowl on her face, Adrienne stopped in the middle of the room and just managed to wait until the door closed before she exploded.

"Where the hell have you been?"

"Out," Jenny responded sullenly.

"Out? Out where? Are you okay?" She'd never seen Jenny so…*angry*. Jenny was practically seething with it. "What's going on?"

"Oh, yeah, that's the big question, isn't it?" Jenny snapped. "God, how stupid was I? I believed all that crap you told me about trusting me to handle Miami on my own, and it was all just a bunch of bullshit!"

Adrienne blinked, her mind completely unable to connect all the dots. "What are you talking about? Of course I trusted you with Miami! I've seen the footage. It's great."

"I'm not talking about the footage!" Jenny's voice rose. "I'm talking about *her*! About you manipulating me, lying to me, making sure I was out of the way so you could make your move. You hypocrite!"

Holding out her hands in a gesture she hoped would be received as peaceful, Adrienne spoke quietly, unable to comprehend what had worked her assistant into such a state but determined to get to the bottom of it. "Please help me out here. I honestly don't know what's got you so upset and—"

"Oh, don't be ridiculous! Don't lie to me anymore." Jenny glared at her then paused as she studied Adrienne. She took one step closer. "Morgan! You wanted her for yourself, didn't you? So you gave me that whole speech about knowing the boundaries and keeping it all professional, then got me out of the way and took her for yourself!"

"I… What? That's simply not true. I would never do—"

"I saw you," Jenny spat. She shook her head. "This morning. All cozy outside that store, holding hands, looking all gooey at each other. Don't try to deny it!"

Oh. Shit.

Adrienne exhaled slowly, then lowered her hands. "If I promise to tell you the truth, explain to you what's happened, will you please come and sit down to hear it? I hate seeing you so upset like this. Truly."

"I don't need to hear any more lies. I'm—"

"Jenny," Adrienne said firmly, "you need to hear my side of this story. You and I have worked too closely together for you to deny me that, haven't we?"

Something shifted in Jenny, firstly in her eyes, then in the set of her shoulders, and finally in the angry scrunch of her face. She blinked a couple of times, then walked two paces across the room to the nearest chair and threw herself into it.

Adrienne followed and pulled up a second chair to within a few feet of her. She leaned forward, her elbows on her knees, and looked into Jenny's eyes. Her stomach knotted, knowing she'd done exactly what she'd told Jenny not to do and how bad that must look to her assistant.

She's right, you are a hypocrite.

"Morgan and I are seeing each other, yes," she began, and Jenny blew out an explosive breath. "But it certainly wasn't anything I deliberately set out to make happen." Adrienne continued, keeping her voice calm. "I know this looks bad. I know it is everything I told you not to do but... We just ended up spending more time together and realized that there was a mutual attraction we couldn't fight. And I did try to keep it within the boundaries I spoke to you about, I really did, but it was...too strong."

"Oh, please," Jenny said snidely, "you're, like, *twenty* years older than her. This is just some midlife-crisis thing or something."

Adrienne's smile was sad. "You know, it might be easier if it was. But it isn't. She's...very important to me, and I'm sorry that you found out the way you did and interpreted it the way you did. I honestly didn't mean to hurt you. But what Morgan and I have is serious, and it's not something I'm going to give up."

"What about your job if anyone finds out?"

Was that a veiled threat? God, I hope not.

"We've agreed to keep it secret until the project's over. Then I will inform Daniel, and hopefully he will realize it didn't impact my work in any way and give me his blessing."

Jenny snorted, but there was now a haunted look in her eyes. She stood.

"I really liked her, Adrienne." Jenny's eyes filled with tears. "I...really liked her."

Before Adrienne could stop her, she walked quickly to the door and left the room.

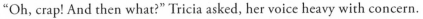

"Oh, crap! And then what?" Tricia asked, her voice heavy with concern.

"She messaged me about half an hour later, telling me she was unwell and needed the rest of the day off. What could I do? I can't accuse her of lying about that and force her to work. So I gave her the day, told her I was there for her if she wanted to talk again, and haven't heard from her since."

Adrienne sighed and leaned back against the headboard of her hotel bed. It had been one hell of an afternoon. With Jenny gone, she'd finalized the schedule with Toby and Diane and e-mailed it to her missing-in-action assistant in the vain hope she'd still turn up for work the next morning. Then she'd holed up in her room with a meal and a glass of wine and called her best friend.

"And does Morgan know any of this?"

"No! She doesn't need to be involved. She's got a first round to play in the morning and needs all the concentration she can muster. Besides, this is my problem to fix, not hers."

"Ah, well, that's only true if Jenny keeps the knowledge to herself. I'll be honest, Addy, I'm concerned she's going to do something with this."

"Yes, the thought's crossed my mind too." She closed her eyes. "You know, I really, *really* hope that everything we've achieved together will give her pause. I get that she's young and she feels like I made a fool of her, but I suppose I hope she'll remember everything else and eventually write this off as an unfortunate stumble between us."

"You think she'll still want to work for you?" Tricia sounded skeptical.

"I honestly don't know. I hope so. If nothing else, I'd still like to mentor her even if she asks to move teams."

"Well." Tricia exhaled loudly. "I guess now all you can do is hope."

"Indeed. Oh God, what a mess."

"Hey, don't panic. Let's hope for the best, but you know, if this does all come out, you'll ride it out. I know you will. And Morgan will help you, I'm sure."

At that thought, Adrienne glowed. "Yes, she would. She's very concerned about my position with the company, and I know she'd support me 100 percent."

"She sounds like a keeper."

Adrienne smiled. "I really think she is."

"This!" Charlie exclaimed as she grabbed Morgan's biceps and squeezed excitedly. "This is what I wanted for you! Look at you. You're all aglow!"

"Aglow?" Morgan rolled her eyes, then laughed when Charlie tutted at her.

They were outside the clubhouse, stood in a quiet spot away from the busy comings and goings of all the players, officials, TV crews, and reporters—the usual circus that surrounded a major tournament. Charlie had found her in amongst the melee and hauled her off to interrogate her about the latest developments with Adrienne, having learned the basics via text messages the previous day or so. Their busy schedules in the lead-up to today's first round had, however, prevented them from finding some private time to actually talk.

"Yes! Don't try pretending you're not." Charlie smiled warmly at her. "God, I'm so happy for you!"

"Thanks, Charlie." Impulsively Morgan pulled her friend into a hug.

"Can I meet her properly now? Maybe we could all have breakfast together on Monday?"

Morgan pulled out of the hug. "That's a great idea. I'll check with Adrienne, but I'm sure she'd love to get to know you."

Charlie grinned. "Look at you with the whole 'I'll check with my girlfriend' thing going on."

Morgan chuckled. "It feels kinda weird to hear her called that. It'll take some getting used to."

"Well, get used to it. I've got a feeling this one's going to last."

"I really hope so," Morgan said fervently.

"Aww." Charlie squeezed Morgan's arm again, then sighed. "Okay, I guess we need to go do our respective things."

"Yeah. I'm glad we found even this time to catch up. How are you feeling?"

"Pumped! Just so excited to be here again, and this time knowing if I keep everything steady, I've got a good chance of playing the weekend."

"I think there's every chance of that! I really hope you do well, Charlie."

"You too!"

They hugged once more, then went their separate ways.

Morgan spent the morning with a mix of press interviews and some putting practice; she was playing in the afternoon, teeing off at 1:30 p.m.

Harry was in a good mood—he'd found an "awesome" spot for some fishing in his free time—and they joked around a little as she putted, which helped quell some of the jitters that had crept in through the morning. They weren't necessarily bad jitters, though. Morgan didn't want it to get out of control, but an excited buzz ran through her. She knew she had played well these past few weeks, and she knew her mind was in a great place too.

What a contrast to the same time the previous year when Naomi had ripped their relationship apart only a week before they flew to Europe.

As if reading her mind, Harry asked the one question he'd probably been building up to all morning. "You feeling okay about your playing partner today and tomorrow?" He tried to make it sound casual, but concern shone in his eyes.

Morgan shrugged. "Ideally it wouldn't be her. But that's the luck of the draw and nothing I can do anything about." She exhaled slowly. "I'm just there to play my golf, and I hope she is too."

"Hm."

"What?"

Harry shook his head. "I don't trust her. If she starts trying to get under your skin, you just—"

Morgan held up a hand. "It's okay. She can talk all she wants. I'm not going to let her get to me. Trust me, I am totally focused on my game and nothing else."

He gazed at her for a few moments. "All right," he said eventually, nodding. "Then let's get some lunch before we need to get out there."

Morgan watched from the edge of the sixteenth green as Naomi attempted a long putt to save her par. She missed wide right and shook her head as she walked to her ball and marked it. She was now three over par, having a nightmare of a round. With anyone else, Morgan might offer a few words of sympathy, but she knew she'd be wasting her breath with Naomi.

They'd been professional with each other and nothing more. And despite what Morgan had said earlier to Harry, she *was* relieved that Naomi hadn't felt the need to be a bitch again. There had been a small part of her that dreaded any kind of confrontation to upset her balance, but it seemed Naomi had also turned up focused to play. Unfortunately for her, two awful drives on the sixth and ninth had left her in a precarious position from which she'd not really recovered.

Morgan, on the other hand, was completely in her zone and currently three under par, with a birdie chance facing her here on the sixteenth. She pushed all thoughts of Naomi out of her head as she approached her marker, a mere three feet from the hole, and replaced it with her ball. Harry walked around and eyed the putt from the opposite side, while Morgan crouched and viewed it from the playing side. If there was a buzz of chatter from the crowd, or birds chirping in the nearby trees, Morgan couldn't hear them. She straightened again, then waited for Harry to join her.

"You got this," was all he said before walking away to the edge of the green.

She smiled briefly, then stepped up to the shot. Thirty seconds later, the ball rolled effortlessly into the center of the cup, and the crowd erupted. She mentally fist-pumped, then acknowledged the crowd's applause before retrieving her ball and throwing it to Harry.

Four under, two to play. Couldn't have asked for better.

"*Yes!*" Adrienne said softly, watching Morgan go four under, one shot ahead of the rest of the field. Morgan was playing so well, and Adrienne burst with pride and excitement.

She eased her way through the crowds, who were staying to watch the next pairing arrive on the sixteenth, and reached the path that led to the seventeenth tee.

It was a glorious summer's day, and she reveled in the sun's warmth on her face as she walked. Her steps were light, which she knew came from the excitement of watching Morgan do so well. She refused to let the sour situation with Jenny spoil her day. Thankfully, her assistant, while still clearly pissed at Adrienne, had woken up with her professional persona in place and was now ensconced on the eighteenth green with Toby and

Diane, capturing the top players' final shots of this first round. Adrienne could have stayed with them to oversee but had made her excuses and left them to it. If Jenny suspected what Adrienne was going to do instead, she gave no obvious sign, focused on the schedule and keeping her head down.

It was probably the best Adrienne could hope for.

"Ms. Wyatt?" a voice asked from her left side.

Adrienne turned and found Bree Spencer strolling toward her, a warm smile on her face. She was casually dressed in capri pants and a summer sweater, both in a rich blue, but she still looked classy and poised. The breeze lifted her hair, and she absently patted it back down with one hand while the other removed her sunglasses.

"Mrs. Spencer!" Adrienne halted her steps and held out her hand. "It's lovely to meet you."

Bree smiled and shook her hand firmly. "And you. I was hoping I would find you today. Do you mind if I walk with you to the seventeenth?" Her blue eyes shone in the bright sunshine, and Adrienne noted that Bree had the same long, lush eyelashes as her daughter.

"No, not at all!"

They fell back into step beside each other. Adrienne found herself unusually nervous. She knew Bree knew about Morgan and Adrienne's burgeoning relationship, and Morgan had assured her Bree was happy for them, but…

"I'm going to come right out and say it," Bree said, and although quiet, her voice carried more than a hint of excitement. "I'm so happy for you and Morgan!"

"Oh." Adrienne's heart thumped, and she smiled. "Well, thank you. That's wonderful to hear."

"I've never seen her so happy." Bree leaned in and kept her voice quiet—she clearly knew they were still keeping it on the down low. "She didn't stop smiling the whole two days I was in her house."

Adrienne shook her head. "I really don't know what to say, but thank you. I…I'll be honest, I worried you would think I was too old for her. I mean, *we're* nearer in age," she said, motioning between herself and Bree, "than myself and Morgan."

Bree chuckled. "Sorry, dear, I'm already spoken for." Adrienne nearly choked, and Bree patted her arm. "Was that too much?"

Adrienne laughed. "No, you're fine. I... Thank you for coming over to say hi."

"It was important." Bree shrugged. "Morgan's had a hard time this past year or so, longer if you count all the ways her father has let her down since she turned professional. I'm determined she knows that at least one of her parents supports her in every aspect of her life. Especially," Bree said with a warm smile, "when she's found herself such a lovely partner."

"Mrs. Spencer, you're making me blush."

"Oh, please call me Bree."

"Okay, then please call me Adrienne."

They smiled at each other, then Bree, to Adrienne's joy, linked her arm through Adrienne's.

"Right, now that we've got that all worked out, let's go support our Morgan together, shall we?"

Overcome with emotion, Adrienne merely nodded and allowed Bree Spencer to lead her to the seventeenth tee.

Chapter 19

YOU'RE PLAYING SO WELL! I'M so proud of you. x

The message from Adrienne was one of many Morgan had received from various people that Friday evening, but it was the one that warmed her heart the most. Although the one from her brother, Jack, was right up there too.

Best I've ever seen you play! I'm glad I got knocked out on the quarters yesterday. Now I can watch you all weekend, haha!

She'd chuckled at that one. He would have been pissed not to make it to the semis of the Rogers Cup, but given his ranking, the quarters was a great achievement. Her message back to him had been full of praise, and they'd chatted via text for a couple of minutes.

Her mom had called, and Morgan had taken that one, letting everyone else who'd tried go to voice mail. Being two shots in the lead overnight going into the third round of the Women's British Open, Morgan didn't want any distractions. But talking to her mom didn't count.

"Oh, and I found Adrienne again, and we had a lovely time together," her mom said after they'd chatted a little about Morgan's second round.

"You're seeing her more than I am," Morgan grumbled.

Her mother laughed. "I know, dear, but I think it helps her having someone she can talk to about you."

"I hope you're not giving away all my secrets, Mom."

"Only a few, darling."

Morgan had groaned, her mom had laughed, and they'd said good night at that point.

Her last message of the evening had been from Hilton.

Superstar! Loving what I'm seeing out there. So are S Pro.

He'd finished that with a winking emoji, and Morgan had to admit his hint of good news about a major sponsor gave her a flutter of excitement. If she was signed by S Pro, all sorts of things would be possible, never mind the money she'd earn. For starters, she could begin to ease up her schedule somewhat—more time at home would be wonderful, especially if Adrienne was part of that picture. At that thought, her stomach flipped.

Whoa, slow down! You haven't even started dating properly, and you're already thinking of living together? She chuckled ruefully. *I'm so far gone it's crazy.*

Morgan put her phone down and concentrated on getting ready for the morning. She'd be playing with Kim Lee, who was one shot behind Morgan. So Park was in third place, a further shot back, tied with Laurie Schweitzer, so they'd be the penultimate pair going out. Naomi hadn't even made the cut and had glared at Morgan as she left the referee's office, as if somehow it was Morgan's fault. Morgan had ignored her.

According to things Morgan had overheard, Kim Lee apparently wasn't firing on all cylinders. Morgan had heard rumors of Lee having an ankle injury this week, and while Morgan felt sorry for her, she had to admit a less-than-100-percent Lee was good news for herself.

Yeah, but you *still have to play your game, so focus only on that.*

With her brain firmly back in the right place, Morgan concentrated on her course notes for the third round and sipped at a chamomile tea.

Adrienne pushed her way into the back of the press room on Saturday evening, more than a little surprised to see it so busy. Sure, Morgan had fired another impressive round to maintain her position in first place at the end of the third round today, and Laurie Schweitzer had played even better to be only two shots behind Morgan overnight, but the press hadn't seemed this interested even at the PGA. Keeping herself against the rear wall to ensure Morgan wouldn't see her through the crowd, Adrienne watched the session unfold.

The top four—Morgan, Schweitzer, So Park, and Charlie McKinnon—were just taking their seats up on the raised platform. A sound technician fussed around with the microphones, then hurried away. That was the signal for the questions to start, and at a prompt from the tour official acting as moderator, Patty from CBS got them underway.

"Morgan, how does it feel to be leading a major going into the final round?"

"It's not bad," Morgan said with a wry grin, which earned her a laugh from the room.

Laurie looked pissed, and Adrienne couldn't help the small measure of delight that gave her.

"But seriously," Morgan said, "it was another good day, and that's all you ever want."

A slew of hands shot up. The moderator pointed at a man in the fourth row.

"Tom Harrison, Sport Today dot Net," he announced loudly above the clamor in the room.

Adrienne tutted. Sport Today were renowned for including large doses of gossip and speculation about stars' private lives in amongst their actual coverage of the main sports played in the US. Their presence in a press room was always treated with a certain level of derision by the rest of the journalists.

Someone near to Adrienne muttered, "Asshole," but she forgot all about seeing who that was as Tom asked his question.

"Morgan, I'm guessing having a new woman in your life has helped your preparations for this week, yes?"

The room fell eerily silent for a moment.

Morgan blinked, and Adrienne wanted to climb over the ten rows of chairs in front of her and strangle Tom Harrison with his own tie.

"Even if there was something new in my private life," Morgan said in a tight voice, "I don't think this is the place for me to discuss it. If you want to ask about my round today, then—"

"Is it true she's working on a documentary with you?" Tom interrupted. "That despite there being very clear ethical issues around being involved with someone she works with, she's pursued you to each tournament and—"

Adrienne didn't hear what else he said. She froze in place, her heart thudding painfully. How dare he? And where the *hell* had he gotten his information?

Oh God, no. Please, not Jenny. Her stomach dropped to her knees. *Surely she wouldn't.*

Would she?

Suddenly aware that a few pairs of eyes now looked in her direction, Adrienne inhaled deeply. She willed her face not to color and lifted her chin in defiance. On meeting her calm, level gaze, most people looked rapidly away.

One person, however, locked gazes with her and didn't flinch.

In fact, she looked highly amused.

Cindy Thomson.

Morgan's heart raced so violently she wondered how everyone in the room couldn't hear it. How the hell had Harrison found out?

"I'm not going to answer questions about my private life," she repeated through gritted teeth.

Where was Adrienne? *God, please don't let her be here, having to listen to this.*

"Next question!" the moderator called. He sounded flustered and out of his depth.

Harrison opened his mouth, but a woman from the UK newspaper *The Times* stood up from two seats away and practically yelled her question over whatever Tom was trying to say next.

"Do you think a two-shot lead is enough going into tomorrow?"

Thank God. Whoever you are, British lady, I love you.

Morgan exhaled slowly and cast a quick glance at Laurie Schweitzer, whose face was set in a grim mask of disapproval.

"Well, I'd like it to be more, of course," Morgan said, and hoped her voice didn't wobble with the stress. "Laurie's a tough player, as are all the women in the top six or seven. I know I'll have to play my very best to maintain that lead."

Laurie shifted in her seat, and a smile finally graced her face as she leaned forward into her microphone. "Yes, you will."

Some of the tension in the room broke with light chuckles scattered here and there.

"What she said!" Charlie said.

The laughter that had started gently with Laurie's comment turned into a full wave of mirth around the room.

The woman from *The Times* turned her next question to Laurie, and Morgan only just stopped herself from slumping back in her chair. *Professional, remember?* But God, that was so hard right now when all she wanted to do was, first, punch Tom Harrison and, second, find Adrienne and make sure she was okay.

They all endured another twenty minutes of the press before the moderator called a halt. Thankfully, all further questions had purely been about the golf, with every other reporter in the room, it seemed, determined to keep Harrison quiet. Morgan thought she caught more than a few looks of disgust thrown his way by his peers as they all stood to leave.

Morgan couldn't get off the stage quick enough but kept her back straight and her pace even as she did so. A warm hand took hold of her elbow. She turned to see Laurie looking at her with, much to Morgan's surprise, sympathy on her face.

"You didn't deserve that," Laurie said. She shrugged. "I mean, I'm still going to kick your ass tomorrow, but what he did back there was bullshit, and I'm sorry you had to go through it."

Morgan was stunned. "Thanks, Laurie." She grinned. "And we'll see about that ass kicking."

Laurie chuckled, released Morgan's elbow, and walked away.

"What did *she* want?" Charlie asked as Morgan drew level with her at the doorway.

"Actually, she was nice. Told me what Tom did was crap."

"And she was right!" Charlie's eyes narrowed. "What the hell *was* all that? I was very close to leaping off the stage and punching him."

Morgan shook her head, and her dread for Adrienne swamped her, turning her blood cold. "Yeah, I can relate. I have no idea what he thinks he knows or how, but I have to find Adrienne."

"Come on, I've got no plans right now. Let's search together. Four eyes are better than two, right?"

Adrienne scrolled through the article on the Sport Today website and didn't know whether to scream or cry or both. The information they'd received from whoever their source was clearly had enough meat that they'd been able to fill in the gaps and present a fairly accurate picture of what had happened between her and Morgan. Now pretty much the whole golfing world knew about them, and it would only be a matter of time before her phone started ringing.

She sighed as she looked out over the eighteenth green. Having managed to extricate herself from the press room shortly after Harrison dropped his bombshell—neatly sidestepping Cindy and her vicious smile before she could open her nasty mouth—Adrienne had fled to the only place she knew would be empty. There were a couple of course grounds staff clearing up after the day, but tucked beside the seating stand, Adrienne was out of sight and could at least breathe again.

How had this unraveled so spectacularly? And what did it mean for them? For herself?

Right on cue, her phone rang, with Daniel's number in the caller display. She had to talk to him, she knew that, but not right now. She needed time to gather her thoughts, to understand within herself what she was comfortable doing about this situation.

And to find Morgan, make sure she was okay, and talk it through with her. Adrienne couldn't make this decision alone; she was in a partnership, albeit a sparkly new one, but what Morgan thought counted for much.

She declined Daniel's call to send it through to voice mail and slipped her phone in her purse.

A quick glance at her watch told her the press call should now be finished. Time to head back to the hotel and take some time to calm down before she found Morgan.

Finding Jenny was also on her list. Although ripping off her assistant's head wasn't going to solve anything. The story was out, whether it was Jenny who had provided it or not. She was high on Adrienne's list of suspects simply because of what had come to pass over the last couple of days. But also high on the list was Cindy Thomson—that smirk she'd given Adrienne in the press room had been way too knowing.

Adrienne sighed. Cindy she could deal with. But if it was Jenny, then that was, unfortunately, the end of their working relationship. There would be no way back from this.

217

Morgan and Charlie stood on the front steps of the clubhouse, hands on hips.

"She must have gone for a walk," Morgan said as she scanned their surroundings.

"Well, I can't blame her for wanting some privacy after that," Charlie replied softly.

"No, nor can I." Morgan sighed. "I hope she's okay."

"Still no answer to your message?"

"No." She shrugged. "Hey, she's a grown-up. When she's ready to talk, she'll find me."

Charlie grasped her arm. "She will. I wouldn't be surprised if she's just staying out of your way, thinking you need some time too."

"Yeah, I know. I just hate that it happened this way. Outside of a tournament, I could, I don't know, whisk her away somewhere quiet where we could just be…us. Here, I'm totally exposed and supposed to be focusing on the final round tomorrow."

"And she'd want you to do that, you know that, right?" Charlie stared intently at her. "That's what's so good about what you two have already—you both get what's important to each other outside of what you share."

Morgan's mood lifted at the words. "Yeah, that's absolutely true."

"Big change from what you had with Naomi, huh?"

Morgan snorted. "Very true."

"So, um, who do you think gave them the story?"

Morgan exhaled slowly. "I guess probably Naomi. I still can't believe she'd go that far, though."

"Oh, come on, she's totally capable of something like this." Charlie's mouth twisted in disgust.

"Ugh, I suppose you're right."

"Morgan, I'd like a word with you, please." Her father's voice from behind her made her jump, and she spun round.

"Dad?"

"Hi, Mr. Spencer," Charlie said breezily.

Morgan's father merely nodded in Charlie's direction, and Morgan's tension ratcheted up.

"Um, well, I guess I'll get back inside," Charlie said. She caught Morgan's eye and raised one eyebrow.

"Sure. I'll catch you later."

Charlie gave Morgan's arm a quick pat, then trotted back into the clubhouse.

Morgan studied her father. The telltale signs of anger were written all over his face—jaw set hard, eyes narrowed, one vein throbbing on the left side of his forehead.

"And you wonder why I don't give you more support," he said, his voice like iron.

"What?" Morgan went from worried to angry in less than two seconds.

He stepped closer. "This is exactly why. You're nothing but a trashy story now. Your TV producer. Really, Morgan?"

"Now wait a minute, Dad, you have no—"

"Where's your professionalism? Where's your respect for the game? You think anyone will take you seriously as a golfer after this?"

"Well," Morgan spat, the dam that had held back her anger all these years finally bursting, "you've never taken me seriously, so why should I care what opinion you have of me now, huh? And talk about double standards."

She stepped up to him, looking him straight in the eye from her position of almost equal height with the man who had fathered her in pretty much name only. Her blood was hot in her veins, her skin almost crackling from it. "I don't remember you saying anything like this about Woods when he made the headlines for all the wrong reasons. *I* seem to remember you saying that he needed everyone's support to get him through a difficult time. How come the rules are different for him, Dad? How come your own daughter doesn't warrant the same courtesy?"

He flinched, and his jaw trembled slightly. "Because…because you *are* my daughter," he said. He pushed one hand roughly through his hair in obvious frustration. "Because what you do reflects on me."

"So, what, I'm supposed to be perfect, is that it? Because anything else looks bad on you? Jesus, no wonder I never made it in your eyes. What an impossible standard to set for someone. Does Jack have to live by the same measure, huh?"

"You leave Jack out of this."

"Oh, no, I think we definitely need to bring Jack into this. You've always treated us differently, and I never wanted to believe the reason why, but it's so clear now. Jack was born perfect because he was a boy. I was born far from perfect because I wasn't. That's what it boils down to, doesn't it? That's why Jack can be number 108 in the world of tennis and you still treat him like a hero, while I'm close to being world number one and you won't give me the time of day." She stared at him in disgust. "God, Dad, I'm your *daughter*. I'm your flesh and blood, yet all you've ever cared about is my gender." She stepped back, her anger spent. "You and I are done, Gordy Spencer. I don't owe you anything anymore, nor do I have to prove anything to you anymore. I see now there's literally no point." She laughed, feeling freer than she had in years. "All this time I wasted trying to impress a man who couldn't even see me. Not anymore. Now I'm going to play my game for *me* because I love it and because I'm damn good at it."

Without waiting for him to respond, Morgan pushed past him and strode back into the clubhouse.

Chapter 20

ADRIENNE MADE IT TO HER room with only one person attempting to stop her for a comment. She politely brushed them off and breathed a sigh of relief as she closed her room door behind her.

She set her purse on the desk and retrieved her phone. Daniel hadn't called again, so at least he wasn't pestering her. His voice mail was short and to the point.

Adrienne, please call me as soon as possible. We obviously need to discuss what has been revealed, and I think it would be best for all of us if we did that sooner rather than later.

He sounded much the same as always, which gave her a little comfort. However, he wouldn't be hearing from her until she'd had some time with Morgan. And given Morgan had the small matter of the final round of a major to play tomorrow, Adrienne was more than okay with putting off all other matters until after then. Of course, she still had to decide whether to show her face in public again tomorrow, but that could be a decision for the morning.

Right now, she wanted a large glass of wine and a shower, in that order. She called room service and placed her order and was pleasantly surprised when the knock on her door came only a few minutes later.

"Well, that's great serv—" she said as she opened the door, only to break off when she found Jenny waiting on the other side.

"Hi," Jenny whispered. She looked drawn and tired, her normally vibrant, spiky hair lying flat, her skin pale.

"Oh. Hello."

"Can I...can I come in? It's important."

I really don't think I'm up for this now, but…

"Okay."

Adrienne stepped aside, and Jenny walked into the room.

"Are you okay?" Jenny asked as soon as Adrienne joined her in the center of the room. Jenny had her hands clasped in front of her, and her entire body was rigid with tension.

"I've been better," Adrienne replied coolly. Feeling no need to pussyfoot around, she said, "Was it you? Will you tell me why? I know we inadvertently hurt you, but I don't think—"

"It wasn't me! I swear it. But I can totally get why you think it would have been." Jenny's eyes filled with tears, and seconds later, they overspilled, trickling down her pale cheeks. "I was such an idiot, Adrienne. I'm so sorry. But believe me, it wasn't me who gave that prick, Harrison, the story."

She seemed sincere, and Adrienne's fears that Jenny had been their leak started to abate.

"Look," Jenny said, a little more firmly, "just listen to this."

She pulled her phone from her pocket, tapped the screen a couple times, and then Cindy Thomson's voice came from the speaker.

"Sick of her acting all superior because she works on films like that. I could do that. I just need my chance. I need some way of getting her brought down a step or two, and your news might just be the way to do it."

"And we'd both get something out of it."

That was Naomi Chase's voice. A chill raced down Adrienne's spine.

"Wait," she said, and Jenny stopped the audio. "What is this? Where did you get it?"

"Yesterday I stumbled across the two of them talking in a small meeting room at the back of the clubhouse." Jenny blushed. "I was…um, trying to avoid you, to find somewhere quiet to work where you wouldn't be looking over my shoulder. Anyway, I was going to back away and find somewhere else when I realized they were talking about you and Morgan." She sighed. "I was already feeling pretty stupid for the way I treated you, and I knew I'd need to apologize, but when I heard them badmouthing both of you, I listened in. As soon as I realized *what* they were talking about, I started recording them." Jenny looked at Adrienne. "Shall I play the rest?"

Adrienne nodded, her hands trembling.

"I do like a win-win situation." Cindy again. "Now, obviously we need to make sure this does not come back to bite us on the ass. So who's gullible enough to break this for us?"

There was a pause. "Tom Harrison?" Naomi said. "That asshole would sell his own grandmother for a story like this."

"Oh, yeah. Perfect! And I know just the person to deliver the message. There's a runner for our channel who's desperate to get a step up. If I hint to her that some sort of promotion might be coming her way if she helps out, I bet she'd grab that chance with both hands. I do like an ambitious young woman." Cindy's laugh was almost evil.

Naomi laughed with her. "You know, Cindy, I thought I was a bitch until I met you. Something tells me I could learn a lot from you."

"Oh, you could, I'm sure," Cindy purred.

"Enough!" Adrienne held up a hand, and Jenny stopped the playback once more. "God, I feel nauseous from that last exchange."

Jenny laughed. "Hell yes. Trust me, the rest of it got pretty gross, and I stopped recording anyway. Couldn't quite get the image of those two out of my head for the rest of the evening."

Adrienne walked unsteadily over to one of the chairs in the corner of her room and sat. A knock sounded on the door.

"Want me to get that?" Jenny asked.

"It'll just be room service, so if you don't mind…" Adrienne wasn't sure she could stand again any time soon. How the hell could Cindy and Naomi do this? How could anyone be that filled with envy and jealousy that they'd try to ruin two careers? "Hey, Jenny, take my purse. There's some cash in there for a tip."

Jenny returned with Adrienne's wine, handed it to her, then took the other chair. She flopped unceremoniously into it with a big sigh.

"I'm really sorry they did this to you."

Adrienne waved her words off, drinking heartily from her wine. "God, I needed that."

"And I'm sorry I didn't bring this recording to you earlier. I was sure I had more time to play with. It never occurred to me they'd get the story out that quickly. I guess that's another sign of my naivety when it comes to this business. And my immaturity around the whole situation with you and Morgan."

Adrienne placed her wine carefully on the small table between their chairs, then leaned over and waited until Jenny met her eyes before speaking. "We've all done things we've regretted, and, yes, usually when we're young, but trust me, age is no protection against stupidity. I'm sorry I suspected you."

Jenny smiled. "It's okay. I would have too."

"And I appreciate you coming to me with this and your apologies. That's the end of it as far as I'm concerned, okay?"

Tears leaked from Jenny's eyes again, but she nodded furiously. "Yes, yes, thank you." She rubbed her eyes. "So how's Morgan taking it all?"

Adrienne sighed. "I haven't actually spoken to her. She needs to focus on tomorrow. Whatever we need to discuss can wait until after the tournament. It's not like we could change the story now."

"God, I'm so angry on your behalf!" Jenny picked up her phone and spun it in her hands. "Adrienne…" She pursed her lips. "We do have a story of our own here, you know."

It took a moment for Jenny's suggestion to register, then Adrienne shook her head. "No. Absolutely not."

"But we could totally nail them both! Don't you want some sort of revenge after what they've done? I mean, I really hope they don't, but TC could fire you for this, couldn't they?"

"They could," Adrienne said quietly, "but that's even more reason not to stoop as low as Cindy. It's not my style, Jenny. Though I appreciate your anger on my—our—behalf."

Jenny looked as if she wanted to say more, then exhaled in a loud huff. "Okay, okay. God, you're so grown up." She pouted, but her eyes glinted.

Adrienne chuckled. "It's a cross I have to bear," she said sadly, then laughed when Jenny rolled her eyes.

"On that overdramatic note, I think I'm going to get going." Jenny stood and smiled at Adrienne. "Thanks for hearing me out."

"Thanks for making the effort."

They nodded once at each other, then Jenny left, quietly shutting the door behind her.

Adrienne picked up her wine and took a long drink. She closed her eyes. *Jesus, what a mess. And I still have to speak to Daniel. Ugh.*

A minute later there was another knock on her door. She opened her eyes and looked around, assuming Jenny must have left something behind, but there was nothing obvious lying anywhere.

Groaning softly, Adrienne rose out of her chair and walked to the door. When she opened it, she came face-to-face with a scowling Morgan.

"Oh," Morgan said, her tone sharp, "you are alive, then?"

"Morgan," Adrienne cautioned, glancing up and down the hallway, "don't you think you'd better come in?"

Morgan huffed but strode into the room as Adrienne stepped aside. Somehow finding the entire situation funny, Adrienne bit back a chuckle as she closed the door and faced her.

"Stop smirking, Adrienne! This isn't funny." Morgan planted her hands on her hips. "I've been looking for you everywhere!"

"You...you have?" Adrienne's mirth died. "Why?"

Morgan shook her head. "Seriously?"

And suddenly she could see it all in Morgan's face. The worry, the concern, the fear. God, how could she have been so stupid?

"Oh, Morgan, I'm sorry." She stepped over to her and tentatively reached out her arms to pull Morgan close. "I didn't mean to worry you. God, I'm really sorry."

Morgan finally relaxed into the embrace, her cheek resting on Adrienne's hair. "You disappeared on me. I didn't know what to think."

"I just assumed you'd need to focus on the tournament. I...I thought you'd want to shut this all out until after tomorrow."

Morgan held her closer. "You are just as important to me as my career, okay? 'All this' is *huge* for us and especially for you. No way do I want to only focus on tomorrow. I also want to focus on you. On us." She kissed the side of Adrienne's head. "I know you thought you were doing the right thing keeping away, but I never want that, you hear? Remember how I said you didn't get to make all the decisions in this relationship?"

"Yes," Adrienne acknowledged meekly. Shame prickled at her skin for misreading the situation and Morgan's feelings for her so badly.

"Well, then," Morgan said, and there was a smile in her voice. "Don't forget it, okay?"

Adrienne placed a gentle kiss on Morgan's earlobe and thrilled at the shudder that ran through the woman in her arms. "I won't. I honestly thought I was doing the right thing, and…" She sighed.

Morgan raised her head and looked deeply into her eyes. "What?"

Adrienne was now wonderfully aware of how close they were, of how their bodies were connected from breasts to thighs. Of how soothing yet exhilarating it felt to be held by Morgan.

She sighed again. "And…I'm still getting used to the idea that *you* care about *me*. That there is an 'us.' And it's not because of anything you've done or not done." She released one arm to tap the side of her own head. "It's all in here."

Morgan's breath, released in a long sigh, was warm on Adrienne's face. "Okay, I understand. I think." Then she smiled playfully and quirked one eyebrow. "I suppose that just means I have to keep working on selling it to you, huh?"

Smiling, Adrienne shook her head. "I don't want you to have to work that hard. You shouldn't have to, anyway. I suppose I just need a little more faith."

"In me?" Morgan's face fell.

"No! God, no." Adrienne drew her near again and kissed her softly. "In myself. In the possibility that you, you amazing woman, can feel as strongly as you do about little old me."

Morgan kissed her, a longer kiss, her lips moving gently, sensuously over Adrienne's. "I really do, you know."

Her voice was husky, and she lowered her mouth to Adrienne's again, this time kissing her with more ardor, pulling Adrienne in a little tighter.

Warmth swept through Adrienne. Morgan's tongue met hers, softly stroking, and it was as if she had applied a lit match to kindling. The warmth transformed to crackling heat. It seared Adrienne's limbs and swept down and inward, focusing between her legs.

She moaned low in her throat, and Morgan shuddered once more.

Raising her head, Morgan gazed at her, eyes heavy with desire. "I…I need you," Morgan whispered. "I *want* you."

There were so many reasons to say no, not least of which was Morgan's big day tomorrow. But every reason that presented itself in the next few moments simply turned to ashes on the fire that burned between them.

Adrienne knew there was nothing that could stop this, not even her own fears of finally doing this again: letting someone close, letting someone have every last piece of her. Because in doing this now with Morgan, there would be no holding back. Morgan deserved nothing less than *all* of Adrienne.

And Adrienne wanted to give it, heart and soul.

Adrienne trembled in Morgan's arms, and her eyes were wide with what Morgan could only assume was fear.

Morgan's stomach plummeted as she wondered if she'd pushed too hard. She hadn't meant to. It was simply that her desire was too strong, all encompassing, enflaming every inch of her, inside and out. Adrienne was everything Morgan had ever wanted in a partner and then so much more besides. She'd not lied to Adrienne when she'd told her about her physical response—she had genuinely never felt so in need of climbing inside someone, of learning everything that would make Adrienne feel cherished and…loved.

Fully prepared to take back her words, suspecting it really was still too soon for Adrienne, Morgan thought her heart would stop when Adrienne's eyes softened and a hint of a blush stole across her cheeks. She raised one hand to stroke gently along Morgan's jawline.

"Yes," Adrienne whispered, and she smiled.

Morgan's knees weakened, but her arms strengthened, crushing Adrienne to her, much as she had done all those weeks ago in the elevator in Williamsburg. There was one exquisite moment where they simply stared at each other, then they both moved at once, their mouths meeting and opening once more, the kiss hard but not bruising, intense with the heat that blazed between them.

Adrienne caressed Morgan's back, her fingertips skimming over her spine and sweeping down her sides. Even through the cotton of her shirt, Morgan could feel their heat and strength, and her mind nearly exploded at the thought of those fingers on her naked skin and everywhere they could travel.

Morgan relaxed her arms, keeping Adrienne close but freeing her hands to go on their own journey. Their first stop was Adrienne's hips, wide and firm, and the perfect spot to dig her fingers into, eliciting a delicious gasp as she did so. The noises Adrienne made could be Morgan's undoing on their own. Every sound seemed to be infused with an intense kernel of desire and passion, barely contained, threatening to detonate and bring them both crashing down.

Adrienne pulled back for air, and she looked gloriously disheveled as she stood, panting, in front of Morgan.

It only made Morgan want to unravel her more.

"Bed," Adrienne croaked.

All Morgan could do was nod, take Adrienne's hand when it was offered, and allow herself to be led to the large bed on the far side of the room. The sun was setting outside, and its golden light filtered through the gauzy curtains that covered the two windows, bathing the room in a sensual glow; there would be no need for lamps. As they reached the bed, Adrienne turned, her nervousness obvious.

"It's…it's been a while. And you know I have some, um, issues," Adrienne said haltingly, but her eyes held Morgan's.

"I know," Morgan murmured. "We don't need to rush anything. We don't even need to, you know, go all the way." She smiled as Adrienne chuckled lightly. "But know this, Adrienne—you are beautiful in my eyes, and I want you so badly it hurts."

She brushed her thumb over Adrienne's lips, and Adrienne's eyes fluttered closed as she leaned up, forcing Morgan to move her hand away so their lips could press tightly together. Adrienne's tongue begged entry, and Morgan sighed with sweet desire as she allowed it, bringing both hands up to cup Adrienne's face, to feel the warmth of her skin beneath her fingertips.

Adrienne sucked in a breath, then brought her hands to the buttons of Morgan's shirt. They both watched as she slowly popped each fastening open, but it was Morgan who moaned first as the fourth button fully revealed the curve of her breasts to Adrienne's gaze. When Adrienne licked her lips, Morgan's pulse jumped in her throat, and she had difficulty breathing normally.

"May I?" Adrienne asked as the final released button allowed the shirt to fall open and she tugged gently at the hem on both sides.

"Hell yes."

Adrienne smiled, and despite a deep ache to start undressing Adrienne too, Morgan willed herself to patience, to allow Adrienne's comfort to rise by being the one to take the lead.

Moments later, Morgan's shirt fluttered to the floor, and she watched as Adrienne's gaze slowly swept over her exposed torso and up over her bra. Her chest heaving, she concentrated on staying upright and relaxing into the moment, even as she silently begged Adrienne to reach out and touch her. Somewhere.

God, *anywhere*.

"You are stunning." Adrienne's voice was a ragged rasp in the quiet room.

Morgan's face heated. There was something about compliments from Adrienne that carried more depth than any she'd received before.

Adrienne lifted her hands once more, letting her fingertips come to rest on Morgan's ribs just below her bra, before slowly, tantalizingly, drifting them upward, with no set pattern. She ran over the softness of the bra, skimmed the exposed curve of each breast, then trailed back down again to finally scratch over Morgan's nipples.

Morgan groaned. Her body, on autopilot, lunged forward into the caress, desperate to make Adrienne's touch harder, firmer.

Adrienne obliged, seemingly not wanting to deliberately tease and instead to give Morgan exactly what she wanted. Through the thin fabric of the bra, Adrienne rolled and pinched Morgan's nipples, each touch an exquisite agony, every moment increasing the throb between her legs. Then she reached behind Morgan, and leaned in to kiss her neck as she undid the bra and dragged it down Morgan's arms.

Her lips scorched a path down to Morgan's chest to brush softly over the topmost swell of her breasts, before her tongue licked a torturous circle around each one.

"Adrienne." Morgan clutched at Adrienne's shoulders.

"I know. I know."

When Adrienne finally licked a long swirl around a nipple, Morgan gasped from the pleasure. Adrienne repeated the gesture; Morgan repeated her vocal appreciation.

"Lie down," Adrienne said, and when Morgan looked into her brown eyes, she saw intent and need, and it robbed her of breath.

She sank onto the edge of the bed, then wriggled back a little to lie down, all the while keeping her eyes on Adrienne, who crawled seductively toward her across the covers. The looseness of her top afforded Morgan a delicious tease of what awaited her when Adrienne was naked.

Adrienne's hands were at the zipper of Morgan's pants. As soon as they were undone, she quickly stripped them from Morgan's body, taking her panties and her sneakers with them. She inhaled sharply at the sight of Morgan now laid out before her, and Morgan swallowed hard at the desire painting Adrienne's expression.

Adrienne lay down beside Morgan, then inched closer until her still fully clothed body pressed against Morgan's. She laid one hand on Morgan's stomach, her fingers gently caressing in small circles.

"I will get naked at some point," Adrienne said quietly. She stared at her own fingers as they moved over Morgan's skin. "But if it's all right with you, I think this will help my comfort level. You know, being able to touch you first. Is that okay?"

Morgan nodded. "Very okay."

"Well, good." Adrienne smiled.

And without any hesitation, she pressed her hand flat against Morgan's belly and swept it down into the wetness that Morgan knew awaited her. They both moaned at the contact, and Morgan's hips surged off the bed in response to that first electric touch.

"Adrienne!"

The sound Adrienne made wasn't a word or a groan but something in between. Then her mouth was back on Morgan's, and her tongue stroked sweetly against Morgan's while her fingers mirrored the motion through Morgan's wet folds.

It was beyond exciting, beyond the level of good that Morgan had even remotely anticipated would occur by being with Adrienne. She wasn't holding anything back, couldn't do so even if she tried. Adrienne had her completely at her mercy, and it was all Morgan wanted. Here and certainly for as long as she could imagine.

"You feel so good," Adrienne murmured against Morgan's mouth. "So wet. So soft."

"Please, Adrienne."

Adrienne shifted, bringing one leg over Morgan's, pinning her down. It only increased the level of torture. Without being able to thrust her hips as much as she would have liked, every sensation engendered by Adrienne's gentle but persistent strokes was exponentially increased.

"Oh God." Morgan moaned, her head moving on the covers beneath her, her eyes squeezed shut as waves of pleasure rolled through her body.

Adrienne increased the speed of her strokes, and Morgan knew a moment later that Adrienne was going to achieve something that had rarely happened for Morgan before. She clutched at Adrienne's back, pulling her down for a searing kiss. All the while keening, whimpering sounds escaped her throat as Adrienne stroked faster and firmer and—

Morgan cried out, her entire body shuddering as a tsunami of pleasure swamped her. She held Adrienne tightly, one hand on her back, the other gripping Adrienne's arm. Morgan kept her right where she was for some time, Adrienne's fingers wetly enclosed, the mere pressure still eliciting aftershocks that rippled through Morgan's legs.

Adrienne kissed her lips, her cheeks, her jaw. "Oh, Morgan," she whispered. "That was…"

"Yeah. It was." Morgan chuckled and shook her head. She let go of Adrienne's arm. "You can, er, come out now."

Adrienne smiled warmly at her and slowly eased her hand away from its resting place. Then she flopped onto her back beside Morgan and turned her head to gaze at her.

"Thank you," she said, "for letting me do that my way."

Morgan grinned and kissed her. "Funnily enough, I really didn't have an issue with it."

Adrienne rolled her eyes but laughed. "Good."

Turning so that she could lean up on one elbow and look down at the gorgeous woman who lay beside her, Morgan wet her lips. "And how about you? How are you feeling?"

"I am…feeling…good." Adrienne bit her lip. "I'm, um, rather turned on."

Joy suffused Morgan, but she took care not to act like an asshole about it. "Well, that's good, right?"

Adrienne nodded. "I might, um, start taking off some clothes."

"Do whatever you feel most comfortable with. And let me know if you need any help."

Adrienne leaned up and kissed her gently. "Let's see how I do."

Okay, you can do this. She thinks you're beautiful, and besides, she's all wrapped up in the afterglow of that wonderful orgasm, so anything would look good right now, right?

Almost groaning out loud, Adrienne mentally rolled her eyes at herself and sat up. *Come on!*

Trusting Morgan to remain where she was until told otherwise, Adrienne shifted to face her, and knelt beside her. She'd start with her top and bra—she'd always been happier with the top half of her body, and if that was as far as she got, well, so be it. Except…the thought of Morgan touching her, of being inside her, burned Adrienne up from the inside out. And if she wanted to experience *that*, she'd really need to get out of her jeans too…

All right, one step at a time.

She took hold of the bottom edge of her summer-weight sweater and lifted, going for the swift action rather than a sensual strip. Her confidence really wasn't high enough for the latter. Before she'd even passed the clothing over her head, a low moan reached her ears, and her confidence rose a little. She peeked out from the neck of the sweater as it passed over her eyes, and her heart began pounding.

Morgan gazed at her breasts, which were encased in a pale-green lacy bra, with what even Adrienne could recognize as pure, unfettered desire.

Swallowing hard, she finished removing the sweater and threw it somewhere behind her. She waited a moment, if only to try to regulate her breathing, then reached for the clasp at the front of the bra.

Morgan's gaze flicked up to meet hers briefly, then returned, as if magnetized, to where Adrienne fiddled with the clasp. It popped at last, and she shyly drew the bra open.

"Adrienne." Morgan's voice was strained, and once again her gaze flicked up to meet Adrienne's. "God, you're beautiful."

Adrienne risked a quick glance down at what Morgan could see. Her breasts were about the same size as Morgan's, and now that she looked properly, they didn't actually look much less firm. *Hm, okay, that's a nice surprise.*

Morgan's breathing was heavy in the still of the room. The light from outside had all but fallen now, but it was still enough to see her by this close, and Adrienne noted how her eyes smoldered, how tense her jawline was. Then she noticed Morgan's hands clenched at her sides, and she knew and, more to the point, *believed* that what she displayed to Morgan was something she wanted very, *very* much.

Rational thought took a vacation, and desire moved in.

Within a minute, she was completely naked.

She lay down again next to Morgan and reached for one of her hands.

"Please," she whispered. "Touch me."

Morgan groaned and covered Adrienne with the whole length of her body.

It was glorious. She reveled in Morgan's softness mixed with muscular firmness. The heat of her skin sparked tingles of excitement up and down Adrienne's limbs.

Then Morgan kissed her, plundered her mouth as if there were no tomorrow, and Adrienne became nothing but emotion and want and need. Her hands were everywhere on Morgan's body; her lover's mouth explored every inch of Adrienne.

She didn't flinch when that mouth alighted on the wide set of her hips or the gentle creases where her thighs met her hips. She didn't comment or move away when Morgan stroked her rounded belly or kissed a line down her less-than-smooth neck. None of it mattered, not anymore. She was being worshipped, of that she was sure, and when finally, after an excruciatingly long wait, Morgan ran her fingertips up the inside of Adrienne's thighs and into her wetness, she moaned, long and loud.

Morgan stroked slowly. "Is this okay?"

"Yes." Adrienne glanced down to watch Morgan as she moved through her wetness. "Very okay. But...oh God, go inside me, please."

Morgan crushed her mouth to Adrienne's, at the same time entering her with one finger. It was more than enough to make Adrienne clutch at the bed covers, her hips undulating to meet Morgan's gentle thrusts.

"More." She groaned. "Another...finger..."

Being filled by Morgan was an entirely different level of pleasure. Adrienne couldn't help the almost constant groans and evocations to a God she didn't believe in as Morgan gradually increased her pace.

Everything was on fire. Everything throbbed with the need to get *there*. To get to that point of utter release and ecstasy. When Morgan changed her position slightly so her thumb could press exactly where Adrienne needed it, it took only a few seconds to send her spinning and spiraling into the blissful abyss.

Chapter 21

ADRIENNE WAS DELICIOUSLY WARM. A soft weight pressed against her back. As she stirred, her memories flared to life, and warmth of a different kind spread over her body, bringing forth a smile of wonder.

Morgan.

Last night.

Oh. My.

Morgan's arm curved over Adrienne's hip, her fingers splayed lightly on Adrienne's belly.

"You awake?" Morgan mumbled against her shoulder.

"I am. I hate to move you, but I need the bathroom."

"Mm-hm," was her only response as Adrienne slid carefully out of her embrace to pad across the room.

The bathroom light was too bright, and Adrienne startled in shock at her reflection.

I look like I've been... She snorted softly. *Yeah, that's exactly what I look like.*

And then she grinned because damn if it didn't feel incredible.

After taking care of business in the bathroom, she walked back to the bed. Morgan was now flat on her back, arms out to the side. Her light-brown hair was a messy halo on the pillow; one cheek was creased and reddened from where she'd presumably laid on it for a good part of the night, but Adrienne honestly didn't think she'd seen a more beautiful sight in her life.

Morgan cracked open one eye and squinted at her. "What?"

Chuckling, Adrienne walked to the edge of the bed and sat down. "Nothing. You're beautiful," she said with a brief lift of her shoulders.

Morgan smiled, blushed, and passed one hand over her face. "I'm quite sure I'm not. I know what I look like in the mornings, and it's not good."

Feeling bold, Adrienne leaned over and kissed her, lingering for a few moments.

"Now I know you're crazy," Morgan said, when Adrienne pulled back. "Risking my morning breath like that."

Adrienne laughed and ruffled Morgan's hair. "You're fine." She sighed. "Look, it's just past six. Please don't take this the wrong way, but I think you ought to get back to your room."

Morgan's eyes opened wide. "Crap, sorry, I didn't think of that." She smiled sheepishly. "To be honest, I wasn't thinking of much at all last night when things, you know, started happening."

Adrienne cupped her chin and kissed her softly again. "Me neither. But even though the story's out now, I still think it would be better if you weren't seen leaving my room."

"I understand." Morgan paused, then let out an extended breath. "God, I still can't believe Naomi and Cindy did all this. Or that you're the one who seems to be being punished for it." Her eyes widened. "Mind you, I haven't spoken to Hilton yet. For all I know, I'm in deep trouble too."

Adrienne smiled wanly. While most of their late evening together had been spent exploring each other, bringing each other pleasure with passion and tenderness combined, they had eventually discussed the day's events. How could they not? Morgan had been stunned at the revelation of what Jenny had overheard, cursing Naomi in some rather inventive ways before her anger was all blown out.

"Will you say anything to Naomi?"

Morgan looked troubled. "I really don't know. Part of me wants to confront her. The rest of me thinks it's probably not worth it." She sighed and rubbed her eyes. "Have you decided what to do about Daniel?" She pushed back the covers.

Adrienne climbed back into the bed and pulled the covers up until they hid her breasts, still not 100 percent comfortable displaying everything so brazenly in front of her new young lover.

Morgan stood, stretched, then started searching for her clothing.

"I'll call him as soon as I've had some coffee and breakfast. There's no point putting it off any longer than that."

"And you're sure about what you're going to say? You're risking a lot."

Morgan, dressed only in her panties, her bra held in one hand, fixed her with an intense stare. It was a tad disconcerting, and Adrienne had to work hard to concentrate on the question rather than the view.

"I know, but I'm sure. It's what I truly believe and... Well, I think you, and what we're becoming, are worth it. And I know I don't have it all worked out for plan B, but I've always wanted to run my own company one day, so if this is the catalyst..." She knew Morgan was concerned on her behalf, having heard what Adrienne planned to say to her boss, but Adrienne was comfortable with her decision—and what she might have to do if the company asked her to leave.

Morgan finished fastening her bra, then knelt on the edge of the bed and crawled over to where Adrienne leaned against the headboard, opening her arms once she reached her.

Adrienne slipped into Morgan's embrace.

"Thank you," Morgan said into her neck. "And you know I feel exactly the same way, about us being worth it, right?"

Adrienne nodded, and her heart swelled with the intensity of Morgan's words. "Yes, I do. And no, I haven't changed my mind about that recording of Jenny's before you ask *that* question."

Morgan chuckled. "Dammit, we've only been dating a couple of weeks. How can you already be reading my mind?"

Lifting her head and gazing at Morgan, Adrienne smiled. "Well, correct me if I'm wrong, but I think last night went a long way toward building some kind of connection between us, hm?"

It was as if Morgan melted in her arms. "Oh yeah..." A dreamy look stole over her face, and Adrienne laughed. "Okay." Morgan sighed. "I respect your decision on this point."

"Good." Adrienne kissed Morgan's nose, then pulled away. "Now, go on, go."

Morgan rolled her eyes but smiled, then clambered off the bed. She retrieved her pants and shirt from the other side of the bed and eased into them before slipping on her shoes.

"Get some more sleep," Morgan said, gazing at her with an expression that sent tingles tumbling over every inch of Adrienne's bare skin.

"I will. And you. We need you fully rested for this afternoon." Her stomach clenched at the thought—the final round, yet another chance, a very good chance, for Morgan to win her first major.

Morgan grinned. "Trust me," she said, stretching her arms wide. "I'm feeling *very* relaxed already."

Adrienne shook her head and laughed softly. "Get out of here."

It was another gorgeous day, and after being confined to her room for over twelve hours—confined in the most delicious way, of course—Adrienne decided to call Daniel from somewhere quiet outside the hotel complex. It was 6:00 a.m. back in New York, but she knew he'd answer.

She grabbed a large takeout coffee from the hotel's espresso bar, put on sunglasses and a wide-brimmed summer hat, and left the hotel by one of the doors that was used to access the gardens. It might have been overcautious, but she had no idea how big this story was being treated by the press and no desire to detract from Morgan's big day.

God, I hope they leave her alone to get on with her game.

As she walked the perimeter of the gardens toward the main gates, her mind insisted on teasing her with images and memories from the night before. She hadn't really believed she'd be able to do this again and certainly not with someone whose body was, quite frankly, a work of art. That first time had all been rather a rush, the floodgates of her desire crashing open so rapidly she couldn't help but touch Morgan once she was laid out before her in all her glory.

But the second time... She shuddered at the thrill that ran through her. Yes, the second time had been...wondrous. She'd taken her time, learned Morgan's body, her responses, her needs. Touching and tasting Morgan had driven Adrienne wild with desire. When Morgan had then returned the favor tenfold, Adrienne had fallen asleep moments after her own extraordinary climax.

Their physical relationship, while still fresh and new, already matched their emotional connection in ways Adrienne could never have imagined.

And that only made what she was about to do easier, much to her surprise.

She found a small empty churchyard at the far end of the village and sat on a rough wooden bench overlooking a rose garden before pulling out her phone.

Daniel answered on the first ring.

"Adrienne, good morning." His usually strident tone sounded flat and tired.

"Good morning, Daniel." She inhaled—there really was no point in prolonging this. "I hope you'll forgive me for not calling you back sooner. I needed some thinking time." He grunted, and she took that as her cue to continue. "I assume you saw the article yesterday evening that Sport Today dot Net put out?"

"I did." He sighed. "Adrienne, I—"

"Daniel, forgive me for interrupting, but I think I can make this a very easy conversation for you." She paused for a moment.

Last chance to change your mind. Are you sure?

An image of Morgan laughing in her arms the evening before was her answer. "Whatever that article may imply," she continued, her voice firm, "what has happened between Morgan and I is not a sordid affair, with one of us being sleazily pursued by the other or forced into a situation they didn't want. We're in a relationship. A very committed one. However, I know that such relationships are frowned on in our business and that the resulting publicity is bad for TC Productions. I've therefore decided that if you and the rest of the board want my resignation, you'll have it first thing tomorrow."

"You... What? You'd quit? For her?"

She'd never heard him sound so shocked. "If that's what it takes. I'm certainly not going to stop seeing Morgan, so if you make me choose, I'm afraid TC loses."

There was a moment of silence, then Daniel cleared his throat. "Let me talk to some people. Adrienne, you're one of our best. I'd hate to see this one lapse of judgement—"

She bristled at his words. "We fell in love, Daniel. I'd hardly call that a lapse in judgement."

Then she realized what she'd said and nearly choked on the emotion that coursed through her chest. In love? *Well, yes, I suppose I am.* Heat raced through her at the affirmation.

"Okay, okay, poor choice of words perhaps. But listen, don't do anything crazy, you hear? Give me today. I'll speak to you tomorrow."

Before she could reply, he hung up.

Her hands trembled as she shoved her phone back into her purse. When it was safely stowed away, she slumped against the hard wooden back of the bench.

I'm in love. Good grief.

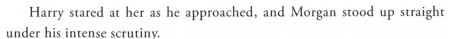

Harry stared at her as he approached, and Morgan stood up straight under his intense scrutiny.

"What happened?" he asked as he drew level. "I mean, I know that dick Tom Harrison wrote that story about you and Adrienne, but anything else I need to know about?"

Morgan shook her head. "Definitely not. But it's all good. Trust me."

Harry snorted but said nothing, and Morgan hoped that was the end of it, at least until after the round.

She glanced around at the bustle and buzz of the final few players heading out on their rounds. The leaderboard showed no great movements from the players behind her, although Charlie was already one shot better off from yesterday's score, and Morgan fervently wished her friend a great round. They'd swapped a couple of text messages over breakfast and planned to meet for a drink at the tournament close.

"Morgan! Morgan! Got anything to say in response to the story about you and the woman from—"

"Oh, shut up, will you? You press are all the same. Scum, every last one of you," a woman shouted.

Morgan looked round at the commotion. A reporter she didn't recognize leaned over the rope separating the players from the crowd with what looked like a recording device in his hand thrust in her direction.

Next to him, and clearly the one who'd interrupted his attempt at questioning Morgan about Adrienne, stood a tall, heavyset woman with close-cropped blonde hair. She glared contemptuously at the reporter, who looked more than a little nervous at the woman's commanding presence.

"Yeah, get lost, you arsehole!" a man yelled. "Leave her alone!"

"Yeah!" yelled a chorus of other members of the crowd.

Morgan smiled and nodded briefly at the blonde-haired woman. She gave Morgan a thumbs-up, then maneuvered herself to stand in front of the reporter, her arms folded across her wide chest.

Chuckling, Morgan decided it might be best if she stepped away from the situation and motioned to Harry, who grinned, to follow her over to the assembly area behind the first tee.

They ran through their usual preparations for the start of a round. Morgan tried to ignore the flutter of excitement in her stomach at what today could mean. She hadn't, in fact, gone back to sleep after she'd snuck back to her room—unseen, as far as she could tell. Her excitement level was too great, both at what today might bring but also, and perhaps even greater, at what she and Adrienne had shared.

She exhaled slowly, her gaze losing focus. God, that had been... incredible. She hadn't known it was possible to feel so many wonderful things all at once with another human being. Everything physical seemed amplified by their emotional connection and vice versa.

"Hey, where are you?"

Harry's rough voice interrupted her musings, and she turned to look at him, embarrassed to have been caught daydreaming.

"Come on, Spencer, I know you're in love and all, but this is where you should be right now." He pointed in the direction of the course. "And nowhere else."

She nodded. "You're right. Sorry, Harry."

He blinked at her quick acceptance of his scolding. "Look, I ain't heartless." He smiled conspiratorially. "I'm happy for you. But here and now, this is—"

Morgan held up her hand. "I'm good. I get it. I'm here."

"Well, that's, um, good."

Laurie Schweitzer appeared at Morgan's side with no warning. Morgan only just avoided jumping in response.

"Spencer," Laurie said, her eyes narrowed.

"Laurie," Morgan replied, smiling brightly, refusing to play Laurie's stupid game of only calling her opponents by their last name when on the course.

Laurie huffed and stepped back. "Better have brought your A game today," she said, a sly smile splitting her lips. "'Cause I am *so* ready to take you down."

Morgan shrugged, knowing her nonchalance would drive Laurie insane. "May the best player win," she said and tapped a two-finger salute off the edge of her sun visor.

Laurie scowled and turned her back on her.

Harry looked like he was going to give himself a hernia, trying not to laugh too loudly.

"How are you holding up?" Bree asked as she linked her arm with Adrienne's.

They'd agreed to walk the course again together but had also agreed to stay well out of Morgan's sight, even if it meant they wouldn't necessarily have the best vantage point to see all of her shots.

Adrienne was grateful for Bree's offer. They'd bumped into each other in the lobby of the hotel when she'd returned from her call with Daniel, and Bree's sunny disposition was the perfect tonic to lift Adrienne's mood.

Jenny was with the crew today—Adrienne had stepped back, leaving her in charge. For all she knew, come tomorrow morning she would no longer be involved in this project anyway, so it made sense to have Jenny take the lion's share of the work today, just in case she needed to finish it all off in France. Adrienne was actually relieved. She wasn't sure she could have concentrated on her work at all today, given how tense she was about Morgan's chances to finally win a major.

"I'm nervous," Adrienne admitted.

Bree's laugh was light. "I know! I don't know if I want to watch or not."

"Oh, no, you have to!" Adrienne smiled. "What if she does it?"

"I know." Bree sighed and shook her head. "When she does, I really want to be here to see it."

"Me too."

"Okay, then let's do it!"

They walked round the back of the crowd that lined the first tee. People were ten deep in places, and it lifted Adrienne's heart to see so many spectators invested in the women's game. After squeezing themselves into a group who occupied a slightly higher vantage point to the left side of the tee, they craned their necks to see the first shots from Morgan and Laurie.

They watched Morgan's ball sail off down the center of the fairway.

"Oh, that's a great start," Bree said.

"Phew." Adrienne mimed wiping her brow, and Bree chuckled. "How do you get used to this? I mean, you watched Gordy all those years too."

Bree was quiet for a moment. "You know, I believe it's even worse watching Morgan. Something about her being my child. I feel the same when I watch Jack play too."

They headed off with the rest of the crowd once Laurie Schweitzer had also successfully teed off. Adrienne was inordinately grateful she wasn't going to endure the next three hours or so on her own.

"All right," Harry said, crouching down next to Morgan as she lined up her eight-foot putt at the sixteenth. "This one turns about halfway. See that little break just there?" He pointed, and she nodded. "That's your sweet spot. Hit that and you'll be good."

He stood up and walked away without waiting for Morgan to say anything. She didn't need to, though—she and Harry had been completely in the same thinking zone all day.

Laurie had caught Morgan up from her two-shot deficit overnight, but Morgan was still calm. They were now on the same score, eight under for the tournament, having both played exceptional golf for the last three hours. Morgan had politely applauded her opponent's good shots, including the two incredible putts she'd sunk on the tenth and twelfth to tie their scores. Laurie, however, the longer the round had gone on, had become nastier and grumpier. She openly scowled when Morgan sunk a birdie and scoffed if Morgan missed a green or hit a slightly wayward tee shot.

Harry had whispered early on, just once, that Morgan should "ignore her," and Morgan had done just that, focusing solely on her game and how damn good it felt today. She'd made par or birdie on every hole, not a single dropped shot, and that felt *amazing*. Now she had this shot to go back into the lead by one. Laurie had just missed a ten-foot putt for birdie and would more than likely make her par, given her ball had finished a scant twelve inches from the hole.

Morgan stood and took a couple of deep breaths, then walked up and addressed the ball. A slight shimmy to her right improved her stance. A flex of her fingers improved her hold on the putter's grip. Two more deep breaths calmed her mind. She swung back, then forward and knew the minute she'd hit it that another birdie was going on her card.

The crowd shouted and applauded as the ball dropped into the cup. She calmly acknowledged their plaudits and grinned at Harry as she handed him the putter.

"Good," he said. "The seventeenth, remember, doesn't need any heroics." He handed her the driver and picked up the bag.

She grinned even wider. Trust Harry not to go all gushy on her just because she was now back in the lead after sinking a tricky putt.

The next hole belonged to Laurie, though, and Morgan had no problem applauding her, along with the rest of the crowd, when a brave third shot gave her a great chance for birdie, which she took with aplomb. Morgan made a comfortable par, and they were all tied again, heading to the last hole.

"Oh, gosh, I don't think I can watch!" Bree's eyes were wide, and her hand clutched Adrienne's arm.

"I know what you mean." Adrienne swallowed hard. This was ridiculously nerve-racking. Her stomach was tied in so many knots she didn't think she'd be able to eat anything for the rest of the day.

She sipped from her water before she and Bree headed off to the eighteenth tee. Thankful for the wide hat, both for keeping the sun off her face and ensuring she received no unwanted attention from anyone in the crowd, fans or reporters alike, she wiped at the back of her neck with a Kleenex. How could Morgan look so cool in this heat and under that pressure? Once again, Adrienne was in awe of her girlfriend.

As they had done on each of the previous seventeen holes, Bree and Adrienne found a spot at the back of the crowd where they could just about see the top of Morgan's head as she teed off, her ball chasing Laurie's up the center of the fairway to nestle only five feet behind by the looks of it. As they had been for the whole round, Morgan and Laurie were neck-and-neck.

The crowd surged around them, jogging up the pathways that lined the final hole in a multi-colored stream of humanity. Adrienne led Bree to follow them, but when they drew level with the spot from where the players would hit their second shots, she tugged on Bree's arm to pull her to one side. Her heart pounded with the tension and excitement of the moment.

"How about we go on ahead, try to get a good spot at the green? We've both got credentials that allow us to be close, and don't you think for the final hole we should do that? We can still stay out of sight of Morgan so that she can focus, but I know I'd like to have the best view possible of what could be an incredible finish."

Bree's smile was delightful. "That's a wonderful idea!"

And with that, she was off, pulling Adrienne along with her.

Morgan watched her fourth shot fly over the creek at the ridiculously long eighteenth hole and then drop down from the sky toward the green.

"Be right," she muttered, her club clutched in her hand, eyes narrowed as she tracked the ball. "Come on, be right."

She hadn't had the best lie after her third shot, somehow finding the one small patch of scuffed turf in the middle of the otherwise pristine fairway, which caused her ball to falter and stop suddenly.

Laurie was already on the green with her fourth shot, about six feet away from the hole, so Morgan needed to get as close, if not closer, and—

The groans and muted applause from the crowd told her before her own eyes did that she'd not managed that. From the looks of it, she was at least twenty feet away, if not longer.

"Crap."

"It's fine," Harry said quietly as he approached to take the club from her hands. "Stay focused."

She gave him a smile, even though her stomach flooded with butterflies. They walked to the green, Morgan absentmindedly waving to the crowd who cheered her on.

When she reached the plateau of the final green, she could see her ball was more like twenty-five feet from the hole. Long but not impossible. She stood, hands on hips, and surveyed the lie, the path her ball would have to take. It would be her turn to putt first, being the farthest from the hole.

So probably one chance, and that's it.

As she let that thought settle in her mind, she calmed, and her shoulders relaxed. She'd sunk longer putts many times in her career. Granted, not for something quite as important as her first major, but her body would remember and know what to do. She allowed herself a small smile.

This, right now, is what I've been training for. This is what I've worked so hard for and put up with all the negative crap from my father and others for. This, right now.

Harry approached with her putter in his hand. He opened his mouth to speak, then looked into her eyes before he closed his mouth again and grinned. He backed away without saying a word.

She took the putter and walked around the shot a few times, making sure of the flow of the green and keeping her breathing calm and even.

A hush fell over the crowd. Even the birds in the nearest trees seemed to fall quiet.

She addressed the ball, once again moving her feet, knees, hips, and shoulders by tiny increments until she knew she was perfectly balanced and ready to hit.

The ball began its path toward the cup.

Screams of "*Get in the hole!*" assailed her ears.

The speed was good.

The direction looked good…looked good…looked—

The crowd erupted, the noise almost deafening, as the ball skimmed the left rim of the cup and then dropped slowly, teasingly, into it.

She took a step forward, lunged into her front knee, and fist-pumped three times in quick succession. Her scream of joy was almost primal, but soon her professionalism resurfaced. She stood quickly before walking to the hole to retrieve her ball.

The purest sensation of relief flooded her veins. She'd done everything she could, everything that was within her control, to try to win this tournament.

Now it was in the lap of the gods and whatever Laurie could conjure up from the significantly shorter distance of six feet.

"Perfect," Harry said, his voice breaking, as she reached him at the edge of the green. "Fucking perfect."

She drew him into a quick hug, then stepped back, her heart racing. Should she watch or not? If Laurie sunk her putt, they were going into a playoff. If she missed…

Morgan shuddered. She didn't dare believe.

Damn, I have to watch. I have to see for myself.

Squaring her shoulders, she raised her head.

Her gaze landed on the deep-brown eyes of Adrienne, who stood across the green with Morgan's mom clinging to her arm.

Adrienne made no move to smile or nod or lift her hand. She simply kept her gaze locked with Morgan's.

They stayed like that while the crowd hushed once more, while the shouts of "*Get in the hole!*" reverberated around the stands, until the shocked gasps and groans, quickly followed by the roar of everyone who realized it, announced that Morgan Spencer had just won her first major.

Chapter 22

MORGAN FELL INTO HARRY'S HUG, but she still had her gaze locked with Adrienne's.

Bree screamed next to Adrienne, pulling at Adrienne's arm as she jumped up and down next to her, but Adrienne couldn't, *wouldn't*, tear her gaze away from Morgan's.

Even as Morgan briefly shook hands with a sour-looking Laurie Schweitzer, she kept the corner of her eye on Adrienne. Even as the press swarmed over the green, TV cameras circling Morgan like hyenas honing in on a lion kill, their gazes found each other and held.

And then Morgan moved, slowly at first, then faster, a smile finally creasing her shocked face as she jogged across the green and pushed her way through the crowd.

Adrienne waited. She gave Bree a quick hug and a smile, then let her go and stood steady in the craziness around them.

When Morgan reached her and pulled her into her arms, Adrienne's tears finally came. She clung to Morgan, vaguely aware that they were kissing, that people were shouting, a multitude of cameras flashing.

She pulled away from the kisses with which Morgan peppered her lips and held her face in her hands. "You did it. And I am so proud of you."

Morgan cried now, and she dropped her head and pressed her face into Adrienne's neck, sobbing against her skin.

"Oh, darling!" Bree exclaimed, and her arms reached around them to encapsulate them both in her warm embrace. "Congratulations!"

Morgan lifted her head, her eyes red, and grinned at her mom. "Thanks, Mom. I'm so glad you're here."

"Oh, me too, darling! I wouldn't have missed this for the world."

Adrienne gently released Morgan and nudged her into Bree's arms. Cameras flashed madly again around them. Adrienne pulled a clean Kleenex from her pocket and pressed it into Morgan's hand when her mom released her.

"Thanks," Morgan said, lifting the Kleenex and smiling ruefully. "I don't normally do this." She wiped her eyes and snuffled a little.

"I think you're entitled, today of all days," Adrienne replied, stroking her back.

"I still can't quite believe it." Morgan's expression was one of awe and wonder.

"Believe it." Adrienne pressed closer to her. "You are the Women's British Open champion. A major winner."

Morgan laughed and shook her head. "Okay, you might need to keep saying that to me for about, um, a week?"

"Whatever it takes."

They smiled at each other, then Morgan exhaled loudly. "Okay, I guess I better go do things." She waved behind her at the green.

"I guess you do."

"We'll be here when you're done," Bree said, dabbing at her eyes with a delicate silk handkerchief.

Morgan grinned at them both, then turned to face the huge bank of press and TV—Jenny among them, right at the front Adrienne was pleased to note—and the table already being set up for the presentation of the trophy.

Bree grabbed hold of Adrienne's arm again and, when their eyes met, let out a squeal. "She did it!"

Adrienne laughed and hugged her. "She sure did."

"And it gives me great pleasure to present this magnificent trophy to our incredible winner, this year's Women's British Open champion, Morgan Spencer!"

The club president smiled warmly at Morgan as she stepped over to receive the elegant silver trophy, thunderous applause seeming to come from every direction as she did so.

"Very well played, Morgan. That was a superb win," the president said as they shook hands.

"Thank you. Thank you very much."

And then the silverware was in her hands, and she held it aloft.

Innumerable flashes from the press cameras and those of the spectators blinded her, but she didn't care. It wasn't the first trophy she'd ever held, nor, hopefully, would it be the last, but she knew this one she'd never forget.

She turned in a slow circle at the gentle prompting of a tour official to ensure that everyone could get their shot of the newest champion.

Adrienne came into her field of view again. She stood at the edge of the crowd, looking serene and beautiful. Her mom was there beside her, applauding vigorously. Harry gave her a wink and a grin, and Charlie stood next to him, arms raised high, fists clenched, a huge smile on her face.

Morgan grinned, then laughed.

This is surreal.

A gentle hand from the tour official guided her to the trophy table, and Morgan placed the cup next to the poster-sized check for a sum equivalent to about $650,000, an amount that made her eyes water.

"Ready for the interview?" the official asked her quietly.

Morgan chuckled. "Not really, but I know I have to."

The official, a kind-looking woman about her mom's age, smiled. "Yes, I'm afraid so."

Morgan patted her on the arm. "I'm good."

She exhaled and faced the cameras. *Please don't let it be Cindy.*

To her immense relief, it was one of the British sportscasters, a woman she'd met the year before, who would do the lead interview.

Morgan smiled at her as they shook hands.

"Well, Morgan. How about that, then?" the interviewer said, earning a ripple of chuckles from the crowd.

"Not bad, huh?" Morgan replied, and the crowd whooped and hollered.

"What a day. What a round, from both of you."

"Oh, I know." Morgan shook her head. "Laurie played some incredible stuff out there. That putt on twelve was one of the best I've seen." The crowd applauded. "And while I'm happy with the win, obviously, especially after all this time"—more laughter from the crowd—"I think I'm equally happy that we showed you all how good our game is. Some people still seem to think our game isn't a match for what the men can produce. Hopefully today has helped dispel that way out-of-date myth."

The interviewer smiled and waited until the loud cheers and applause died down. "I think everyone here would agree with that sentiment. How did you feel, though, on that last hole? You're twenty-five feet away. She's only six…"

The interview went on for a few more minutes, Morgan earning more laughs and cheers from the crowd with her answers. She knew she'd never come across as so relaxed in front of a camera. *Amazing what kicking a monkey off your back can do.*

After the interviewer had thanked her and walked away, it was the turn of the other, lesser broadcasters and print press. The tour official was excellent at her job, moving Morgan from one to another, ensuring everyone got to ask two or three questions but keeping things moving along at a good pace.

Once it was over, Morgan made her way over to her own special set of supporters. She gave Adrienne a quick kiss again, which elicited childish sniggers from Harry and Charlie, and gave her mom another hug.

"Way to go, Spencer," Charlie said when they finally hugged.

"I didn't even see where you finished," Morgan said, eyes wide. "How did you—?"

"Third place!" Charlie yelled.

Morgan's tears threatened again, and she swallowed them back. "Oh my God, Charlie, that's amazing!"

"I know, right?" Charlie danced on the spot.

"So can we finally have a beer tonight? A real one, not one of those lame-ass light beers?" Harry stood with his hands on his hips, glaring at her, but she could see a twitch in his left eye and knew he was only just holding it together.

"I might even have *two.*" Morgan winked at him, then laughed when he pulled her into a bear hug and lifted her off the ground.

"Fucking perfect," he said, looking intently into her eyes before bringing her back down to the ground.

"Thanks, Harry. Couldn't have done it without you."

"Oh, well, I know *that.*" He puffed out his chest.

Morgan snorted.

"So do you want to hear some more good news?" Charlie asked.

Morgan spotted Adrienne and her mom shaking their heads even as they smiled. "What?"

"Did you realize you weren't interviewed by Cindy at all out there?" Charlie asked.

Oh, yeah, she's right.

"Uh-huh." Charlie nodded, then grinned. "It's really strange. Out of the blue, a Golf Channel runner came forward to speak to Patty at CBS about being threatened with her job if she didn't give your story to Tom Harrison. Allegedly it was Cindy Thomson who threatened her, and I know this part will break your heart, but poor Cindy's been suspended while the Golf Channel investigates."

Morgan blinked, trying to absorb the news. She spun round to face Adrienne.

"But I thought—? Did you—?"

Adrienne held up both hands. "Nothing to do with me."

"Jenny?"

"I presume." Adrienne smiled ruefully. "It was her recording, after all."

"I need to buy her a drink. A large one. Or six."

Adrienne chuckled. "I'm sure she'd be happy to accept." She glanced at her watch. "I suppose you'd better get inside and change, ready for the evening, yes?"

Morgan ran her hands through her hair, suddenly exhausted. "I guess so."

She looked round at the four of them and was overwhelmed with emotion at the joy and love on each of their faces. Even Harry's.

"Thank you. All of you. This…" She swallowed hard. "I…I really appreciate your support today."

Without a word, all four of them stepped forward and joined together to hold her in a long group hug.

AWESOME!!!!!

The first message from Jack, which appeared on her screen as soon as she switched her phone back on in her room, made Morgan smile. She scrolled down to the one he'd sent a couple of minutes later.

And listen, I know you don't need me to fight your battles, but Dad called and was being an ass. I might have said some things. Don't know if it will help but I want you to know I tried.

She blinked, then read the message again. Before she could absorb what it might mean, her phone rang, Hilton's name in the caller display.

"Morgan!" he boomed. "Congratulations! I am so proud of you!"

"Thanks." She moved the phone away slightly to give her eardrum a chance of surviving.

"And I understand why you didn't call me about that Sport Today dot Net article, given you had a major championship to win, but we do still need to talk about how S Pro will—"

"Hilton, I'll tell you right now, if S Pro has an issue with me being an out lesbian, then I'd rather not have them as a sponsor. This is my life, and they can either accept that or—"

"Whoa, whoa, Morgan! Slow down! It's nothing like that. That's what I wanted to talk to you about." He chuckled. "S Pro *love* the fact that you're an out lesbian. They've been looking for someone to be their LGBT poster person for a couple of years now. They're delighted to learn the vague rumors they'd heard were true."

"Wait, you never told them?"

"Of course not! That's your private business. And you've never gone out of your way to be truly out, so I assumed you wanted to keep it quiet. I've never pushed you on it for that reason."

Morgan chuckled. "And here I was thinking it was going to cause you problems with sponsors, et cetera, so I never brought it up."

Hilton laughed ruefully. "Well, you know, it might have with some of them. But not S Pro. They want to sit down with you as soon as you're back from France. They are loving this new Morgan, the one who's relaxed in front of the cameras and smiles a lot. And wins majors!" He laughed, then said in a more somber tone, "Thank you for pushing through with the film. I know it wasn't easy for you."

"Well, I must admit, Adrienne made a little difference there."

Hilton laughed. "I'm not going to say anything to *that*." He paused. "We can work out a very sweet deal here with S Pro, you know. *Very* sweet."

Morgan sat on the bed with a thump. "I think my head's about to explode."

"Quite the weekend, huh?"

"Yeah, definitely."

"So, um, the thing with Adrienne. Is it...?"

"Serious? Oh yeah."

Hilton's laughter this time was gentle and understanding. "Good for you, Morgan. Right, go out and celebrate! I'll talk to you in a couple of days, okay?"

"Thanks, Hilton."

They hung up, and Morgan flopped back on the bed, her mind spinning. She wanted to talk to Adrienne, to tell her all of this, to have Adrienne hold her and kiss her and bring her back down to reality. Because all this talk of massive sponsorship deals and being a major champion was making her feel like she was somewhere above the Earth, looking down on someone else's life, a life that hadn't seemed possible only a few months before.

But then, being with someone as wonderful as Adrienne hadn't seemed possible back then either. *Amazing how your life can be turned so upside down so quickly in so many ways.*

The tears that flowed now were gentler than the ones she'd shed back on the course. They were almost cleansing, easing her heartaches from all the times past, leading her into a new, calmer state, where the life she had now was the one she knew she never wanted to let go.

The speeches were over, as was the meal. Adrienne longed to kick off her heels and find a soft couch somewhere to sink into, preferably with a good glass of Merlot to finish off the evening. However, the party was still in full swing, and there was no way she would leave here without Morgan.

They'd had to sit apart for the formal part of the evening, seating arrangements having already been planned months in advance, of course. And it would be a while yet before they could spend any quality time together.

Morgan, as newly crowned British Open champion, had plenty of obligations this evening and was busy working her way around the room. She had, however, found a couple of moments to swing by Adrienne's table to talk with her for a few moments or simply to brush her fingertips across Adrienne's bare shoulders. Her glance of admiration at Adrienne's sleeveless black dress—packed on every trip just in case she ended up at an event such as this—sent shivers down Adrienne's spine.

They weren't pretending to hide the fact that they were a couple, even though they hadn't spoken about that in advance. There really wasn't any point after making it so public on the eighteenth green earlier that day. Pictures of them wrapped up in each other's arms straight after Morgan's win were all over the internet, and to her surprise, Adrienne wasn't bothered. *Que sera sera* seemed to be her motto of the weekend. It was rather lovely to feel so relaxed, despite what might befall her in the morning.

Tricia had messaged just as Adrienne had been dressing for the evening event and had made Adrienne smile with warm gratitude at her encouraging words.

You two look SO good together! I didn't catch that first nasty reveal last night, but I'm glad because tonight's pictures show me the true story. Can't wait to meet her. xx

Jenny returned to the table, a glass of something vividly blue—matching her hair color this evening—in one hand, Adrienne's wine in the other.

"Here you go," her assistant said, placing the wine in front of her.

"Is that a real drink, or are you and the bartender having some fun making them up?"

Jenny snorted, then mock glared. "Of course it's a real drink! It's called a Blue Lagoon, and it's awesome."

Shaking her head, Adrienne reached for her wine. "I'll stick to this, thank you."

They drank in silence for a minute or so, then Adrienne finally asked the question that had been on her lips all evening.

"So do you know anything about how Cindy's runner managed to end up talking to Patty from CBS?"

Jenny nearly sprayed her blue concoction all over the pristine white tablecloth. She wiped at her mouth, her eyes wide, then slumped in her chair.

"I couldn't let them get away with it," she mumbled, not meeting Adrienne's eye.

"Jenny, I'm not mad at you."

Jenny's head whipped up. "You're not?"

"Not really." Adrienne sighed, then rolled her eyes. "I can't lie. Knowing Cindy's in some trouble over it *does* give me more than a little satisfaction. I want to be a better person than that, but much to my surprise, I find I can't be, given the circumstances."

Jenny stared at her, then they both burst out laughing.

Morgan finally completed her last circuit of the room and almost jogged back to her table in relief. *Maybe I don't want to win any more majors. I had no idea how much extra work it was after picking up the check.* She snorted softly at herself. *Yeah, right.*

She found her mom in what looked like earnest conversation with Lou Thomson, Cindy's father, of all people. Morgan wondered about staying away until her mom caught her eye and motioned for her to join them.

"Darling, you remember Lou, don't you?"

Lou stood and shook Morgan's hand. "Fantastic win, Morgan. I'm so pleased for you." His words were heartfelt, but there was a sadness in his eyes as he spoke.

Morgan regained her seat next to her mom. "Thank you, Lou."

Lou sat back down again on her mother's other side and clasped his hands together on the table. "I was just telling your mother how sorry I am for what else has happened this weekend." He sighed and blinked a few times. "My daughter…" He shook his head. "She always wanted to be the best, I know that. I guess I just didn't realize how hungry she was and what she'd do to get ahead. I'm very sorry, Morgan."

Morgan placed one hand over his joined ones and squeezed gently. "You don't have to apologize for her. But thank you."

He nodded. "I just hope she learns a lesson from this."

"She's young," Morgan's mom said gently. "She has plenty of time to learn."

Lou nodded again, then pushed back his chair and stood. "Well, I just wanted to say what I've said. Enjoy the rest of your evening."

"That was sweet of him," her mom said as he walked away.

"It was. Makes you wonder how Cindy turned out the way she did with a father like that." Morgan sipped at her water.

Her mother sighed. "I know. But you—"

A throat cleared nearby. Her mom turned her head to look over Morgan's shoulder, and her eyes widened.

Morgan swiveled in her seat to find her father standing behind her. Everything in Morgan tensed as he looked from her mother to her.

He motioned to the chair Lou had just vacated. "May I sit?"

Morgan looked at her mom, one eyebrow raised in silent question. Her mom nodded.

"Sure," Morgan said, sounding much calmer than she felt.

What does he want now?

Silence fell over them as he took his seat.

Her father's face, set in its usual cast-iron mask when he'd first appeared at the table, now seemed to soften slightly, and he shifted in his seat. "I just wanted to say that was very well played today, Morgan. You held your nerve in a tight situation and deserved the win."

Morgan's breath stalled in her chest. It wasn't the most glowing of praise, but he actually sounded like he meant it. For the first time in her life.

Her mom let out a small gasp and laid a hand on Morgan's forearm.

"Th-thank you," Morgan said.

He fiddled with an empty glass left on the table. "Yes, well. Praise where it's due." He sat up a little straighter, his glance flicking between Morgan and her mom, and cleared his throat once more. "I have been doing some thinking this week. I hope to prove to you that I've made some progress on the things you asked me to think about. One of them is your game, Morgan. I've spent a lot of time with Lou and my other colleagues this week, and they have all told me the women's game has more than I probably gave it credit for in the past and—"

And there it was. The kicker.

"Dad," Morgan said, shaking her head. "I think you'd better stop right there. I accept your congratulations, but I won't sit and listen to you tell me that now, because all of your male colleagues have told you how good our game is, suddenly you're a changed man." She snorted. "Seriously? You'll believe their opinion over mine and any other woman playing the tour? Do you not see how little that indicates to me that you've made any progress at all?"

He blinked rapidly, confusion etched on his weathered face.

"Oh, Gordy," her mom muttered, also shaking her head, a sad smile on her face.

"What?" he said sharply, staring at his wife. "I just said I know the women's game is better than I previously thought and—"

Morgan sighed and pushed back her chair. "Nice try, Dad, but you've got a long way to go. Excuse me, I'm tired and I'd like to spend some time with Adrienne before the evening is over."

She kept her tone as polite as she could manage, but her shoulders ached with tension. Would there ever be a time when her father *didn't* have this effect on her?

She looked up, and her gaze was held by a pair of beautiful deep-brown eyes. Adrienne tilted her head in concern, but when Morgan nodded, she visibly relaxed.

"Morgan, I—" her father began, his voice showing his irritation, but his wife's hand on his arm stopped him mid-flow.

"Have a lovely evening, darling," Morgan's mom said, smiling warmly. "Perhaps we can meet for breakfast tomorrow?"

Morgan nodded. "As long as you don't mind sharing me with Charlie and Adrienne?"

"Not at all." Her mom gave her a quick nod, then turned back to Morgan's father.

Morgan stepped away but risked one look back. What she saw made her chuckle.

Her mom had a stern expression on her face and ticked off whatever points she was making with Morgan's father on her fingers.

Morgan almost felt sorry for him.

Chapter 23

"YOU MUST BE EXHAUSTED," ADRIENNE said, as she and Morgan made their way, hand-in-hand, to the elevators.

"I think I'm having an out-of-body experience," Morgan replied and laughed.

"What happened with your father?"

Morgan sighed and shook her head. "I'll tell you later."

"Okay."

Adrienne squeezed her hand, then pressed the call button. They waited in silence until the elevator doors opened. They had the car to themselves, and Adrienne reached over to the panel to press the numbers four and five.

"Adrienne," Morgan said softly.

"Hm?" Adrienne faced her.

"Why did you press for both floors?" There was, despite her obvious tiredness, a sparkle in Morgan's eyes.

Adrienne chuckled. "Because you need some sleep. We'll have plenty more opportunities to spend the night together in the—"

Morgan's lips on hers cut her off, then Morgan's tongue, gently seeking permission to enter, stopped any thoughts she may have had about protesting.

The kiss was incendiary. Morgan's hands roamed firmly over Adrienne's torso as her mouth owned Adrienne. Her fingers brushed scandalously close to Adrienne's already hard nipples.

Adrienne moaned into Morgan's mouth, and it only seemed to spur her on.

Morgan cupped Adrienne's breasts, rubbing her palms over Adrienne's nipples, until the ping announcing they'd arrived on the fourth floor pulled them apart.

Morgan grabbed her hand and pulled her from the elevator. She strode down the hallway, tugging Adrienne along with her, toward Adrienne's room.

"Key card," Morgan said as they reached the door.

Adrienne fished it from her purse and handed it over, lost in a daze of desire, all thoughts of insisting Morgan get some sleep left behind in the empty elevator car that now rode a lonely journey up to the fifth floor.

The door was open, they were in the room, and Morgan had her pinned against the wall next to the bathroom, her hands insistent at the zipper on the side of Adrienne's dress.

Morgan stepped back slightly and kicked the door closed, then said, her voice husky, "Off. God, Adrienne, I need to touch you."

Adrienne's knees weakened as she obeyed Morgan's command. She wrestled the zipper down, then quickly peeled the dress from her shoulders to pool at her feet.

"Jesus," Morgan hissed.

Her gaze raked Adrienne's body, taking in the red lacy bra and panties and the black pumps that still adorned her tired feet.

The need in Adrienne, sparked by the kiss in the elevator, ramped up under the heat of the look on Morgan's face. Everything, everywhere, ached for Morgan's fingers, her mouth.

"Morgan, touch me. Now."

Morgan didn't need telling twice. She bent forward and ran her tongue swiftly over a lace-covered nipple.

Adrienne arched her back and cried out softly as sweet pleasure rippled down her body to settle somewhere deliciously low and deep. Morgan did it again and again, and Adrienne's pleasure reached fever levels in a ridiculously short span of time.

"Morgan..." she begged, though for what she wasn't really sure.

It didn't matter. Morgan understood.

She dropped to her knees. With her nose first, then her lips, she nuzzled Adrienne's belly, just above the waistband of her panties. Then she licked delicately at the skin at the top of Adrienne's thighs, where the lace edge of the panties lay, and Adrienne reached out blindly to find Morgan's shoulders.

"Morgan, I'm not sure I...can stand...for..."

Her protests died on her lips the moment Morgan swept her tongue downward over the lace, stroking softly yet insistently. Small moans of delight escaped Morgan's throat as Adrienne bucked against her. Then Morgan's fingers pushed the lace aside, and her tongue met Adrienne's wetness unimpeded, and Adrienne knew her lover was about to set her world on fire once more. Seconds later, embarrassingly quickly in her opinion, Adrienne fell apart as her orgasm turned her entire body to molten liquid.

She stumbled unceremoniously toward the floor, Morgan helping to ease her down before covering her with her own body, her hungry mouth plundering Adrienne's once more.

After a minute or so, Morgan broke the kiss and gazed down at her. "I…I love you. I love you so much."

There was a hint of fear in her eyes.

Adrienne reached for her, cupped her face with one hand, and pulled her even closer with the other.

"I love you too. Completely. Utterly."

Morgan gave a small cry, then held Adrienne to her, their hearts pounding in perfect synchronicity.

The loud, insistent buzzing pulled Morgan from sleep. She reached behind her to switch off her alarm clock, then realized her clock was missing and sat up in confusion. A few moments later, her brain caught up.

Oh, yeah, I'm in Adrienne's bed. Last night.

Oh, yeah…

"Wassat noise?" Adrienne mumbled.

Morgan smiled down at her sleepy lover and planted a soft kiss on her shoulder. "I think it's your phone, my love."

"Ugh."

As Adrienne made no move to move, and as her phone kept buzzing, Morgan sighed and pulled herself out of the bed. She found Adrienne's phone in her purse and blinked as she read the caller display.

"Um, Adrienne. It's Daniel. I guess you'd better take this?"

Still not opening her eyes, Adrienne held out one hand above the covers.

Grinning, Morgan returned to the bed and pressed the phone into her hand.

"Daniel," Adrienne said, her head half buried under the sheets. "Yes. Yes. Really? Well, okay then. Sure. Bye."

Adrienne held out the phone again, and Morgan took it, bemused. "Well?"

"Still have a job."

"Yes!" Morgan leaped onto Adrienne, who grunted in protest as Morgan kissed what parts of her face she could actually see.

"Ugh, stop being so…*young* this morning," Adrienne growled.

Morgan threw back her head and laughed.

"How are you feeling?" Adrienne asked Jenny as they made their way out to the Evian Resort Golf Club for the final time. The last two weeks, since all the drama in England, had passed in a blur, and Adrienne, for one, couldn't wait for it all to be over. "After today, the project is pretty much over, and we'll have to return to the office."

"I'm happy! I know everyone says travelling for your job is glamorous, but it really isn't. I'm sick of living out of my suitcase. I want to go home. I'm really ready."

"Yes, me too."

"And how are *you* feeling?" Jenny asked. "Going out there today to watch her try and do it again?"

"You know, not as nervous as I was at Wentworth. Not because I think it's a foregone conclusion—we both know anything can happen on the course. But more because she's just so perfectly in the zone this week and yet so relaxed, that whatever happens, she'll be fine."

"I'm so happy it's all working out." Jenny blushed. "I'm really pleased for you both."

"Thank you."

They met Toby and Diane, ran over the schedule one more time, then got to work. Adrienne kept one eye on the filming and one eye on Morgan, marveling again at how effortless she'd made golf seem these past few weeks.

By the time Morgan played—and birdied—the fifteenth, it was obvious that nothing short of a meteorite strike on the course would keep her from winning her second major in a row. When her final putt dropped on the eighteenth, and the crowd erupted with joy on Morgan's behalf, Adrienne made her way slowly through the throng of people between her and her love with a broad smile on her face.

Morgan swept her up in her arms, lifting her a few inches off the ground.

"Good God, put me down," Adrienne exclaimed, shaking her head as the cameras flashed all around them.

"All right, all right. Spoilsport." Morgan grinned and kissed her softly.

"Well done, my love," Adrienne said quietly, then kissed her back.

"Thank you."

The presentation, interviews, and evening event all passed in one big, tired haze for Adrienne. She was exhausted—the last few weeks had been a physical and emotional rollercoaster.

Morgan was feeling it too. Adrienne had seen her this morning, pushing herself to be as awake and alert as possible. But as soon as she'd gotten out on the course again, she'd found some hidden depths and pushed on through to claim the top prize once more.

Back-to-back majors. Astonishing.

As the formalities began to wrap up at the end of the post-tournament dinner, Adrienne caught Morgan glancing more than once at her watch.

"Got a hot date?" she asked.

Morgan colored, and Adrienne feared her heart would stop. "No, not that, but..." Morgan glanced around. "Can we get out of here? I really need to be alone with you."

Adrienne's libido tried to stir but didn't quite manage it. "I'm happy to leave, my love, but I'll be honest, I'm not sure I've got the energy for anything more tonight."

"What?" Morgan looked confused for a moment, then her blush deepened. "Oh! No, I, um...that isn't quite what I meant." She sighed. "Can we just go?"

Even more confused than she was a minute ago, Adrienne nodded and allowed Morgan to take her hand and lead her from the room.

Charlie threw them a wave as they passed, smirking knowingly at them.

They took the stairs up one floor to Morgan's room. Once they were inside, with the door closed behind them, Adrienne couldn't hold back her nervous curiosity a moment longer.

"Morgan, please, what's going on?"

Morgan held up one finger, then walked to the desk by the window and pulled a large envelope from the top drawer. She twirled it in her hands as she walked back over.

"I was…" she began, then cleared her throat as her voice croaked. "I was doing some thinking yesterday before we met for dinner. I'm pretty sure you're as tired as I am after the last few weeks, yeah?"

"I am." Adrienne grinned wryly.

"So I was thinking, wouldn't it be nice if we could have a little break now? I was penciled in for the first tournament in China, but I've made my apologies and will join the Asia circuit at the second one in three weeks' time."

"Oh?"

Morgan nodded and took one step closer, then held out the envelope. "So here's the thing. I kind of booked us a trip. Together. Starting Thursday."

Adrienne blinked. She was so tired she wasn't sure she'd heard Morgan correctly. "A trip? Thursday?"

"Uh-huh." Morgan sighed. "I think we could both use a break. Time to be together." She pushed the envelope once more in Adrienne's direction, and this time she took it. "Open it, please?"

Shaking her head in mystification, Adrienne slid her thumb under the seal and opened the envelope. Inside were three or four sheets of paper, which she pulled out and turned toward the light from the desk lamp.

It was a travel itinerary, but only the odd word here and there leaped out at her, as her eyes and brain struggled to take it all in.

Caribbean. First class. Private villa. Jacuzzi. Beach view.

"Morgan." Adrienne's voice sounded strange even to her own ears. "What is this?"

Shuffling, Morgan thrust her hands into the pockets of her dress pants. "Well, you know, Charlie said I should keep doing that wooing thing. So this is me, you know, wooing you." She blinked a couple of times. "Adrienne, I'd love to see you on a quiet beach, the sun in your hair, the sand at your feet. I'd love to make love to you in a jacuzzi under the moonlight. I'd love to spend fourteen uninterrupted days with you by my side, showing you how much I love you." She inched closer. "And I'd like us to have time to talk about what we do now, how this"—she motioned between them—"will work, given how far apart we live, how much travelling we both do. I mean, only if you're ready to talk about all that. We don't have to. Not yet." She rolled her eyes. "God, I'm rambling, sorry."

Adrienne gazed up at Morgan. Her mind whirled with all the thoughts Morgan had just planted about their future together. Her hands clutched at the papers as if they would somehow anchor her against the storm of emotion threatening to floor her.

Morgan pulled her hands from her pockets and carefully tugged Adrienne into her arms. "What do you think?" she finished quietly. She gazed down at Adrienne with a hopeful expression on her beautiful face.

Adrienne breathed deeply, willing herself not to ruin her makeup by crying, but it was a hard-fought battle. "I think," she said, tossing the papers on the floor, "that you are without a doubt the most wonderful woman I have ever met. I…I can't believe you've done this."

Morgan's face opened up with a beam of a smile. "Is that a yes?"

Adrienne chuckled and leaned up on her toes to kiss Morgan softly on the lips. "Oh, my love, that is most definitely a yes. And Daniel can go to hell if TC Productions won't let me take the time off."

Morgan grinned, then dipped her head and kissed her deeply. She enfolded Adrienne in her strong arms and pulled her close.

When they eased apart some moments later, Morgan had a sly smile on her face. "Of course, there is one condition."

Adrienne quirked one eyebrow at her, on full alert given the playfulness written all over Morgan's face. "And what might that be?"

"Well, it *is* a beach holiday. And that means you have to…wear a bikini."

Adrienne snorted. "I haven't worn a bikini in ten years."

"Then it's about time you started again."

"Morgan…" Adrienne sighed and closed her eyes for a moment.

"Adrienne," Morgan whispered, before tracing the tip of her tongue along Adrienne's cheek to the top of her ear, where she licked delicately, making Adrienne's knees go weak. "You know you are the sexiest woman I've ever met. The thought of seeing you in a bikini drives me crazy, but if it's too soon, I'll understand. No pressure."

"We'll see," Adrienne offered. She smiled. "Maybe I could wear one when we're in our villa. It might be a little too much for me to cope with wearing it on the beach."

"Hm, I could live with that," Morgan said. She kissed a trail down the length of Adrienne's neck. "Probably best for all of us, actually. I doubt I'd last five minutes before I'd want to rip it off you anyway."

Adrienne shook her head. There were still some things she was getting used to about being with this amazing young woman, and Morgan's desire for her body was one of them. But still, she knew she had plenty of time to adjust and all the time in the world to learn to revel in it and to revel in what being in love with Morgan Spencer was all about.

Because each of them knew this was going to last for a very long time.

"You still tired?" Morgan asked, her hands coming to the back of Adrienne's dress.

Chuckling, Adrienne reached for the zipper on Morgan's pants. "It seems not, no."

"Good."

Morgan's lips returned to hers, and as the contact deepened, Adrienne sunk into the kiss and lost herself once more in the heady feeling of being loved by Morgan.

About A.L. Brooks

A.L. Brooks was born in the UK but currently resides in Frankfurt, Germany, and over the years she has lived in places as far afield as Aberdeen and Australia. She works 9–5 in corporate financial systems and her dream is to take early retirement. Like, tomorrow, please. She loves her gym membership, and is very grateful for it as she also loves dark chocolate. She enjoys drinking good wine and craft beer, trying out new recipes to cook, and learning German. Travelling around the world and reading lots and lots (and lots) of books are also things that fight for time with her writing. Yep, she really needs that early retirement.

CONNECT WITH A.L. BROOKS
Website: www.albrookswriter.com
Twitter: @albrookswriter1
E-Mail: albrookswriter@gmail.com

Other Books from Ylva Publishing

www.ylva-publishing.com

Up on the Roof
A.L. Brooks

ISBN: 978-3-95533-988-3
Length: 245 pages (88,000 words)

When a storm wreaks havoc on bookish Lena's well-ordered world, her laid-back new neighbor, Megan, offers her a room. The trouble is they've been clashing since the day they met. How can they now live under the same roof? Making it worse is the inexplicable pull between them that seems hard to resist. A fun, awkward, and sweet British romance about the power of opposites attracting.

Code of Conduct
Cheyenne Blue

ISBN: 978-3-96324-030-0
Length: 264 pages (91,000 words)

Top ten tennis player Viva Jones had the world at her feet. Then a lineswoman's bad call knocked her out of the US Open, and injury crushed her career. While battling to return to the game, a chance meeting with the same sexy lineswoman forces Viva to rethink the past...and the present. There's just one problem: players and officials can't date.

A lesbian romance about breaking all the rules.

Romancing the Kicker
Catherine Lane

ISBN: 978-3-96324-129-1
Length: 314 pages (86,000 words)

Parker Sherbourne, the new rookie kicker for the High Rollers, Las Vegas's pro football team, is hot property. When athletic trainer Carly Bartlett signs on, her boss has one warning: don't get involved with a player. That's no problem—until Carly has to treat seductive Parker and sparks fly. With the macho world of football against them, can they beat the odds in this lesbian sports romance?

Food for Love
C. Fonseca

ISBN: 978-3-96324-082-9
Length: 276 pages (96,000 words)

When injured elite cyclist Jess flies to Australia to sort her late brother's estate, the last thing she wants is his stake in a rural eatery. She'd rather settle up, move on, and sidestep the restaurant's beautiful owner, Lili, and her child. Given her traumatic life, Jess isn't sure she'd survive letting her guard down.

A lesbian romance about how nourishment is much more than the food we eat.

The Long Shot
© 2019 by A.L. Brooks

ISBN: 978-3-96324-247-2

Also available as e-book.

Published by Ylva Publishing, legal entity of Ylva Verlag, e.Kfr.

Ylva Verlag, e.Kfr.
Owner: Astrid Ohletz
Am Kirschgarten 2
65830 Kriftel
Germany

www.ylva-publishing.com

First edition: 2019

Credits
Edited by Miranda Miller and Amanda Jean
Cover Design and Print Layout by Streetlight Graphics

Made in the USA
Monee, IL
07 November 2020

46952031R00166